AN IRRESISTIBLE ATTRACTION

To avoid a scandal that would devastate her family, Riona McKinsey has agreed to marry the wrong man—though the one she yearns for is James MacRae. Had she not been maneuvered into a compromising position by a man of Edinburgh—who covets her family's wealth more than Riona's love—the dutiful Highland miss could have followed her heart into MacRae's strong and loving arms. But alas, it is not to be.

A man of the wild, tempest-tossed ocean, James MacRae never dreamed he'd find his greatest temptation on land. Yet from the instant the dashing adventurer first gazed deeply into Riona's haunting gray eyes, he knew there was no lass in all of Scotland he'd ever want more. The matchless lady is betrothed to another—and unwilling to break off her engagement or share the reason why she will marry her intended. But how can MacRae ignore the passion that burns like fire inside, drawing him relentlessly toward a love that could ruin them both?

"A WRITER OF RARE INTELLIGENCE
AND SENSITIVITY."
Mary Jo Putney

"RANNEY IS A RICH, RARE FIND!"
Judith Ivory

KAREN RANNEY

The Irresistible MacRae

BOOK THREE OF THE HIGHLAND LORDS

An Avon Romantic Treasure

AVON BOOKS
An Imprint of HarperCollinsPublishers

This is a work of fiction. Names, characters, places, and incidents are products of the author's imagination or are used fictitiously and are not to be construed as real. Any resemblance to actual events, locales, organizations, or persons, living or dead, is entire coincidental.

AVON BOOKS
An Imprint of HarperCollins*Publishers*
10 East 53rd Street
New York, New York 10022-5299

Copyright © 2002 by Karen Ranney
ISBN: 0-380-82105-2
www.avonromance.com

First Avon Books paperback printing: December 2002

Avon Trademark Reg. U.S. Pat. Off. and in Other Countries, Marca Registrada, Hecho en U.S.A.
HarperCollins® is a registered trademark of HarperCollins Publishers Inc.

Printed in the U.S.A.

10 9 8 7 6 5 4 3 2 1

To Mary Gabehart,
one of the neatest people I know.

Chapter 1

May 1778

"**Y**ou'll marry him," Mrs. Parker said sternly.

"I'll not," Riona replied, just as forcefully.

That had been the extent of their conversation all the way from Edinburgh.

The world had gone mad; Riona McKinsey was sure of it. Should she forget that fact for even a moment, Mrs. Adelaide Parker, late of London, was there to remind her. The formidable woman sat opposite her in the darkened carriage, her arms folded across her chest, her toes tapping against the floor, her heavy sighs making Riona feel alternately uncomfortable and beyond irritated.

Mrs. Parker had declined to light the lamps, no doubt reasoning that since Riona was going to perdition she might as well have a taste of it beforehand.

1

Riona's sister sat beside her in the darkness, daintily sobbing into her handkerchief. Of the two of them, Maureen made her feel worse.

The coach rumbled on, despite the fact that it was a moonless night. Landscape, however, was no obstacle to the redoubtable Mrs. Parker. She had stared down kings and queens of society. What was a treacherous road in comparison?

Riona wedged herself more firmly into the corner, using a finger to lift the leather shade. There was no scenery to observe other than shrouded bushes and darkly shadowed trees.

She should, perhaps, be formulating a plan, thinking of some words to assuage her mother. Her throat was hoarse from speaking blandishments to Mrs. Parker, and attempting to make her see reason.

Mrs. Parker had declared her ruined, and so she was.

Her mother, however, was not so devoid of sense as her chaperone. Susanna would see the situation as it was and judge her accordingly.

Why was it that a woman had to prove herself twice over and a man's words were taken at face value?

She'd had absolutely no intention of slipping into the garden with Harold McDougal. Nor would she have willingly remained there and agreed to the ruination of her reputation. But the man had neatly captured her with words. Not those of a romantic nature, but of a sisterly one.

"My dear Miss McKinsey, your sister is in the garden, weeping. Could you not lend her your aid?"

She'd not thought twice. Maureen had been emotional of late, believing herself in love with the dashing Captain Hastings. To make matters worse, the young man had not been able to attend the gathering that evening, being newly posted to Fort George. She'd seen Maureen dabbing at her eyes herself, and never thought twice about going to her side.

Except that Maureen was not in the darkened garden sitting on a stone bench.

She whirled on Harold, only to have him grip her bare arm with his damp hand. Deliberately, she pulled away.

"I have been captivated by you from the first, Miss McKinsey. Say you feel the same and I'll be the happiest man in all the world."

"I have met you on but two occasions, sir," she said. "Have I given you any indication that such familiarity would be welcome?"

"You have smiled at me, Miss McKinsey." His voice was low and soft and no doubt meant to be seductive. Instead, it was merely repellent. "And I have been fascinated by the sparkle in your beautiful eyes. I have never been privileged to see such a shade of silver before."

"They are gray," she said flatly. "A simple gray." She took the precaution of stepping backward.

"I would have you know of the respect and admiration I feel for you."

Holding up one hand, palm toward him, she hoped to stop his advance, but like most ardent suitors, however, he heard encouragement in her words and coyness in her silence.

"I have startled you with my impetuousness," he said. "There is but one cure for it, my dearest Miss McKinsey. We must marry."

She was in Edinburgh to attract a husband, and the fact that she possessed a legacy from her mother's great aunt made the task less onerous than it might once have been. Riona was under no illusions as to her attractiveness, since the attention paid her was in direct proportion to rumors of her dowry.

None of the men she'd met had made her daydream as Maureen did over Captain Hastings, or sigh in wonder at the thought of living with him all the days of her life. Not one man stood apart from any other. Not even Harold, although she was beginning to think that he would forever be memorable for the sheer tenacity of his suit.

"I thank you for the honor of your declaration, sir," she said by rote. One of many lessons she'd learned from Mrs. Parker.

Taking one step back, Riona encountered the trunk of a large tree. Harold wasted no time placing one hand at either side of her waist. She didn't feel threatened by him as much as annoyed, an emotion that only grew as he leaned down and breathed against her cheek.

"I'll love you for eternity," he said, panting heavily. She pushed against him, but he didn't budge.

Suddenly, he reached out with one hand and squeezed her breast, for all the world as if he'd found a peach to pluck. She slapped him away, but he refused to stop pawing her.

"You have a passionate nature. I've seen evidence of it in your eyes, Riona."

Raising her slipper, Riona stomped on his boot, but it seemed to have no effect on him at all. He only leaned forward and tried to kiss her in response.

Most of her life had been spent in Cormech, a small coastal town, as the daughter of a widowed woman. She'd learned early how to protect herself. Riona raised her knee and assaulted him.

When she'd returned to the others, irritated and beyond angry at Harold, the guests had stopped speaking. Instead, they'd begun to stare at her, the murmuring growing as the moments passed. She looked down at herself to find that the lace on her bodice had been torn. Three dozen people immediately viewed her as a harlot, and what was worse, according to Mrs. Parker, they were correct in their assumption. Although she was as chaste and virtuous as the day she was born, Riona was ruined.

Yet Mr. Harold McDougal, guilty of being a liar, an abductor, and a man with busy fingers and intrusive hands, was seen as innocent, overcome by a passion she had deliberately incited.

Which was why she was now sitting here in disgrace on her way back home to Tyemorn Manor, with Harold in a carriage following them.

A rider had been sent on ahead with word of their arrival. Riona could only imagine what her mother was going to say when she returned from Edinburgh in disgrace. Susanna was not overly reticent in her opinions.

It was all Great Aunt Mary's fault, Riona thought sourly.

Until a year ago, they had been living a quiet existence in Cormech. But then the elderly woman had died and left her mother a manor house, a series of farms, and a significant fortune, along with a bequest to both daughters. For that reason, her mother had invested a goodly amount of money in the employment of Mrs. Parker, a woman of excellent reputation who was rumored to have been behind some of the best matches made in Edinburgh in the past five seasons.

The Englishwoman's duty had been to groom Riona and Maureen for presentation to Edinburgh's eligible men. At times, Riona felt like a suckling pig, delivered up for the delectation of any man with a good family name, a favorable appearance, and an offer.

The fact that the woman had accomplished part of her goal was evident in Maureen's silent grief. The young captain in the Fencible Regiment had fallen as desperately in love with her sister as she him.

Evidently, however, Captain Samuel Hastings was the last male descendant of a long and distinguished line. Despite the fact that the coffers were empty, the Hastingses prided themselves on their great lineage. Any hint of scandal would quash the hope of a betrothal between Maureen and Samuel more effectively than poverty.

She was not a terrible person, Riona thought, only one trapped in circumstance. Was that a reason to ruin the rest of her life?

These past few days she'd thought of nothing but marriage. Her father had died when she was young, but she could still recall the sounds of his boots tapping on the stairs or echoing on the upstairs floor. He had a voice so low that it sounded as if a pond of bullfrogs had taken up residence in his chest. There had been amusement and joy in their house, great guffaws that made her wonder if God laughed, and if He did, would the sound be the same?

Sometimes, she and Maureen had sat on his lap, perched on either leg with his arms wrapped around their backs while he told them stories of places he wanted to see. Wanderlust, her mother had called it. Dreams, he would say. But they would always share a look and a smile. Despite her father's frequent absences, it was a happy home, made even more so on his return.

More than once, she'd interrupted a heated kiss between her parents, and sometimes, at night, she would fall asleep to the sound of their voices in the parlor as they talked of subjects too grand for a ten-year-old girl to understand.

That was the kind of marriage she wanted. One of perfect accord, of friendship, perhaps. What kind of marriage could she expect with a man who thought so little of her as to trap her this way?

The coach abruptly shifted, the angle indicating that they were traveling uphill now. Tyemorn Manor was situated in the bowl of a glen with lush farmland all around. A few moments later, Riona peered from behind the curtains again, this time viewing the blur of lights as they neared the manor house.

Her prayer was easily summoned. Please let her mother's good sense prevail over Mrs. Parker's outraged sensibilities or Maureen's grief.

The coach slowed before the house. Mrs. Parker was the first to disembark. Before leaving the vehicle, Riona turned and stared into the shadows at Maureen. Her sister remained silent, no more communicative now than she'd been during the entire journey.

"Do you think I should marry him?"

Nothing but silence.

"Tell me truthfully."

"I cannot, Riona," her sister said faintly. "Your future is tied to my own happiness. It would not be fair for me to tell you what to do. You must make your own choice."

"Even if it makes you miserable?"

Another pause. "Yes," Maureen said finally.

Riona left the carriage, fervently wishing that her sister wasn't such a very nice person.

The knock was loud enough to be heard on the second floor of the manor house.

"They're here, mistress," Polly said.

Polly's soft blue eyes looked worried as she chewed on her bottom lip.

The woman was past the first blush of youth, her shape once as rotund as an apple. Over the past year, however, she'd lost weight. Along with the reduction in her girth had come a new nervousness. She was constantly wringing her hands or tapping her foot. Once, she'd worn her hair tucked neatly into a bob behind her head. Since she'd come to Tyemorn Manor, however, the style was more severe, pulling at Polly's temples until her blue eyes appeared forever startled.

Susanna McKinsey calmly finished tidying her hair as Polly fidgeted beside her, first standing on one foot, then the other. With the ease of practice, Susanna ignored her, finally moving her brush to where it belonged on the lace-covered dressing table.

Staring at herself in the mirror, she surveyed her appearance. Her face was narrow, but relatively unlined. Her eyes were the same shade of blue as Maureen's. Her chin was, perhaps, too pointed. There was nothing at all she could do about her high forehead and widow's peak except ensure that her hairstyle was flattering. Her lips, in better times, were acceptable, she supposed. At the moment, however, they looked thin, almost disappearing into her face. As if she were as worried as Polly.

"I'm in no hurry to greet them, Polly," she admitted. "I cannot imagine what Riona has done."

"Nothing, I'll wager," Polly said loyally. "That Mrs. Parker grates on the nerves, she does. No doubt our Riona simply had enough."

"She was never a wild child." Susanna met Polly's gaze in the mirror. "In fact, of the two girls, Riona was always the more responsible."

"Well, something's happened, that's for sure, else the woman wouldn't have sent you that letter."

Mrs. Parker's note still remained on the top of her dressing table, having been delivered only a few hours ago. The contents left nothing to the imagination as far as the woman's feelings about her older daughter. The only thing lacking from the missive was the exact nature of Riona's failing.

The knock came again, imperious and impatient. Susanna sighed and stood.

"Your daughter is a wayward young woman," Mrs. Parker said a few moments later as she sailed over the threshold.

As a greeting, it was terse and to the point, Susanna thought, following the woman into the parlor.

"How is she wayward?"

Mrs. Parker resembled a plump crow in her severe black. No, not a crow, but a disapproving bird of prey with an angled beak and beady, focused eyes.

Susanna managed to compose herself, standing with hands folded decorously in front of her as both her daughters entered the room. There wasn't time for a greeting because Mrs. Parker raised her hand and shook her finger in Susanna's face. "If you do not curtail her now, she will ruin everything we have worked so hard to achieve. My reputation is at stake, madam."

"What has she done?" she asked, glancing at Riona.

"Allowed a young man the freedom of her person."

Susanna sat heavily on one end of the settee, the fingers of one hand clenched around the brooch at her neck. "Is this true, Riona?" she asked her elder daughter.

Riona said nothing in response, a telling absence of explanation. Mrs. Parker nodded, appearing vindicated, while Maureen, who'd come to sit beside her, looked merely miserable. Her eyes were reddened from weeping, and her hands clutched a sodden lace handkerchief.

"Tell me the whole story," she said, turning to Mrs. Parker once more.

The older woman related the tale, halting at frequent intervals to frown at Riona.

"She and Harold McDougal were seen entering the garden and leaving some five minutes later. Riona's dress was torn, and her hair askew. Not only did she show a lack of decency in refusing to absent herself from the guests, she acted in the most forward manner, almost daring anyone to chastise her for her behavior. When I insisted that she should at least demonstrate a little shame, she told me some story about being lured into the garden. It matters little why she was there, madam. All that is important is her behavior while she was alone with a young man. That was, and remains, deplorable."

"How many people know of this encounter?" Susanna asked.

Mrs. Parker responded quickly. "All of the guests at the party. Maureen's betrothal is in jeopardy. There are too many proper young women in Scotland for Captain Hastings to settle for one whose family is tinged by scandal."

How many of them were possessed of a considerable fortune? A question Susanna decided not to ask.

"If she marries the young man, we can let it be known that she was carried away with an excess of youthful exuberance, predating the marital bed by some weeks. But if she steadfastly refuses to marry, the world will see her as a strumpet, a young woman of loose morals. That will surely seal Maureen's fate."

"And who is this Harold McDougal?" Susanna asked.

"I am, madam."

To her surprise, a young man stood in the doorway. At first glance, he looked amenable enough. Of average height, with brown hair and flashing hazel eyes. But there was something about him that she didn't like, an instantaneous feeling that had less to do with logic and more to do with instinct. She'd been a widow for some years, had relied upon her own judgment when boarders had come to her small house in Cormech seeking a room. On more than one occasion, she'd turned away a potential source of income simply because of a first impression.

"I was the one who led her into sin, madam," he confessed, looking down at the floor, studying either the oak boards or perhaps his dusty boot tops.

Strange, but he didn't look all that contrite.

Sly, but not clever, for all that.

"I cannot deny that there was an attraction between us, ma'am," he said, his eyes still downcast. "But I was wrong to encourage it. Of the two of us, I should have been stronger."

That statement had Mrs. Parker nodding in agreement.

Riona, however, snorted in a thoroughly unladylike manner.

"But I've come to make amends now," he said, and for the first time raised his head to stare directly at her. "I would take your daughter to my wife."

"I agree that my daughter's behavior sounds dreadful," she said calmly. "However, you will grant me the license to speak with her before I make a decision."

"I would be a good husband," he continued, as if she hadn't spoken. "I've some family property. And plans for the future."

"Do any of those plans include my daughter's fortune?" Susanna asked bluntly. She could hear Mrs. Parker's indrawn breath.

Neither she nor Mrs. Parker had been born to wealth. Mrs. Parker made her living as a matchmaker, chaperone, and governess of sorts, escorting young women through the perils of society. For that she was paid a handsome sum.

As to Harold, Susanna wasn't naïve about the effect of Riona's inheritance on a young man's fancy. Harold's heart might be engaged, but she would wager that he had found it easier to fall in love with an heiress than a woman without a fortune.

"I am aware that your daughter is an heiress, ma'am," Harold said stiffly, all righteous anger and indignation. "But I would have loved her had she been penniless." His words met with Mrs. Parker's murmur of approval.

"A pity that we can't test your fidelity," Susanna said dryly.

She stood, nodding to Polly. "The decision will be made, but it will not be made tonight," she said. "For now I think it would be better if we retired to our rooms." She nodded to Harold. "If you will give us a few moments, I'll have a chamber prepared for you."

He bowed smartly and smiled his acceptance, the expression no doubt meant to be disarming.

She sent Maureen to her room with a whisper that she'd visit her later, then turned to Mrs. Parker. "Shall I send a slight repast to your chamber?"

"You're not putting me where I stayed last, I trust?" the other woman asked querulously. "The wind is simply too fierce. I would prefer a south-facing room."

Susanna didn't bother telling the woman that there were no south-facing rooms. She only nodded, resigned to having Mrs. Parker as a guest once again. Glancing at Riona, she summoned her with a nod. They met in the hallway outside the parlor.

"I cannot marry him, Mother," Riona said stonily, after the double doors were closed. "I won't. I've done nothing wrong."

"Sometimes the appearance of impropriety is all that's necessary," Susanna said. "There is Maureen's happiness to consider."

The fact that Captain Hastings was visibly in love with Maureen was the only bright spot in the entire situation.

"Is there nothing else I can do, short of marriage?"

She glanced at her daughter, sighing. For the first time in many months, she wished Fergus were near. Her former boarder and longtime friend would have advised her on how to handle this situation. Riona and Fergus had always been close, her daughter coming to view the older man almost as the father she missed so much.

"If there is something, I cannot think what it might be."

There were Captain Hastings and Maureen to consider. What man in good standing would wish to align himself with a family riddled in rumor and innuendo? A fortune could not purchase respectability.

"I want more in my life," Riona said, her contempt for Harold McDougal showing in her eyes, and her stubbornness in the set of her chin. Susanna could not honestly blame Riona for her feelings. A lesson in human nature she'd learned long ago. The more flattering the prose, the less substance the remark. So far, Harold had not impressed her with his sincerity.

"Your father once said much the same thing to me," she said. "Before he went to sea again. He never found what he wanted, but I could never have stopped his looking. Nor would it have ever occurred to him that following his dreams would pain those he left behind."

Riona looked stricken. Harsh words, perhaps, but the truth was often cruel.

"Sometimes," Susanna added, "we must put our own happiness aside for those we love."

She left Riona then. After arranging for the comfort of her guests and visiting with Maureen, Susanna retreated to her own chamber. This room was her haven, the place where no problems intruded, no cares were allowed past the door. Between the two long windows was a large, comfortable chair and there she sat and sewed most days.

"Why do you not come down to the parlor?" Polly had asked her a few months back.

A moment had passed before she'd realized the answer. In Cormech, the parlor had been a communal place for her boarders to sit in the evening. She'd become accustomed to the sanctity of her chamber. Even after all this time in a new house and with only her family in residence, she still found herself coming here. Perhaps because the sheer size of Tyemorn Manor was disconcerting. Or it might simply be that she had become a creature of habit after all these years.

There was only one exception, and that was when she and Old Ned discussed the ledgers. Susanna found herself sitting companionably with him in the library on those nights. Almost as she and Fergus had once done around the kitchen table.

Sitting in her favorite chair, Susanna pulled her lap desk close. She didn't know quite what to do, and there was only one person whose judgment she trusted implicitly. Fergus MacRae. If anyone could talk some sense into Riona, he could.

Swiftly, she began to write, each word interspersed with a sigh, and the whole of it blessed with a prayer.

Chapter 2

The great hall at Fernleigh was an ugly place, one that was in the process of being painted and refurbished. The once brightly hued brick had been allowed to fade over the years to a dull gray. Above him, the stained-glass window that must once have been magnificent, detailing the story of the first Drummond laird, had been left to neglect. What panes weren't damaged had been loosened by winter winds and summer storms. The stone floor was equally as ill cared for, being pocked and worn. A difficult place for him to walk.

Yet he wouldn't have traded being here for anyplace on earth.

"What is it, Fergus?" Leah said, coming to stand beside him. Her hand trailed across the back of his neck, enough that his concentration ebbed. Smiling, Fergus McRae put the letter down on the table in front of him and reached for her.

"You'll shock all the servants, my dearest," she said, allowing him to pull her down on his lap.

Grinning, he bent to kiss her, and when that was done refused to release her once again. But then, she wasn't trying to escape all that hard.

She was in his arms, as he'd dreamed all these years. Separated by war, they had found each other again only a year ago. They had waited to marry until her widow's mourning was done, and the ceremony, mutually anticipated, would occur soon.

"It's a letter from a friend of mine," he explained, reaching for it and holding it open so that she might read it along with him. "It's from Susanna McKinsey, my landlady when I lived in Cormech."

One eyebrow rose, but Leah said nothing. Still, he caught the glint in her eyes.

"She was a friend, Leah," he said, smiling gently at her. "And I felt like an uncle to her daughters."

"What does she wish of you now, Fergus?"

"It seems as if one of her girls has gotten herself into trouble," he said, frowning as he continued to read the letter. "Riona refuses to wed a young man who compromised her."

"Is she of a nature to be led astray?"

He smiled, remembering Riona. "I've never thought her to be so."

"What does Susanna want you to do?" Leah asked, not bothering to read the letter. Instead, she concentrated on his features, staring at his face as if she couldn't get enough of the sight of him. She did that a great deal, and well he knew the feeling, since he'd often caught himself doing the same to her. Neither one of them could quite believe in their good fortune in finding the other after all these years.

"The young man in question is not a match Susanna would have chosen, evidently. Yet at the same time, it seems that the other daughter's betrothal is in jeopardy if scandal erupts."

"It sounds as if there isn't much choice for her." Leah moved to a more comfortable position. Not for her, but for him. He had but one leg and a stump, and she was forever conscious of it, trying not to cause him pain or discomfort.

"She sounds like a willful girl," Leah said.

"I knew another like her," Fergus teased. "This girl met me in secret places because our parents disapproved."

"And fell in love with you." She stood, bent to kiss him full on the lips. "For that reason alone, I sympathize with the young man's plight."

"It's not as simple as that, Leah," he said, putting the letter on the table again and placing both his hands on either side of her waist. "Evidently, he is more enticed by Riona's fortune than he is Riona. She knows that and refuses to marry him."

Leah laid her hands on his shoulders and leaned into him for yet another kiss. He would never grow tired of kissing Leah, not after thirty years of missing even the sight of her.

"What is she to do if not marry?"

"Exactly Susanna's dilemma. She wants me to come and see if I cannot talk some sense into the girl. Riona and I have a great fondness for each other."

"Would you leave me so close to our wedding?" Leah asked carefully.

"No," Fergus said firmly. "Not after all these years and not after all this waiting. Unfortunately, I cannot help her in this instance."

She seemed to contemplate the matter. "Will you send her a letter to that effect, Fergus? Or choose a gentler way?"

"What do you mean?"

"It seems a harsh thing to simply send her a letter explaining the matter. I believe you should send an emissary. Someone who would explain your absence so that she is neither hurt nor offended."

"Who would you send, Leah?" he asked, amused. She had someone in mind or she would not have suggested it.

"James."

His eyebrows rose. "James?" he repeated.

"Why not? Who else could plead your case so well?"

"And doing so would absent him from our wedding," he said, understanding immediately.

She smiled, but the expression was tinged with sadness. "He cannot help but feel bad on such an occasion. Even though I bless him for saving my life."

Perhaps it would be better if James were gone from Fernleigh on the occasion of their wedding. Taking a life was a difficult thing, regardless of how villainous the victim. The ceremony would, no doubt, remind James of the death he'd caused.

"If you can convince him to go," she said, grabbing her basket. She'd been on her way to another room when she'd stopped to kiss him, and now her chore needed to be completed. She turned and glanced back at him, her expression amused. "He is as stubborn as you, my dearest."

"A challenge, Leah?"

"If you choose to take it that way," she said, and left the room with a swish of hips.

"He'll do it," Fergus announced to the empty room. "He's family."

Picking up the letter again, he read it once more, feeling Susanna's worry in the words she hadn't said. He truly had no answers for her dilemma. Foolish girls must pay for their foolishness. Still, he found it difficult to believe that Riona had been so lax as to allow herself to become the source of scandal. A person did not change character that much in the time since he'd seen her.

"You want me to do what?" James MacRae asked incredulously. "I can't leave Gilmuir now; the hull of the new ship is being water tested."

"It can wait a week or two," his brother, Alisdair, said easily.

Their uncle, Fergus, sat between them, smiling. "That it can," he said in agreement.

James looked at the two men with narrowed eyes.

The day was bright, the last of the sunshine pouring down into the unfinished great hall of Gilmuir Castle. A long scarred and well-used table had been moved into the space for the convenience of the workers, and it was here the three of them sat.

Once, the castle had sheltered generations of their clan, only to have fallen into ruin in the last thirty years. Alisdair had it in his head to rebuild the old fortress. The work, although having progressed for more than a year, was nowhere near complete. The priory had been rerooted and the foundations shored up, and now scaffolding supported the stone masons as they built towering walls. The constant ringing noise of chisel against stone resulted in frayed nerves and a fine mist of dust permeating everything around Gilmuir.

Once councils of war, gatherings to discuss raids and retribution, had been held in this place. Along the south wall, his grandfather had sat in the great stone chair the MacRae lairds occupied when adjudicating punishment. Flags and pennants had flown above long trestle tables, and torches flickered from sconces mounted in the brick.

Now there was nothing but rubble, the signs of construction obliterating any hint of a glorious past. Alisdair, the current laird, sat at the head of the table, Fergus to his left and James to Alisdair's right. Each man drank from a tankard—one of the first provisions to be purchased in Inverness had been supplies of excellent whiskey.

"What is this rush to send me from Gilmuir?" James asked.

"I wish you to do an errand for me," Fergus said, his grin replaced by a frown. "A task that I would entrust to no other person but you. Or," he amended with a glance at Alisdair, "your brother if he could be spared."

"Chinese gunpowder could not move me from this place," Alisdair announced. "Not with Iseabal so close to her time."

"Nor would I ask it of you. Not when there is someone else who can help," Fergus said, sending an irritated glance toward James.

James studied the other two men in silence. Alisdair had an air of satisfaction about him nowadays, possibly because the work in the shipyards and the restoration of Gilmuir was going so well. Or perhaps it was simply because he was married and happy, and Iseabal, his wife, was heavy with child. Fergus looked equally as content, but then he was due to marry a rich widow soon.

Of the three of them, he was perhaps the most unsettled, both in temperament and in purpose. A year ago, he'd captained his own ship, but he'd chosen to leave the sea, working at Alisdair's side to create a shipyard in the cove below Gilmuir. He'd been content for the most part, satisfied that the first MacRae ship was out of the design stage and into construction. Yet now he felt curiously detached. Adrift.

Despite the fact that Gilmuir was the ancestral home of the MacRaes, he didn't feel the tie to the castle that either of the other two men did. The shipyard, although important and the source of his labor all these past months, failed to hold his continuing interest. Perhaps he missed the sea, although James doubted that was the reason for the dissatisfaction with his life. Captaining one of the MacRae vessels had been a challenge, but he'd not been born for a life aboard ship like his brothers.

"What do you want me to do?"

"Offer my apologies to Susanna, explain that I'm to be married."

He lifted an eyebrow and stared at both of them. "If all you want is a messenger, Uncle, send Rory."

The older man fixed him with an intent look. "I wish a representative," Fergus said shortly. "Anyone can deliver a letter. I wish someone to stand for me. She is a kind and gentle woman, and I would not have her hurt by my inability to aid her now."

"How far away is this Tyemorn Manor?" James asked, feeling as if the noose of responsibility was tightening around his neck.

"A few days' ride, no more. It's a landlocked place, so you cannot take a ship, but you know your way on horseback well enough."

"Any MacRae does, Uncle," Alisdair said in reproach.

James nodded reluctantly, pushed his tankard across the table. "Very well. I'll go."

"And Rory?" Alisdair asked.

"I'll take the pup. If for no other reason than to keep him occupied."

The former cabin boy, the same age as his youngest brother, Douglas, had sprouted up in the past year, his appearance altering along with his interests. He'd recently discovered females, evidenced by the fact that he often stopped work to stare at a woman if she came into his range of vision.

Alisdair grinned at him, the expression reminding him of their boyhood. As the two oldest MacRae sons they'd grown up together, becoming adept at managing bothersome younger brothers.

Yet James had the feeling, however ill placed it might be, that he'd been manipulated by his honor. The quick glance between the other two men did nothing to dispel the notion.

Riona entered the parlor, shutting the door behind her. She made her way to the settee and sat, folding her hands on her lap. Even though Harold stood at the window, his gaze intent on the view, she knew his attention was on her movements.

"I cannot imagine that a marriage based on duplicity would be a happy one," she said as a greeting.

"A man in love can be desperate, Riona," he said slowly, turning to face her.

Harold saw himself as a financier, someone who spent a great deal of time in meeting rooms in order to advance his family's fortune. At least, that was what he'd told her on the one occasion she'd met him prior to the debacle in the garden. Only later had Mrs. Parker informed her that there was no family fortune to increase—Mr. McDougal was in the market for a rich wife, and it seemed he'd found one.

" 'Gi'e me a lass with a lump of land, and we for life shall gang thegither; Tho' daft or wise I'll never demand, or black or fair it maks na whether.' "

"I fail to see your humor," he said stiffly.

"I think Allan Ramsay's words say it best, don't you? You haven't the slightest affection for me. It's all for my fortune."

"If you feel that way, Riona, then there is nothing more for me here. I shall return to Edinburgh immediately."

He knew very well that she couldn't allow him to do that. But it was, nevertheless, a cunning ploy.

"If I do not marry you, Harold, my sister's life might well be ruined." Maureen's silence weighed more effectively on her than Mrs. Parker's irritation, Harold's cloying pleas, or even her mother's censure.

"People have a way of talking," he agreed. The ease with which he said the words warned her.

"Your tongue will be among those telling the tale, won't it, Harold?" she asked, forcing herself to remain calm. "Are you that desperate for money?"

His face didn't change. He still looked agreeable enough, but his eyes seemed to shift, revealing another man beneath the affable exterior of Harold McDougal. This man was not nearly as pleasant or as patient.

"Again, Riona, a man in love will do what he thinks necessary."

"I do not love you."

Silence.

"Nor do I think I ever will."

"Perhaps I can convince you in time, my dear."

"No," she said, standing, "I don't think you can. Are you willing to trade a life of misery for my fortune?"

He smiled, the expression strangely unsettling. "Only a woman would think her life ruined because of lack of love."

How refreshing that he'd finally dropped his act of pining lover.

"If I do not marry you, you'll see us ruined," she said, certain of it. He would, she suddenly understood, go out of his way to create rumor and innuendo, destroying Maureen's chance of happiness. As to her own? She'd be just as happy remaining here at Tyemorn Manor the rest of her days. Without a husband, especially if the candidate was similar in character to Harold McDougal.

She resented being trapped into marriage, and although no one had asked such a sacrifice of her, it was clear they expected it. Maureen wandered through the house like a wraith, and her mother had taken to mumbling to herself. At first Riona thought her praying, but her name had come up too often for Susanna's words to be invocations to the Almighty. The past week of obstinacy had accomplished nothing but to bring misery to her family.

Harold was still here, Mrs. Parker was still obdurate, and the situation was still bleak.

"Very well," she said ungraciously. "We will marry."

The expression in his eyes lightened as he bowed in front of her. "A wise decision, Riona. Shall we set the date?"

"A year from now."

He smiled, the expression oddly cool. "I believe not. A month."

"I cannot marry you that soon," she said, feeling a surge of panic.

"You will have to become accustomed to the notion of it."

He bowed slightly, then leaned toward her as if he meant to kiss her. Riona stepped carefully away.

"I shall inform your mother, my dear." His expression was once again affable as if she'd not rebuffed him. "Until that blessed day," he said.

Smiling brightly, he turned and left the parlor.

In less than a day James was ready, his bag packed and carefully tied to his saddle. Fergus had penned a letter and it lay, folded with a map, inside his jacket.

At the moment Alisdair was at the shipyards, some hundred feet below the castle walls. Half the men of the MacRae clan were with him, the others occupied with rebuilding Gilmuir. The sounds of chisels against stone, hammers against nails, and spikes being driven into wood had awakened him at dawn as it had for the past year. If for no other reason than quiet, James should welcome this errand of his.

His sister-in-law, heavy with child, waved at him. He waited patiently for Iseabal to approach.

Her condition had changed Iseabal from the shy and diffident woman she'd once been. Now she was more a termagant, surprising all of them with the force of her character. Iseabal, of the soft voice and winsome nature, could yell when she chose, and Alisdair, after his initial surprise had faded, tended to shout right back. Their disagreements, oddly enough, centered around their worry for each other. She was concerned about the danger he put himself in at the shipyard or scrambling up the scaffolding, while he wanted her to rest more than she did and cease placing herself in harm's way around Gilmuir.

Iseabal saw nothing wrong with waddling through the

construcfion site of Gilmuir Castle with one hand pressed against her back. Or in giving the men occasional orders while sitting in the middle of the courtyard and studying the work of the stone masons. More than once she'd called one down from the side of the wall to ask questions or obtain advice.

"I do not wish to take any of your time for more important thIngs," she said now when she reached him. "But I'm wondering if you could add my errands to Alisdair's list. Only if you have time," she added, patting his knee as he sat on his horse.

"You know I will, Iseabal. What is it that you want?"

"I need a new carving tool," she said, handing him up a drawing of a crescent-shaped hook. "Fergus tells me that it's too fine an instrument to be crafted by a smith, but perhaps a goldsmith might have some familiarity with it."

"For your stone work, Iseabal?" She spoke deprecatingly of her talent, but she was capable of creating wondrous works of art simply from a block of stone and her imagination.

She nodded. "For the eyes, most particularly."

Tucking the drawing into his jacket, he smiled down at her. "I'll do my best. You realize, of course, that he might need some time to craft such a tool?"

"I'll have the time," she said, returning his smile. "Your nephew is sure to make his presence known soon enough. I'll no doubt be away from my carving for a while."

"Fare you well, Iseabal." He placed his hand on her arm, wished her ease in her travail with an unspoken prayer.

"Hurry back, James. What will the women of Gilmuir do without you?" she teased.

He shook his head at her, but she didn't look the least abashed.

"Alisdair needs you also," she added, serious once more.

Smiling again, he motioned to Rory to mount, leaving unspoken the thought that occurred to him. *Alisdair could do without anyone but you, dear Iseabal.*

He and Rory rode through the glen, once filled with great flocks of Drummond sheep. Over the past year they had been winnowed to make way for people and crops. Where other parts of Scotland were lonely and isolated, this corner of the Highlands was burgeoning with new life. Three babes had been born in the last month alone.

At the top of the rise, James turned and looked back toward Gilmuir. He had grown up in Nova Scotia, a land not dissimilar to this one. Yet neither place inspired in him the sense of home Alisdair felt. That lack left something missing inside him, a hole that desperately needed to be filled.

"I'm thinking that a horse is not unlike a ship," Rory said from beside him. The boy was staring intently at a spot between the ears of his mount. "It takes a certain getting used to, all this swaying back and forth."

James turned and smiled at his companion.

"I'm not saying I dislike it," Rory added, still frowning down at his horse. "But, all the same, I'd prefer climbing the rigging."

Rory had not yet made the transition from cabin boy to carpenter. Yet he had a natural affinity for building things, a talent that seemed to surprise him as much as it had anyone else.

A noise had James jerking in his saddle in time to see the branch of a nearby tree shatter before his eyes. Without thinking, he threw himself from his saddle, reaching Rory's side and dragging the boy from the horse. Using their mounts as cover, he pulled Rory into the woods, knelt and looked around.

"Who's the fool shooting at us?"

"A question I can't answer. Stay here," James said, leaving the cover of the underbrush. To his left was the promontory of Gilmuir, the bright golden light of morning illuminating the scaffolding surrounding the castle. To his right was the glen stretching up to a hill and beyond to another growth of trees. Behind him lay the forest, topped by a knoll they'd begun to call Iseabal's Hill since she had a liking for that one spot.

Nowhere, however, was there a sign of another person.

"Is it a Drummond?" Rory asked.

For generations there had been a feud among the MacRaes and Drummonds, but that had ended a year ago with the death of Magnus Drummond. A few diehard supporters of the old laird had left, choosing to emigrate or live in Inverness rather than to accept the new order. His uncle would become, by marrying Leah Drummond, the virtual, if not titular, head of the Drummond clan.

Fergus was universally respected. None of the Drummonds currently residing at Fernleigh expressed any discontent about his presence or his rule. But silence can sometimes hide a man's true thoughts. James knew that as well as any other leader of men.

"I don't know who it is," James said, scanning the countryside.

"Well, someone's shooting at us, and no one else hates us that much."

"Perhaps we weren't the target." There was a time when he and his brothers had accidentally shot the door of a neigh-

bor's cottage while hunting. Their father had meted out punishment swiftly—they'd been forced to replace the door, and
spent hours at target shooting before being allowed to hunt
again.

"It could be an accident," James said now, more to allevi-
ate Rory's worry than because he actually believed it. His
years of travel in foreign places had made him cautious by
nature.

James returned to the boy's side, retrieving his mount,
anxious to be about this errand so that he could return to
Gilmuir once more.

Thomas Drummond cursed the musket's limited range
and his own ineptitude with the weapon. He was more profi-
cient with a pistol, but the man he'd robbed on the road from
Inverness had been armed only with this useless bit of iron
and wood and brass.

He would have to get closer.

Below him lay the place he'd dreamed about, had held in
his memory all these days. Gilmuir Castle, the ancestral
fortress of the MacRaes and the place where the Drummond
clan had been defeated.

Here Magnus Drummond, his laird and cousin, had died.
Here they had trussed Thomas up like a fattened goose and
sent him to London aboard an English ship.

The wounds on his ankles and his wrists were barely
healed, and they would forever bear the scars from English
ropes. The whip marks on his back bore testament to the
many times he'd been lashed in the service of His Majesty's
Navy. They'd impressed him as a sailor, and he'd never forget. The whole of the MacRaes would pay for his months of
slavery.

A fortuitous accident had beached the hell ship Thomas was on, and he was one of fifteen sailors who had managed to survive. While the others had sought out another English ship, he and another man had taken advantage of the opportunity to escape. The two of them had made their way back to Scotland after many months, funding their expedition home by robbing those unwary travelers in their path. They'd parted ways weeks ago, Thomas's destination the castle that lay before him.

For months he'd kept himself alive with a simple vow. One by one, he would kill them all, beginning with the one who'd murdered Magnus Drummond. As he watched, the MacRae and his companion mounted again. Placing the musket in the sling he'd devised, Thomas turned his horse and followed them.

Chapter 3

Riona sat beneath a venerable oak, her skirts arranged
artfully around her. If a casual onlooker could ignore
the streaks of dirt on her garments, the unkempt state of her
hair, and the fact that her nails were dirty, she might have
been considered one of Mrs. Parker's prize pupils. But she'd
helped deliver a calf this morning, and Riona doubted very
much if that ability ranked highly in the older woman's lexi-
con of acceptable behavior.

Tugging on her lopsided braid, she pulled it free, wishing
again that there was some way of controlling her hair other
than the heavy plait. Tying the ends again, she tucked the
mess up on her head with what hairpins still remained, hoping it looked like a crown of sorts. A moment later, it came
tumbling down again. Giving up on any semblance of propriety, she unplaited the whole thing, letting it frizz around her
face like an auburn cloud.

Sitting back against the trunk of the tree, she surveyed the cloudless sky, marveling at the beauty of the day. In front of her was the lane and beyond it a meadow blooming with hardy flowers and tall grass. Sometimes, sheep foraged here, but it had been left to go wild these past months. On the other side of the expanse of land grew a series of hedges, kept neatly trimmed by the gardener and his boy. Oddly enough, the juxtaposition of the two, hedges and meadow, reminded Riona of herself.

She would dearly love to be left wild, but she was being trimmed all the time.

Take this morning, for example. She desperately wanted to discuss the birth with someone, but she wasn't supposed to have been present, let alone to have placed her hands on the cow's belly to gently urge the contractions.

Why should she be left in virtual ignorance of nature when she was going to give birth herself one of these days? Riona could only imagine the reaction should she ever voice that comment.

There was a book in her lap, one of those Mrs. Parker thought acceptable, but she wasn't in the mood for Milton.

Regions of sorrow, doleful shades, where peace
And rest can never dwell, hope never comes
That comes to all, but torture without end
Still urges, and a fiery deluge, fed
With ever-burning sulphur unconsumed.
Such place Eternal Justice has prepared
For those rebellious; here their prison ordained
In utter darkness, and their portion set,
As far removed from God and light of Heaven
As from the center thrice to th' utmost pole.

Paradise Lost seemed a fate similar to what Mrs. Parker would have decreed for her, had not Riona chosen to wed Harold.

Riona stared at the page for a long moment, wondering why she suddenly envisioned Mrs. Parker as Milton. Perhaps it was because the older woman had not ceased in her endless complaints and dire predictions, despite the fact that Harold had announced their betrothal. All was still not well at Tye-morn Manor and would not be, evidently, until Riona—an immoral creature of sin—was safely married.

Putting the book down on the ground beside her, Riona folded her arms around her drawn up knees, staring off into the distance. The village was beginning to prepare for Leth-son, the ceremony marking the summer solstice. Ayleshire had created its own celebration around the date, and this year would mark the first time the manor inhabitants would participate. At least she would be here for Lethson, she thought dispiritedly. The bonfires, the horse fair, and the blessing of the fields would take her mind from her coming nuptials.

Unless Mrs. Parker disapproved of Lethson as well.

As if she'd conjured her up, Riona heard the sound of a stick pounding on the lane. Twice a day, the Englishwoman took a bracing walk during which she quoted soul-elevating verse. "A time to exercise the spirit as well as the limbs, my girl," Riona had been told during similar constitutionals in Edinburgh.

Mrs. Parker was making vigorous progress, striking the whins on either side of the lane with her stick until the air was perfumed with almonds. As if she were reprimanding the brilliant yellow flowers on their posture.

Realizing that she could be seen if the other woman glanced to the left, Riona looked around for a place to hide, finally choosing the hedge that bordered the edge of the front lawn. Throwing herself behind it, she lay at ground level, watching Mrs. Parker's shoes through the gnarled branches as the older woman made her determined way to the front door.

The remainder of the journey to Susanna McKinsey's home was uneventful; however, James took the precaution of doubling back several times to see if they were being followed. Twice he suspected as much, and twice nothing had come of it. If someone was acting as his shadow he was being extraordinarily cautious.

He was familiar with the scenery of the Highlands, from the stark jagged peaks of the mountains to the brilliant French blue of the skies. Yet this part of Scotland was all rolling wooded hills and lush green glens. James felt as if he were back at his father's childhood home in England.

The River Wye ran between the four hills surrounding Ayleshire. To the southeast was a cliff face that reminded him oddly of Gilmuir, only not as severe or stark. The ruins of an abbey were all that remained, sitting atop the plateau like a guardian of old.

He and Rory descended to the village, following a well-worn path that widened to form the main road. Ayleshire seemed a prosperous place, with blocks of houses merging together just behind the main street. James found himself nodding to people, surprised at their smiles of greeting. Rory began to wave as if they were a royal procession. James noted, with some amusement, that more than one of the village girls waved back.

Crossing the small bridge that spanned the river, they turned toward the west and Susanna McKinsey's home.

Situated in a depression of earth, Tyemorn Manor was an odd little place. The main part of the red brick structure reminded him of homes he'd seen in Surrey, making him wonder if the original builder had taken his inspiration from the English. But subsequent owners had evidently continued with construction until the house was now a hodgepodge of styles. A small tower jutted from an abutment to the right, and a long flat wing to the left added to its disjointed appearance.

A small garden, formal in appearance, fronted the structure, while the lane that led to the front door was flanked by blooming yellow flowers.

Instead of taking the road to the house, however, James obeyed an impulse, giving his horse its head across the meadow, leaving Rory to follow as well as he could. Over a series of hedges they flew, and James felt exhilarated for the first time in months. The sound of his own laughter surprised him. A last bit of freedom, then, before he dusted off his clothes and adopted the sober mien of a responsible MacRae once more.

James cleared another hedge, the muscles of the horse beneath him arching and flexing. He didn't see the woman on the ground until it was almost too late. For a second, a horrified instant, James thought she would move, thereby putting herself even further in danger. But she remained still as he sailed over the hedge. Hurriedly dismounting, he raced back to see if she had been injured, kneeling at her side.

She had a look of dazed amazement on her face as she lay there, hair spread around her head like an auburn pool, her arms stretched outward, palms up. Her gaze was on the sky, but slowly her eyes moved until she focused on him.

"I've never been quite that close to the underside of an

animal before. How illuminating. Your horse is a stallion, isn't it?"

Her comment caught him off guard, and for a moment he could only stare at her.

"Do you always ride like that?" she asked, sitting up slowly. Her eyes, the color of clouds before a storm, were steady on his.

"I would have been more cautious had I known you were there," he said. "Do you always hide behind hedges?"

"Only when I'm trying to avoid someone." She brushed a twig from her bodice, made a sweeping inspection of herself, and seeming to find everything intact, got to her knees.

He wanted, suddenly, to know whom she might be hiding from. But that was as inappropriate as watching her tidy herself.

"Are you certain you're all right?" he asked, standing and extending a hand to help her rise.

Ignoring it, she stood, brushing her skirts down. "I believe so." She seemed to consider the matter for a moment. "Yes, I'm fine."

She glanced at him and then away, making him wonder what, exactly, she was thinking. He grabbed the reins of his horse, hesitant in a way he'd rarely felt.

"If you're certain—" he began, only to have her interrupt.

"Most assuredly," she said, watching him mount.

He inclined his head, and she smiled lightly. Two perfect strangers engaged in exquisite politeness. But he couldn't help but look back once he'd reached the road. She was gone, only the lingering echo of her voice remaining, making him wonder, idly, if he'd imagined the entire interlude.

* * *

Riona watched in dismay as he dismounted at her front door.

Who was he? Why was he calling at Tyemorn Manor? Was he one of the innumerable messengers who ferried letters between Captain Hastings and Maureen? A visitor come for Lethson? He might be filling one of a hundred roles, and would soon be gone from here, him with his amazing blue eyes and easy grin.

If it were possible, she'd stay hidden behind the tree for the rest of the day. She wasn't a hoyden, truly. She had learned her lessons well from Mrs. Parker and, before that woman's tutelage, had always been a proper young woman. She could now walk with grace across wooden floors without her heels clunking at each step. Although not as delicate as Maureen, she was not a clumsy oaf, either. She could dance in a fashion, although she admitted that the more complicated steps were beyond her. She was expected to silently count them in her mind while remaining outwardly flirtatious and charming. One or the other always took precedence. More often than not, her partner heard her mumbling to herself.

Now she'd been found in a hedge.

He'd only stared at her when she'd made that remark about his horse. No proper lady ever commented upon the gender of an animal. Which was absurd, of course, but it was one of those innumerable rules that everyone obeyed. Even living on a farm, she was supposed to pretend that she'd never noticed animals copulating, or even the fact that a male was a male. Not that she was given to studying the nether regions of horses, but in this instance she hadn't exactly been able to ignore it.

He'd known right away what she was doing. *Do you always hide behind hedges*? Her suitors in Edinburgh would never have dared say such a thing. Even if they had suspected, they would have fawned all over themselves to excuse her behavior.

Are you looking for mushrooms, my dear? Or have you gotten yourself entangled in the brambles? Or were you, perhaps, indisposed, having twisted your ankle or torn your skirt on a wayward branch?

She'd been so flustered that she'd told him the truth. Riona closed her eyes, wishing that she'd had the presence of mind to say something witty, instead.

Peering around the tree again, Riona discovered that he'd disappeared into the house.

She had seen attractive men before, in Inverness and Edinburgh. Not once had she been tempted to stare. Until now.

Would she have been as shamed if their guest had been a troll? If he had been Old Ned, for example, would she feel this flush of heat? Or even the parson? She doubted it, and it was that knowledge that further added to her irritation.

Looking down at herself, she frowned. Grass stains marred the front of her skirt, and her arm had a streak of mud on it. A leaf clung to a tendril of her hair, and she brushed it free impatiently.

She could march into the parlor in her current state and pretend that nothing was amiss, but such behavior would shock her mother. Or she could retreat to her room, clean herself up, and present herself to their guest, thereby impressing him with her manners and grace. Annoyed with herself, she chose yet another option, that of returning to her room and remaining there.

* * *

A young maid answered his knock, stepping aside before he gave her his name.

"Welcome to Tyemorn Manor," she said with a little curtsy. "Come and rest yourself in the parlor while I let the lady of the house know you've come." The greeting, evidently recited from memory, was offered with a cheerful smile.

Smiling back at her, he turned to look at Rory, who cantered up behind him. The young man dismounted, but didn't move toward the door.

"If it's all right with you, sir, I'd rather wait here."

James nodded, hiding his smile. Rory was staring at the young maid as if he'd never seen a woman before.

Entering the paneled hall, he gazed at the staircase directly in front of him. Soaring high above the foyer, the polished expanse of wooden steps seemed to entice the eye. Two intricately carved lions' heads began the banister that curved upward in a delicate arch of wood and workmanship. A beautiful creation, obviously built with as much care as the hull of a MacRae ship.

He followed the maid into one of the two rooms flanking the entranceway. Two settees, both upholstered in a deep blue fabric, sat opposite each other in front of a large white marble fireplace. The chamber walls were covered in the same dark blue material, as were the curtains on the two long windows. The monochromatic scheme was oddly comforting.

The drapes were open, and streaks of sunlight illuminated the richly patterned carpet on the floor. A silver bowl filled with flowers occupied the table between the settees and perfumed the air.

The only sound in the room was the lulling tick of the

mantel clock. For the first time in months, James felt himself relax and wondered at the skill of his hostess in wordlessly conveying welcome.

Walking to the windows, he stared at the hedge to the right of the front walk. Who was she? He smiled, thinking of her words. *Your horse is a stallion, isn't it?* Her gray eyes had been filled with a succession of emotions—surprise, wonder, embarrassment. Her face had, at first, been too pale before warming with color.

Conversation with a beautiful woman normally consisted of compliments or a series of witty verbal thrusts and parries. But with her he'd been startled into silence.

He was accustomed to feminine gestures, womanly traits. Just the right profile or angle of head, an extended hand, an artfully placed foot, a demure yet teasing smile, each one designed to attract and entice. This woman had lain beneath a hedge staring up at the sky.

Who was she?

He realized that he very much wanted—and perhaps needed—to know.

Chapter 4

Abigail bobbed in front of her, a smile on her round face.

"Ma'am," the young maid announced, "you have a visitor."

Susanna didn't bother looking up from her sewing. "If it's the parson again or his wife, Abigail," she said firmly, "then please tell them I am unwell at the moment." Not exactly a lie, since Mrs. Parker had just left her with a new list of complaints.

She'd managed a house with three boarders for over twenty years, but Susanna had never had a more disagreeable person living under her roof than Adelaide Parker. Something was always wrong—either wet or dry, hot or cold, soft or hard. Susanna closed her eyes and leaned back against the chair.

Why had she ever thought of employing the woman in the

first place? Because she had been recommended by the pastor's wife, a sweet and endearing woman who must not be related in any fashion to Adelaide Parker.

Abruptly, she realized that Abigail was still patiently standing in front of her.

A year ago she'd hired Abigail from the village. Her smile was always in attendance. Even the gloomiest of days had no effect on her mood, and as far as she knew, Abigail liked everyone. She was one of those genuinely good people who made others consider their own flaws simply by entering a room. Laughter halted, gossip stopped, and people glanced from one to the other as if ashamed of their own verbal viciousness. Susanna wondered if God created people like Abigail to make the rest of the world a better place.

Small in stature, Abigail had blond hair and soft blue eyes, and her cheeks seemed perpetually pink. She had a habit of brushing at her face with the backs of her hands as if to wipe the color away.

"It's not him at all, ma'am." Abigail said. "Nor any of the villagers come to call."

Or gossip, Susanna silently amended.

"It's a tall man with the most beautiful blue eyes you've ever seen and a smile that warms your heart just to look at it."

Susanna looked up curiously. Abigail seemed caught up in some kind of daydream. Her eyes were vacant, her smile oddly crooked, and she breathed in deep gusty sighs.

"Did he give his name?"

"No," Abigail said, looking disconcerted. "I've gone and forgotten to ask him, ma'am." She turned as if she would rectify the matter this very moment.

"Never mind, Abigail." Susanna stood, setting aside her

needlework. "I shall attend to our visitor." *Before he strips another thought from your mind.*

Truly, she should have taken Abigail's words to heart, Susanna thought a few moments later. She had no one to blame but herself for the surprise she felt, or the strange fluttering in her chest. For a moment she chastised herself, because the visitor in her parlor was much, much younger than she. But should she be denied an appreciation of masculine beauty simply because she was getting older?

She thought not.

He was as tall as Abigail had said, and slender, with broad shoulders straining the fabric of his buff coat. His face was narrow, ending in a squared chin and graced with an aquiline nose. Eyes of startling blue, so pale they looked almost transparent, stared back at her, divulging intelligence as well as force of character. His hair was black and unruly in the front where it fell over his forehead, and as she watched, he brushed it back impatiently.

Abigail was indeed correct. He was quite the most handsome man ever to stand in her parlor.

She inclined her head, realizing that she had been staring. "Forgive my rudeness, I'm Susanna McKinsey. May I be of some service?"

He smiled then, revealing white, even teeth, and for a moment she felt as if she were no more than a young girl herself. Flattening her hand against her midriff to ward off a quivery sensation, she counseled herself against such foolishness.

"I am James MacRae," he said, his voice low and resonant. "My Uncle Fergus sent me here with a message."

Until this moment, she'd forgotten the almost desperate letter she'd sent to her old friend. Riona had reluctantly acceded to the betrothal a week after she'd implored Fergus to come to her aid.

"Oh dear," she said, embarrassed that she hadn't informed Fergus of the new development.

Turning, she gave instructions for refreshments to be brought to the parlor. For a second, Susanna thought her maid had lost her wits entirely. Abigail only continued to stare at their guest before Susanna cleared her throat. The young girl finally giggled and left the room.

Shaking her head at such foolishness, she waved James to one of the settees.

"I hope Fergus is well." Sitting opposite him she wondered at the fact that there was no resemblance. Fergus was as tall, but stockier, and his hair had been a red to rival the setting sun.

"He is indeed well, and regrets that he could not come to your assistance himself."

"I did not think Fergus had any relatives."

"We believed him dead as well," he said, flashing that astonishing smile. "His sister immigrated to Nova Scotia years ago, thinking all of her family dead. Fergus had no idea that she survived, wed her childhood sweetheart, and became the mother of five sons."

"And you are one of the five?"

He nodded. "The second oldest of the brothers."

"I am so happy for Fergus," she said. "The loss of his family weighed heavily on him."

"He is about to acquire even more kin. He is due to be married soon."

"Married?" How curious that she felt no jealousy. For years, she had nursed a fondness for Fergus, but it was all too evident that he had loved another, a woman lost to him years before. The reason that, more often than not, there was an air of melancholy about him.

James nodded. "To a woman he's known for a great many years."

He handed her a letter, and she opened it with fingers that suddenly trembled.

Instead of reading it in front of him, she walked to the window, spreading open the paper and fingering the broken seal. There had not been that many occasions to witness Fergus's handwriting, but the bold strokes seemed so much like him that Susanna felt a catch in her heart.

My dearest Susanna,

I am saddened to hear of your dilemma with Riona, and pray for you and her in this hour of indecision and strife. She is a level-headed girl, and I have no doubt that she will make the right decision in the end. In the meantime, please note that my heart and my prayers are with you.

Forgive me for being unable to call upon you myself, but I know that you wish me the greatest of happiness. I have been reunited with the woman I once lost and have loved all these many years. Please know that you can count both Leah and me as your friends.

Yours in friendship,
Fergus MacRae

She stared out the window, thinking that she was not quite done with envy after all. Fergus and she were not that different in age, yet love had come to him once more.

Had she truly forgotten to write him again? Or had she secretly wished that he would call on her?

The sight of a boy standing beside two horses drew her back to the present.

Turning, she addressed James, "I am sorry he was unable to come himself," she said honestly. "But I'm glad for the reason that he was not. How kind of him to have sent you in his stead."

Polly entered the room with a tray on which a pitcher and two glasses rested, the giggling Abigail blessedly absent. "There is a young man outside," Susanna said before the housekeeper could leave the room, "who looks tired and dusty. I have no doubt he would be grateful for some refreshments as well."

"Indeed he would," James said, smiling. "Thank you."

Waving away his thanks, she sat once again. "We make a fine cider here at Tyemorn," she said, pouring from the pitcher on the tray. She handed him a tumbler and sat back against the settee.

"Tell me, how did you find yourself back in Scotland?"

"It is a long and complicated story," he began, his words interrupted by Abigail's entrance into the room. Her knees were nearly buckling beneath the weight of the tray she carried. Bemused, Susanna stared at the array of dishes aligned there—slices of the cake Cook had made a few days ago, a selection of dried fruit, and an assortment of cheese and hard crackers. The larder had been emptied. Or, at the very least, severely depleted.

James stood, helping her lower the tray to the table. Abigail bobbed another curious curtsy, her legs bowing out. Taking pity on the girl, Susanna dismissed her with a smile and a fervent wish that Polly would send her upstairs to dust.

"May I serve you?" she asked, already preparing a selection of delicacies for him. "I would dearly love to hear the tale," she said as he took the plate from her. "I must confess that I am somewhat lacking in news from time to time in this out-of-the-way place."

Now, that was a blatant falsehood since the inhabitants of Ayleshire were remarkably informed as to events transpiring in the world. No doubt due to the trade for which the village was known, linen so finely woven that it attracted buyers from a dozen nations. After politics, talk of rebellion, and news of far-away wars were exhausted as topics, there was always gossip.

"My brother was heir to an earldom," he said. "On the way to England to decline it, Alisdair found himself married. Consequently, he returned to Scotland with both a wife and a title, intent on rebuilding our ancestral home. I chose to remain at Gilmuir in order to help him build his shipyard."

"And your other brothers?"

"Douglas is too young to be of much use to anyone," he said, smiling. "But Hamish and Brendan command their own ships, as I did once."

"My husband was a sailor," she told him. "He would have been miserable on land."

"I've merely traded my captain's duties for those of a shipbuilder. At least for the moment."

She took a slice of the jewel cake, thinking that Cook had outdone herself.

"Have you traveled far from Gilmuir?"

"A matter of a few days only," he said.

And all for naught, she was afraid. She sighed, wishing again that she had thought to send word to Fergus. "Did Fergus tell you of our troubles?"

He shook his head. "Only that he regrets not being able to assist you himself."

"He said nothing?" she asked carefully, sipping from her tumbler of cider. An inkling of an idea began, was ruthlessly smothered, yet was reborn just as quickly. Fate and Fergus had delivered James MacRae to her, the answer to a prayer she hadn't dared to utter.

"It is not nearly as fascinating as your story, I'm afraid, James." She smiled at him. "May I call you that? I am, after all, a longtime friend of your uncle's." How odd that her heart was racing and her palms felt damp. "Please, call me Susanna."

Pouring herself another glass of cider, she feigned a relaxed pose. If he looked carefully, he might see that her fingers trembled as she lowered the pitcher. A point in her favor, that she did not lie easily or well. "You'll stay a few days, I hope. Just to rest from your journey."

"Perhaps overnight. I'm anxious to return to Gilmuir."

"Yes, of course. You must not wish to be away from your wife." She smiled gently, holding her breath.

"Alisdair is the only MacRae brother who is married," he said, smiling.

She lowered her eyes and exhaled. "I was hoping . . ." she began, allowing her words to trail away into silence. "Never mind." She looked up, smiled, then glanced away. "It would be too much an imposition."

He didn't look all that eager for her to continue. Another sigh didn't elicit his curiosity, either, so she was forced to lower her head and look at him below her lashes. A rather pathetic pose. "You are, no doubt, a busy man. Far be it from me to inflict my problems on you." *Oh dear, Susanna, you are billowing up the sails*, using a favored expression of the long-departed Mr. McKinsey.

"How may I be of service, Susanna?"

Finally.

She smiled brightly at him, this expression less one of deception than of burgeoning relief.

"I hope you do not think the task onerous, but I am in need of a man unknown to my workers."

He said nothing, but the look in his eyes was calm and waiting. Not a man to fool.

"You see," she said, rushing to finish her request before she lost her nerve, "someone is stealing from me. The losses have not been large, I confess. A few sheep here, a goat or so there, a bale of hay. But if it continues, I could be rendered penniless. I need help ascertaining who, exactly, is behind these heinous deeds."

She seemed to have rendered him speechless. He blinked a few times, took a drink, but still said nothing. Finally, he spoke. "I am not a magistrate, Susanna."

"Oh, but I would not wish one. You see," she said, leaning forward, "Tyemorn Manor is actually a series of farms, James. We employ twenty people here. If one of them is stealing from me, I want to know why."

"But you don't want him punished?"

"Indeed not," she said, gripping her hands tightly together. The falsehood was only minutes old, and already she was becoming ensnared in the details of it.

"A few days," she urged. "It would take no more than that."

He didn't say a word for a few moments.

"I truly wouldn't ask if you were not a friend. Dear Fergus." She sighed again, looking toward the window as if in yearning.

"If you think I can be of service," he finally said.

"One more thing." She hesitated, wondering how, exactly, she might request such an odd thing of him. Just ask. "If you would, please, James. I'd prefer that you not divulge the reason for your being here. Let's just keep it between the two of us." She wished that he weren't looking at her so strangely. As if he saw through her ruse.

"Doesn't your steward know of the thefts?"

She felt cold. "Of course," she said, smiling forcibly. "But only Old Ned."

"Then I shall direct my inquiries only to him."

Susanna stood, began to move toward the door before he could change his mind. "I'll have Polly prepare a room for you and your companion. Today is too late to be about any investigation, but you could start in the morning. Until dinner, then," she said, making her escape.

A short, profound oath escaped him after Susanna closed the door behind her, leaving him alone in the parlor.

For the first time in his life he felt the burden of family. *Someone to stand for me.* Fergus's words were irritatingly loud in his conscience.

She'd been trembling, her hands clasped tightly together as if she were frightened, and she'd asked for his help almost timidly. How could he refuse?

He swore once more and resigned himself to a few days at Tyemorn Manor. He walked to the window, watching Rory talking to the young maid. He turned bright red as she spoke to him, then looked bemused as the girl curtsied.

Rory evidently wouldn't mind remaining here for a few days.

As for himself? There was only one bright spot in this cntire situation, and that was the woman he'd met. He didn't doubt that she was one of Susanna McKinsey's daughters. There had been a resemblance about the eyes and chin.

He smiled, conceding that investigating some missing livestock was the least he could do for Fergus's old friend.

Susanna flattened her back against the closed parlor door, motioned to Abigail standing outside. "Go find Old Ned," she whispered in desperation when the girl reached her. "Have him meet me in the kitchen."

"The kitchen, ma'am?"

Susanna refrained from rolling her eyes. "Yes, the kitchen. And quickly!"

That errand done, she went in search of Polly to have her prepare a chamber for James MacRae and the young man who'd accompanied him.

The house was a warren of various-sized rooms connected by narrow hallways and a wide staircase. Susanna had never visited her great aunt; in fact, prior to her death she'd not known of the other woman's existence. But she wondered from time to time, especially in walking from one section of the house to another, if Mary had found Tyemorn Manor as charmingly odd as she did.

A small octagonal tower had been constructed on the south side of the manor, adding two odd-shaped chambers to the house. Mrs. Parker was now installed on the second floor. She would have Polly prepare the third-floor chamber for James. The breeze from the two facing windows cooled the space, and the view of the farms was breathtaking.

"I hope he's not as rude as Mrs. Parker," Polly said, fluffing up a pillow.

"No one is like Mrs. Parker." A lamentable truth. The

woman greeted her every morning with a litany of complaints.

"How long will they be staying?" Polly asked, reaching into the press for another set of linen.

"As long as possible," Susanna replied. "As long as possible."

She left Polly looking after her with a quizzical expression. There was time enough to explain it all later. For now she needed to convince Ned to cooperate. When she entered the kitchen, he was sitting there at the table, his cap removed, his nose buried in a cup whose contents smelled suspiciously like whiskey.

The room wasn't empty. Cook stood at the stove, stirring a stew for dinner. But instead of asking her to leave, Susanna realized that if this impromptu plan of hers was to succeed she would need the help of her entire household.

She sat beside Old Ned, waiting patiently for him to finish his whiskey. There wasn't any point in fussing at him; Ned did what he wanted when he wanted, regardless of her wishes.

Cook, however, despite her appearance, was a much more congenial person. She was tall for a woman, with broad shoulders that could rival any man's. Her form attested to her skill at her job, however, but since she was such a large woman she carried the extra weight well. Her cheeks, far from being plump, were marked by high bones, giving her an almost Slavic appearance. Her thin lips were almost always narrowed until her mouth was a mere gash in her face. Her nose was truly spectacular, pointed and narrow, as if God had taken two fingers to it and pulled with all His might. Her true name was Feona, and she was a widow Susanna had hired from the village, but she preferred to be called Cook.

The kitchen was larger than the house decreed, as if the builders had constructed this room first, foreseeing a much larger home. Two large tables stretched the width of the room, each equipped with benches. Along one wall was a huge fireplace, tall enough that a man might stand within its arch. But they did most of their cooking on a new iron stove nestled against one wall.

Finally, Old Ned finished his whiskey with a loud, satisfied sigh.

"I was getting ready to muck out the irrigation ditch when you summoned me," he said. "I hope it's for a good enough reason I'm here."

He didn't seem to understand that she employed him, but then neither did Mrs. Parker. Of the two of them, however, she much preferred Old Ned's stubbornness. At least he had Tyemorn's best interests at heart.

Although his brown hair was only lightly salted with gray, the pointed beard falling to his chest was white and matched in shade by a bushy mustache and eyebrows. His skin had been weathered by the elements into a leathery patchwork of lines, but his brown eyes appeared almost youthful at times.

"Ned," she said conspiratorially, "I need your help. What I am about to tell you must not leave this room." She caught Cook's eye, and the other woman nodded. "Have I your word of that?"

He studied her over the rim of his cup, then nodded, albeit reluctantly.

Accepting that this was the best she was going to get, Susanna explained what she needed.

"There are no lambs missing."

"I know that. But for now you must pretend that there are."

Polly moved into the room, eyeing Susanna with a frown.

"Why would I be doing that?"

"It is the only way I can keep James McRae here," she said, explaining about their guest.

"And why would you be wanting to keep a stranger at the manor?" he asked, narrowing his eyes.

Perhaps it was better not to admit the truth, Susanna realized. Not at this precise moment. After all, she needed to see if there was a chance of success for her plan.

"I can't tell you that right now. You will simply have to trust in me."

The old man didn't move a muscle. Nothing in his craggy face altered, as if he had passed the point of being surprised by anything he saw or heard. Polly, however, narrowed her eyes as if she'd divined Susanna's intentions. Cook only shrugged and turned back to the pot.

"Well?"

"Women," he finally said in disgust.

She sat up straighter, frowning at him, not having expected quite this response.

"Show a woman a straight line and she'll make a circle of it."

"What is that supposed to mean?"

He glanced over at the door when Abigail entered, bearing the tray from the parlor. Evidently, the girl had taken the opportunity to ogle James MacRae again.

"Men are direct, women aren't. You've got something on your mind, it's better for it to be out in the open."

She frowned at him. A quite quelling expression. How vexing that he simply ignored her.

He narrowed his eyes. "What else are we supposed to be missing?"

"A little of this and a little of that," she said, wishing he wouldn't frown at her so. "A few lambs, a few cows, perhaps some hay."

"You'll never fool Riona," he said, and for the first time since the meeting began, his voice warmed. "She knows the stock like I do."

"Then come up with a story for her," Susanna said, irritated by his continued stubbornness.

"Who've you picked for the thief?"

"Since there isn't really a theft," she said, standing, "there's hardly a necessity for a thief."

She fluffed her skirt, smoothed down the fabric with both hands. "So you'll help me?" she asked.

He nodded, not bothering to put his assent into speech. Standing, he left the house the way he came, through the side door. She could not have run Tyemorn Manor without him, but that didn't negate the fact that Ned was sometimes cantankerous and difficult. He'd been with her great aunt for years, and most of the information she'd learned about him had come from Cook and Abigail.

A most valuable man, but a most annoying one.

She dismissed thoughts of Ned and concentrated, instead, on her plan.

Chapter 5

"**S**upper is to be held in the red dining room, Riona," Polly announced, after knocking on her door and poking her head inside.

Riona turned, surprised. "The Red Room?" Her mother never used the cavernous room that seated thirty-five, preferring instead the more intimate family dining room. Susanna had named it the Red Room because of the predominant color of the massive tapestry in the room.

"What is the occasion?" she asked, even though she had her suspicions.

"We've a visitor," Polly said. "Fergus's nephew." Polly's smile seemed younger than her years. She'd been with them for a decade now, and on their arrival at Tyemorn Manor had been promoted to housekeeper. Although not exceptionally skilled at all her tasks, she made up for any lack of expertise with a boundless enthusiasm for her new position. Now she consulted the brooch watch pinned to her bodice. "Your mother's invited the parson and his wife, too."

"And Mrs. Parker will be present, no doubt," Riona said. The hope that the older woman was somehow indisposed was dashed the moment Polly nodded.

"You're to wear one of your Edinburgh gowns and to mind the time." All her instructions delivered, Polly left the room.

They were keeping town hours in honor of Mrs. Parker. Normally, at Tyemorn, they ate but two meals a day, a large breakfast midmorning and then a second meal late in the afternoon. As long as Mrs. Parker was in residence, however, they kept to Edinburgh hours, which meant that three meals needed to be served, since dinner was not eaten until much later in the evening.

Now they were hosting a visitor. An attractive man with a smile that was too charming, and blue eyes that seemed to see into her very thoughts. She really should have planned for such an eventuality. Her mother was famous for her hospitality.

Fergus's nephew? Strange, she'd not seen any resemblance, but then she'd not been looking for any. *No, Riona, you were too occupied in making an idiot of yourself.*

She had fond memories of Fergus and had missed him greatly this past year. But he had left Cormech before they had, heading back to his childhood home.

"I'm for changing the way I've lived my life all these years, lass," he'd said the night before his departure.

"In what way?" she asked, sitting beside him and carefully ignoring his wooden leg as she always did. He wore the appendage casually, even though it was, to her way of thinking, a badge of honor. The wound that had eventually led to the loss of his leg had been inflicted thirty years earlier. Culloden and all the battles before it were not subjects he spoke about, however. Still, there were times when she wanted to ask, to know what it had been like to be truly Scots on that one fateful morning.

"I've lived more cowardly than I should have. Fixed in myself and not thinking of others."

She'd glanced down at his leg, understanding what he didn't say. After Culloden, he'd refused to return to his home because of what the war had done to him. For the same reason, he'd lost his sweetheart, preferring to let her think he was dead rather than maimed. She'd married another, and he'd grieved for her all these years.

"Don't you live your life the same way, lass," he'd said earnestly, and she, just as sincere, had agreed with a smile.

What would Fergus say now to see her cowering in her chamber, almost afraid to meet his nephew again?

Go and face the man, Riona. He'll not bite your head off. Fergus's voice boomed loudly in the recesses of her imagination. *No, Fergus,* she answered silently, *but he might smile at me, and that would be just as frightening.*

Perhaps she should take a bit more care with her hair to ensure that the unruly tresses stayed in place. She pushed at the right side and then the left, making the tiny muslin cap on top of her head list like a sinking ship. Abigail had helped with her hair tonight, but no amount of pomade could keep her curls where they were supposed to be. Perhaps more pins were the answer, but she had used all that she had and borrowed most of Maureen's.

A knock on the door was her final summons as her

mother's voice came from the corridor. "Hurry, Riona, the guests are already assembled."

At least she was dressed well. Her soft green gown had a low square neckline edged with a dark green pleated fringe. Her looped-up skirt revealed a quilted underskirt of cream silk. Her sleeves were gathered and tucked, adorned with small embroidered flowers to match those on her bodice.

Of all the nights for her complexion to be sun-brightened. Her gray eyes were a bit too bright, as if she were a mischievous child holding a secret. In actuality, there was nothing even remotely amusing about this moment, and yet she still looked curiously pleased with herself.

"Cease," she said to her reflection, but the Riona of the mirror stared back, a small smile curling up the corners of her lips. She held her shawl, crafted from the same brocade fabric as her overskirt, closer about her shoulders in an effort to compose herself.

She wanted him to see her differently. Not a hoyden hiding behind a hedge. Someone who'd recently spent five weeks in Edinburgh. A woman the match of his attractiveness.

One more glance at herself in the mirror. When she smiled, her lips curved pleasingly over white, even teeth. All except the front one that overlapped its neighbor by a tiny bit. Her nose wasn't memorable, but neither was it pointed nor overly short. The chin, however, hinted at her stubbornness with its square appearance.

There was nothing she could do about her accent. She would always sound Cormech born and bred. But she could show him that she'd been English trained. The merriment gone from her eyes, she tilted her head up and surveyed herself, regal pose and all. No, she abruptly decided, that would not do at all. She wasn't the regal sort. But neither was she the kind of woman who skulks about in bushes.

Or perhaps she was, thinking of the calf she'd helped birth earlier.

What she needed to do was show him some sort of happy measure between the two. Herself, perhaps, dressed for dinner with her best manners showing.

She pushed at her hair again, adjusted her shawl, powdered her neckline, pressed a cool cloth against her cheeks. One last glance in the mirror, and she sighed in resignation.

As she walked through her door and closed it softly behind her, Riona couldn't help but wonder why it mattered so much. He was, after all, only a visitor, and however embarrassed she was by their meeting, he would soon be gone from their lives.

In three weeks she was going to be married. That fact alone should render her more circumspect.

"My daughters," Susanna said as Riona and Maureen entered the room a few moments later.

Riona inclined her head in greeting as she'd been taught. Until a man's rank was ascertained, it would never do to slight him. Therefore, an inquisitive look was always better than a snub. Mrs. Parker's words.

"My dears, may I present James MacRae of Gilmuir. He's brought news that our dear friend Fergus is to be married."

"Fergus? How delightful," Maureen said, stepping forward with a smile. "How is he?"

With Riona's marriage soon to occur, Maureen's betrothal to Captain Hastings looked secure. Over the past week, Maureen's grief had been replaced by an effusive happiness in direct proportion to Riona's misery.

In all honesty, Riona could not blame her sister. Maureen had had nothing to do with that night in Edinburgh. Nor should she be restrained from feeling happiness now. No one, after all, had pressured Riona into marriage. There was simply no choice. Still, she felt as if she'd been asked to surrender her glass of wine while there was a full cask remaining in the butler's pantry.

Their guest was dressed in a buff coat with a high standing collar and deep cuffs, one on which the lapels had been folded back to reveal a rather splendid waistcoat of crimson. His blue breeches were fitted into tall, immaculate black boots. The severity of his attire was offset by gold buttons bearing the image of a thistle.

Not one speck of dust clung to him. Not one leaf or spot of dirt. Even his boots gleamed.

"Fergus is well and happy," James said. "I have been instructed to give both of you his compliments and best wishes."

Maureen was an excellent conversationalist, easily describing the sights and entertainments in Edinburgh. As for herself, it was better if she said nothing at all. Before she'd gone to Mrs. Parker's house, her companions had been Old Ned and the workers of Tyemorn Manor. And prior to that, the maids in their Cormech home. She was not, as the older woman had once ruefully stated, very well suited for polite society.

When MacRae glanced at her curiously, she only smiled slightly at him. A glance that in no way gave him any encouragement. The kind but distant look Mrs. Parker maintained was the kindest way to quell any hopeful, but unsuitable, suitors.

For the first time, she was grateful for the Englishwoman's lessons.

He didn't look in her direction again, concentrating his attentions on her sister, instead. Maureen's laughter was especially annoying, Riona discovered. How odd that she'd never before noticed that her sister seemed to end each sentence as if it were a question.

Had Maureen suddenly forgotten the good Captain Hastings?

"We have missed you, my dear," the parson said from beside her.

Startled, Riona turned to smile at him and his wife.

"We've not seen either of you for months it seems."

She had thought from the moment she'd met Reverend and Mrs. Dunant that these two people were admirably suited for their roles in life. Mrs. Dunant was childless and showered the children of Ayleshire with enough attention to make up for the lack, while her husband was as gentle from the pulpit. His sermons were genuinely uplifting, making Riona feel that perhaps she was capable of earning a place in heaven. The pastor at the Edinburgh church Mrs. Parker favored made her certain she was about to perish in hell, and that any thought of aspiring to a hereafter was futile.

Mrs. Dunant smiled at her, nodding at her husband in that way long-married people have. "Now I understand felicitations are in order."

Riona smiled, which surely must have been a pale imitation of her usual expression, but no one seemed to note the difference. A disconcerting revelation, that she was thought to be content with her future. So pleased, in fact, that not one person had wished to discuss it. Not her mother, not Maureen, not even the formidable Mrs. Parker. Her future as Mrs. Harold McDougal simply was, like the dawn or the sunset, expected and assured.

"You'll be married at Ayleshire, surely?" Mrs. Dunant asked.

"Of course." In fact, she'd given little thought to where her wedding would take place. Strange, how the details had not yet been finalized.

I'll return in a month, Riona. Harold's words replayed in her head. *I've matters to attend to in Edinburgh.*

Take your time, Harold. I am in no mood for marriage.

Ah, but I am, he'd said, chuckling when she frowned at him.

Until he returned she was, no doubt, supposed to wait as any expectant bride, with a bright smile and starry eyes and a giggle not unlike Maureen's.

She bit down on her tongue at that thought, forced a smile to her face, and nearly sighed in relief when the doors to the dining room were opened.

MacRae led her mother into dinner, followed by Mrs. Parker shepherded by the pastor. She, Maureen, and Mrs. Dunant were left to bring up the rear.

"Will the manor be participating in Lethson this year?" Mrs. Dunant asked.

"The solstice?" Riona asked.

The pastor's wife kept her gaze on her husband's back as she whispered to Riona. "It's best we don't use that term. Robert has learned to turn a blind eye to such festivities but such a pagan word should be avoided."

They'd settled in to Tyemorn Manor in October, too late to participate in the ceremony that marked the first six months of the year, but she'd heard Cook and Abigail discussing it recently. Evidently, the entire village joined in the celebration. Shops were closed, and every other occupation was delayed until the festivities were complete.

"The village elders coordinate everything. It's best if you speak with them and volunteer yourself before too much more time has passed." With a pat on her arm, Mrs. Dunant stepped forward, leaving Riona to follow.

The dining room was one of those odd chambers at Tyemorn Manor that was too large in proportion to the rest of the house. A red and tan striped silk lined the walls, and crimson curtains hung from the solitary narrow window. A large tapestry dominated the west wall, the scene one of a crowded courtyard filled with knights, horses, and ladies in waiting. A gate stood open, and through it came a score of hunters, bearing several dead deer between them. The animals' glassy eyes stared sightlessly toward heaven while blood dripped from each carcass to pool on the ground.

As she did every time she entered this particular room, Riona glanced at the tapestry, marveling not at its artistry, although it was expertly crafted, but its ugliness.

Three silver epergnes filled with candles were set in the middle of the long table and on each of the two sideboards. Despite the candlelight, however, shadows still loomed in the corners.

The parson sat to her right, with Mrs. Parker to her left. Across the table, Maureen was flanked by James and Mrs. Dunant, with her mother seated at the head of the table. At least this way, MacRae would have to look up from time to time and see her. After that first glance at her, he'd not deigned to look in her direction.

She only wished he was as easy to ignore.

"I look forward to officiating at your wedding, my dear,"

the parson said, smiling at her. "Although I'm surprised at the suddenness of it."

"A love match," Mrs. Parker hurriedly offered from Riona's left. "They fell in love so quickly it made my head spin. She could not wait and neither would dear Harold."

Mrs. Parker smiled toothily at the parson, who had no choice but to smile back.

James glanced in her direction, then looked away as quickly, bending his head attentively to something Mrs. Dunant said.

Recalling one of Mrs. Parker's lessons that a lady never appeared to have an appetite, Riona pretended not to be hungry. She ate barely three spoonfuls of soup, and waved away the wine, choosing cider instead.

"A most charming man," Mrs. Parker whispered to Susanna.

Susanna glanced at their guest and, finding him occupied in conversation, whispered back. "He is a ship's captain."

Mrs. Parker narrowed her eyes. Evidently, not an occupation she considered suitable.

"And the brother of an earl," Susanna added.

Mrs. Parker's frown eased as she considered MacRae with a softer gaze. No doubt the woman considered him a matrimonial candidate. Riona could almost see her running through the list of available women, clients who might pay well to be united with such a man.

She hoped he hadn't overheard their comments. Yet she couldn't imagine that it was the first time women had speculated about him. Men as attractive as James MacRae must become inured to attention.

Her soon-to-be husband's face floated in the air as if she'd summoned him there. Harold's complexion was pale, almost waxen, while James was sunburned brown as if he spent all his time out of doors without a proper hat. Harold's eyes were hazel, his hair brown, his height average. In fact, everything about Harold was unremarkable. Unlike the man who sat opposite her, with his black hair, blue eyes, and wondrous smile.

She herself had never been entranced by a man's looks, believing that character was more important. But in that respect, Harold was also lacking. A man who would ensnare a woman in marriage had little honor.

Concentrating on her plate, Riona wished that she didn't feel so excluded. The parson and Mrs. Parker were discussing the sights to be found in Edinburgh, while her mother was engaged in listening to Mrs. Dunant's tales of plans for a new communion cloth. Laughter and conversation swirled around her as if they were clouds and she a lone tree beneath them.

She could have saved herself the effort of her toilette, since their guest had looked only once in her direction.

Suddenly, he glanced at her again. His face was immediately stripped of emotion, his mouth losing its smile, his eyes suddenly growing colder. Blue ice, she thought, startled by the indifference of his look, and wondered why she didn't become chilled from his expression.

Just as quickly, James looked away again, leaving her with the notion that of all the people in the room, he found her the most lacking.

She was to be married.

The idea rankled him. But she was, after all, a stranger. However much she incited his curiosity, he would be wiser to take no notice of her.

She looked almost forlorn sitting there silent among the others. Not the woman he'd met a few short hours ago. Somewhere in between the hedges and this dinner she'd changed. He doubted this woman would comment about his horse with such candor, or stare at him with wide eyes.

A love match.

No doubt she was pining for her intended.

Of the two women, Maureen was, perhaps, the prettier. She had a delicate sort of beauty, her ivory features and black hair reminding him of his sister-in-law. But where Iseabal's eyes were a vibrant green, Maureen's were blue, the mirror of her mother's.

Riona was unlike either her mother or her sister in her appearance. Although some of the features were the same, her eyes were gray, a color so fascinating that he found his gaze returning to her face time and again. What he had thought was embarrassment earlier must be her natural coloring. Her cheeks were pink, her eyes bright and luminous. The picture of joyful health for all that she sat immobile between the two older people, clenching her shawl so tightly it looked as if she were strangling it. Occasionally, she would look up from her meal, frown at her sister, and then look away.

While Maureen was a charming conversationalist, Riona had said little during dinner. Any personality she might have possessed was well hidden beneath a surface amicability. Riona. The name was as unusual as the woman had been. A pity that she'd disappeared. Or perhaps she was simply a wraith, lasting but a moment near the hedge.

He was, he suddenly realized, being asked a question. Mrs. Parker smiled at him expectantly. Maureen answered, deftly hiding the fact that he had not been paying attention.

"Yes, please tell us about some of your voyages. How exciting to be a sea captain."

"Not all excitement," he said, smiling. "There are days of tedium waiting for a wind."

"Or cleaning tack and decks," Riona said.

Surprised, he glanced over at her.

"We come from Cormech, Mr. MacRae," she explained. "It's a port town, and there are more than enough sea captains and ships to observe." She sent a fulminating look at her sister, then studied her plate again.

"Riona is correct, sir, in that we are not unfamiliar with the sight of a ship," Susanna interjected. "But that does not mean we are not curious as to your travels."

"A dangerous occupation surely," the parson said.

"There is more jeopardy on land, sir," James told Mr. Dunant. "At sea one is subject to nature and rarely to man."

Mr. Dunant smiled. "I minister to mankind, and have no sway over nature, so perhaps I'm biased in that regard."

"But to have seen all those sights was surely exciting," Maureen said.

"I have heard of many strange customs in the Orient," Susanna said, nodding when Abigail brought another bottle of wine. She came to his side, pouring his glass first and giggling when he smiled his thanks. "Have you traveled there?"

"Yes, often."

Riona looked up, then away again, her lips thinned. He couldn't help but wonder what words she'd bitten off without speaking.

"I've a cousin with the East India Company," Mrs. Parker said. "Have you traveled there?"

James nodded, hoping someone would change the subject.

But she persisted. "Do you know any of the British in India, Mr. MacRae?"

"I've met a few, madam," he said. He'd delivered three ships under charter to the Company, but he had no love for the English association.

"God has seen fit to convert many of the heathen in those lands," Mr. Dunant said.

For a moment he considered not answering, but the pastor and his wife were looking at him expectantly. "Yes, they have." Although he'd striven for a noncommittal tone, James could hear the disapproval in his own voice.

"Do you not believe we should attempt to introduce God to such a heathen land?" the pastor asked.

Mrs. Parker was likewise curious. "Or bring them British trade?"

This was not the first time he'd entered into such a discussion. Nor, James suspected, would it be the last. But, as in arguments about the weather, there was rarely a definitive winner. Each man had his opinion, and each opinion was simply that.

"I don't believe that it's wise for anyone to go to other countries," James answered carefully, "and interject one's beliefs to the exclusion of the native population's. It is one thing to teach faith, another to belittle others' culture."

"And you think we do?"

"I know we do," James said. "I've seen the East India Company at work. They've no feel for India, no respect for its inhabitants." The British would not be satisfied until every man, woman, and child was trussed up in English clothing, spoke English, and carried a King James version of the Bible to prove that they had indeed been anglicized. Thoughts he would never convey to the assembled guests.

Mr. Dunant was not to blame for the excesses of those in his calling any more than Mrs. Parker was responsible for the wrongs perpetrated by the East India Company. Their only fault was to admire the institutions that so effortlessly conveyed contempt while ostensibly trying to do good.

"Would you have no foreigners in India?" Riona asked quietly.

Her question was an act of defiance, James thought, if the look from Mrs. Parker was any indication. He smiled and answered her, his response no doubt as ill advised.

"I would feel the same if a man came to Scotland and claimed me ignorant of knowledge, forced me to speak his language, wear his clothing, and believe in what he did, ignoring thousands of years of my history and my own antecedents."

"You've just described the English presence in Scotland," Riona said, her look somber and intent.

Mrs. Parker gasped, and even the parson and his wife appeared shocked. Only Susanna looked amused, but that expression was quickly wiped from her face.

"However," he added, changing the subject quickly. "I have not been aboard ship for nearly a year."

"I thought those born to the sea always longed for it," Riona said.

"Perhaps I was not born to the sea." Their gazes locked, and for a moment he thought that she might say something else, but she evidently thought better of it.

Mrs. Parker, seated beside her, whispered something he could not hear. Her blush intensified, and this time he did not doubt it was caused by embarrassment. Yet he'd enjoyed her probing questions and saluted her courage in voicing what others might feel but not say.

Another course was served, and he noted that Riona ate even less this time. He wanted to ask her if she had no appetite for this meal, if something was disturbing her, or if discomfiture had stripped her of hunger. A paradoxical woman. She was, truly, as fascinating as he'd earlier thought. Yet now she sat opposite him, eyes once more downcast and staring at her plate.

"You have an interesting accent, Captain MacRae. Where are you from?"

He smiled at Mrs. Parker, wondering at her fixed look. The woman was staring at him as if she were a starving cat. Evidently, her disapproval of his opinions was transient and to be forgotten. Or supplanted beneath a respect for his heritage. He couldn't help but wonder how she would have treated him had he been the oldest son and an earl.

Not for the first time, he blessed the fact that Alisdair was the firstborn.

"From Nova Scotia, madam," he said, "although I've recently moved back to Scotland."

"Do you live near Ayleshire?"

"A few days' distance," he answered, wishing that she would not survey him quite so avidly. "Gilmuir." At her blank look, he continued. "Not far from Inverness. Gilmuir is our ancestral home."

"A castle, I understand," Susanna contributed.

"A castle?" Mrs. Parker sat back in her chair, her plump face wrinkling into a smile.

"My brother's land," he said firmly. "He is rebuilding the structure, and I am only assisting him."

Her smile subsided somewhat, but not enough to reassure him.

"May I offer you felicitations on your wedding," he said, raising his glass to Riona.

She looked startled at his words, but recovered quickly enough.

"Thank you," she replied, looking not in his direction but at the wall behind him and the hideous tapestry mounted there.

His curiosity surfaced once again, and just as before he ruthlessly tamped it down. She was to be married, and any thoughts about her were unwise.

Chapter 6

"**H**ow long is he staying, Mother, and why is he staying at all?" Riona asked, as her mother closed the heavy front door behind the parson and Mrs. Dunant. Mrs. Parker had retired for the night, and Maureen was in her room dreaming, no doubt, of the worthwhile Captain Hastings. Their guest had likewise retreated to his chamber.

Susanna whirled and stared at her. "Is this what I get for spending all that money to have you educated in manners?" She swept past Riona, walking back into the dining room. Riona had no choice but to follow her.

"If so, I've not received my money's worth at all," Susanna said, moving the epergnes to the sideboard.

Riona felt a spurt of shame. "Forgive me, Mother. I only wished to know why he's here."

"Is it any of your concern?"

Taken aback, Riona could only stare at her mother. In the past, Susanna had never hesitated in sharing the business of the estate with her. In fact, she'd even come to ask her advice in certain matters, as if to second Old Ned's recommendation.

"Evidently it's not," she said, stepping away from the table.

"Fergus sent him," Susanna said, gathering up the used silver from the table and placing it in the basket Abigail held. The cutlery would be the first to be washed, then dried and put back into the cedar-lined box for the next important occasion. "He has agreed to help me with a problem I've been having."

"A problem?"

"Nothing you need be concerned about, Riona."

"Is it Great Aunt Mary's legacy?"

Her mother looked startled for a moment before quickly recovering. "No, do you wish there was a problem with it? Sometimes I think you would have been happier if there never had been a legacy."

"I would have been content without Mrs. Parker," Riona admitted, "and without those weeks in Edinburgh. But I would not have missed this year at Tyemorn."

Susanna halted beside a chair and studied her. "Will you be happy living in Edinburgh?"

No, but the truth would serve no purpose in this instance. Riona dreaded the idea of moving to Edinburgh, but there was no question of living elsewhere. Harold had made that point clear the day he'd left Ayleshire.

"I'll need to locate a place for us, of course," he'd said matter-of-factly. "My bachelor quarters will never do. Something with a garden, perhaps? You'd like that, wouldn't you, Riona?"

She wouldn't like it at all, but she'd only smiled, determined to be resigned to her fate. After all, she had to marry someone. But the fact that her money would pay for his new style of living was rancorous. Perhaps her mother was correct after all, and she wished that their newfound wealth would disappear.

"Then we're not poor again?" she asked in an attempt at humor.

Susanna only smiled, continuing around the table removing the silver, inspecting the crystal, duties she hadn't relinquished no matter how large or wealthy their household.

"Is there a problem with the farms?" she asked.

"Do not tax yourself, Riona," Susanna said, reaching over and patting her arm. "It's nothing that should worry you."

In other words, her mother had no intention of telling her. Strange, since Susanna was very bad at keeping secrets.

"Let me help you," Riona said, picking up a few of the plates and following her mother into the kitchen.

"Nonsense, this is my job, and Polly and Abigail and I will do it well enough. You should be readying yourself for bed since you rise at dawn." Her mother's words were uttered with a smile, an unspoken apology for the sharpness of her earlier comments.

Sleep, however, had been elusive for the past week. Instead of returning to her room, Riona grabbed a bannock from the tray on the table and left the kitchen by the side door.

Walking away from the house, she took the path leading up around the barn to a spot overlooking the pastures. She began to stroll between the night-shrouded trees, feeling the heat of the day still present in the dirt beneath her shoes. At Cormech, she'd never noticed the seasons in the way she did here, or felt so close to the earth.

A bird called and was answered; a few crickets chirped a greeting. The gardener's dog barked from his cottage on the other side of the manor house. Night sounds that comforted her. She'd left her shawl behind in the dining room, but the night was warm, the breeze gently brushing against her cheek.

The bannock was a poor substitute for dinner. When it was gone she wished for another, but was in no hurry to return to the kitchen.

Staring up at the stars, Riona wished that the moon was full. Instead, it was only a crescent, half obscured by wafting clouds.

She'd acted the fool again, hadn't she? She should have remained mute instead of saying anything that popped into her head.

What had happened to her? Her sister's politeness had grated on her, Maureen's gentle welcome of James MacRae acting as an irritant. She loved her sister, and Maureen had done nothing more than either of them had been taught to do—converse politely on a variety of subjects while complimenting a man every other sentence. Riona should have acted in the same manner.

Instead, she'd been almost rude.

"It's not as if I wanted to act the idiot," she explained to the moon. Evidently, there was something about James MacRae that brought out the worst in her. At least she'd not spilled soup on her bodice. "Please, let him leave soon." Less a plea to the stars, she realized, than a prayer.

"I think now is a good time to announce myself," James said, stepping out from behind one of the trees.

She felt a prickling of embarrassment, but reassured herself that he couldn't know she'd spoken of him. Wrapping her arms around her waist, Riona stared at the dark shadow emerging from the grove.

"What are you doing here?" she asked, then winced at the abruptness of the question. "Could you not sleep?" There, she sounded almost polite.

"I'm used to more activity than I've had today."

She nodded, understanding. While in Edinburgh, she'd found herself constantly restless simply for that reason. Being an heiress didn't require very much effort.

"I would give you a chore to do," she said, "but the cows have all been milked and the animals fed."

"Perhaps a walk is all I need." There was amusement in his voice, and for the first time tonight, she smiled genuinely.

"This path leads to the top of the hill. At night there's a lovely breeze."

"Would it be proper to ask you to come with me?"

A hundred responses came to her lips, but they all fell beneath a greater truth. She was betrothed, and being here alone with him was vastly improper.

"No," she said, acting wiser than she wished to be, "it wouldn't."

"Because you're about to be married."

"It would be untoward at any time."

"Then I shall leave you," he said. The shadow moved and she wondered if he bowed to her.

"My father was a sailor," she said, in order to keep him here. "He died at sea. I always wished that he would stay at home, but he told me once that a man is born to be what he will, and neither wishes nor weeping will ever keep him from it."

"A wise man, your father."

He said nothing further, and she smiled again. Must she pluck the words from him? Very well, it was little enough penance for her earlier rudeness.

"Do you not miss the sea?"

"I've been a builder for the past year, but that does not mean I've given up my occupation."

Riona decided that she preferred James MacRae in the darkness rather than in daylight. With only the quarter moon as illumination, she wasn't flummoxed by his attractiveness, didn't wonder at the color of his eyes, and wasn't rendered wordless by his smile.

"Rebuilding your castle?" She wondered if he were punishing her after all, or if James was simply not used to speaking of himself. That would be refreshing after the men she'd met in the last five weeks.

"The castle is Alisdair's. I've been occupied with the shipyard."

"You've been building ships?"

"For a time."

For a time. A tenuous answer, leaving the future open and uncertain. She couldn't help but wonder if he would return to Nova Scotia one day, but it was a question she would not ask.

"What kind of ships are you building?"

"For the India trade, mainly. Perhaps for the Orient."

"All ocean vessels."

"The fastest ships afloat." He turned, facing toward the house.

"Forgive me," she said, the words released from the depths of her conscience. "I was rude earlier."

"I found your comments refreshing. Perhaps it's being raised with all my brothers, but I find total agreement suspect."

"While I have been lectured on the advisability of never speaking a cross word."

"Perfect harmony might be pleasant for a few days, but a lifetime of it would be dull. I would much prefer honesty to politeness, Riona."

He spoke her name slowly, extending the syllables until it sounded almost foreign. Or perhaps it was simply his accent that made it sound so exotic.

She wanted to ask him to say her name again, but that would be another forbidden act. Even standing here with him in the darkness would be frowned upon if others knew about it. Yet she couldn't bring herself to move or return to the house.

"Tell me about your castle," she said, walking to the side of the path. There an old oak stood, once struck by lightning and now growing in an odd shape, the heavier branches low to the ground. She leaned against the trunk, watched his shadow as he followed her to rest one hand against a branch.

"Not mine as much as Alisdair's. If affection is ownership, he is the rightful heir to Gilmuir."

"But you share its history, do you not? Will you tell me of it?"

"What I know comes from tales my father and mother told," he said. "The castle itself is at least five hundred years old, but it was built on the site of another structure, one that predates it by several hundred years. A shrine, I believe, the home of Ionis the Saint."

His resonant voice carried well. She found herself leaning back against the tree, staring up at the sky as he spoke.

"My ancestor saw the promontory, the story goes, and decided that it would be a good defensive site for a fortress. There are those among my clan who would tell you that God looked after the MacRaes on that long-ago day, and ever since. That we are a prized group of Scots, fierce and fabled."

"But you don't think so?" she asked, smiling.

"I do. After all, I'm a MacRae."

"You MacRaes are not guilty of pride, are you?" she teased.

"One of our overweening faults," he said easily, but there was a tinge of humor in his voice.

"I envy you your heritage. My father had no siblings, and my mother's family immigrated to the colonies. There are few McKinseys left to whom we can claim kin."

"While there are plenty of MacRaes."

"Tell me about them," she said, then realized she'd phrased her request wrongly. She should, if she'd been as avid a student of Mrs. Parker as Maureen, batted her eyes at him and implored in a soft and sweet voice, "Pray do tell me all about them." Instead, she'd blurted out the words.

Perhaps in her sleepless hours she should practice her tact.

"There is my brother Alisdair and his wife, Iseabal; my Uncle Fergus, whom you know. The rest of our clan are sailors who have chosen, like me, to temporarily retire from the sea. My other brothers, Hamish and Brendan, both have their own ships while my youngest brother, Douglas, alternates and travels with either of them."

She should not be thinking of a man's voice, of the way he said his words. Nor should her heart be beating so wild and free.

Riona looked toward the house, knowing that she should leave. Wanting to remain here was foolish. Why? To become more certain that she liked him? To become enchanted by the sound of his voice? To be amused by his tales or charmed by his self-deprecating humor? No, it was better to leave now and limit her association with James MacRae until he was gone from Tyemorn Manor or she was married.

"I must return," she softly said. "And you must continue your walk."

"Yes." He remained a motionless shadow against the branch.

Twice she looked back at him as she headed homeward. Regret was an emotion she'd learned well, but it had never seemed as sharp or painful as it did now.

Chapter 7

Morning came early to Tyemorn. Rosy fingers of light stretched across the horizon, peering gently over the hills as if to lure the sleeper awake.

Riona was up before dawn, donning her most comfortable gown, an often mended dress of brown linen with half sleeves that she could push out of her way and a skirt that reached only to her ankles. Her oldest leather shoes were a concession to her mother, who had been horrified the first time she'd gone barefoot like the milkmaids.

She'd slept well, a surprise since she'd thought to be awake all night. But on waking she was suffused with the same feeling she'd had ever since agreeing to wed Harold McDougal—a near-suffocating dread.

Work was the only way to ignore it, otherwise she would spend the entire day in contemplation of her future life and waste the gift of these last days at Tyemorn.

If she had been born to wealth, Riona doubted the farms would be as familiar or special to her. But she had not been reared to believe herself exempt from work, and from the very first, she had wanted to learn everything she could about Tyemorn Manor.

When she'd first arrived, Riona had been ignorant of so much, including caring for the animals. The chickens were a fearsome bunch, coming at her with their strutting walk and their razor-sharp beaks. But she had learned that they were more interested in the food she scattered over the yard than in her ankles.

A year had taught her so many things. Now she knew how to move a flock of sheep from one pasture to another and how to divert the irrigation channel from the Wye. In the evening, when the cows were brought home, she could hook her hand in the collar of one and escort it back to the barn, whereas when she'd first come to Tyemorn she'd been overwhelmed by the sheer size of the animals.

In the spring she'd helped in the planting, walking the rows, dropping seed into holes she made with a tall stick. Now the long, thin leaves of the seedlings were visible, a tenuous promise of a good harvest. She never failed to delight in a single sprouting seed, viewing life where only bare earth had existed before.

Each morning at dawn she walked the farms, following a routine proscribed for only a year. Today, however, her journey seemed almost bittersweet as she waved to the people working in the fields.

Tyemorn was a prosperous holding, a true legacy from a woman she'd never known. But sometimes, as now, Riona felt close to Mary.

"She loved the land, she did," Old Ned had once told her.

"Up until the time she couldn't walk she'd take the path of a morning and survey all that was hers. Knew every lamb born, every calf. Even when she was confined to a chair she knew more about Tyemorn than most people who were able-bodied."

Mary, too, had been wed to a man she disliked. Instead of the marriage mellowing into respect and admiration and even a type of love over the years, it had evidently remained the same as it had been in the beginning, a union of two people with nothing in common.

At least Mary had had Tyemorn Manor.

Times had not changed much since her mother's great aunt had been a young woman. Women were still expected to marry. A scoundrel for a husband was better than remaining a spinster. A foolish notion, but one society embraced wholeheartedly.

Riona halted at the top of the hill, looking back at the house. A funny-looking place and one filled with history. A book in the library stated that it was two hundred years old, having had at least three owners.

Time was passing too quickly, and this morning was a precious memory. The breeze was cool, belying the heat to come in a few more hours. The cows were being led to pasture after milking, the chickens squawked in a hundred discordant sounds, the pigs rooted around in their pens.

She had become accustomed to the dullness of the air in Edinburgh. At Tyemorn, it was sparkling clear as if having been cleansed each night. In Cormech, the sound of seabirds cawing overhead woke her, and the scent of the sea permeated everything. In both places, she'd grown used to the noises of carriages, and wagons, and people moving from one place to another as if eternally restless.

Here, amid the hills and glens, there was a silent kind of peace, interrupted only by the screech of an eagle soaring above her head.

A place she belonged.

What a pity she was to leave it soon.

Rory MacRae woke feeling like a king. For the past year, the accommodations at Gilmuir had been stark at best, and prior to that he'd spent years aboard ship where a hammock was the most he could expect. Last night, however, he'd slept on a real mattress, one that felt as soft as a cloud. Standing, he turned and looked down at it, still in awe.

Not that he'd been treated badly at Gilmuir, but everyone had shared in the deprivations. Building the old castle meant that they all slept in communal quarters. All except Alisdair and Iseabal, of course. Even James had, more often than not, taken to sleeping aboard ship rather than sharing the crowded barracks.

True enough, he shared the chamber with the other man, but the bed was all his.

This room was grander than anything he'd had in his life. Besides his bed and the one James had slept in the night before, there was a bureau and a place to hang his clothes along with a washstand. Behind a folding screen was a cunning little chair with a hole cut in the top and a chamber pot affixed to it.

The knock on the door surprised him, enough that he squawked out a greeting before realizing he wasn't fully dressed. He dashed behind the door as it opened, holding the latch firmly in his hand, pressing against it so that the girl on the other side couldn't open it more than she did.

Abigail stuck her head in the opening, peering around the

door and then darting back just as swiftly, her eyes wide. That's what she got for not giving a man time to put his clothes on, Rory thought irritably.

"You're to come and eat your morning meal," she said, her voice somewhat muffled. He peered around the door to see her standing there, hand over her mouth, eyes gleaming brightly. "Unless, of course," she said, removing her hand, "you'll be wanting a tray."

He shook his head. Last night, he'd not felt comfortable dining with the rest of them, him being a MacRae by default as it were. He wasn't exactly sure who his father was, but after his mother's death he'd been found by Alisdair in a wintry port in Nova Scotia, and given a job as cabin boy. Ever since then, he'd called himself a MacRae and had been welcomed into their midst as if he truly were one of them. But when the invitation had come to join the others at dinner, he'd stayed in his room, expecting to spend the night hungry. Instead, Abigail had brought him a tray of food, and he'd eaten his fill.

"I am hungry at that," he conceded, "but I'll not make you wait on me again."

"Well, come down to the kitchen. But only after you've had a chance to put your trews on." With a muffled giggle, she left him.

Smoke billowed up from the kitchen stovepipe, indicating that the household was up and awake. All going about their daily business while she wasted the morning away. Returning to the house and slipping into the kitchen, Riona greeted Susanna with a kiss to her cheek and a smile to Polly and Cook. Stealing a rowdie from Susanna's plate, she took a bite of the soft dark brown roll, then stopped abruptly as the door opened and James walked over the threshold.

Last night he had looked the picture of a sea captain, and in the darkness he'd been a wraith, but one strangely companionable. This morning he looked impossibly handsome, a man steeped in power and authority even without a ship to command. He was dressed simply, in dark breeches and a white shirt with flowing sleeves. His tall black boots had been replaced for shorter ones of worn brown leather, and his hair had been queued at the nape with a black ribbon. But for all the casualness of his clothes, one would never mistake him for a field hand.

He looked, she thought in amazement, like a lord of the manor. As if he belonged here more than they did.

"You're up early," she said, startled at his appearance.

He smiled. "I am used to being up at dawn. At sea it seems we're always pursuing the sun. Let's say I anticipated morning."

"As we have anticipated you," Susanna said, standing and smiling at him. She pulled out a chair, a wordless invitation to sit at the head of the table.

"You will have some oatcakes, of course," Cook said, loading a plate with the triangular slices along with a few chunks of their own cheese. A warm venison pastry lay on a platter along with a large portion of ham. Flanking the meats were several pots, one each of butter, cream, and honey. A selection of bannocks and a small wheaten loaf completed the breakfast, to be washed down with his choice of beverages, either whiskey, ale, tea, or cider.

"And a cup of tea?" Susanna asked, pouring from a squat little ceramic pot.

"Cook makes the finest jam," Polly offered, holding out a small silver bowl and a long-handled spoon.

Riona hadn't seen her mother so solicitous since Fergus lived with them. And the other women? She looked at the roll in her hand and smiled, thinking that she'd never been the recipient of the treatment James MacRae was now receiving.

"Riona will show you about the farms," her mother said, glancing toward her. "She knows the manor lands better than anyone. You would have thought her born here."

James looked in her direction, then away. "Wouldn't it be better if I spoke with your steward?"

"Riona will direct you to him as soon as you've seen the farms."

She glanced at her mother, but Susanna carefully avoided her gaze. Why should she give him a tour of Tyemorn?

Riona sat, waiting until James finished breakfast amid the fluttering of four females. Abigail had joined them, evidently preferring to tend to their guest than to dust the upstairs rooms. With her was the young man who'd accompanied James to Tyemorn.

Riona waved him to her side of the table, smiling her welcome.

"Did you sleep well, Rory?" she asked.

"I did." He looked, however, as if he wished to be anywhere but here.

Abigail served him, then turned her attention back to James.

Riona could understand why they fawned over him. He was charming and handsome, smiling his thanks for each task done for him. His cup was filled twice, and his plate would have been replenished as well if Cook had her way. But he shook his head, smiling his refusal.

Rory acted as if all this fluttering attention was nothing

out of the ordinary, as if James received the lion's share of female adulation as a natural course of events.

Impatient, Riona finally stood and walked to the door,
waiting for James to notice her.

He finally looked in her direction again, then back at
Rory. The younger man nodded, finished up his breakfast,
and stood.

"No," Susanna said hastily before the three of them could
leave the kitchen. "I mean, would you allow Rory to remain
here?" She looked pleadingly at the young man. "I could use
the services of a stalwart lad." She smiled again, the expression holding an edge of desperation to it.

A glance between James and the young man ended in
Rory's shrug.

"Then I'll leave you here," James said, and held the door
open for Riona.

"The curtains in the parlor," Susanna abruptly said. "I've
long been wishing to clean them properly. Rory, it's too big a
chore for Abigail. Could you assist her, please?"

The young man nodded, looking as bemused as the young
maid. After they'd left the room, Polly turned to her.

"Well, what do we do now?" Polly asked, having been ap-
prised of Susanna's plans the night before.

"Worry about Mrs. Parker. I have never seen a more curious or intrusive woman."

"Can't you simply dismiss her?"

Susanna looked askance at Polly. "According to the terms
of our agreement, she will remain until both marriages are
celebrated."

"Do you not mind Maureen marrying an Englishman?"

"Who am I to stand in the way of true love, Polly?"

Polly snorted, a thoroughly rude gesture, and even Cook smiled.

"You'd do everything in your power to change her mind if you thought he wasn't good enough for her," Polly said, a decade of service giving her the freedom to speak the truth. "Is that why you invited James to stay?"

Susanna nodded in rueful agreement. "Do you think I'm wrong to want someone better for Riona? Did you see the way they acted toward each other?"

"Riona hardly said a word, and James didn't notice her."

"Exactly," she said brightly.

"What are you going to do about Harold?"

"I'm not exactly certain," she said, having come to no clear resolution of the problem. If Harold could be convinced to give up his suit, the situation would be perfect, of course. But she frankly doubted that he would, given the size of Riona's fortune. Something, however, would have to be done.

Polly shook her head. "Mrs. Parker won't be happy with your plan. What are you going to do about her?"

She sighed heavily and shook her head. "It's a pity she can't be ill. The woman feels every draft and every chill. How odd that she's never truly sick."

"She could be," Polly said.

Susanna glanced at the woman who'd become her friend over the years. "Are you suggesting that I poison her?" she asked, shocked.

"A simple matter of a few herbs brewed in a tea. It would be enough to make her ill for a few days, that's all."

"And where did you acquire this knowledge?"

Polly shook her head, meaning that the answer wasn't going to be forthcoming. Susanna glanced from Polly to Cook, wondering if the other woman had passed on this wisdom. If so, was it altogether a good thing to have a woman with such talents acting as her cook?

"Perhaps it would be better if we considered other alternatives for the moment," she said, banishing the thought of that option.

"My dear Mrs. Parker," Susanna said, entering the woman's bedchamber a few moments later, "how are you faring this morning?" Placing the breakfast tray down at the foot of the bed, she went to the window and drew back the curtains. "The day promises to be a sunny one, if a bit chilly for this time of year. I've heard my share of coughs this morning and cannot but wonder if the weather is responsible for it. My own throat seems a bit sore as well."

Mrs. Parker raised herself up on one elbow, blinking at her like a mole. "I slept as well as can be expected in this dreadful air, Mrs. McKinsey."

"You do look the worse for the night," Susanna said, peering around the bed hangings. Over her thinning hair Mrs. Parker wore a huge yellow lace cap with deep flounces, making it appear as if a large flower were sitting up in the middle of the commodious feather bed.

"Are you feverish?" she asked, picking up the tray. "I do hope not. I've heard that once this cough gets in the lungs it takes a few days to expel it."

"I do not feel ill," Mrs. Parker said.

Susanna reached out and touched Mrs. Parker's cheek lightly with her knuckles. Shaking her head from side to side, she sighed heavily as if worried.

"I'm sure you're correct," Susanna said, placing the tray on the bedside table. She deliberately did not look in the other woman's direction. "It is just that you look a trifle pale. Have you any joint pain? Or difficulty rising?"

Mrs. Parker was, generously put, a large woman, and the bed was absurdly soft. A thin person would have to push his way through the mountain of feathers. Mrs. Parker must be forced to roll to the edge and simply fall to the floor.

"Now that you speak of it," Mrs. Parker said, frowning, "I have had some pain in my joints of late. I've taken it to be the Scottish air."

Susanna smoothed her face of any expression. Mrs. Parker conveniently forgot that she was an inhabitant of the country and the widow of a Scot. In fact, in all the time she'd known the woman, Susanna had yet to hear of her departed, but evidently not lamented, husband. But the older woman never let it be forgotten that she was London born and bred. Some in Edinburgh might conveniently forget that antipathy had existed between the countries for centuries, but here in the country, memories were longer.

"I cannot think that this air is good for one's lungs. And I did ask you to ensure there was no draft in my chamber."

"I am sorry that there is not another room for your use. But I would be happy to close the curtains so that you might rest for a while."

"I'm certain I'll be fine," Mrs. Parker said, leaning back against the pillows and tucking into her breakfast.

"Perhaps it would be better if you remained in your chamber today," Susanna suggested.

"Nonsense," the other woman replied, looking up from her sausages. "A good breakfast, a brisk walk, and I'll be as good as new."

"I have a restorative tea that will do wonders to fight off the ague. May I send it up?"

"That would be wise, I suppose."

Susanna nodded, her hand on the door. Looking back at the older woman, she wondered if she were destined to hell for her actions. Praying that God would understand her motives, she went in search of Polly and the herbal potion.

Chapter 8

~~~∽◯◖◗◯∽~~~

Riona led the way, thinking that she should have balked at the task of showing James the farm. Even now, she could feel him behind her, as if he were staring at the middle of her back. How silly, to think that she could feel a man's gaze. She glanced over her shoulder at him to find that she was correct, after all. He was indeed looking at her, and his expression when she caught him didn't alter. There was something somber and altogether disturbing about his look.

"You have very unusual eyes," she said, a remark over which Mrs. Parker might have fanned herself vigorously. Too intimate, she would have whispered vehemently. Too much interest implied.

"My mother is beautiful and my father garners his share of attention from other women. I cannot help how I look."

What had she done to anger him? Gone was the man she'd talked with the night before, and in his place was this creature of icy stares and clipped sentences. At least toward her. He'd been excessively cordial with the other women of her household.

Annoyed with herself for having felt the first inklings of friendship for him, she turned and led the way once more.

"I would think that you would not object to your appearance. After all, even in nature the more attractive of specimens captures attention. Bees, for example, will seek out the prettiest flowers."

His bark of laughter startled her. "I've never been likened to a flower before. All in all, I'd prefer the role of bee."

He would.

Facing him, she folded her arms. "What am I supposed to show you?"

"Everything."

She smiled, thinking that he didn't know exactly what he was asking. "Very well," she said, more than willing to walk him over every inch of Tyemorn Manor.

The path was one she knew well, leading through the woods that intersected the property. Pointing to a cultivated patch of earth, she said, "There is no kitchen garden, so we grow our herbs here."

He nodded, and she wondered how interested a man could be in spices and medicaments.

"Tyemorn Manor is actually seven farms," she said, leading the way again. The path sharply rose, following the curve of the hill. At the top she halted, waiting for him to catch up with her. "The land here is more fertile than any near Ayleshire. We grow barley, oats, wheat, hay, and potatoes. In addition, we have over a hundred head of cattle, fourteen milk cows, four hundred sheep, seven goats, two hundred three chickens, and several barn cats and shepherding dogs."

"An impressive litany. How are you so certain of the numbers?"

She turned and glanced at him again. His expression had thawed somewhat, a small smile playing around his lips. "I know Tyemorn," she said simply.

At the top of the hill, along the ridge, was another path, this one leading to the falls. She hesitated, wondering if she should show him her favorite place at Tyemorn, then reasoned that if she didn't someone else would. The view was not, after all, her domain, any more than if she owned the sky or the clouds billowing white on the horizon.

The path was wide enough so that they could walk abreast, and he slipped into place beside her.

"Our cheese is sold at market in Inverness and commands a good price," she told him. "I'm not as familiar with the making of it as I should be, but I'm sure Old Ned can inform you."

"Old Ned?"

"Our steward," she said, staring at him curiously. "The man you need to see. He's been here since Great Aunt Mary was alive and knows Tyemorn better than anyone."

"You seem to be as well versed."

She smiled at him, wondering if he knew what a compliment that was. He turned away from her, intent on the view. They had climbed to an elevation where the lower farms could be seen. They sat like squares of brown and green next to the undulating River Wye.

"Most of the farms are irrigated with canals leading from the river, but two of the pastures are too high and need water pumped up to them in dry months. But the spring has been wet and the summer looks to be as plentiful with rain."

"Will you be here in the summer, Riona?"

The question caught her off guard. She answered him too honestly, her voice not schooled in deception.

"No," she said, hearing her own regret. "Why are you here at Tyemorn Manor?" There, a question as sudden and blunt.

"Didn't Susanna say?"

She suspected that he knew only too well that her mother had been mute on the subject.

"Will you tell me?"

"Regretfully, I cannot."

"Tyemorn Manor isn't to be sold, is it?" she asked, making no effort to hide the panic in her voice.

"No. At least, not that I'm aware."

She didn't know him, couldn't trust him with something so important. The very fact that she was tempted to believe him concerned her. Her judgment had been appalling of late, witness the fact that she was soon to be married to Harold McDougal.

"Will you give me your solemn word of honor that it is not?"

His eyes, oddly enough, seemed to warm the longer he observed her. As if he were measuring her worth in a glance. *Is this a woman I should give my word to?* the look seemed to say. A reassuring notion, that his honor might be so valuable that he did not treat it lightly.

"I give you my solemn oath that I know nothing of the sale of the property, Riona. It is not for that reason I'm here."

"But you will not tell me why you are?"

"I've given my word."

She changed the subject for the moment, fully intending to return to it. "As far as people at Tyemorn, Polly is our housekeeper. Abigail and Cook are the only other servants in the house. The gardener, who also serves as our coachman, lives with his wife and three children in the poultry yard. His widowed father has a small dwelling behind the henhouse. Is there anything else you wish to know?"

"Have you no information about Ayleshire?"

Once again he'd surprised her. She'd been quite proud of her recitation, and any Cormech or Edinburgh man would have ladled her with praise. Not, however, James MacRae.

"Ayleshire?"

"Are you never teased, Riona?"

She considered the idea for a moment. "Rarely," she admitted, a little disconcerted to realize that it was the truth. But then she had little patience with courting games.

"I wonder why?" he asked.

Turning to look at him was not a wise decision. He was smiling directly at her, his lovely eyes gleaming as if he knew an amusing secret.

"Perhaps I've not the wit to understand a jest. Or the time to appreciate it."

He reached out his hand and gripped her wrist before she could move away.

"Forgive me."

She nodded quickly, anything to make him release her. But he wasn't satisfied.

Reaching out his other hand, he tilted up her chin, touching her in a way no man ever had before and perhaps should not now.

"Forgive me," he repeated. "I was very impressed by your knowledge of Tyemorn. I chose a poor way of demonstrating it."

"I took no notice of your comment," she said, secretly appalled at how quickly the lie came to her lips.

He studied her for a moment as if doubting her words,

then released her. But he didn't step away. Suddenly, she wanted to ask him to move, to put some distance between them. For a moment she thought of placing her hand flat on his chest to keep him at bay. But she didn't wish to create a bridge of either words or touch.

Long ago, someone as appreciative as she of the view of the falls had erected a few stones so that they formed a bench. She walked to it now, sitting and pulling her skirts aside so that he might join her.

To their right, water emerged from the ground soundlessly and tumbled down over a succession of rocks towering nearly twenty feet in the air. The pool at the bottom was black and deep and ringed by vegetation. Where they sat was midpoint, a place misted by the eternal falling water. A perfect spot for solitary reflection.

"Doran's Falls," she said as he joined her. "No one knows why it's called that, but I hope it's not because someone named Doran decided to do himself in here."

"All for the loss of a ladylove?" he asked, and it took a moment for her to realize he was teasing again. She wished he wouldn't. His charm was disconcerting. His earlier coldness was easier to bear.

She glanced at him, thinking that their paths would never cross again, This moment in time, as fleeting as it was, would be all they would share in life.

Celebrate the temporary, lass. Sometimes it's all you have. Her father's voice, rarely recalled of late. His advice was wise, if a little sad.

They sat for a moment, listening to the fall of the water over the rocks. Riona folded her hands together on her lap, staring at the plume of mist rising like smoke from the pond. Day after day, regardless of the weather, the water plunged over the embankment. Only during the coldest winter days did the waterfall freeze.

"This is my favorite place at Tyemorn," she said, wondering why she divulged that information to him. "I think it's because it's possible to feel out of yourself here."

He raised one eyebrow, and she explained. "Sometimes I'm quite tired of my own thoughts. Have you ever felt that way?"

"As if there is a dialogue in my mind?" At her nod, he smiled. "Too often."

"I haven't decided why it is. Perhaps I spend too much time arguing over something I don't want to do and yet must."

"What is it you must do?"

She shook her head, unwilling to confide in him. Speaking of Harold would only tarnish the days she had left.

Closing her eyes, Riona listened to the sound of the water. Sometimes she thought that if she kept her eyes closed long enough, she might be transported to another time. At this moment, it wouldn't be so difficult to believe herself a Roman maid or one of the Picts who tinted themselves blue and were so fierce that stories were still told of them.

She opened her eyes, conscious of the passing of time. Standing, she looked down at him, wondering at the companionable silence that had sprung up between them.

A disturbing man. He'd started the morning by being unapproachable and had reverted to charm only too quickly. She was unwisely curious about him, and more interested than she should be. The sooner she was rid of him, the better.

"You need to meet with Old Ned, do you not? Come, and I'll introduce you."

The barn was a commodious rectangular structure that looked as if it predated the manor house by a hundred years or more. Constructed of gray stones that had rounded over the years, the building showed its age. The mortar between the stones had begun to crack and disintegrate in spots, allowing weeds and moss to flourish, thereby weakening the integrity of the walls. An especially large gap appeared at the roof joint on the west side.

James was surprised that work hadn't been done to repair the building, but he said nothing as he entered, following Riona to where an older man was building a pen.

Old Ned reminded him of his Great Uncle Hamish, who had died when James was just a boy. Ned's beard was as white as his uncle's had been, and there was something of Hamish in Ned's speech, too, a rolling accent that was peppered with enough Gaelic to make James grateful he understood and spoke the language.

"This is Ned," Riona said, introducing them. "Evidently, James needs to speak with you."

"And why would you be wanting to do that?" Ned narrowed his eyes at James.

His promise to Susanna hampered him from speaking in front of Riona. But she didn't move, merely stood there looking interested.

After several moments of silence, she finally smiled. "He is sworn to some vow of secrecy, Ned," she said, staring straight at James. "Evidently, I'm not to know."

"Well, I haven't time for games," Ned grumbled. "I've chores to do."

"I'm sure James would be glad to help," she said, her eyes twinkling with mischief.

"Would he now?" the old man said, eyeing him from beneath bushy brows.

"I would," James said, noting Riona's amusement and Old Ned's sudden sharp look. He had four brothers, all of whom bedeviled him from time to time. After the many pranks played on him in his life, he was capable of enduring any mischief.

"I've a bit of plowing to do at the end of the south farm."

Silence was the best recourse, especially as they were both looking at him expectantly.

"Very well," Old Ned said. "I'll take him."

With that, Riona left, sending a smile to both men as farewell. He caught himself watching her walk away.

She had prepared herself well for the chores of this day. Not one single hair was loose from the tight coronet of braid. Leather brogans, well worn at the heels and scuffed at the toes, covered her feet. Her dress was of a dun-colored linen, the threadbare nature of the hem attesting to its long wear and serviceability.

The sun had added color to her cheeks, her lips were red, and her eyes were the color of cannon shot. She was, simply put, beautiful.

Her skirt swayed in a gentle arc as she made her way out of the barn. Her head was bent, and it seemed to him that she was intent on her thoughts rather than her footing.

Until this moment, he'd never felt such curiosity about a woman. What was she thinking? Why did she look so relieved to rid herself of him?

He was appreciative of the companionship and grateful for the generosity and talents of those women who'd shared his bed in the past. But James had never before found his mind engaged in a way that was almost equal to a physical response.

Mental seduction. He'd never thought it possible.

He had tried to hold himself aloof, but had warmed to her too quickly, charmed by her abrupt comments and obvious love of her home.

Being interested in a woman promised to another man was foolish. Wanting her to be free was even more ill advised.

Old Ned kept working on a pen he was constructing, intent upon that chore even as Riona left them.

"You know about the thefts," James said, grateful to be talking with someone who could shorten his visit.

"I do," Old Ned responded.

"Who do you think might be behind them?"

The older man stood, taking his time, as if the movement pained him. "I thought that's why you were here."

"How many of the livestock have been taken?"

Ned didn't answer.

"Have you any idea when they were taken?"

Still no response.

If the old man was trying to irritate him, he was succeeding admirably. "Are you going to tell me anything?"

"Herself told me to help you, but she didn't tell me to solve the riddle for you. I'm thinking you're smart enough to do that on your own. For now I've chores to do, and you'll help." He headed for the door, glancing over his shoulder. "Or was your promise just a way of impressing Riona?"

James found himself torn between active dislike and amusement. Like Hamish, the old man bedeviled him, and was staring at him now with humor in his gaze.

"I'll help," he said, moving to follow him.

The room in which Harold McDougal stood was opulent by any standards. A richly patterned carpet lay on the dark oak floorboards. Crimson silk fabric stamped with small gold medallions adorned the walls. A portrait of a man sitting in a high-backed thronelike chair, its wooden arms ending in carved lion's heads, dominated the wall above the cold fireplace. Below it, sitting like an aged and malevolent replica, was the same man and the identical chair. Of the two, the man had suffered the passage of the years with less grace. His hair was no longer dark, but streaked with gray, and the face that had once been lean, but not unattractive in its way, had grown gaunt and saturnine with age.

There were some who said that William Sinclair had become even more vicious over the years. Harold McDougal doubted that the man had ever been less than evil.

Gambling had begun as a way to keep body and soul together, and had become a habit that ruled Harold's life. A few months ago, he had come to the man for help in paying his debts, never realizing that a reputation for being unable to pay a gambling chit was preferable to owing any sum to William Sinclair.

"You'll have my money, then?" Sinclair asked, his voice a gravelly echo.

"I will," Harold said. "As soon as I marry the girl."

"And when will that happy event occur?" the other man asked.

"In less than a month."

His major creditor nodded his head, sitting back in his chair. "I will wait until then. But I'll have my money a day after the ceremony and not a moment later."

"It might be a bit longer than that," Harold said, feeling sweat trickle down his back. "I have to get control of her funds first."

"How long, then?"

"A week. No more."

He hated the man sitting in front of him for a variety of reasons, the first being the ease with which he inspired fear. A friend of his had appeared at Harold's doorstep one night with a broken arm, a blackened eye, and a curiously cryptic account of what had happened. Later, he'd learned that Sinclair had ordered him beaten because he'd been two days late with a payment.

Sinclair wouldn't hesitate to cripple him, or worse, if Harold didn't make good on his promise.

The date of his wedding couldn't come fast enough to suit him.

"You'll be beating the fabric to bits," Abigail said, peering over the line at Rory.

"If I'm poor at this task, it's because I've never done such a thing before. It's woman's work."

"So being clean is a womanly thing, now?" she asked, frowning at him. "I doubt the MacRae feels the same. The man is a beauty, he is, what with those eyes and that smile." She sighed, which made Rory strike the curtains even harder.

He'd been given a wooden tool that looked like a paddle with bands of wood stretched over a frame. They'd placed the curtains over a rope strung in the yard, and were now thrashing the dust from them.

Abigail, however, was taking the opportunity to badger him with questions.

At Gilmuir, he was accorded respect due to his newly discovered carpentry talents and his acquaintanceship with the MacRaes. Here at Tyemorn Manor, he was only the person who had accompanied James McRae across Scotland. When Rory wasn't being suffused with questions, he was being told how wonderful James was. He found it a perplexing experience to be wanting to talk to a girl, only to have her giggle about another man.

One thing he'd learned over the past year was that females were a changeable lot, and it was best to view them with caution. Abigail had a laugh that made him want to smile, but still and all, she was a woman.

You never knew what they were going to do.

Experience told him that it was better to be a bit standoffish, which wasn't a problem since all she wanted to talk about was James.

"Will you be here at Lethson?" she asked.

"When is it?"

"A few weeks from now," she said, looking at him as if he were the most daft person on earth. "The longest day of the year."

"I doubt it," he answered, not at all sure why they were remaining there at all. A few days, that's what James had said. Only a few days.

"Well, I for one hope that you are. It would be a shame for you to miss all the fun."

It was the first time she'd not mentioned James. He felt a little more hopeful.

"What's there to do?"

A spate of giggles answered him. "You must dance, of course."

He felt his heart sink. Only aboard ship did he have perfect balance. Months of practicing on the rigging had given him a sense of confidence that didn't translate well to land. He felt like a clumsy oaf at times, one with too many feet.

"I hope you stay. I, for one, would like a chance to dance with James." Another sigh had him frowning at her again.

"Or with me." The words were blurted out before he thought them.

"Or with you," she said pertly, smiling at him.

He began to smile, forgetting for the moment that he had never learned to dance.

Chapter 9

Old Ned might look ancient, but he did the work of a much younger man. At the end of a few hours, James had an even greater appreciation for the man's stamina.

He found himself behind a plow as Ned gave the horse a swat on the rump. The old man thought it uproariously funny when his arms were nearly jerked from his shoulders. Once he'd become accustomed to the strain, however, James found the chore no more difficult than pulling in a full-bellied sail.

In addition to plowing, they unloaded wheat from the granary, sent it to the mill, and inspected the irrigation ditches. James talked with the smith, the gardener and his son, the shepherds, and the young men repairing tackle. Nothing seemed amiss at Tyemorn Manor.

At noon they halted, but instead of returning to the house for their meal, a basket was brought to them by a smiling

Abigail. She tarried long enough that even Ned noticed. When the lunch was consumed and the girl gone, Ned turned to him with a frown.

"She's a young lass and silly. Best you remember that."

"And young enough to remind me of my childhood," James said calmly, understanding the protectiveness of the old man. Girls like Abigail were more foolish than wanton and needed to be protected from the world. Unfortunately, there were men who would prey upon that innocence. He wasn't one of them, but Ned had little way of knowing that.

"No one seems alarmed at Tyemorn," James said. "I would think the drovers would be more cautious with animals being stolen."

"There's a few sheep missing," Ned answered. "Fewer head of cattle. I've no knowledge of the chickens. I don't count the fool things."

"Two hundred three, according to Riona."

Ned smiled, looked off into the distance. The mist had been burned off by the sun, and now the air was clean and clear. Before them lay the south pastures, the crops already to his waist.

"She's a marvel, that girl. City bred, but she's taken to the farms as if they're her own. Pity they're not. She'd make a fine mistress for Tyemorn Manor."

"You don't feel the same about Susanna?"

Ned shook his head. "Now that one. I've yet to make my mind up about her. She means well, but I don't think she knows the difference between a bull and a goat."

"She's fortunate to have you to help her."

"I've lived here all my life. It's home."

His words reminded him of Riona's earlier statement.

"Are there any other chores you need done?" he asked the older man.

Ned looked at him, his full beard obscuring any expression. "The cows need milking. We're shorthanded today since one of the girls is visiting her sick mother."

He'd never milked a cow in his life, but there wasn't any way James was going to confess that to the old man. "Lead the way," he said, squaring his shoulders.

Thomas Drummond stared at his target. How easily he wandered over the pasture and followed the paths around the farm. Not once had MacRae realized that he was being observed.

He didn't know if these people were kin or not, hampered as he was in his discovery of information. The area was so sparsely populated that he couldn't move around without being noted.

Yesterday, he'd waited for the MacRae to leave, only gradually realizing that he was staying the night. Nor did it appear that he was in any hurry to return to Gilmuir, a development Thomas had not anticipated.

His escape had trained Thomas to blend in with the landscape rather than call attention to himself. For that reason he'd chosen a ruse suitable for travel, stealing not only his money, but a grinding wheel from an itinerant knife sharpener. He'd already made a few coins from a goodwife who'd spotted him in Ayleshire. But she'd frowned at the job he'd done, so he'd spent an extra hour trying to please her rather than have her comment about his poor work. She'd finally taken her newly sharpened knives and axe away, leaving him blessedly alone.

Last night, he'd used a few of his coins to rent a room above a local tavern. He'd hoped that being a stranger wouldn't cause comment, but the people of Ayleshire, while friendly, seemed otherwise occupied and not overly curious.

Another lesson he'd learned from the English—to focus on one thing above all others, his survival. Although he could have killed the MacRae at any time today, he'd have been discovered only too quickly. Thomas had no intention of dying until every MacRae was dead.

Tonight he would wait and watch for the man to be alone. Tonight he would rid the world of one MacRae before he returned to Gilmuir for the others.

James entered the three-sided milking shed to be greeted by the sight of fourteen cows all lined up, headfirst, in individual stalls. Two young girls standing shoulder to shoulder giggled when they saw him.

As the second oldest of five boys, he was familiar with being dared by his brothers. This activity was no different, he realized, as Ned took up a position at the side of the shed, leaning against one of the supports. The two milkmaids, both of whom were more than happy to help him with the rudiments of this chore, fetched a stool and sat it down on the left side of the cow. Beyond that, he was left to his own devices and a basic knowledge of what was required.

He heard Riona's laughter before he saw her. Stiffening his shoulders, he wished she weren't here. Not because he was reluctant to be viewed as inept at a task, but because he wished to keep some distance between them. The more time he spent with her, the more time he wished to spend with her. That circle of interest and curiosity was unwise. Twice today he'd become ensnared in the sound of her laughter and had looked for her. More than once, he'd wondered at her self-imposed duties and her whereabouts.

"Ned, that is too bad of you, to expect our guest to know how to milk." She placed her hand flat on the cow's flank and glanced down at him. "You don't, do you?"

"I regret that I do not," he said, wise enough to admit to lapses in his learning.

She grabbed another stool and placed it beside him. "Do you want to learn?"

"Not necessarily," he answered honestly. "But I suppose my honor is at stake if I do not." He glanced over at Ned, whose beard quivered as if he laughed softly.

"This is Marybell," Riona said. "A very sweet lady." The cow chose that moment to turn her head and placidly stare at him, as if they were being introduced.

"You grab the teats," Riona said serenely, smoothing her fingers over the cow's distended udder.

In his youth, he and his brothers had been given the task of looking after the sheep or fishing to feed the village. He'd never been asked to plow a field, or seed it, and only rarely assisted in the harvest. Even at Gilmuir, he'd been more involved in constructing the shipyard and occasionally helping in the rebuilding of the old castle than in tending to the animals.

James didn't think he'd ever been this close to a cow.

"Use this part of your hand." Grabbing his hand, Riona slid her fingers over the heel of his thumb. "Here," she added, closing his fingers tightly in demonstration.

Leaning forward, he placed both hands around the teats as instructed. Pull. He knew that much. He pulled, but the only response was the cow's interested glance.

His dilemma was attracting more than its share of onlookers. Even Marybell was evaluating his performance, and judging it poorly if her low mooing sound of displeasure was any indication.

"I did the same as you the first time," Riona remarked, placing her hands around his. "I was terrified I'd hurt the poor thing. But she's more likely miserable waiting for it. Aren't you, girl?" This last remark was directed toward the cow, who was looking vastly relieved now that Riona was assisting.

"It's not a pulling motion," she instructed. "But a squeezing one. Squeeze and then roll." She demonstrated, and milk streamed into the wooden pail. "Squeeze and roll."

"Squeeze and roll," he repeated, following her lead.

He could smell Riona's sun-warmed hair amid the scents of new hay and warm milk. Her hands, soft yet strong, lay atop his. He could feel the exhalations of her breath against his cheek. If she whispered he would be the first to hear, and the only one to feel her tremble.

Who knew that such a moment would be so sensual?

"There, that's it," she congratulated him a moment later as another thin stream of milk hit the wooden pail.

The others, surrounding them, clapped their hands, and he grinned at their good-natured teasing.

She withdrew her hands, making him regret that he'd learned so quickly. Dipping one finger into the pail, she held it in front of his lips.

"The taste of your success," she teased.

Warm milk and Riona.

His thoughts, at the moment, weren't concerned with theft or even milking. They centered on Riona smiling at him, her full lips curving in an enchanting expression. Her eyes were alight with humor, making him wish she'd share her thoughts even if he was the brunt of her amusement.

Abruptly she stood. "You have the way of it now," she said, her voice suddenly quick and impatient. Before he could say a word, she was gone from the shed.

Chapter 10

"You look very peaceful."

Riona didn't turn, knowing who it was by his voice. How could anyone not recognize James? In the three days he'd been here, she'd heard him speak often.

"I am planning things in my mind," she said, feeling guilty for the laxity of the past hour. "It is the only reason I was sitting here with my eyes closed."

She opened her eyes, glancing up at him with a smile.

"Why close your eyes when the falls are so beautiful?" he asked, sitting down on the bench beside her.

"The better to hear the water. It sounds like the voice of God."

He looked over at her, his smile broadening. "I never know what you will say, Riona."

"I should, perhaps, be more circumspect with my words. But it is too late to fool you now. You have seen me at my worst." Today she wore her most mended dress, with her hair askew. Yet she felt perfectly at peace. There was little to be gained in pretending to be someone else.

He studied her intently, but didn't say anything. A lapse in his manners that she readily forgave.

"Try it," she dared him, closing her eyes again.

She didn't peek to see if he was obeying her, but a moment later she asked, "Do you hear the sound?"

"A deep rumbling? Is that your voice?"

"Or the sound of the earth," she said. "Perhaps all we have to do to understand it is keep quiet long enough."

Riona opened her eyes to find him studying her. She felt her cheeks warm. "Do you think I'm foolish?"

"No," he said softly. She had the impression he wanted to say more, but he remained silent.

"I haven't seen you often in the last few days," she said. "Has your task kept you that busy?"

"That and Old Ned," he said. "But I've seen you everywhere on the farm. You seem to have a hand in all sorts of duties."

Keeping her hands busy kept her mind occupied. In less than three weeks she was going to be Mrs. Harold McDougal, and there was nothing anyone could do to stop it.

Her nightly prayers had begun to reflect that fact. She didn't seek an escape from her marriage as much as the strength to be a good wife. When James's face appeared a little too often in the midst of her reflections, she'd prayed about that, too.

"You are welcome to play truant with me," she said. "I shall not tell Ned that you're here. Or Mother, for that matter." That was as close as she would come to querying him about his reason for being here.

"They both know where I am," he said, smiling at her as if genuinely amused by her remark. Of course, a man like James wasn't the sort to be given orders. Instead, he gave them.

"Ned seems to like you very much, which is a very great compliment."

"Doesn't he like many people?"

She turned and looked at him. "I suspect he is much more amenable than he would like to appear, but he doesn't mention his feelings. The fact that he singled you out for comment is high praise indeed."

A telling fact, that he didn't seek to know what Ned had said. Had she ever been that supremely confident? Perhaps if she were as beautiful as James was handsome. Or imbued with that aura of authority seeming to surround him. She couldn't help but wonder if it was because he'd been a sea captain and accustomed to being in command.

Such questions were permissible between them, but the interest they indicated was perhaps wiser to hide.

She didn't ask him why he'd sought her out, because she didn't truly want to know. There might have been an errand that sent him to her, a message to deliver, a dozen people might need her.

Or he might have simply wished to spend time with her.

More dangerous thoughts.

In her pocket was a letter from Harold. She should think of that, perhaps, more than James. She'd felt nearly ill when opening it. Her first prayer had been that he'd changed his mind and found another heiress to wed. The second was that he'd been irretrievably delayed and the wedding must be postponed.

Unfortunately, neither was the truth. Harold's letter was simply informing her that he'd found suitable lodgings.

The house has a small garden to the rear, where you might like to plant flowers. The aspect is pleasant, overlooking a main thoroughfare, although the traffic is not such that it will disturb sleep. I trust you will approve of my decision when you see it as my bride.

His bride. She should be thinking of the role to come rather than the man sitting beside her. James fascinated her; being Harold's bride filled her with dread.

"How is Fergus?" she asked, instead of thinking of Harold and her wedding. "My mother tells me he is marrying his Leah after all these years."

"You know the story?" He sounded surprised.

"I know enough to wish him well," she said, grabbing her arms beneath her shawl. How odd that the sound of his voice should have such an effect on her skin, rubbing against it as if the syllables and crisply enunciated words had the power of touch. She felt attuned to him in a way that both disturbed and saddened her. A mystery why he, above all the men she'd ever met, would have this effect on her. A riddle she wouldn't have time to solve.

"He loved her before the war," she recounted from memories of the tale Fergus had once told her. "But he was thought dead and never returned to her. I think his pride kept him away." She smiled fondly, thinking of her friend. "I take it Leah cares not about the loss of his leg but rather for the man?"

"Yes." James smiled.

"How wonderful that fate worked for them and that she was free to marry."

He didn't answer her, yet the silence wasn't an easy one.

"Do you not think so?" she asked, curious as to why there was this sudden tension between them.

"Fate has less to do with it than her husband's greed," he said. "Magnus Drummond chose to march on Gilmuir. A matter of some territorial dispute. He believed our land to be his. He was killed in the battle."

For a moment she studied him, wondering why his expression had grown so fixed. He stared at the waterfall, but she had the impression that he didn't see it. Instead, she wondered if that battle was intent in his mind. There was more to the tale, she suspected, that he hadn't told her.

"Tell me how it happened."

He glanced at her. "It is not a story for this beautiful day."

She wouldn't let him escape so quickly. He couldn't hint at something and not fill in the gaps. Especially since his voice had changed so oddly and his expression was so altered. Somehow she'd created a wall between them by her questions.

"Tomorrow might prove to be as lovely," she urged. "But I'm not so certain this opportunity will come again. Tell me what happened. Please."

"I killed him."

She held herself in check so as not to ask a question or make a remark. Instead, she waited for him to continue.

"The battle was not going well for the Drummonds, and their hired soldiers had been beaten back. Magnus raised his pistol, and I saw that the target was his wife, Leah. No one else was close enough or knew what he had planned. I shot him through the heart."

"Did you mean to kill him?"

He made a noise that sounded like a mirthless laugh. His eyes warmed the longer he looked at her. "You're the only person who has ever asked me that question, Riona. No, I didn't. But intent matters little when a man is dead at your hand."

"But you still castigate yourself for it," she guessed.

"What kind of man would I be if I didn't question my own actions?"

"You shouldn't blame yourself, James. Think of Leah, instead. You saved her life."

She wanted to comfort him, and wasn't that a foolishness? But the impulse to place her palm on the curve of his cheek, press her lips against his forehead, was strong. All forbidden gestures.

"You sound like my sister-in-law. Iseabal said much the same." He hesitated, then spoke again. "Drummond was her father, so perhaps I should heed her words."

Riona had nothing to say in the face of such goodness. Heaven was witness to her own weaknesses. One of them being another errant and wicked thought. If she had to be ruined, then why could it not have been with this man? Let him have lured her to the garden, and she might willingly have gone and gloried in her disaster.

Fate, however, or her own foolishness, had given her Harold McDougal, and she must make the best of it.

She stood, wishing that she could find the words to speed him back to his castle. He was a dangerous distraction, a perfectly charming man with a wicked smile and devilish eyes, and a face that no doubt fueled many a woman's dream.

"I have work to do," she said, almost rudely. As she walked away, she decided that it would be best if she pretended he'd never come to Tyemorn Manor at all.

Now, if only she could.

Chapter 11

Maureen watched as her sister made a studied effort to ignore their guest.

Sometimes she felt as if she didn't know Riona at all, even if they were sisters and the closest of friends. There was something almost passionate about her sister, something feckless and free just beneath the surface. Except for tonight. This evening she was acting very oddly. She kept her eyes directed at her plate, and her speech, when it came, was monosyllabic and diffident.

Mrs. Parker, if here, would certainly be pleased at the sign of Riona's demure behavior. But the older woman was in bed, dreadfully ill.

"An attack of gout, perhaps," Susanna had said earlier. "Or indigestion. Or the fever."

She'd looked at her mother curiously, which made Susanna only sigh. "A temporary indisposition, I'm sure, Maureen. Our Scottish weather proves difficult for her."

Riona, however, wasn't celebrating the other woman's absence from the table. In fact, she seemed hardly to notice. No, her sister was definitely not behaving like herself.

In Edinburgh, Riona had chafed at her daily restrictions. When Maureen would just as soon be abed, Riona was up at dawn. She wanted to talk about subjects that no one else wished to discuss. Barnyard prattle, Mrs. Parker called it. There were too many times when, in the midst of a polite gathering, Riona would simply not be there. Her gaze would be on a far wall, but Maureen knew that in her mind she was seeing Ayleshire, or a pasture or paddock, someplace at Tyemorn Manor far removed from the ballroom or dining room or parlor in which they sat.

Where Maureen would just as soon be sitting with her needlework or reading a novel, Riona was all for exploring the woods or visiting the animals. Sometimes she patted them on the rump fondly, addressing them by name. Once, when she'd watched Riona bringing in the cows, it looked as if her sister were conversing with one of them.

Mrs. Parker was forever comparing the two of them, holding her up as an example for Riona to follow. Every time the older woman did that, she could feel Riona almost physically step away. By the time they'd returned from Edinburgh, they were almost strangers. Maureen might have told the older woman that it was foolish to expect her sister to be someone she was not. But Mrs. Parker and, in a way, their own mother tried to ignore Riona's true nature.

She reminded Maureen of those women about whom stories were whispered, women who'd followed their sons and brothers, husbands and fathers into battle, who had hidden a prince and defied defeat.

Riona was unlike anyone she knew. Her sister's laughter seemed so much louder, her smile more amused. Her anger was deeper, and her tears, although rare, seemed to emerge from a wellspring of grief.

She herself had a gentler relationship with the world.

Conversation was stalled, the long silences between questions and answers inordinately long. Remembering her lessons, she turned to James.

"Where are your brothers now?" she asked him.

"I'm not certain of their exact location," he said. "But they should be returning to Gilmuir within the year."

"Are they planning on settling in Scotland?"

"I would be surprised if they did so," he answered, glancing at Riona and then away.

"I hope that you'll be able to stay long enough to celebrate Lethson," Maureen said. "The entire village participates."

"Indeed," Susanna added. "The festivities are planned for months."

Even that comment did not elicit a response from her sister. This was definitely not like her at all.

Riona had surprised her by agreeing to marry Mr. McDougal. Only in these past few days had Maureen begun to realize that she was truly miserable about the decision.

The candle burned long into the night in Riona's room, and too many times Maureen had heard her sister open the window, and wondered if she sat there looking out into the darkness. Maureen had not spoken on those occasions, sensing that Riona preferred the solitude of her own thoughts to conversation.

"What do you think of Tyemorn Manor?" Susanna asked now.

"What I've seen of it is impressive," James replied. "But I'll confess to knowing little of farming. We maintain some cows and sheep at Gilmuir, along with our crops, but I have been more involved in building in the last year."

"Do not let our gardener hear you say that," Susanna chided with a smile. "Else he will have you building a new winter house for him. And a new chicken coop as long as you're at it."

"It's your barn that needs work," James said, surprisingly.

Riona looked up, their gazes meeting across the table. "The west wall," she said, animated for the first time tonight. "I've noticed it needs shoring up."

"It would be better to replace it."

Riona returned to her soup, concentrating on it with an almost desperate intensity.

Maureen felt as if she were balanced on a fulcrum. On one side was her happiness and on the other Riona's. But now there was no choice, was there? Riona had agreed to marry the determined Mr. McDougal.

He was, on the surface, a favorable enough husband for any woman, yet she doubted that the union would be a happy one. There would be nothing for Riona but cramped living quarters in Edinburgh. No fields, no woods to explore, no Ayleshire.

What a shame that Riona's decision had been made. Especially now, when James MacRae and her sister were each trying to pretend that the other wasn't in the room. As if no one could sense the emotions flowing between them.

Her mother glanced toward her, and they shared a look.

Instead of appearing concerned, Susanna seemed inordinately pleased.

Another reason to worry.

After dinner, when Riona would have dearly liked to escape to her room, Maureen surprised her by asking for help.

"We've a pupil," she said, "who needs our assistance."

"A pupil?"

"Rory," she explained, walking down the hallway.

The young boy refused to join them in the dining room for the evening meal, choosing instead to eat dinner in the kitchen with Abigail and Cook. Now he waited outside the double doors of the parlor, straightening when he saw both of them.

"Are you sure I'm not a bother, Miss Maureen? I've no one else to ask."

"We're happy to help." Maureen turned to Riona. "Rory wants to learn how to dance."

A few moments later, some chairs and a table had been moved aside to give them room, and Maureen was leading Rory in the first movements of a country dance.

"I was a fool, Miss Maureen. I'll never learn it."

"Nonsense, Rory," Maureen said. "Simply extend your right leg forward, then swing it in a gentle arc to the right. That's it," she added approvingly. "Now put your left foot forward, move your right foot right behind it, and then take a small hop."

"On the right or the left?" he asked helplessly, looking down at his feet.

Riona smothered a smile. "It's a lot easier than it sounds, Rory," she said, taking pity on the boy. There was something sweetly innocent about his eagerness to learn.

"It doesn't matter," Maureen said, holding out her hand. "We'll get to that part later." She glanced over her shoulder at Riona. "What do you recommend, Riona? A reel?"

She nodded. "It would be the easiest, don't you think?"

"Can you hum a tune?"

"Better than I can dance," she admitted. She sat in the corner on an ottoman, watching as Maureen led Rory through the first part of the reel. Humming a tune, she clapped her hands to the rhythm.

"I'm awful at this," he said, stopping a moment later. Maureen had a pained expression on her face. No doubt Rory had stepped on her toes again.

"You're doing better," Maureen reassured him. "Truly you are."

The young man looked mutinous.

"Perhaps it would be better if we discussed proper comportment," Maureen said diplomatically.

Stepping in front of him, she smiled and extended both her hands. "The man offers his hand palm up and the woman puts hers in it."

"Except when actually doing a movement," Riona offered, remembering her lessons from Mrs. Parker. "Then pretend as if you're shaking her hand."

"Or, if you're wearing sharp buttons, you should hold her wrist and she'll hold yours."

Rory looked increasingly confused.

"I've seen you climb the rigging, Rory," a voice said. "This will be no challenge for you."

The young man flushed, his gaze flying to James standing in the doorway.

"You're doing quite well considering that you've never danced before," Maureen said.

Riona stood, moving to James's side. "Do not laugh at him," she whispered. "He is trying his very best."

"I have nothing but admiration for him," he said, smiling easily. "I cannot help but recall my own dancing lessons. He is much more adept than I."

"Where did you learn to dance?" she asked.

"France," he said surprisingly. "Paris, to be exact." His smile altered in character, but he didn't offer any details.

"You're the one who should teach us," she said.

"I'm content to stand and watch."

He leaned against the doorframe, arms folded in front of him, looking as if he were indeed happy to remain as he was.

She glanced at him surreptitiously from time to time and then away before he could catch her watching him.

His lips curved into an easy smile, and she realized how fond he was of Rory. His smile was not strictly for the boy, she realized, but also for her sister. There seemed to be a sparkle in his eyes as he watched the two dancing in the middle of the room. Maureen was gently instructing Rory, her kindness showing through her soft blue eyes.

She'd been envious of Maureen before, but never so acutely as now. Her sister's black hair did not frizz. Her eyes weren't a plain gray but a lovely blue. Even her smile was different, easily summoned and generous.

But it was in her nature that the two of them were truly different. Maureen was more accepting, sweeter, and undoubtedly kinder.

She moved to leave the room, but was captured by a question from James.

"Are you going walking, Riona?" he asked softly.

She had not planned on it. In fact, she would be unwise to do so. But she nodded.

"Perhaps I will as well," he said. A warning. A promise? Wordlessly, they stared at each other.

A wiser woman would have escaped at that moment, returned to her chamber, and sought forgiveness in a prayer. Instead, she left the house and stood in the shadows of the trees waiting for him.

"Mrs. Parker would say that it's improper to meet you here," she said, as he emerged from the house a few moments later.

"Do you always listen to what Mrs. Parker says? Is she that great an arbiter of behavior?"

"She is exactly that, and more," she said. "It's for that reason that my mother hired her. She has a reputation for making great matches."

"And is your match one of them?"

She didn't answer him. One more word about Harold and she would go screaming off into the woods. Even the condemned were not incessantly reminded of their sins prior to their hanging.

"When is your wedding?"

"Soon." She didn't want to enumerate the days, count the hours.

The evening breeze stirred the hem of her dress, slipped inside her skirt to caress her ankles. She clasped her shawl closer to her as she turned, walking up the path away from the house.

Unwise, this was unwise. But oh so tempting to be here with him. She'd tried to ignore him, but it was too difficult. His eyes attracted her attention, his smile summoned forth her own. Who could ignore the sound of his voice? Or the intelligence of his discourse?

He followed, but they did not walk together. At least ten feet of shadowed night separated them. They were each steeped in propriety even if she rebelled against it. Especially since she'd obeyed all the rules dictated to her and had subsequently been trapped by them.

"How soon?"

How obstinate he was.

"A matter of weeks," she said, staring down at the shadow of her shoes. How odd that she knew they were there, but could not see them in the gloom. She could not see her heart, yet knew it beat in her chest. She could not see humor, yet felt amusement.

She could not see James, but felt him near. How foolish to feel anything for a man she'd known for only days.

She doubted that Harold would tromp through the woods as James had done, or look as interested as he had when she'd pointed out the various foraging areas for their sheep. Or keep silence with her at the falls, allowing nature to speak for them.

Sometimes curiosity was a troubling trait to possess. Especially about this man. She wanted to know everything about him. What colors he liked, what season was his favorite. Was there a poet he read or a novelist he preferred? What occupations did he prefer in the evening? Gaming or reading, conversing or spending time in solitary pursuits? Did he play cards? What amused him or made him thoughtful? None of those questions was intrusive by its nature, but taken all together they were too personal.

She should want to know such things about Harold. Instead, her mind darkened when thinking of her betrothed as if he were no more substantial than a shadow.

James suddenly closed the distance between them, coming so close that she could feel his warmth, smell the scent of the soap he'd used for his evening shave.

He raised his hand, and before she could react, skimmed his fingers over her face, tracing a path from temple to chin. Shivers followed in their wake as if he were a sorcerer and had summoned lightning in his touch.

Instead of turning away, she remained like a porcelain figurine, never moving. When his finger stopped at her chin, she should have smiled or teased him about his solemnity. But she remained in place, fixed and rapt, even as he withdrew his hand.

"Why did you do that?" she whispered.

James looked down at her, making her wish that she could see his expression. "An impulse. Forgive me."

That was all the explanation she was to have? What would he have done if she'd followed her whim? Stroked her fingers over his face, or traced his lower lip with the edge of her thumb, wondering at its fullness and softness?

Harold. There, his name. By invoking it, perhaps she would bring some sense and decorum back into her life. Yet she could ignore him only too easily. She tilted her head back, wishing it were light so that she could see James's beautiful eyes.

But if it were day she wouldn't be standing there, would she? She would be wise and proper, and all those qualities of character that seemed so difficult in his presence.

Chapter 12

O ne moment his attention was on Riona. The next, he heard a rustle of leaves, then the flash of gunpowder. At the same time James heard the shot, he pushed Riona into the safety of the trees, kneeling beside her.

"What was that?"

"Someone is shooting at us."

"Shooting at us?" she asked in disbelief.

He felt the same incredulity, but his was lessened somewhat by the fact that this had happened before. And, as before, the musket was badly aimed.

"Stay here," he said, leaving the cover of the trees. He was tired of being a target. Even worse, the bullet could as easily have hit Riona as him.

"What are you going to do?" she asked, following him.

"Stay here," he repeated. "You'll be safe as long as you remain in the shadows. Promise me that." Reaching out, he

133

touched her face, his palm cupping the edge of her cheek, feeling her nod.

Following the path that stretched along the ridge of hill, he halted, hearing the sound of running footsteps. A shadow emerged from the copse of trees, and he pursued it down the path to the granary. Before the intruder could slip from sight, James launched himself at him. They both fell to the ground with a thud and a tangle of arms and legs.

He pulled back his fist and slammed it into the other man's jaw, feeling the pain vibrate across his knuckles.

"Who are you? And why the hell are you shooting at me?"

The man struck a blow of his own, connecting with James's cheekbone. He winced, then threw the stranger to the ground again, straddling him. Gripping his shirt with both fists James picked the man up and then slammed his head down against the dirt.

"Who are you?"

Instead of answering, the man spat at him. They were evenly matched in size, but James hadn't expected that the man would suddenly grab a rock with an outstretched hand. The glancing blow to his head dazed him for a moment, blood flowing from a cut above his left eye. He pinned the man's wrists to the ground and used his forearm to press against his throat.

"Who are you?"

"Drummond," the man rasped. "I'm a Drummond, you spawn of Satan."

"James?"

He turned to find Riona standing there, her pale yellow dress light enough to be seen in the darkness. His inattention was rewarded with a second blow to the side of his head. A third. He heard her scream and realized that he had lost the battle just as Drummond twisted and rose to his knees, the rock descending once more.

Reaching for the dirk he kept hidden in his boot, James armed himself with the knife just as Drummond lunged for him again. He felt the blade enter the other man's body, heard his muffled oath as he staggered back several feet.

Rising to his knees, James watched as the man scuttled from the clearing like an insect in the light.

Riona reached his side just as the man disappeared.

"What was that?" Susanna asked, hesitating at the door of the library.

Ned was already standing, moving around the desk.

"A shot," he said abruptly, brushing past her.

"Who would be shooting?" she asked, following him.

"Exactly what I intend to find out," he said, grabbing the lantern from the desk.

She jerked her shawl from the peg in the kitchen and hurried after Ned, following the lantern bobbing from his right hand. Catching up with him, she walked by his side on the well-worn path.

"Riona and James are out walking."

"Another of your plans?" he asked disparagingly.

She glanced at him. The faint light revealed his irritated expression.

At times, it seemed as if he didn't like her at all, and then there were occasions when they got on very well together. They often spoke in the evening, she confiding in him of her concerns about her new wealth and her daughters. In the past, he'd listened intently. Lately, however, they grated on each other's nerves. Strangely enough, she missed the times of accord, having become accustomed to his companionship.

At the top of the hill, he halted before striding down to the granary. The lantern illuminated a scene she could not have imagined. Riona knelt beside James on the ground, using her shawl to stem the blood pouring from a gash on his head.

"What is going on here?" Susanna asked, somewhat impatiently. Fear, however, underscored her words.

"James was attacked," Riona said curtly.

"Attacked? Who would dare?"

"A Drummond," James said, standing. Handing back her shawl to Riona, he seemed oblivious to his injury. "A legendary enemy, I'm afraid."

"Here?" Susanna asked. "What is he doing here?"

"Exactly what I would like to know," James said.

They made their way back to the house, none of them speaking.

Riona wanted to press herself against James's side, extend her hand around his waist, offering support. But he didn't need her assistance, and her actions would only be seen as wrong rather than helpful.

Ned parted from them at the door, returning to his own cottage.

In the kitchen, Susanna lit a few of the lanterns until the room was as bright as day, before leaving to fetch the basket of medicines.

James sat on the bench beside the table. Riona went and stood at his side, gently tilting his head to the light. Among her failings, she counted the fact that she disliked the sight of blood. Yet now that flaw wasn't as important as James's injury.

"A little harder and we'd be fitting a shroud for you."

"I think that was the intent," James said dryly.

"Why was Drummond shooting at us?"

"He was shooting at me," he said bluntly. "You were only in the way."

"Why?" Susanna said, coming back into the room. In her arms she carried a basin, a basket, and several cloths that she placed on the table.

James turned and glanced at Susanna. "A feud that's been carried further than it should have."

Susanna frowned and opened the basket. Tucked inside the various glass bottles were remedies of every sort. Now she retrieved a bit of moss and a mixture that looked as green but smelled worse. She waved Riona aside.

At any other time she would have relinquished her position, but now Riona only stretched out her hand for the vials. Surprisingly, her mother didn't argue, only gave her what was necessary and retired to the other side of the table, smiling slightly.

"Have you brought danger to my doorstep, James?" Susanna asked.

The two of them waited for his answer. "I don't know. But it's possible that I have. But I will ensure that it doesn't touch you or those you love, Susanna."

Riona busied herself preparing a poultice. Before applying it, she bathed the wounds on his face. Drummond had struck him at least three times, each blow harder than the last. After she applied a salve, she mixed a drink, a noxious potion that smelled heavily of onions. Her mother nodded in approval as she handed James the cup.

He eyed it dubiously.

"You'll find that it will ease the pain," Riona said.

"I'll be fine," he said.

"Yes," Susanna agreed, "as soon as you drink it."

Riona wanted to warn him that even a grown man was no match for her mother when she was determined, but he managed a faint smile then. A weapon of his own, one with the power to charm even Susanna.

"Leave it on your bedside table, then," Riona said, taking pity on him. She remembered the drink from her childhood and had felt the same aversion to it. "At least I'll have given it to you."

"You should rest," Susanna said, standing. She bustled around the table, gathering up the ingredients Riona had used. "Do you need some assistance, James?"

He stood, steadying himself on the edge of the table. Pride kept him upright, Riona thought. Or a strong constitution.

"I'll be fine. Thank you for your ministrations." He sent Riona only a cursory glance before he bid them both good night.

But she wasn't content with that. "Sleep well, James."

He looked at her, his gaze long and intent. "And you, Riona," he said, in that deep, well-modulated tone of his.

Only her mother's presence made her turn away.

The tower room Susanna had prepared for them, with its facing windows and high ceiling, revealed her hospitality as nothing else. On the bureau was a vase filled with fresh flowers. The bedside table held a small jug of cider, along with two crystal tumblers. Abigail had turned down his bed earlier, fluffing up the pillows. She'd prepared the desk for him also, the crystal inkwell and newly sharpened quills luring him to write.

James hoped that Rory was asleep. The wish was half fulfilled when the boy woke as he lit a candle. He sat up, leaning on one elbow and gaping at him.

"Was it a fight I missed?"

"It was," James answered, placing the crystal shield around the candle and settling it on the desk.

"It's rare to see a MacRae with a battered face," Rory said admiringly, examining his wounds. "Especially you. Who did it to you, sir, and how?"

"Drummond," he answered, finding it painful to talk. Relating what had happened in the briefest of terms, he pulled out the chair and sat at the desk. "I have the answer to who shot at us, at least."

Rory sat up on the edge of his bed. "Are you going after him? If so, I want to join you."

"No. It would be foolish to do so at night. Besides, I wounded him well enough," he added, thinking of that moment when he felt the knife slide between the man's ribs. "I'll do some investigating in the morning, go into the village and see if there's a stranger wandering around."

"I hope you killed him."

Looking back at his companion, James almost smiled. There was so much ferocity in the boy's eyes, but it was born of loyalty. "It's a better idea to discover why he hates me enough to try to kill me twice."

"Because of his laird, of course," Rory said easily.

"I'd believe that if one of Magnus Drummond's men had shown any grief at his death," James said. Picking up the quill he began to write. "I want you to be a messenger for me." He'd give Rory a letter to Alisdair, impart the information about Drummond, and warn him to be on his guard.

"Am I to return?"

There was a hint of wistfulness in the question, no doubt because of the absence of young females at Gilmuir.

"Yes, Rory," he said. "It would be a shame not to put those dancing lessons to good use."

The young man's face relaxed.

"You're sending word about Drummond, then?"

James nodded. "And asking for information about anyone with a grudge. Even though I think it unlikely that we wouldn't have been aware of some discord before now."

"There be rats in the cleanest hold."

"True enough, Rory," he said, again concentrating on his letter to Alisdair.

Once he finished, James turned his attention to his journal. He had not written in the book for months, but prior to that he'd often made a nightly habit of recording his thoughts. Smiling at the impulse that had made him tuck the journal into his pack upon leaving Gilmuir, he opened it and began to write.

Magnus Drummond has haunted me overmuch. I have spoken of his death for the first time and feel a curious release.

He dipped the quill into the inkwell again, thinking of Riona's earlier words. Did he blame himself? Yes, perhaps. Taking a man's life could not be undone.

At least one mystery has been solved. Drummond has evidently followed us here. Why now, when there is peace between our clans?

He paused, disturbed by the fact he had no answers. Thank Providence that the man had been such a poor marksman. Not once, but twice.

The moment of the shot seemed fixed and clear. His first thought had been of Riona, and relief that she'd been unhurt. Through it all, she'd remained composed, offering neither hysteria nor argument when he'd left her.

I would be foolish to state that my only interest in her is as a companion, although she is a pleasant one. She has a way of lifting her head when she asks a question. Or looking away when thinking of an answer. Both gestures fascinate me, and I find myself looking for them.

Neither am I a saint that I can ignore the way she walks or the smile she bestows on the object of her amusement. She has a way of pointing her finger into the air to accentuate her words that I find charming. I have not heard her laugh but I most definitely wish to, to see if her humor matches her as well as her solemnity.

There would be no more nightly walks, Drummond's appearance making him more circumspect than his own wishes.

How intimate could friendship be? Did Riona know that she'd surmounted the barrier he'd erected around himself? Or that he wished to tell her even more of his life?

But she loves another. I find myself goaded to question her, yet I don't want to know more about this paragon of hers. I cannot help but question the timing of my arrival. Why have I found her now, when it is too late?

Sleep would come late tonight, if at all, Riona thought, leaving her mother. She entered her bedroom, closing the door behind her and leaning against it.

He would have killed the man. She knew that, just as she knew that he had killed before. In a way she wished he hadn't told her, hadn't divulged that secret. Doing so had changed him. He was no longer simply a handsome man, but a warrior who protected himself and those under his care.

In this part of Scotland, the world was civilized. Their social behavior, like it or not, was more patterned on life in England than on Scotland's heritage. But in certain places old feuds were still remembered and a hundred years was only a moment in the mind. At Gilmuir.

She walked to the window seat and stared into the darkness. No candle lit the gloom, and the night seeped into her chamber. She heard the window open in the next room, wondered if Maureen also sat staring at the moonless night. Saying nothing, Riona remained where she was. She wanted no company, no sisterly confidences.

"Riona? Are you awake?"

She remained silent, wishing her sister to bed. Finally, Maureen moved away from the window, leaving Riona free to sit in the darkness.

A year ago she didn't know this place, had been content enough to live in Cormech. But in one short year she'd come to love Tyemorn and Ayleshire, its inhabitants and customs. She'd learned the seasons and become enthralled with a life she'd never before known. Now she would have to leave it all again, going to live in Edinburgh with a man she barely knew. Even as she mourned the loss of a man she wanted to know only too well.

What a pity that her life had already been ordained before she met James MacRae.

Chapter 13

Abigail looked as if she were going to cry. Even Cook halted in her pot stirring to stare at him. Susanna stood, sat down heavily before standing once more. Only Ned didn't look horrified. He grinned as he left the kitchen. No doubt in commiseration for what was to come, James thought later.

What faced him in the mirror was a daunting sight even for someone expecting it. One of Drummond's blows had struck him above his left cheek; another had peeled the skin from his forehead. Between the two, his left eye was badly bruised and swelling, and his right was bright red.

He looked like some sort of variegated sea monster.

"You'll sit and let me look at your head," Susanna said. Her tone of voice was one his mother might have used. But he towered over his mother as he did Susanna. The time to coddle him had long since passed.

"I'll be fine, Susanna."

"You'll sit right down, James MacRae."

When a woman frowned so fiercely, it was wiser simply to obey her. Words his father might have said. Or even Alisdair this past year, as his quiet bride had turned demanding at times.

But he startled Susanna by leaning over and kissing her cheek in genuine appreciation for her worry. "I'll be fine."

She sputtered a little but didn't attempt any further cosseting.

He waved Cook away when she would have served him breakfast. He had no appetite this morning.

"Will your attacker come again?" Susanna asked.

"I'm not entirely certain," he said, giving her the truth. One thing about the Drummond clan: they were rarely convinced to give up their hatred. The fact that his sister-in-law, Iseabal, was a Drummond was a constant surprise to him.

"Did you deliver him a mortal blow?"

The question surprised him, but perhaps it shouldn't have. Susanna had a bluntness that he recognized in Riona. In addition, both women, when asking a question, wanted a direct answer in return.

"I can't tell you that, either." He walked to the door, impatient to be about his task.

"You should rest today. The thefts will wait," she added, following him as he left the kitchen and entered the yard.

"It would be best if I cleared up the matter as soon as possible," he said, "and returned to Gilmuir."

If nothing else, the events in the past day had proven that it was unwise for him to linger at Tyemorn Manor. Not only might he have unwittingly brought danger to the McKinseys, but a hazard also lurked there for him as well.

Riona.

He had to keep reminding himself that she was betrothed, that she was soon to be a wife. Each day it grew harder to remember.

Susanna watched James walk away, feeling terrible. Worse than terrible. Her conscience was grating at her so fiercely that she had barely slept the night before. She really should tell him the truth. But if she did, he'd leave, and all her plans would disintegrate into nothing.

But that was not, regretfully, the only reason that her better nature was up in arms.

She was worried about Mrs. Parker. The herbal tea had worked only too well. The poor woman had been dreadfully ill the day before, and it looked as if today would be no better.

What had she done?

"They are spending a goodly number of hours together," Polly said, joining her and staring after James. "Is it what you intend?"

"I'm not entirely sure," Susanna said, her façade of calm abruptly disappearing. "On the one hand, I would much rather have my daughter aligned with Fergus's family than that dolt from Edinburgh. But I haven't the slightest notion of what to do about Harold McDougal."

As if she'd summoned the sound, a bell rang from the upper floor as they returned to the kitchen.

"Nor can I keep Mrs. Parker ill forever."

"Why not?" Polly asked.

She sent her housekeeper a censorious look.

The bell rang again, and not one person in the kitchen made a move to answer it.

"I was the last to wait on her," Polly said, backing away.

Now was not the time to remind Polly of her position, Susanna thought. After all, her housekeeper had taken the brunt of Mrs. Parker's temper for the past few days. And Abigail looked as if she would mutiny if asked to serve the woman again.

"Very well," Susanna said, sighing. She picked up the tray. "I will take her breakfast."

The other women in the room only nodded, as if she deserved such punishment.

"Good morning, Mrs. Parker," she said in greeting as she entered the room. "I trust you are feeling well?"

"I'm feeling wretched," the other woman complained, "just as you warned. But my health must suffer for a greater errand. I have a letter that must reach Edinburgh."

The woman was attired in her usual nightgown over which she wore a beribboned bed jacket. "Here," she said, weakly waving a letter in the air. "You must promise me that it will go today."

Carefully placing the tray down on the table at the end of the bed, Susanna nodded.

"You do have a post in the country, I trust," the older woman said. "I must get word to my housekeeper that I've been taken ill and have been delayed. There are several social events where I must make my appearance."

No doubt trolling for clients. Mrs. Parker did know a great many people in society. Had she not sent her daughters to the woman, it was doubtful that Maureen would have ever met Captain Hastings, let alone be on the verge of betrothal. Nor would Riona be marrying Harold McDougal, but she put that thought far from her.

"I will have it taken to the village this morning," Susanna said, nodding and placing the letter in her apron pocket. "I am truly sorry you are not feeling well. Is there anything I can bring you?"

"You can ensure that it is quiet outside," Mrs. Parker said crossly. "How you manage to get any sleep at all with all that bleating and neighing and mooing, I don't know. Indeed, the streets of Edinburgh are less noisy than that barnyard of yours only feet from my window."

The barn was located nearly half a mile away, and the air was fresher here than in the crowded streets of Old Town, but Susanna said nothing, only smiled determinedly.

Her years of experience handling boarders had taught her that people would complain if you allowed them, and certain people would grumble more than others. Mrs. Parker was most assuredly in the latter category, choosing complaints over any other topic of conversation. Which was just as well, Susanna thought, laying out the breakfast dishes. She didn't want to talk to the woman anyway.

"You look terrible," Riona said, staring at James in awe. She stood outside the milking shed, in the act of handing two filled pails to one of the milkmaids when the sight of him halted her. Beside her the milkmaid gaped. "Does it hurt as bad as it looks?"

His mouth moved in what might have been a smile. "I will be a brave and stalwart MacRae and say no."

When it was all too obvious the answer was just the opposite.

"I am so sorry. What can I do?"

For a moment he didn't answer, and when he did she had the impression the words weren't those he truly wished to say.

"It will get better in time," he said, smiling.

She'd never seen anyone look so bad and still be walking around.

His forehead was badly abraded, his left eye bulging and shut, while his right was bloodshot. The area around his cheek was tinted various colors, but mostly crimson.

If she had been Drummond, she would have fled simply from his expression.

"Are you certain you feel well enough to be about?"

"No more onion possets," he said, holding up his hand.

"Very well," she said, taking pity on him. "But should you not rest?"

"Your mother said the same." His glance was filled with irritation. "I was only in a fight, Riona. Shall I do something to prove my strength?"

"What, exactly?" she asked curiously.

"A labor of Hercules. Give me a list and I'll perform any manner of tasks."

She shook her head at him. "I think standing would be beyond you. I am already impressed."

"We MacRaes are hardy."

A bit of a boast that amused her. Right now he looked less hardy than simply stubborn.

"Have you seen the Roman wall?" she asked suddenly.

He started to shake his head, then resorted to speech. "No."

"Then that is something we should amend." Stretching out her hand to him, she said, "You should see one of Ayleshire's most famous sites."

"Are you attempting to lure me from my duties?" he said, taking her hand. His fingers curved around hers.

"What exactly are your duties?" she asked.

"Has anyone told you that you're inordinately obstinate?"

"Only a few people," she answered. "Those who know me well."

There was a pause between them that she was in no hurry to fill with words. Neither, it seemed, was he.

"I have things I must do," he said, pulling his hand away. "Chores I've been given by Ned."

"And your secret task."

"Yes," he said, smiling once again.

"Then I will leave you to them." She turned and began to walk away.

"Where are you going?"

"To the village," she said over her shoulder. "I have to meet with the elders."

"Is it wise to go alone?"

"You could accompany me." She turned and faced him, certain that behind those bruises was a frown.

His injuries had robbed his face of beauty, yet she was even more intrigued by the man. He acted as if the distortion of his appearance was unimportant. James MacRae, for all his attractiveness, was not vain.

Shrugging at his silence, she turned and continued striding down the hill. Glancing over her shoulder, she realized he was following her. There was no longer any doubt about the frown.

"Another way of keeping me from my duty?"

"Whatever that might be," she said blithely.

"Very well." An ungracious response, one that amused her. He didn't like being pushed into behavior. Who was more stubborn of the two of them?

She stood and waited for him, looking out over the vista. To her left were the farms, showing square and perfect in the morning mist. To her right was the manor house. Ahead, the River Wye undulated through the pasturelands. Even farther, a distance of a mile or so, past the woods and down a well-trodden road, was the village of Ayleshire.

Tyemorn Manor was situated, if one was looking at a map, in the southwest quadrant and occupied most of the land to the west of the river. Opposite and across the river was a large hill on which the abbey ruins were located. North of that was the village, the church, and the Roman wall.

"Do you think Drummond is out there?"

"Men like Drummond slink in the shadows, preferring to ambush rather than fight directly. I doubt he'll show himself in the light of day."

"Still, we'd be wise to set guards around the property at night," she said calmly.

"I have already taken the liberty of speaking to Ned about that. They'll stand watch beginning tonight."

She glanced at him, surprised. "You and Ned have a great deal in common, then. He takes it upon himself to manage Tyemorn and does. I doubt my mother knows half of what he accomplishes."

"There's more to managing an estate the size of Tyemorn than what appears on the surface, I suspect," he said.

"Could you not say the same about a ship at sea?" she asked. "I used to stand at my window and watch as the ships came into Cormech. They always seemed to glide by as if the water were glass. But if I looked closely I could see the sailors scrambling in the rigging and pulling at the sails. The captain would stand there observing, but I always knew that he had planned the entire voyage and the docking in his mind."

"If he hadn't, he wouldn't have turned a profit."

She smiled. "Of all the people I might meet here, isn't it strange that it should be a sea captain?"

"You'll miss Tyemorn," he said, his gaze shifting to her. She wished that he hadn't learned her so quickly. Was it because he studied her with such intensity? Or simply because she had allowed it?

"Yes," she said. "I'll miss it." Turning, she began to descend the path. "I feel at home here as I never did in Cormech. Perhaps each person finds a place like that in his lifetime. Do you think so?" She glanced back at him. "One special place that makes him feel at ease?"

"My brother has. Alisdair has an affinity for Gilmuir that I don't share. A comfortable place is not always simply a location, Riona, but the people who reside there, too."

"Perhaps the location shapes the people. In a village you know the people better than in a town. For example, at Ayleshire, there is a certain sticky-fingered lad who has a tendency to take what is not his. And a woman who has a habit of spying on her neighbors. But I think she does so because she is lonely and their lives seem so much more lively than her own."

"Do you think your sticky-fingered lad and your nosy neighbor are that way because they live in Ayleshire? Would they not have been the same in Inverness or Edinburgh?"

She considered the question. "You could be right. Perhaps I'm the only one who is different."

"What were you like in Cormech?" he asked, and she glanced over at him, surprised into smiling.

"What was I like?" She thought of the years growing up in the coastal town. In that time she had passed pleasantly enough from child to woman, the span marked only by a feeling of waiting. As if she'd known that life wouldn't truly start until she'd left Cormech. "Not appreciably different from what I am now. Of course, I knew nothing of farming then. Or of goats and chickens, unless it was something I bought at the market."

"If you had no such duties then, what did you do with your time?"

Her amusement deepened. "I was as busy even though my chores were different. We took in boarders in order to keep a roof over our heads, a secret Mrs. Parker would be horrified to hear me divulge."

"You forget that I know your tale from Fergus."

"And all our secrets?"

He smiled. "Are there any more?"

She shook her head. "Not truly. We lived quietly, another fact Mrs. Parker would hate for me to admit. She believes that anyone not living in Edinburgh is hopelessly countrified."

"Soon you will be free of her dictates," he said.

She didn't want to discuss Mrs. Parker or Harold.

He fell into step beside her as she descended the hill and crossed the footbridge. Below them the river looked peaceful only because it had already passed through the mill, slowing in an effort to turn the huge millstone.

Once on the other side, the earth curved up to the hills, creating a natural basin that shielded the area from the most severe weather and fierce winter winds.

Aylshire was a tidy little village whose prosperity was readily apparent. Adding to the village's wealth was the fact that a century ago a group of Flemish weavers had settled in the vicinity. Over the years the industry had thrived until Aylshire linen had developed a reputation as some of the finest and most tightly woven cloth in the world.

"Why are you meeting with the elders?"

"I shouldn't answer you," she teased. "Since you've not been forthcoming with me. I will tell you, if you divulge your task."

He remained silent and she realized he wasn't going to respond.

"They are the ones appointed to hand out tasks for Lethson," she told him. The elders were the arbiters of all that went on within the village. A marriage needed to be arranged? The elders negotiated between warring parents. A man was a poor provider? The committee arranged for a quiet talk. Any number of complaints was handled by the seven members, and each seemed to revel in the authority conveyed by age. Perhaps their influence was so great since the village had no commanding castle or great house nearby. Nor was there a lord in residence to instill authority.

"I'm to receive my duties from them. Each villager is expected to participate in the ceremony."

He raised an eyebrow and winced, abandoning that expression. "Haven't you enough to do?"

"If someone from the manor doesn't volunteer, there will be no end of resentment."

"What about Susanna? Or your sister, for that matter?"

She wondered what he might do with the truth—that she truly wanted to stay busy to keep her mind from the proximity of her wedding. Each morning she clenched her eyes shut and prayed that a day had not passed again. But it had, and time was speeding along regardless of her wishes.

Did brides cry? She felt as if she would. In fear, panic, and remorse.

"Maureen will help, and my mother has given the approval for the celebrations to be held on Tyemorn land. But I have volunteered to appear before the committee." She smiled at one of the occupants of a pony cart. A few curious looks were directed toward James and his battered face, but for the most part the women looked away. Little did they know the surprise they had in store for them once his bruises faded.

"I'm surprised that Mr. Dunant would allow such a festivity," he said.

"Ayleshire is renowned for its stubbornness. Did you know that once the entire village was shunned by the Synod? Our minister at the time was a freethinker, but much beloved. They came to take him away, but the villagers stoned the church authorities when they approached. Of course, that happened a hundred years ago, but the sentiment still abides here."

At the inn door she hesitated. "Would you like to come inside with me?" The establishment served a multitude of purposes, from communal meeting place to tavern. At the beginning of June, the meeting rooms were given over to the elders and the procession of villagers began, each one arriving for his assignment. Even now there were a few people ahead of her, a matron she recognized and greeted with a smile, and a young boy who looked rebellious about being forced to participate.

"I have some questions to ask," he said, accompanying her inside.

"About Drummond?"

He nodded, and she watched him enter the tavern part of the inn. Turning left, she walked into the meeting room and waited her turn.

When it was time, she greeted the elders, taking her place at one side of the long table in the middle of the room. Sitting with knees together, and hands on her lap, Riona felt like a penitent or a child who'd been summoned for her punishment.

Three wizened old men and four equally ancient old ladies sat facing her.

"You are new to Ayleshire," the eldest of them said. "And you do not know our ways. Is the manor prepared to assist us this year?"

At first Riona had been taken aback not only by the curiosity of the villagers but by their blunt way of speaking. Now, of course, she understood their suspicion and their fear. Tyemorn was an important employer and source of income.

"Indeed we are, sir," she said respectfully. "We would have done so last year had we known of the ceremony." They'd not moved here until after Lethson, but she didn't remind him of that fact. "It is an oversight that will not occur again, I can assure you."

The gentleman, who had a long flowing white beard not unlike Old Ned's, surveyed her critically as if testing the mettle of her words. Finally, he nodded, before turning to look to the others for their assent. Approval came soon enough in the quavery voice of an elderly lady who managed to smile at the same time she spoke, unfortunately giving her kind face an almost malevolent appearance.

"We will, of course, use Bonfire Hill."

Riona nodded. The property, the highest point of land near the village, belonged to the manor.

"Do not forget the peat wagons," another elder contributed. "They need the right of way on Tyemorn's roads."

Again Riona nodded.

"What duties do you wish to perform?" the elder asked.

"Whatever you feel might be of benefit to the village," she said diplomatically.

"You will gather the birch branches," one old lady said, and the first gentleman nodded sagely. "We will need a hundred of them, collected a few days before Lethson."

"They're to be nailed above the doorway of each house, but you needn't be concerned about that. You must, however, get them to the villagers on time."

She nodded, thinking that with some help from the farm boys the task would not be so difficult. She hesitated, wondering if questions were permitted. Finally, curiosity won out over prudence. "What is the purpose of the branches?"

One of the elders looked at her approvingly. The others, however, seemed disconcerted by her question.

"We've always done it." A consensus of nods.

"A way of demonstrating our thanksgiving for a bountiful first half of the year," one man added.

"And to demonstrate our hopes for a good harvest," another contributed.

"Is that all?" she asked, relieved to have been given only one chore.

"No," came the answer. "You must bake the cake."

"A cake?" she asked faintly. "For the entire village?"

"For the elders," one of the men stated.

"The making of the midsummer cake is a sacred duty." This admonition came from one of the women at the table.

"Very well," Riona said, attempting to smile, but failing at it. "I will do the birch branches and the cake."

"The cake shall be made of the finest flour," another elderly woman said. "And made with the dew gathered the morning of the last quarter moon before Lethson. Mixed with honey, eggs, and spices, it will produce the most superb cake in all of Scotland."

Riona thought there might be more optimism in that state-

ment than warranted but nodded anyway. What was the punishment for failing in such a task? Would she be banished
from the rest of the festivities?

What Riona wanted to do was to beg for mercy, ask for a
reprieve, argue that she would be better suited for almost any
other task. But she stood and smiled weakly, thanking the
elders for their time and their faith in her.

She hoped that James had greater success in his errand.

Chapter 14

A yleshire was crowded, the inn filled to the rafters with people, most of whom had come to the village for the horse fair. James stood in the tavern, the object of a few curious stares. But no one ventured a comment about the state of his face. Nor were there eyes filled with hatred staring back at him. He was hampered in his task because he'd never seen the man who attacked him in the daylight. He might be talking to Drummond and never recognize him.

His discussion with the innkeeper yielded nothing in the way of information.

"Have you seen a man recuperating from a knife wound?"

"A knife wound?" The innkeeper scratched his grizzled chin as he thought about the question.

"Well, now, I cannot say I have. But I've got every room rented, and even the attic is being shared by twenty or so men. The villagers are making a pretty penny for themselves offering a bed and a meal. The man you seek might well be staying with one of them."

"Are they all here for Lethson?"

"No, for the horse fair. If I were you, I'd go to the fair. It's the first event of the Lethson celebrations. You're bound to find the man you seek there."

James nodded, deciding to do just that.

A few moments later, Riona emerged from the meeting room, a dazed look on her face.

"You look miserable," he said gently when she joined him. "Did you receive your task?"

"Yes, but what about you? Did you find Drummond?" She looked less worried about Drummond than the duties she'd been given.

"No. It's been recommended that I attend the horse fair."

"Will you?"

"If Drummond doesn't appear before then."

"Can you spare the time from your duty?"

He sent her a sideways glance as an unspoken rebuke for her curiosity.

"Tell me this, if you can do nothing else. Is your task something that would worry me if I knew?"

He studied her. "No, I don't think it would." She would, he thought, simply solve the mystery of the thefts and then handle the problem of what to do about the thief.

"Very well, then," she said. "I shall not ask any further, but when you can, will you tell me?"

"I can agree to those terms," he said, touched by her loyalty to her family and Tyemorn. "But tell me what the elders said."

"I have two duties. The first is not onerous. I have to

gather birch branches for all the village doors. The second, however, has me troubled."

He remained silent, waiting.

"I have to bake a cake."

They left the inn and began walking back to Tyemorn. The path she took, however, was not the same as the one that led them to Ayleshire. He wondered if she were taking him to the Roman wall after all.

"I'm not a very good baker," she explained. "It isn't that I don't measure everything correctly, because I do. But something always seems to go wrong. There is either not enough salt or there's too much honey. I would much prefer to gather the branches and leave the baking to someone else."

"When does this monumental chore need to be done?"

"Which one, the branches or the cake?"

"The branches," he said, one corner of his lip turning up.

"Next week."

"I'll help you with the branches."

"Are you certain you won't help with the cake? I truly need more assistance with that task," she teased.

She bent, picking up a twig lying across the path, and began swishing it back and forth in front of her.

The sky was darkening to the west, but he didn't urge her back to Tyemorn, being as complicit in this truancy as she. They followed a ridge surrounding the village like the lip of an overturned bowl. The wind increased, marking its presence through the tall grass and carrying with it the scent of rain.

Each was content to remain silent. Not once did Riona look over at him, lost as she was in her thoughts, and he in consideration of her.

"This is it," she said a little while later, pointing to a small brick outcropping emerging from the side of the hill. "The villagers say that the wall used to surround Ayleshire hundreds of years ago. Now there's not much left." She led the way through the bracken, glancing over at him to ensure he was following. "We've had visitors from as far away as France come to look at the wall, take measurements and ask questions, but they also take a few stones home to remind them of their journey. A pity, since it is so old."

The wall came barely to his knees, and was constructed of bricks rounded by age and weather.

"I realize it doesn't look like much." She brushed a few bricks clean of thickly growing moss.

"On the contrary," he said. "It reminds me of walls I've seen before. Ancient ruins in Italy."

She laid her hand on the top of the wall. "It must have been taller at one time and more impressive. But I don't know where it begins or why it was built."

"Or what it was meant to keep out? Or keep in?"

"Exactly," she said, smiling at him.

A moment of perfect accord as each looked at the other.

She leaned against the wall as storm clouds raced above them, blowing gusts of heated wind and dust. Impatiently, she tugged at her hair, making him want to grab it between his hands and hold it away from her face to give her some respite for a moment.

"We should go back," Riona said, but she turned her face into the wind and closed her eyes. At that moment, she appeared part of the elements herself. An errant gust billowed her skirt behind her. She smiled, pressing her hands against the fabric to keep it in place. Her hair, loosed of its restraint, flew about her head, tendrils brushing against her cheeks.

He didn't want to leave her, James realized abruptly. Until she wed he wanted every moment she could spare, every instant in which to learn what she thought or believed. What amused her? What saddened her?

"We should go back," he repeated. Her words, but his thoughts hiding behind them.

She turned her head and looked at him, her glance even and steady.

Rain began, falling so lightly that they remained motionless beside the ancient wall. What had it witnessed in all that time? More than one couple standing here, surely. Had a woman tempted a man here a century ago? Two? Had a man ever fought a battle with his honor as he did now?

She was silent, and he wanted to warn her that she was so at her peril. He might begin to believe all manner of things if she did not refute them. That her conscience warred as his did. That her mind was fixed not so much on Harold as on him.

For her safety and his sense of decency, he should encourage her to speech.

Talk to me of Harold. Or Edinburgh. But do not, I beseech you, continue to look at me with those eyes that mirror the sky above us. Do not look as if you might weep at any moment.

The rain began to fall more heavily. Reaching out, he gripped her hand, pulling her to the outcrop of rock and earth that formed a natural shelter.

Lightning flashed on a nearby hill and thunder rolled, echoing on itself until it sounded as if two storms raged above them. The ground trembled in response, as if nature's fury was a lover and the earth itself a receptive partner.

She was to be married. Worse, she guarded the image of

her beloved as if he were sacred, refusing to talk of Harold, as if, in doing so, she might sully his name.

"How many days until your wedding?" he asked her abruptly.

Riona glanced up, her smile fading as she stared at him. She shouldn't have been so lovely in her threadbare dress. The sun had pinked her cheeks, and health sparkled in her eyes.

"Does it matter?" she asked instantly.

"Perhaps not," he said, wishing he had not asked.

"It isn't a love match, James," she said. Words that made him glance at her again, hold her gaze with his. "Rather, it's one of obligation."

What sort of man was he to be pleased to see regret in a soft, gray-eyed gaze, or feel his heart leap at the mournful tone of her announcement.

"What sort of obligation?" His voice sounded relaxed, betraying none of his inner thoughts. He'd learned the trait in the midst of biting gales and deadly ice storms. When everything around him solicited his fear he grew the calmest.

Riona's words had been as powerful as a typhoon. *It isn't a love match.*

She turned away, facing toward the woods in the distance. "Is it important? I must marry him."

"Why?" he said, taking a few steps closer to her. "Is it a familial duty? A betrothal from childhood?"

She shook her head. But still, she would not look at him.

"Why, Riona?"

Finally, she turned and faced him. The two of them stood sheltered beneath an outcropping of shale, an isolated place. Almost an island for as much as anyone could see them. They were together, and dangerously close.

His conscience bid him move back, away. But he didn't, only stretched out his hands to her, gripping her sleeves.

"Please do not ask me, James." Her voice was thick with emotion, and he was startled to see her eyes swimming with tears.

"What is it?"

She shook her head, and one errant tear fell. But instead of taking a leisurely path down her cheek it was swiped away quickly by her hand. An angry gesture, as revealing of her irritation as the thinning of her lips.

He wanted to kiss them until they were full again. Soft and pillowy, slightly parted in wonder. He studied her mouth for long moments as if witnessing the deed, both participant and voyeur.

Slowly, James lowered his head, too close for propriety, too dangerous a position for decency's sake. His honor shouted at him, and he ignored the warning. He flirted with disaster, sailing on the edge of the wind, full-bellied sails unfurled.

Say my name, he commanded her silently. *Summon me with a sound. Just a word, that's all, and I'll cover your lips with mine. I'll give in to the temptation that has dogged my steps all these interminable days.*

But she remained silent, but for a deep sigh.

He pulled her closer, until the tips of her shoes bumped against his boots. A gentle nudge of feet until her hands pressed against his arms. Her head tilted back to see him.

"James," she said softly. A warning.

Where was his honor? His decency? Buried, numbed, hidden beneath an almost paralyzing wonder. Who was she, to do this to him?

He turned her hand in his, marveling at both the differences and the similarities. Each of their fingers was callused, but her hand was small in comparison to his.

The sky above them flashed like lanterns signaling at sea. The storm was above them now. The wind blew his hair about his face, as if in gentle chastisement.

He draped himself over her to protect her from the worst of the weather. She braced her hand against the placket of his shirt, and he wanted to ask her if she did so to keep him at bay. She was safe with him. His thoughts, inappropriate and sinful, would never be translated into action.

But, God, he was tempted.

There were some things, James reasoned, that could not be explained. The source of the wind, the narrow escapes he'd had at sea, the feeling of the Almighty being at his elbow in treacherous conditions. The longing he had for Riona McKinsey.

He'd never felt anything like it before, this absurd desire to be in her company. His lips twitched into a smile just looking at her, and his heart seemed to lighten in his chest at her answering glance. He'd never before considered himself an irrational man, but he was acting the fool. Lovesick and besotted.

How could he feel so much so quickly? A matter of days only. His life, once charted, most certainly planned, seemed adrift now. Vague. Amorphous, like the clouds above them.

Why her? Why not a woman of Inverness? He'd been to the town numerous times in the year he'd been at Gilmuir. Why not a woman he spied in the street? An innkeeper's daughter, an inhabitant of a coach, a woman encountered by chance at the market?

Because as lovely as she was, Riona's attraction wasn't her appearance. She was simply herself, intransigent at times, questioning at others, willful and malleable, simple and complicated.

They had blurred the boundaries between them from the moment they had met. Now, he didn't know where she belonged. More than an acquaintance. Friend? What did he call a woman he wanted but could never have?

A wish unfulfilled.

He took one step closer to her, pressing his hands against the base of her neck and trailing his fingers up to rest at her nape. She shivered, and he almost congratulated her for the freedom and honesty of her response.

Tremble for me. Words he wanted to whisper against her closed lips. And she would gasp and open them, inviting a kiss.

"We should leave," she said, lowering her head a little. If he moved just so, his lips would rest against her forehead. A benediction of touch, a sweetly innocent kiss that was only a prelude to what he really craved.

But he was civilized, wasn't he? There were no more clan raids, no more stealing of women. Instead, they were paraded before men in their pretty frocks, wearing demure looks. Men were sent to bid on them surreptitiously with genteel words like dowries and annual income.

He'd lost her before he ever knew her.

Something in him, old and ancient, surprised him with its atavism. He was no longer James McRae, ship's captain, man of letters and learning, as much as he was the great grandson of the old laird who could ride like a banshee and plunder with the best of them.

He placed his fingers firmly against her mouth, a guard against his wayward lips. Lightning flashed nearby, startling them both. In the bright flash she looked too pale, almost frightened of him. He pulled her gently toward him, curving his body over hers in protection. Only he knew the desperate desire that surged within him at the moment.

Nature had stripped itself of all decorum, and he was following suit, changing the longer he stood here with Riona only a breath away. What separated them, what protected her, was his will, now whisper-thin and flagging.

His imagination furnished thoughts he shouldn't have, visions of laying her down on the grass and loving her there. He would put his hands on her until she grew accustomed to the touch of his palms and fingers on her skin. Then, only then, would he allow himself the luxury of feeling all her separate curves, the swell of her breasts, the enticing sweep of waist to hips, the long line of her legs.

Giving in to the temptation, he jerked her toward him and tilted his head so that his lips slanted over hers. Her lips were warm and full, falling open beneath his tender coaxing. Then his tongue traced a delicate path across her bottom lip. She gasped, and he was inhaling the sound of it.

She clung to him, her fingers clutching his shirt as he bent her backward even farther. There wasn't any room between them for thoughts or even regrets.

Damned, he was going to be damned. The last conscious thought he had for long moments.

Finally, they parted, his breath coming so fast that he felt as if he'd run a race. She was as breathless, laying her forehead against his chest.

"Dear God," he said, the guttural voice unlike his own, the two words uttered in wonder and disbelief. He'd never before been carried away by a simple kiss.

She looked up at him then, her eyes large and wide. Silver in the afternoon sunlight, they sought his gaze and held it.

He should ask her forgiveness. Or explain. But any further words were impossible. He was still reeling from what had just happened.

Riona pulled back finally, her hands trembling where they rested on his arms. She nodded to him as if he'd spoken, or perhaps it was simply an acknowledgment of the power of that kiss.

He caught her hand, brought it to his mouth, slowly kissing her fingertips, feeling her tremble.

"You will make a lovely bride," he said, forcing himself to step back and away from her.

For a long moment, neither said a word. Finally, she pulled her hand free, gripped her skirts in both fists, and began to run. Either toward sanctuary or simply away from him.

Chapter 15

Dinner that night was tasteless, and endless. Riona's behavior garnered several approving glances from Mrs. Parker, who had finally recovered from her bout of illness, and more than one curious look from her mother and Maureen.

Yearning after James MacRae had rendered her silent. Her fingers itched to curve around his. Or to press themselves against his waistcoat. She wanted so desperately to touch him that it was almost a craving.

Every time she glanced up he was staring at her, so intensely that she shivered. She stared at her plate or her lap rather than return his look.

After dinner was done and the dishes washed and put away, Riona knocked on Susanna's door and entered at her response.

Instead of being occupied with her needlework, her

mother was simply sitting, hands folded on her lap, head resting on the back of the chair, a pose Riona had not often seen. Her chair was turned toward the window, and Susanna was gazing at the night sky. When Riona entered, she turned her head and smiled.

"What is it, Riona?" Susanna asked gently. "Are you feeling well?"

Riona nodded.

She went to sit on the footstool beside her mother's chair. She wrapped her arms around her knees and sat staring out the window. Susanna smiled at her and contentedly resumed her study of the stars. For a few moments, they were simply content to be silent with each other.

"Do you ever miss Father?" Riona asked.

"Sometimes," Susanna said to her surprise. "On misty nights especially. He used to tease me then, telling details of brownies and elves and strange creatures that dwelled in the fog. Every time I see an overcast morning I think of your father. And at night, too."

She'd never thought that Susanna might be filled with a sense of grief or loss. Her mother had always seemed so capable, so confident. But she hadn't always been that way, Riona realized. At one point in her life, she had been half of a couple, part of a whole.

"How did you do it?" she asked. "How did you learn to live without him?"

"I had no other choice," Susanna said simply. "I had you and Maureen, and the world doesn't stop because I was stricken by grief. I had rent to pay and food to buy and all those necessities that two growing girls required. I simply had to put one foot in front of the other until it became natural to live without him."

Riona thought it had to be a great deal more difficult than that, but she only smiled in response.

"Polly tells me you've received another letter from Harold."

Riona nodded. "He has purchased some furniture for our house," she said. More expenditures, and before they'd even wed. The creditors of Edinburgh must be counting on their marriage even more than Harold. As it was, it seemed to her that he was doing everything in his power to spend Great Aunt Mary's legacy.

Susanna patted her hand, a way of commiserating without saying anything critical.

"I've invited the McDermotts to dinner," her mother said.

"Why?" Riona asked, frowning.

"I am hoping to interest Mrs. Parker in another commission," her mother said candidly. "The McDermott girls are of an age to be introduced to society."

She wondered if her mother's wish to help Mrs. Parker had anything to do with the fact that Susanna was also a widow, once responsible for making her own way in the world.

"Besides," her mother continued, "the presence of Gorman McDermott will be a welcome change for James. All this female company must be tedious for him."

"You like him, don't you?"

Susanna nodded. "I do. At first because of Fergus, but now because I've become acquainted with him. And you, Riona? Do you like him?"

"He's very charming," she said cautiously. Devastatingly so. Nor could she forget their kiss. How could she?

"If things were different, I wouldn't mind having him as a son-in-law."

But things weren't different, weren't they?

For a long moment, they continued to gaze at each other. Finally, Riona stood, bending forward to kiss her mother on the forehead. She hadn't said the words, but they were there between them, nonetheless.

Is there no way I can escape this marriage?

She knew the answer as well as Susanna.

Harold glanced up, frowning, as his brother entered the room. The sun had been up for nearly two hours, and Peter had not yet been to bed. Morning, in his brother's world, was when he returned from his debauchery, not a time to rise to greet the world.

Ordinarily, Harold would have joined him, but he was being prudent so close to his nuptials.

"You should be a little more careful about the way you spend money, Peter. My fortunes have not been reversed as yet. Why don't you wait until after I've wed to be the profligate?"

He loved his brother, as well as his three sisters. They were, after all, the reason he'd come to Edinburgh and trolled through the recent crop of heiresses. Right at the moment, however, he would gladly toss Peter and all his siblings out the window.

They were spending entirely too much money. He'd just received a letter from his eldest sister demanding a new roof for their house. And new clothing for their youngest sister. She was always whining about the lack of funds.

"Perhaps you should consider a military career, after all."

"Have you the wherewithal to purchase a commission?" Peter asked, brows arching.

"No, but I hear they need cannon fodder in fighting the rebels in America."

Peter laughed, the sound grating on Harold's nerves. "I doubt it's come to that, brother. I'd find an heiress on my own, but my reputation has preceded me," he said easily, falling into the chair beside the desk.

Harold frowned at him.

"Don't worry, isn't your little brown wren worth a fortune?"

"The way you and our siblings are spending money, soon that won't be enough."

"Isn't there property in her family? That charming, pastoral prison where you stayed for a week? Surely that has to be worth something."

"Only when her mother dies, and she looks to be in grand health."

"Yes, but the hint of property is enough to allow you some additional credit. Things are not as dire as you think, dear brother."

"I've already spent as much as I can on promises, Peter." He pushed aside his papers and stood. "Pretend to be a little less vulgar in your tastes, will you, brother, at least until I get the chit to the altar."

Rory reached Ayleshire when dusk was approaching, that time of day between light and dark that always seemed eerie and mysterious to him. At sea, the sun bid farewell over the horizon, streaks of orange and pink and blue warning of night's approach. On land, the end of day was a quieter thing, but longer.

He'd much prefer being at sea, but since the MacRaes had decided to toss their lot in with farmers, he had no other choice but to join them. He didn't think that he could sail with another captain or trust another man as he trusted the MacRae brothers.

James would be surprised at the news he brought. A baby had been born to Iseabal. A sweet little thing with her father's eyes and her mother's firm chin. He'd returned in time to witness the wedding at Fernleigh, too. Fergus looked as proud as any young man, for all that he was grizzled and gray. Leah Drummond, now MacRae, presided at his side, as happy as any woman he'd ever seen.

For years, he'd sailed with a first mate who'd seen omens around every corner. Daniel had chosen to return to Nova Scotia, but there were times Rory could swear, as now, that he heard the older man's voice intoning one of his many superstitions. "They come in threes, my boy. Two sorrows and a joy, or two joys and a sorrow. Never three of the same."

Rory gave a thought to Daniel now, wondering if he still found solace in his shipboard companion, a cat who was known to foretell calm seas or rough winds by the swish of its tail.

If it were true there was a sorrow to come, Rory hoped it was a small one. Despite their wealth and their lineage, the MacRaes had borne their share of hardship.

Recently, however, there was nothing but good news for the clan.

In his pack was a gift from Fergus and his new bride to Riona upon the occasion of her marriage. He also carried a letter from Alisdair to his brother, although he knew the contents of it well enough.

A goodly number of the Drummond clan had left Fernleigh, but they'd done so with no visible rancor. The only man who might have carried on a feud was many miles away.

Thomas Drummond had been given over to the English, and had been impressed upon one of their ships. One of His Majesty's sailors, reluctant as he might be. The attacker might be him or another Drummond, one of those who'd left for Inverness months earlier.

Alisdair, however, had taken the precaution of setting up a guard and watching for any strangers near Gilmuir. There would be no danger to the MacRaes as long as he was laird.

Rory smiled as he neared the village. Preparations for Lethson were well under way. He should be brushing up on his footwork in order to ask Abigail for a dance. A flush of anticipation surged through him. While it was true Rory had been kept longer than he wanted at Gilmuir, he'd made up for the delay in the swiftness of his return.

A few of the villagers waved at him, and although he didn't know any of them, Rory waved back, caught up in the general excitement. Laughter seemed to perfume the air along with the scent of blooms and greenery.

Ribbons had been affixed to various signposts to mark the path of a foot race. Perhaps he'd participate when the time came, especially if the prize was worthwhile.

But the greatest addition to the village was the series of rope corrals filled with horses, erected toward the east. A horse fair—perhaps he'd come and see that, too.

Crossing the bridge, Rory anticipated the moment when he would see the crooked manor house. Darkness was almost fully upon him when he viewed Tyemorn Manor. He grinned, thinking that perhaps Abigail would greet him with some favor. After all, he was a messenger of some importance.

He dismounted in front of the barn and led his horse inside.

Ned was there, currying one of the plow horses.

"It's about time you've returned," he said gruffly. "A certain young lady has been asking every day if I've seen a sign of you."

"Really?" Rory asked, pleased.

Suddenly there was commotion at the front of the barn. He heard a soft squeal and then Abigail came into sight, running so quickly that her feet were a blur beneath her. She skidded to a halt in the middle of the doorway, clasping her hands in front of her.

"Oh," she said, as if she were surprised by his presence, "it's you, Rory. I had no idea you'd returned so quickly."

Rory grinned in response. "I'm back," he said. And glad he was of it. "I wanted to make sure I was here for Lethson. I want that dance you promised me, Abigail. Or have you forgotten?"

She smiled at him, and he realized he would have traveled across Scotland to see one of Abigail's smiles.

"No, I haven't forgotten, Rory MacRae. And have you remembered how to work your feet?"

That question was a little too close to the mark. He might well have forgotten but for the fact that he'd been practicing the steps in his mind.

She giggled at his silence. "Never mind, a few minutes with me and you'll remember it all again."

She disappeared as quickly as she'd arrived. Ned cleared his throat and took the reins of his horse from him.

"Go and find James, lad," he said kindly, "and I'll take care of your horse."

He entered the house by the kitchen door and headed for the stairs. Riona, who was reading in the parlor, looked up as his booted foot touched the first step.

She saw him and greeted him with a smile.

"Rory! You're back. How was your journey?"

He turned and walked into the room. "Not a bit of trouble, miss. Not a squirrel out of place or a sparrow. Nor did I see any sign of Drummond."

"And everyone is fine at Gilmuir?" She closed the book, using her finger to mark the place.

He had a letter for James entrusted to him by Alisdair, but he told her the contents of it now.

"James has a niece," he said. "A plump little thing with a red face and a cry that can be heard throughout Gilmuir. They've named her Aislin Patricia MacRae."

"Have Fergus and Leah married?" she asked.

"They have," he said. "I was there when they recited their vows."

"A happy day," Riona said. "Fergus must be overjoyed."

Rory nodded. "He looked the part," he agreed. "I've brought greetings from all of them for James. Along with a dozen or so requests for his return from the women of the village," he added, grinning. "Half of them imagine themselves in love with him. The other half swear he loves them as well. But that's James. A conquest everywhere he walks."

"Oh?" Riona said softly.

"He's very well thought of by the ladies," Rory said. He began slapping at the dust on his shoulders. "I need to wash the dirt of the road off me."

"It's so good to have you back," she said, smiling.

He nodded, thinking that he had had other homecomings before, but this one seemed special somehow. As if this place nestled in its protective valley was truly home.

Tyemorn's sole inn was a tidy little place with three rooms up the narrow stairs and a common area now crowded with men. For days Thomas had lain abed, struggling with fever, only the kindness of the tavern maid keeping him in water and clean cloths. He had given her most of his money to ensure her silence and her assistance, and now had only enough coins for another meal, or a tankard or two. He settled on the tankard, hoping that the whiskey would dull the worst of the pain.

MacRae had killed him.

There wasn't any doubt of it. If he could have ignored the agony in his side, there was still the stench. The edges of the wound had grayed, red streaks now radiating outward from where he'd been knifed. The smell of death, sickly sweet and cloying, was with him always.

He could barely summon the strength to sit here. But before he expired of putrefaction, Thomas was determined that MacRae would die. The score wouldn't be settled, but he was beyond finding justice for the Drummond clan now. All he wanted was to avenge his own death.

Pressing some clean cloths against the wound had diminished the smell somewhat, enough that he felt comfortable among the group of men in the tavern.

"So, you're here for the fair, then?" one man asked him and he nodded into his whiskey, the effort of pretending to be a peddler beyond him at the moment.

"We used to be renowned for our horse fair," he said, "but it's not the sort of thing it used to be. Once upon a time the world traveled to Ayleshire for our horses."

He continued to mull over the past, staring into his tankard. "Why, they came for days on end they did, so thick over the hills. Nothing but horses, lines and lines of the beauties."

"Sounds impressive," he managed to say.

"Aye, that it was," the old man replied. "Nowadays, however, we spend more time with Lethson." He wearily shook his head over his ale. "Pagan bit of nonsense, that's what it is. An excuse for the girls to act like slatterns and the boys to revel in it." He sighed heavily. "I've a daughter with a daughter, all because of Lethson. And a weak, puling husband she's found for herself, too."

"What's this ceremony, this Lethson?"

The old man looked over at him with a sour expression. "A bit of tomfoolery. Bonfires and dancing, singing and gathering at the well. Foolish stuff, man, that you'd be better off ignoring. You should find yourself far from here before that night. The good folks of Ayleshire lose their minds and behave like idiots beneath the moon."

Thomas motioned to the barmaid. He ordered another tankard and gave her his last coin.

"Even the manor folk are participating this year."

"How, exactly?" Thomas asked, leaning both elbows on the table in front of him. Nausea rolled over him, and he could feel himself grow chilled, even as beads of perspiration dotted his forehead.

Just let me live long enough to kill him. A strange entreaty, but one fervently prayed.

Chapter 16

Any moment now, the McDermott daughters were going to pinch each other and giggle. Riona frowned at them, but her expression made absolutely no difference to their silliness.

They acted as if they had never seen an attractive man before. James's bruises had faded over the last week until only a tinge of yellow appeared on one cheek. Riona found herself wishing that he could have remained battered for a few more days, and then instantly felt ashamed of thinking such a horrible thought.

Mrs. Parker, meanwhile, was looking on fondly as if the two girls were precocious children instead of women old enough to have their own households.

Where was her censure? Her disapproval?

James, to his credit, appeared to pay them no heed, concentrating instead on his conversation with their father.

"I would appreciate it if you could assist me in this matter. I know it's not a large vessel, but I had hoped to be able to use it for river traffic."

"I would be more than happy to take a look at the design," James was saying.

Mr. McDermott was always trying to increase his profits and had hit upon the idea of taking his produce to market using a water route. Their neighbor had proved invaluable this last year. He had loaned them his draft horse when one of theirs had gone lame, and some of his workers had come to help Ned from time to time. The relationship between the two farms went back several decades. The difference now being, of course, that Mr. McDermott was a widower. Riona suspected he looked at her mother with the vision of joining the two farms.

She doubted, quite frankly, that there would ever be an alliance of land or marriage between her mother and their neighbor. Mr. McDermott, kind as he might be, had a rather boisterous nature. His laugh was so loud that the china in the cabinet seemed to shiver whenever he was amused. Susanna treated him like a rather large puppy, kind yet firm.

Upon first meeting Mr. McDermott, Riona thought that his daughters' characters must fade beneath his effusive nature. But instead of being shy, withdrawn women, both Rosalie and Caroline had distinct personalities.

Rosalie McDermott was one of those tiresome individuals who have an answer for everything. Despite the fact that she had no experience or any knowledge, she offered a comment on everything from animal husbandry, planting uncultivated furrows, and sluice drainage, to a score of other farming subjects. In addition, she professed superior awareness about Edinburgh despite the fact that the last time she'd visited the city was two years ago. She was, she said to anyone who would listen, familiar with the fashions, the balls, the dinner parties. In short, she had an opinion on anything.

Her sister, Caroline, was her opposite, but by no means a shadow of Rosalie. While her older sister espoused to know everything, Caroline pretended to know nothing, cultivating a vacuousness she perceived as charming. In addition, she batted her eyes at any available male in the vicinity. Even Old Ned was not sacrosanct. She patted her bodice from time to time as if her heart were beating too fast in her chest and sighed dramatically like an actress on the stage. Whenever anyone would ask her opinion, Caroline would sigh deeply and say, "I truly don't know. What do you think?"

Now both of them were looking at James with greed in their eyes, as if they wanted to add him to their collection of suitors.

She, who had railed so fiercely against society's rules, wanted to dictate a few of her own. James truly should not smile in the presence of other women. Not at the milkmaids or at Polly and certainly not at poor Abigail. Or at strangers, either. Women became silly in the presence of his charm. They lost their senses, evidently, choosing to giggle or stare wide-eyed at him.

Riona wished she could say something, anything to dissuade them from staring at him so, but she was constrained to silence by good manners and one thing more. He wasn't hers. He never would be. The knowledge was like a blow to her midriff. He wasn't hers. He never would be. Maybe if she repeated that to herself endlessly, she might be able to act with some decorum around him.

She concentrated on her plate, the silverware, the damask tablecloth. Anything but across the table at him.

A kiss did not bind them. Even though it was a kiss like no other. But, oh, it was so difficult to sit here and watch as other women admired him, knowing that she could never claim him as her own. She had no right to frown at Rosalie McDermott. Or change the subject, or chastise either of them for their simpering looks and small, coy smiles.

Had she acted as foolishly?

"Perhaps you might come and visit me tomorrow?" Gorman McDermott said.

"I would be pleased to," James said, glancing at Susanna. Her smile was approval enough.

What task did he feel so honor-bound to perform for her mother? She'd agreed to refrain from asking, but she was still curious. Where had he learned his courtly manners? In Paris where someone, no doubt a woman, had taught him to dance?

Rosalie and Caroline were smiling and cooing at James, looking as if he were a sweetmeat and they starving urchins.

But who was she to remark upon their forwardness? She had been guilty of her own wanton behavior.

If anything, she should feel remorse that she'd allowed him to kiss her, feel some sort of regret that it had happened. Or guilt that she felt nothing of the sort and might possibly do it again if the opportunity presented itself. What type of woman was she, that she couldn't cease thinking about it?

"You are very quiet this evening," Mrs. Parker remarked in an aside to her. The older woman's color was high, and she looked inordinately healthy. No doubt from being abed this past week. "Are you feeling ill? One can hardly tell with that brown color you've acquired. Buttermilk and lemon juice applied three times day, and especially at night, will help fade your skin. I doubt Mr. McDougal will find himself pleased to be married to a little brown berry."

Riona smiled her assent. In actuality, she didn't care what Harold thought of her complexion.

"You're looking a little drab," Mrs. Parker continued. "Some color would not be amiss. A pretty little bow in your hair, for example. Flowers like your sister is wearing." Maureen's hairstyle was interspersed with tiny daisies. But then, Maureen's hair didn't have to be tamed as hers did. If she wore daisies in her hair, Riona was certain that she would look ridiculous, rather than fetching.

But Mrs. Parker wasn't finished with her, it seemed. "You should really try to be more animated, my dear," she whispered. "All this silence gives you a sullen disposition. Surely you have something to contribute to the conversation. Something that doesn't have to do with barnyards or animals."

James glanced in her direction and then away, making her wonder if he'd overheard Mrs. Parker's whispered remarks.

"Tyemorn Manor is such a pretty little place," Rosalie said. "Picturesque in its way. Have you given any thought to cultivating the meadow in front of the manor?"

Susanna looked startled at the question and only shook her head.

"I should, if I were you. You might wish to plant potatoes there."

Susanna nodded again, but didn't comment. No doubt she considered a view of rows and rows of potato mounds somewhat lacking, Riona thought.

"Will you be taking your daughters to Edinburgh?" Mrs. Parker asked, directing her attention to Gorman.

Riona stifled a smile. Her mother's plan was working.

"I do so wish to see Edinburgh again," Rosalie said. "There are a series of charming shops that have exquisite fabrics. On my recommendation, of course. I told them that they needed to stock more lawns and laces."

Maureen made some polite comment while Riona resisted the urge to yawn.

"Riona, I would be more than happy to show you my last selection. In fact, we can plan a day when the seamstress will be working. She and I are finishing up the details of an exquisite ball gown that I designed. Will you not come and let me show you?" Rosalie surveyed her from her chin to her toes, her expression leaving no doubt of what she felt about Riona's yellow and blue silk dress. "Perhaps we can find something in a color that flatters you."

Riona nodded politely. An unexpected blessing of being married and living in Edinburgh, she'd never have to see Rosalie again.

A little while later, dinner was finally over and they retired to the parlor, the men joining them. Mrs. Parker bemoaned the lack of amusements, while the McDermott girls entertained themselves by crowding around James.

"You will never guess who I saw in Ayleshire, Maureen," Caroline was saying. "Agnes Haversham. She's the girl I told you about who's gone to live in Inverness. She's back for a visit. You must meet her."

"The horse fair doesn't last long, but it attracts a fair number of visitors," Mr. McDermott was telling James. "A great deal of horseflesh gets sold in our small village."

"Lethson is the most wonderful ceremony. Although, as I told the elders," Rosalie was saying, "perhaps it would be better to have it in the early spring, before planting season."

Riona wanted to ask, but didn't, why Rosalie thought they would listen to her since the celebration was held because of the summer solstice, the longest day of the year. Which oc-

curred in June, not April. Mrs. Parker was effectively dealt
with by ignoring her, a fact that made the older woman cross.

Before she could be singled out for more attention, Riona
stood, excused herself, and was out of the room before anyone could object.

Once the door had closed behind her, she debated where
to go. Drummond's presence had made walking outside unwise. Yet she didn't feel like going to her chamber yet.

Finally, in desperation she walked down the hall, entering
the library.

James had taken to working here before dinner, and after
the meal as well. Taking a few steps inside, she felt oddly like
a trespasser in this room now that he'd claimed it as his. He
had made his mark on the farms; she had seen the result of
his handiwork almost every day. Why wouldn't it be the
same in the library?

The desk bore evidence of his use; the inkwell had been
moved to the right, a selection of quills were neatly trimmed
and lying flat in expectation of his return. On the left corner
of the blotter was a small oil lamp and a few candles sitting in
reserve. She bent and retrieved the flint box, lit a few, and set
them in the iron holder until the room was tinted yellow by
the flickering light.

She noticed the large red leather book sitting in the middle
of the desk. JM. Her fingers trailed over his initials.

A journal, no doubt. What sort of thoughts would a man
like James MacRae write? She realized that she very much
wanted to know. But such a book is intrinsically personal,
almost intimate, and reading it would be an invasion of his
privacy.

Just as he invaded her thoughts.

She placed her hand flat against the books on one of the

shelves, picking one by the shape of it and not its contents. She wasn't in the mood to read, but something should enliven her mind, take her thoughts from that of her own life. Perhaps even transport her somewhere else. To Greece or Rome, to tales so wrought with peril that her own existence seemed tame and mundane in comparison.

Anything but a story, perhaps, of unrequited love. Or loss so painful that it mimicked a burn, blazing away inside the human heart.

She had never felt the way she did now. Every moment seemed crystalline and painful in its intensity. She felt too much, was too aware.

The backs of her hands were somehow sensitive, as were her wrists. The cuffs of her dress irritated them; even lace felt too abrasive. She wanted to be surrounded by something soft and pillowy.

She placed her hand at her throat, wondering if she were sickening. It almost hurt to swallow, as if a hundred unshed tears lingered there. Her eyes felt gritty, as if she had been awake for days. But when she slept, she dreamed. Where once she'd had perfectly ordinary dreams, now they were so much more. Vignettes of James and kisses so exquisite that they awakened her to lie staring at the ceiling, flushed and wanting.

When she heard a noise and glanced over her shoulder to see James standing there, a deep, resigned sigh escaped her.

"What is it, Riona? What's wrong?"

She turned back to the books, studying their spines for the first time. What is it? If she only knew, she might address that problem and find a solution for it. Oh, but she did know, didn't she?

What is it? Infatuation. Love. Desire. All these and perhaps even more. Emotions too late to be discovered, and with the wrong man.

"Go away, James."

"Are you unwell?"

Why was everyone so concerned with her health? She wanted to answer him: *Desperately unwell, my dearest James, and the cure is you.* Such words shouldn't be thought, let alone spoken.

"No," she said softly. "I'm well enough."

"Then what is it? Why did you leave the room so quickly? Why were you so silent at dinner?"

She turned and studied him, thinking that she had questions of her own.

Why, of all the men she might have met, had he come to Tyemorn Manor? Why this man, with his intense blue eyes and his broad shoulders? Why him, with his sense of humor and fairness, loyalty and honor? Why James, with his ability to pluck reason from her with a kiss?

"You should return. Rosalie and Caroline will be missing you. I wouldn't be surprised if they followed you in here," she said, glancing at the closed door.

She turned again, rather than watch him leave. She heard his footsteps, but he came closer.

"Please, James, leave me alone."

He halted and she placed both hands on the bookshelf, her fingers gripping the shelves. With all her being, she wanted to walk into his arms. God help her, because she was too weak to help herself.

"Forgive me," he said tersely. "I was but concerned about your welfare."

She closed her eyes, praying for the resolve she needed.

He placed his hands on her shoulders, and she leaned back

against him. Just for a moment. Just long enough to feel him against her. Resolutely, she straightened and pulled away.

"Do women fall at your feet everywhere you travel, James?"

He looked surprised at her remark. "I don't know what you're talking about, Riona."

"What about the women of Gilmuir? What do you do about them?"

"I treat every woman I meet the same, Riona," he said. "With kindness."

"And gallantry?" she asked. "And charm, no doubt." She glanced at him, her smile fading a little. "From any other man, it would be merely polite. From you, it's devastating."

"I doubt they think so."

"I know they do," she countered. "I've seen the effect of your charm at dinner tonight." *And felt it myself.*

He looked startled at her words, or maybe the tone of them. Too bitter, perhaps.

Taking a few steps back, he bowed slightly to her.

Good, he was leaving, before she humiliated herself by begging him to stay.

"Forgive me," he said once more. "I didn't mean to intrude."

"But you have." The words slipped free of their mooring. She spent too much time wondering about him, thinking about him, looking for him during the day. She'd even taken to dreaming of him.

She heard the door close softly behind him, and only then did she relax.

Rory snored. The young man was obviously exhausted, and the sound indicated a deep slumber.

James lay there with his arms braced behind his head, staring up at the ceiling. The night was one he had experienced many times before. As tired as he was, sleep should have come easily to him. Instead, he pictured Riona in the library tonight. Curt, almost rude, not the woman he'd come to know.

The closer the wedding date, the more she seemed to change. Almost as if she were readying herself to become a shadow of the woman he'd admired. Her laughter was more rare, her comments were tinged with irritation. Gone was the hoyden, and in her place a proper young woman of Edinburgh. An almost wife.

He felt the knowledge press down on him as if it were an anchor he wore around his shoulders.

He sat up on the side of the bed and looked toward Rory's bed. His snores had not abated, but that was not the reason James stood and dressed. Living aboard ship had taught him to sleep in even the most uncomfortable situations.

He closed the door quietly and found his way to the library. There he pushed the door closed silently behind him, his destination the desk. He lit a few candles before drawing shut the curtains to keep out the night. Sitting, he opened his journal and began to write. The thoughts were those he could never convey to another living soul.

It eased him somewhat to write, to purge his mind.

There are times when I want to ask her what she's thinking, or simply sit and listen to her laugh. Sometimes at dinner she captivates me and I lose all thought while watching her. Of all the women I have ever met, none has challenged my heart or my mind as much as she does. She makes me smile and muse on subjects I'd never considered.

At table she does not often look in my direction, but I cannot help but be drawn to her. During the day I stop and look for her and find her diligent at some task. Even that momentary sight is enough to lighten my hours.

A sound at the door made him look up. He'd expected Susanna. Riona entered the room instead.

For a moment they just stared at each other. He wanted to see her above all people, yet at the same time he realized how improper it was to bc alone in the middle of the night, with her dressed only in a thin nightgown and matching wrapper. Her hair was trailing down her back in one long, thick braid. Tendrils of hair had come loose and framed her face. Her hair had always reminded him of her true nature, unable to be completely controlled, almost wild.

Her hand went to her throat, her fingers splayed as if she held her words there before they could reach her lips.

"I couldn't sleep," she said finally.

"Neither could I."

"Forgive me for what I said earlier. I didn't mean to say those things."

"Yes, you did," he said, unwillingly amused. Contriteness did not suit her. "But I would be more interested in hearing why you said what you did."

"A comment of Rory's," she said, shrugging. "I shouldn't have paid it any heed."

"Is that why you're here? To apologize? It was not necessary."

"It was for me."

She was looking at him as if she'd imagined him. He

wanted to tell her that he was only too real. Human, not a ghost.

If he weren't an earthly creature, there would be no constraints between them. He would be able to touch her when he wished, infuse her nights with visitations. His invisible fingers would skim along her breasts, and he would press his unseen lips to her neck just above her collarbone and feel her shiver in delight.

But he was only too corporeal not to notice how the night-gown she wore hid none of her charms from view. Her breasts pressed against the modest material, lifting it, her breath made it rise and fall. One hand still pressed against her throat, the other at her waist as if to further delineate the lines of her figure.

His imagination had already furnished details to his curious mind, and now his eyes verified them.

"I am not a saint, Riona," he said. "But I do not make indiscriminate conquests."

"But you have made some?"

Did she want lies? Or him virginal? He was far from that, but she didn't need to know the details. Only, perhaps, that he had never before felt the way he did with her.

"Do you ever wish to be back in Cormech?" he asked abruptly. The question evidently surprised her. "Do you ever wish to be penniless again and more in control of your own destiny?"

"Without Great Aunt Mary's fortune?" She smiled. "More times than I can tell you. But then I realize how selfish a wish that is. Maureen is happy, and so is mother. Who am I to wish us back to penury? If I still lived in Cormech, it's possible that I would never have wed at all."

"Would you prefer that?"

"Would haves and should haves and could haves are unfair. I know exactly what I would have done a year ago or six months ago or even a month ago. Because I am so much more aware than I was then. But who is to say that I won't regret, a year from now, what I'm doing today? I can only do the best I can each moment."

"Is there nothing you would change about this moment now?"

"Oh yes," she said softly, not attempting to look away from him. "There is something I would change."

Her cheeks flushed; the picture she presented was of indescribable temptation.

He stood and came around the desk, but halted when he was still a few feet from her. There, a test of his resolve, and his honor. He reached out one hand, and she matched the gesture until only their fingertips touched.

"You shouldn't be here," he said, the words both a chastisement and a warning.

"No," she agreed softly. "I shouldn't. Or you should not be. We should not be together, especially on a night like this."

He glanced over his shoulder at the closed curtains. If the moon shone brightly, he could not see it. If the wind was riffling through the trees, he was unaware. The temperature might be chilled, and animals restless, but nothing intruded into this quiet room but their own emotions.

Yet neither of them moved to leave.

They were held together by the simple touch of their fingertips, a bond as strong as iron between them. But more linked them than that, he suspected—curiosity and humor, intelligence and whimsy, desire and need.

A sound outside the door made Riona draw her hand back. She smiled again and went to the bookshelves, blindly grabbing a volume before turning toward the door.

He watched her go, so painfully aroused that he was shaking.

Chapter 17

Every year the sluice leading from the River Wye needed to be cleaned of weeds and debris to ensure that the fields were properly irrigated. At intervals, wooden dams were erected in the channel, each successive board adding height and consequently slowing the flow of water.

The frames in which the boards fit needed to be replaced from time to time, since they swelled from being in the water constantly. Ned was repairing a section just off the river, where the current ran swiftly. Riona was helping, as were several other women, by carrying the baskets of silt away from the sluice and onto the newly cultivated west fields.

She was glad that James wasn't there. The work wasn't prettily done. Her oldest shoes squished with water, and the front of her dress was filthy. Add to that the fact that her hair had come undone once again and her braid was muddy.

Women moved in a line from the sluices to the west field,

each bent under the weight of her basket. Riona joined them again, preferring to stay busy rather than think about James's errand.

He'd gone to visit with Gorman McDermott. Something about plans for a river barge, she'd heard her mother say. She doubted the excuse. Gorman's daughters were of a marriageable age, and he'd be a fool to ignore a prime candidate for a son-in-law in James. She didn't doubt that Rosalie and Caroline had pleaded with their father to think of some reason for James to come to their home.

"Riona?"

She glanced up, realized she was next in line, and gave her basket to one of the men dredging the sluice on the other side of the dam. Ned was hammering the top board into position, softly muttering to himself as the frame, swollen and waterlogged, refused to budge.

Riona was returning from the field when she saw the commotion. The line of women disintegrated into a group crowding around the dam. She pushed her way forward.

"What's wrong?"

"It's Ned. He's gone and gotten his arm trapped."

Ned's face was pale, his body half in and out of the rushing water. "Get the mallet, lad," he said, directing another, younger man. "I dropped the fool thing when the board slipped."

Riona threw her basket down and knelt on the side of the sluice. "How can I help, Ned?"

"Get a wedge from the smith. A long bar that we can use to lever up part of the dam. My arm's caught between two boards." The effort of speaking was evidently costing him.

She nodded and stood. The journey back to the farm was uphill, and she held up her skirts and ran.

There was no one in the smithy, but she looked around for something that would act as a lever. Finally, she found it, hanging next to the door. A long flat iron bar that she remembered was used to help change the wheels on the wagons.

She grabbed it and began retracing her path when she heard the sound of hooves. Turning, she saw James riding into the yard. She flagged him down by waving both arms in the air.

The moment he halted his mount she was beside him. "James," she said, breathlessly, "you must come and help Ned." Quickly, she explained what had happened.

He dismounted, leaving his horse in front of the barn, and accompanied her back to the sluice.

Quickly, he surveyed the situation, then removed his jacket. Taking the bar from her, he jumped into the river. A second later, he disappeared from sight beneath the surface. It was only then that Riona realized the water level was rising.

Ned was paler than he'd been earlier, the thinness of his lips now rimmed with a bluish line. She knelt at his side, then lowered herself into the water, shivering at the chill.

"What do you think you're doing, lass?" Ned asked, but his voice had lost its edge.

"Helping you," she said shortly. She drew closer, using both hands on his back to push him gently upright. The current seemed to be getting stronger, and the water level was at his chin. If James couldn't free him, Ned might drown.

James surfaced, whipping his head back. "Can you hold on for another few minutes, Ned? I've nearly got the board free."

"Do I have a choice?" Ned answered, the surliness of his answer reassuring Riona as nothing else.

She exchanged a smile with James over his shoulder.

He disappeared below the surface of the water again, and

a second later she heard a muffled oath from Ned. One end of the board came free, bobbing to the surface.

Riona moved to his side, following his sleeve below the water.

"Can you release your arm, Ned?"

"I would if I could feel it, lass," he said.

His arm was lying limply on the board. Gently, she pulled on his sleeve as James looked on from the other side of the dam.

"Is he free?"

"Yes," she said.

Ned moved, a grimace shadowing his face. "I'm out of my trap, right enough," he said. "But fool that I am, I've gone and broken my arm."

James scrambled up the bank, coming to the other side of the dam. He knelt, holding out his hand for her.

Riona shook her head. "Help Ned first."

"I'll help Ned after you," he said firmly.

"You're a very stubborn man, James MacRae," she said, frowning at him.

"And you, Miss McKinsey, are my equal in resolve."

She gripped his hand and he pulled her out of the sluice. Her feet began to slip on the muddy incline, but James wrapped one hand around her waist and drew her closer to him.

A slight breeze pressed her sodden skirts against her legs, outlining them. Her bodice clung to her torso, leaving nothing to the imagination.

Riona wished, suddenly, that her stays were made of leather, instead of canvas. They might have been some protection against his quick-shuttered gaze.

James bent and retrieved his coat from where he'd left it on the bank and put it around her shoulders.

"You'll catch cold," he said, not quite looking at her.

She crossed her arms over her chest, grabbing the lapels of his jacket close to her.

"So will you."

He shook his head as if to negate her comments.

James climbed down the bank to help Ned out of the sluice. A cheer arose from the women still watching them. The sound made Riona turn and frown at the assembled throng, wondering if they, too, were fascinated with James MacRae. Or was it simple relief they felt?

Ned's right arm hung from his shoulders, his hand nearly blue.

"I've no time for an injury," he said angrily. "How am I to get everything done that I need to do with a broken arm? You might as well shoot me like you would a horse."

"I'll help," James offered.

"Oh you will, will you? I'm thinking you should get yourself gone from here as fast as you can."

He and James exchanged a look.

"Did you finish your errand at Mr. McDermott's house?" she asked casually as she helped Ned tuck his hand into the placket of his shirt. The arm would hurt less that way, but it still needed to be set quickly before the injury swelled.

"I did."

Nothing more than that. No comment about Rosalie or Caroline, or even McDermott's farm. She glanced at him.

The look on James's face was suddenly indifferent, almost unfriendly, almost as if he were a stranger. Was this the man who'd kissed her so passionately only days before?

Or about whom she'd lusted only minutes earlier?

She was reminded of the day after he'd first arrived at

Tyemorn Manor, when he'd adopted a similar attitude toward her. Was that behavior then and now designed to keep distance between them?

Turning, she led the way back to the manor house, the two men silent behind her. Ned uttered no word of complaint, and from time to time, Riona would turn and look at him. Other than a tight expression around his lips, there was no indication that he was in pain. He was, like the rest of them, soaked and no doubt chilled.

"What on earth happened?" Susanna said, rushing out of the kitchen door. Taking in Ned's disheveled appearance, she clucked her tongue and frowned at him. "What have you gone and done, you foolish man?"

"That's what I need," Ned said, "a lecture. Do you think I broke my arm just to irritate you?"

They exchanged a look, a slight smile finally coming to Susanna's face.

"Whether or not you planned it, you old goat, I have to treat you. As my patient, you'll do as I say."

"I will, will I?" Ned's eyes narrowed as he stared at her.

Riona had the distinct impression that they might have said more to each other if she and James had not been present. She stepped aside as Ned entered the kitchen door.

She glanced at James. "Why do I think he is not nearly as upset with her as he sounds?"

"No man likes to admit his weakness," James said. "Least of all someone like Ned, who hides behind a gruff exterior."

"What about you, James? Do you dislike displaying your weaknesses? Or do you have any?"

Once again his face was shuttered, his glance almost unfriendly. An irritation, that look. No doubt he was far more charming to Mr. McDermott's daughters.

"How are Rosalie and Caroline? Did you find them in good health?"

"Excellent health. They are very charming women."

"Are they?" she said coolly. "Perhaps you'll be seeing more of them in the future."

"Are you jealous?" He looked amazed.

Her laughter sounded brittle even to her own ears. "I have no right to be."

"I am," he said. Words that were perhaps better left unspoken. "I am, Riona. I can't think of another man kissing you or touching you."

"Don't, James. Please." How adroitly he'd turned their conversation.

"You shouldn't stand there in those wet garments, Riona," Susanna said from the open door.

"Or you, James," Riona said, just now realizing that his clothing did little to conceal his physique.

There was something almost delightfully wicked about the male anatomy. Not only was his chest outlined in magnificent detail, but other portions of him as well, protruding and obvious.

She glanced upward to find that James's smile had deepened, but there was a new heat in his gaze.

Her cheeks warmed. She slipped off the jacket and handed it to him, thanking him.

Before he could respond, she'd disappeared into the kitchen and beyond, to her room.

"Well, are you happy now?" Ned asked Susanna as his eyes followed James. The younger man had left the kitchen, no doubt to change his clothes.

He frowned at her, and then down at his useless arm. How was he to do everything he needed to do before harvest? It was all very good for James to offer, but he was thinking that it would be better for all of them if James were gone from here. And soon.

"You have them lusting after each other. Is that what you wanted?"

Susanna looked at him as if she couldn't quite decide whether or not to lie full-faced or to brazen it out.

"I'm sure you're wrong," Susanna said, rolling up his sleeve.

He clamped his lips firmly together, rather than to allow himself a pained gasp as she straightened his arm.

"It's a clean break," he said, staring down at it. "The cold water kept it from swelling too much, and it should be easy enough to set."

"Are you telling me my business in this, too, Ned? I'll have you know I can set a bone well enough."

"You saw the way they look at each other," he said, returning to his original subject.

She stood and left the room, returning with a covered basket. Placing it on the table, she opened it and withdrew a roll of linen and two planed sticks. Susanna McKinsey was prepared for a number of injuries. A good thing, since a farm was often a dangerous place.

"Aye," he said. "If it's lust you want, they feel that well enough."

"Harold McDougal is a toad of a man. Riona deserves better."

"The way I heard it, Riona deserves what she got."

Holding the two sticks on either side of his arm, she bid him hold them in that position as she unrolled the bandages.

"I will grant you that she was foolish," she said, "but a mistake of that caliber does not deserve Harold McDougal for punishment."

She began to wrap the bandage around his arm.

"Then why did you agree to the union to begin with?"

She sighed heavily but answered him nonetheless. "I was balancing one daughter's good against the other's. Maureen is so very much in love with Samuel Hastings. I didn't want any scandal to ruin that for her. But it seems to me that I condemned Riona to a loveless marriage."

"She won't be the first woman to be married for reasons other than love."

"I know that. But on most occasions there is at least respect between the parties. In Riona's case, I do not think that she could love a man who had wheedled his way into matrimony with her."

"What do you want to happen, then?"

"I'm not entirely sure," she said, and he had the feeling it was a grand admission he'd received from her. "When James first came, all I could think about was that he would make a wonderful son-in-law."

"Without thinking how that might come about?"

She nodded reluctantly.

"What do you plan to do about Maureen? It seems to me that you've got the same problem as you did in the beginning."

She shook her head, and he was shocked to see the sheen of tears in her eyes.

"I cannot but hope that somehow everything will work out. Am I foolish for thinking that?"

"I think that you are still believing in something long past the time for it to be abandoned," he said carefully.

"Perhaps you're right," she said.

"I don't have a good feeling about this, Susanna," he said honestly.

She smiled, the effect that of the sun coming out during a brief afternoon storm.

"Ah, Ned, you've always been a dour man. Maybe something good will happen."

While all he could foresee was disaster.

Maureen sat on a bench in front of the manor house, in a secluded place not far from a large oak.

It was a glorious late spring morning, the kind of weather that made her inexpressibly sad. Perhaps because she had no one to share it with, no one to remark upon it at her side. Riona was about the farms, as usual, and her mother busy with chores around the house. Susanna always seemed happiest when she had the most to do.

Maureen had finally finished her wedding gifts to Riona, two nightgowns heavily embroidered with images of the flowers that bloomed around Tyemorn Manor. A small remembrance of things her sister loved.

Once again, Maureen was reminded of their differences. Not just in nature and temperament, but in good fortune.

She stared down at the letter on her lap, smoothing her hands over the black script. She did that to savor the message before she ever opened it.

Samuel's handwriting was so much starker than the rest of him. Samuel, for all that he was a soldier, was of a gentle temperament. He hid his demeanor from most. But with her he'd been honest and open, revealing his love of books and poetry, and other secrets that he'd admitted sharing with no one but her.

What would this letter bring? More details of his post? Of the men with whom he served? She was beginning to know them by their idiosyncrasies and habits. One day soon, she would no doubt make their acquaintance, preparatory to becoming a lady of the regiment.

But Samuel wouldn't always be a soldier. He'd confided that he wanted to go into politics. Perhaps one day he would even run for office. But the future seemed so very distant now.

Finally, she slid her nail into the flap of the letter. He had a great deal of news, it seemed, since he had covered both sides of the paper.

"I'm sorry," a voice said, "I didn't mean to interrupt."

She looked up to see James standing in front of her, a riding crop in his left hand, the reins of his horse in the other.

"I didn't hear you approach," she said, smiling. "Isn't that strange?"

"You looked involved in your letter. Forgive me for disturbing you."

"It's from Samuel," she said in explanation.

"Your intended?"

"No," she said, feeling her cheeks warm. "But I hope that he will be one day."

She glanced down at the letter again. "He has news of his regiment, and I find myself fascinated with the details of soldiering."

"Is he stationed in Edinburgh?"

"He used to be," she said. "But now he is in Inverness. He is part of the Fencible Regiment. Have you heard of them?"

He shook his head.

"Their duty is to patrol the coast of Scotland. Ever since the unpleasantness in the colonies began, the government is afraid the French will try to invade."

She wondered at the nature of his smile, half crooked, as if he were amused at himself.

"My family has built many ships for the French," he said. "I sincerely hope they do not invade, since that will put me in the middle of a quandary. Whom do I champion? Our customers? Or the English?"

She decided that she wouldn't divulge that particular information to Samuel.

"You and Riona would keep old feuds alive, I think. Isn't it time that we simply forgot all that in the past? We are part of England now, you know."

He tied the reins of his horse to a nearby branch. She moved her skirts aside so that he might sit on the bench beside her.

"Injustice is a difficult thing to forget," he said. "But as the years pass, those who were affected personally begin to die off, leaving a younger generation who carry only tales in our hearts. Sooner or later, both adversaries will forget why they ever fought. Unfortunately, that sometimes leads to new battles."

"Do you think that Scotland and England will fight again?"

"Not if the people of Scotland acquiesce to England's rule. My father, however, tells stories of the Highlanders that make me wonder how they can ever forgive the English."

She was not, for all her interest in soldiering, prepared to discuss war. Frankly, she didn't want to think of Samuel being in danger.

"Have you been exploring Tyemorn Manor?" she asked, glancing at his horse.

"I have," he said smiling. "It's a beautiful place."

"I have never learned to ride," she said. "In Cormech we

could not afford a horse, and here they seem to be used mostly for farm work."

They sat in silence for a few moments.

"What do you think of Harold McDougal?" he said finally.

She should have, perhaps, been surprised at the question. But she wasn't. Anyone seeing him with her sister would know why he'd asked. However, she didn't exactly know how to answer.

"Is he a man of honor?"

She didn't think so, but she couldn't say such a thing. After all, he would shortly be her brother by marriage.

"Perhaps that is a question you need to ask Riona," she replied. "She knows him much better than I."

"Would you marry him?"

Now that was a surprising question. She carefully folded her letter, wishing he had left her alone to read it.

"I don't know," she said finally. "I do not think so, no."

"Why not?"

She stood abruptly, aware that she was being rude. But if she stayed, he would force her into admissions that she shouldn't make about a future member of the family.

"I really can't say, James. And now if you'll excuse me, I have things I must do."

She placed Samuel's letter in her pocket and almost fled from him.

Chapter 18

⟨✦⟩

She was standing beside the Witch's Well, attired in a diaphanous white garment. Her hair, for once not unruly, fell straight down her back to end at her waist. Although she could not see her reflection, she felt beautiful, attuned to herself in a way that was oddly strange and yet fitting.

Her skin was ivory, her lips full and red, her eyes sparkling. Her body felt different, aware somehow.

The world around her was hushed and expectant. Suddenly, James was there, striding out of the strange and eerie fog that obscured the ground. He stretched out his arms, and she walked toward him, before realizing that the well separated them. She circled it slowly, one hand trailing on the rough stone ledge, the other at her side.

There were no birds chirping in the silence, no

sound of water dripping from the bucket. No leaves fell, no flowers bloomed. The air was warm, yet chilled at the same time, as if her dreaming mind refused to label a season or mark a time.

James was dressed as a Roman soldier in crimson wool tunic and leather armor. As she watched, he removed his helm, revealing his black hair and perfectly formed face. His pale blue gaze was intent on her as she neared.

Slowly, he reached out and touched her cheek with his fingers. Until that instant she'd no idea how cold she was. She turned her face into his hand, feeling the curve of his palm as he bent to kiss her. Her lips warmed, her breath quickened even as her body readied for him.

She placed her hands flat on his chest, feeling his heart beating strong beneath her palms as if to mock her dreaming state.

His smile warmed her. Softly chiding, it made light of all her worries and all her fears. As she stood there expectant, he lowered his head and kissed her again. She sighed into the embrace, entwining her arms around his neck and holding on as he deepened the kiss.

She tasted tears at the back of her throat. A moment of unexpected grief, as if she'd been afraid this moment would never come and now wept in gratitude. As happened often in dreams, the moment faded too quickly, becoming another scene.

Harold McDougal stood at the entrance to the garden. "Come," he said. "Maureen needs you. She is weeping and I cannot get her to stop." A moment later

*the dream changed again, just as his face altered.
Gone was his surface amiability, and in its place a saturnine mask.*

*Her mind, still in the throes of a dream, summoned
James to her. Like an avenging angel, he appeared between the two of them. With a word, he banished
Harold before turning to her. Suddenly, he was kissing
her again and she was losing herself once more.*

*Then she was in the library, seated on the desk, her
feet placed on the chair. Between them, cradling her
ankles, sat James, his smile wicked as he grinned up
at her.*

*Her nightgown was virginal with rows of buttons
marching from a staid collar down across her breasts
to her waist.*

*His fingers slipped between the buttons of her
nightgown, reaching in as far as the material would allow, stroking the upward slope of one breast. Halfway
to a nipple, and no farther.*

*Her indrawn sigh was nearly a gasp, and he reached
up and silenced it with two fingers against her lips.*

*Gently, he unfastened one button, smoothing his fin-
gers over the base of her neck. But he didn't speak, and
the silence was almost a living thing.*

*Her hand bunched into knuckles and the hard ridge
of them brushed against his shirt. He didn't hurry, however, only smiled at her as if amused at her impatience.*

*Opening the second button, he slipped three fingers
inside, touching the edge of her collarbone, then down
the curve of her breast. Teasingly, he withdrew, smoothing his hand over her nightgown as if to soothe her.*

Her nipples were hard points beneath the material.

In her sleep, Riona moaned.

Another button undone.

She clasped her hands together in the middle of her chest while he stood, bending his head to lay his lips against one nipple and then another.

He speared one hand in her hair, pulled her head up for another kiss. He murmured something, a caution, a warning, an order. She obeyed, quiescent, obedient, trapped by his charm and her need.

That was how she awoke, with the touch of James's lips on hers and his whispers in her ears. For the longest time, Riona lay there clutching her pillow, her eyes clenched shut as if to hold the remnants of the dream tight to her. A drumbeat still echoed in her body, and her breath felt constricted. Finally, she sighed deeply, regretfully, while blinking open her eyes.

Sunlight filtering through the trees outside created lacy patterns on the ceiling.

Sunlight?

One quick look at the window verified it. The golden glow of the sky indicated that dawn had already come and gone.

She scurried out of bed and peeked into the hallway. Maureen was just leaving her room.

"What time is it?" she asked, horrified. Was she too late?

"What's wrong?"

"The Lethson cake," she said, looking back wildly into the room. Where were her clothes? Dear God, the cake. "I have to gather the dew for the elders' cake!"

She slammed the door shut and dressed in a flurry of clothes and mumbling.

* * *

James stood at the window, his attention caught by a movement to his left. Riona was racing to the glen, her skirts above her calves, her hair unbraided and askew. His smile widened as she stopped and, with a large bowl in her hand, twirled in a circle, gathering dew from the top of the grasses.

The elders had given her a bedeviling task.

She selected another spot and did the same dipping and swirling. With any luck, she'd be able to collect some moisture for her cake, but he had his misgivings.

Riona began twirling once more, her skirts billowing around her like a summer flower. On her face was a look of concentration mixed with panic.

Smiling, he went to join her.

"Are you having any success?" James asked, coming up behind her. She whirled, and shaded her eyes with a hand.

Glancing down into the bowl, she ruefully said, "I've only a smattering of droplets. Not nearly enough to add to a batter."

He held up a flask he'd hidden behind his back, poured a few tablespoons into the bowl. The pungent smell of whiskey wafted upward.

"Who's to say what dew tastes like?" he asked with a grin.

"I shall tell the elders that a wicked brownie appeared with a bottle of elixir and forced me to make a cake of it."

"I've no doubt they'll enjoy the taste of it more than simple dew."

She turned and walked with him back to the house, cradling the bowl in her arms.

"What other duties do you have for this day?" he asked.

"We need to set up the tables for the refreshments tomorrow night. And load the peat and wood on the wagons that will come this afternoon." At his quizzical look, she explained. "The lads from the village gather peat from all the farms for a week before Lethson. Tonight is our turn. The biggest Lethson fires will be lit at Tyemorn since we have all the highest hills in the area."

"Why the fires? Signal beacons?"

"No, they're to entice the dragons."

"The dragons?" he asked, holding the door open for her.

"A very long time ago, people believed that dragons lived in the fields and must be convinced to leave in order for there to be a good harvest. At Lethson, each farmer still takes a torch and runs around the perimeter of his land, chasing away any lurking dragons."

"And who will do that for Tyemorn?" he asked.

"You, of course," she said easily. "Since Ned's arm is broken. Do you mind?"

"Not at all," he said. "I'd consider it an honor."

He stood in the doorway and watched her, intent on her chore. Cook was not in attendance, which was strange. Twice Polly entered the room, glancing at them, and twice she'd left, pulling Abigail after her. As if, he thought, the household conspired to keep them together.

"You cannot fail in this task," Riona said, so much consternation in her voice that at first James thought she was admonishing him. Instead, she was giving herself a good scolding. "After all, it is only a cake. Anyone can bake a cake if they set their minds to it."

She peered into the bowl and frowned.

"I can't," he said, smiling at her.

"You haven't been given the duty by the elders, either," she said, transferring her frown to him. She handed him a basket, and pointed to the doorway with her chin.

"I need eggs. At least six of them."

"And I'm to fetch them?"

"If you will." Her smile was dusted by worry, her eyes narrowed by concentration.

"Only if I can claim a payment in turn, Riona," he said easily.

"A payment?" she asked, distracted.

"A kiss."

Her head jerked up. Neither of them said a word.

After the other day, he should have been wiser. But he was surfeited with wisdom, awash in it. He wanted to touch her, kiss her. Love her.

"A kiss," he repeated, leaving the room.

James nodded to a few of the workers as he entered the chicken yard, dipping his head inside the coop to collect a few eggs.

Returning to the kitchen with his bounty, he found Riona mumbling to herself again. "A splash of milk, enough sugar to equal the dew." She looked up at his entrance, put down the flask she'd taken from the tabletop where he left it, smiling unrepentantly at him.

"I didn't think a few more drops would matter," she said, corking the bottle again.

He only grinned at her in response.

After adding the eggs he'd gathered and several other ingredients, she began to stir the mixture with the large wooden spoon, cradling the bowl between elbow and breast. If a creation had ever been commanded to rise or to be sublime in its existence, this cake surely was. She cajoled and convinced and prayed more than once. And all the time, James leaned against the doorframe watching her, amused and fascinated.

He had claimed her from the instant their gazes had locked and their smiles had been exchanged. Riona was his, even if she did not yet know it.

She rounded the table, still beating vigorously, but halted at the sight of him.

"I did tell you what a terrible cook I am, didn't I?"

"You did," he said, smiling and hoping to ease her.

She still looked worried, and the batter was being beaten nearly to death.

"I am better at growing things than I am at cooking them." She halted, finally, pouring the batter into a pan.

"Without one you couldn't have the other. Perhaps growing things is the better talent to have."

"I suppose you're right," she said, as if considering the matter. "It does seem a shame to spend all that time and energy trying to grow something, only to burn it in the end."

His laughter startled him as much as her. But he was, except for a few minor inconveniences, truly happy at this moment.

"It's my impatience. I want everything to be done immediately without having to stand over it. I haven't the time to watch the custard, or endlessly wait for the rolls to bake. I would simply like to place everything in a big pot and come back later when I'm hungry to find it done."

She carried the precious cake to the stove, and carefully opened it. Before inserting the pan, however, she dropped a spoonful of water on the top of the iron surface. The droplets bounced like tiny balls before evaporating; leaving him to guess that by such a gesture the correct heat was gauged.

"I could teach you how to make a fish stew our cook aboard ship concocted. But I believe he used heads and tails, and even seaweed."

She made a face as she closed the stove. The heat had reddened her cheeks, and her hair was a mess, strewn around her shoulders as if he'd threaded his fingers through it. The thought captivated him.

"That doesn't sound appetizing at all." She turned and smiled at him. "I'm quite good at darning socks. And I embroider quite well. Maybe I should be content with those skills."

Cook peered into the kitchen at that moment. "Can I have my kitchen back yet?" she asked. "I've the noon meal to prepare."

Riona nodded. "Thank you for your patience, Cook. And for giving up your kitchen."

The other woman bustled into the room, tying her apron as she surveyed the kitchen, nodding in approval as Riona tidied up. "I was once a young cook myself," she replied. "I know how it feels to have someone looking over your shoulder." She sent a curious glance toward James.

He only smiled and left the kitchen, intent on his investigations and chores.

Thomas's side was throbbing, each spearing ache reminding him of the MacRae. The damnable horse wouldn't move above a trot, and he feared he'd never make it there. Sweat poured from his forehead, stinging his eyes. Occasionally, he was so dizzy that he wanted to stop his mount and rest beneath a tree. Time was running out, but that was one lesson the English had taught him—he could tolerate great pain.

He was going to kill the MacRae. He wouldn't use a musket this time. He'd tried twice with the weapon and missed on both occasions.

The sight of the manor house was a lodestone, taking his

mind from how sick he felt. Death was staring him in the face, but he refused to die until MacRae joined him.

Leaving the horse tied to a tree, Thomas made his way slowly toward the house. He would wait until MacRae emerged from the building and stab him with the last of his strength. He wiped the sweat from his forehead and waited.

Chapter 19

Riona walked toward the barn, intent on her errand. After dinner, Rory had given her a message. James wished to see her.

Why? Especially since they'd said little to each other at dinner. He'd seemed preoccupied, and she had attempted to forget his words of the morning.

A kiss in payment. But he'd forgotten, intent on his day, and she'd been left to sigh in secret disappointment.

Night was draping itself over Tyemorn. The cows were being led from the milking shed, the chickens were settling down. One of the stable boys, lantern in hand, began to close one of the broad barn doors, his actions stayed by a shadowy figure just out of sight.

Suddenly, he moved into the light, the glimpse of him making her heart beat too quickly. James.

The inside of the barn was dimly lit, the smell of thatch as pungent as the scent of the hay piled to one side. Two pens had been erected in the main area of the barn, each containing young or sickly animals. Along the left side of the structure were five bays for the horses, mostly work animals used for plowing or pulling the heavy market wagons.

Riona walked to where James was working, standing outside the stall. He cared for his own mount rather than foist the chore on someone else.

"You wished to see me?" she said softly.

"I did," he answered.

After a few moments, James finished his task, moving past her to place the curry brush on a shelf. As he did so, she reached out her hand, almost touching him, wanting to smooth her fingers over his shirt, not to feel the texture or the fine weave of the material as much as to measure the rise and fall of his chest. She wanted to stroke the edge of his jaw, the curve of his lips. Perhaps even pretend that he was hers and no one else's.

Dearest James.

A friend. Certainly that. A companion. Yes, that, too. A lover? Never. But she could wish it, could she not? Mrs. Parker had thought her behavior shocking in Edinburgh. What would the woman think if she heard that confession?

How strange that Riona didn't care.

What was in her mind before he came? What had she wished for before he arrived at Tyemorn Manor? Now she couldn't imagine a day without talking to him. Who would answer her questions, or listen to her thoughts with such acceptance? Or understand how she felt about Tyemorn? Who would smile at her in such a way that her heartbeat escalated and her palms became damp?

No one.

They would, no doubt, meet each other in the future, and talk like friends, constrained, however, by her bonds of marriage. There would never again be the freedom she had felt to say anything she thought.

He glanced at her. He should not have such lovely eyes, she thought.

How odd that he seemed so much more imposing to her now. Taller, stronger. Even his voice had altered, so that a mere whisper of it sounded resonant and deep. His accent had grown familiar to her ears, but now she noticed it. Perhaps nature or God was demonstrating their differences in a futile attempt to winnow him from her.

Abruptly, James reached out and placed one fingertip on her cheek, a subtle connection, a disconcerting touch. She held herself still, kept by dint of will alone from placing her hand on his.

"I want my payment."

"Payment?" she asked faintly. So he had not forgotten.

"For fetching the eggs. We were interrupted by Cook this morning."

She licked her lips, then lowered her head, studying the floor with great intensity. "You really shouldn't say things like that, James."

He bent until he could meet her gaze, smiling into her face. "I want my kiss, Riona."

She shook her head.

"You are determined to make me a conquest, aren't you?"

"Perhaps I'm the one who's already been conquered," he answered, "and a kiss is my forfeit."

She smiled at that thought, doubting it.

"It's vastly improper."

He remained silent.

"My mind wanders when you kiss me. I can't keep a thought in my head. It's as if I'm getting dizzy."

"That's the way it's supposed to feel."

"Is it?" She doubted that. "I've never heard anyone say so. Not even in Edinburgh."

"Perhaps they don't know how to kiss in Edinburgh," he teased.

She began to smile. "Oh, it's a skill only the MacRaes of Gilmuir have, is it?"

"It might be, if I ever have the opportunity to test it," he teased.

She took one step closer to him, tilted her head back, and closed her eyes. Slowly, she pursed her lips and waited.

Rory grinned to himself. He wasn't the only one being made daft by a woman. James was evidently having some problems of his own. He'd delivered the message to Riona and watched as she entered the barn.

He couldn't help but wonder if the others knew what was going on between those two. It was as clear as the freckles on his nose, but then he'd been around the MacRae men, or at least Alisdair, when he had fallen in love. The emotion had rendered the man decidedly odd.

He was halfway to the cheese house on an errand for Susanna when he happened to glance to his right. Rory halted and frowned.

Although he knew most of the men at Tyemorn, he didn't recall this one, not stooped over as he was and walking unsteadily. As he watched, the man gripped the long wooden bar in front of the barn doors and lowered it, locking James and Riona inside.

He shouted to get the man's attention, but the stranger took the lantern from the hook in front of the structure and disappeared around the corner.

Easing around the edge of the building, Rory was shocked to see the other man extending the lantern upward in several places, catching the thatch on fire.

"Are you daft, man?" he yelled.

The stranger turned, a look of hatred contorting his pale face. "Another MacRae," he said.

Advancing on Rory, he began to smile, the expression malevolent in the glare of the spreading flames.

Rory watched as the man rushed him, the motion slowed by his own shock. He saw the lantern come toward him, then felt the flaming oil. The blow on the side of his head was unexpected. An instant later Rory realized that he'd fulfilled Daniel's superstition after all.

Perhaps he should have been prepared, what with all the warnings he'd taken to Gilmuir about Drummond. But it hadn't occurred to him that he might be in danger. Nor had he thought, on this warm and fragrant summer evening, that death might be lying in wait for him.

The other man leaned into him as his knees buckled.

"Die, MacRae," he rasped, his breath heated on Rory's cheek.

The last words he was to hear. Not Abigail's teasing or James's praise, but Drummond's curse.

His final thought, in the moment before the world went gray, was that he hoped the MacRaes did not think his death a minor sorrow after all.

* * *

Instead of taking advantage of the invitation, James abruptly lifted Riona up, sitting her on the edge of a nearby table. Her eyes flew open and she stared at him.

"Not that way," he said, taking her hands and putting them on his shoulders. "You must kiss me as if you mean it. As if there's nothing else in the world you'd rather do. As if someone might be calling your name and you can't go to him, or a flood is threatening but you can't leave." He placed his finger in the center of her bottom lip. "Until you have that kiss."

He bent, but an inch from her mouth he hesitated. "Relax your mouth, Riona. Just enough for your lips to part."

Her lips fell open, and he brushed his tongue against them, first the top, then the bottom. Slowly, so that she could experience the sensation. Her hands tightened on his shoulders, and he moved closer, standing to the side of her and placing his hands beneath her arms and behind her back.

Her breath was faster than before, her eyes still closed, and there was a look of such rapt concentration on her face that he almost smiled.

His lips touched hers, softly at first, then with more firmness. Her hand wound around his neck as he pulled her even closer. He wanted her breath, her soft gasps. What he received was an interlude of magic. Deep in her throat she moaned, and he felt himself harden at the sound. His hands moved from her back to frame her face, fingers thrusting into her hair as he'd imagined only hours earlier.

Dear God, he wanted her.

Finally, he pulled back, his heart beating rapidly, his erection almost painful. He lay his forehead against hers, heard her breathing, and thought that she was as affected as he was by their kiss.

He should have left upon first meeting her, before she imprinted herself on his mind and his heart. But she would remain there now, a woman with cool gray eyes and a smile that forever hovered over full lips. A woman who yanked at her hair and muttered imprecations when a braid came loose. One who smelled delightfully of cheese and warm milk.

Prudently, he stepped away. She reached out for him, then let her hands drop to her sides. What a sight to see, Riona well kissed, her blush intensifying with his scrutiny. But he couldn't look away. If he did, he might miss a second of her. Gray eyes sparkling and lips curving in a winsome smile.

An expression of horror suddenly transformed her face. "James, look!" she said, raising her arm and pointing. He spun on his heel.

There, in the corner, was a tendril of smoke. Horses whinnied in alarm as James instantly recognized the danger. Fire was a constant threat in thatched buildings, and the barn was no exception.

He went to the closed door and pushed on it. But instead of it opening, he felt resistance.

"It's been barred from the outside," he said as Riona joined him.

The blaze that had begun in the corner was spreading rapidly up the wall. Although the stones didn't burn, the vegetation between them did, resulting in smoke that permeated the interior of the barn. Even worse, he caught a glimpse of a flame closer to the ceiling.

Riona had seen it as well. "James, the roof's on fire!"

The horses were nearly screaming now, and the other animals were desperately kicking or butting at the stalls in an effort to escape. Riona began to pound on the doors with her fists, shouting over the din.

The barn wasn't that far away from the house. Even if no one heard anything, the fire would be seen. But they might not have that much time.

"The only way to save the animals is to get out of here, Riona," James said.

He pulled her away from the door, helping her to the ladder to the loft. She climbed up hurriedly, then stood beside him at the open window. Squares of thatch were beginning to fall to the ground in a rain of fire. The roof was now fully ablaze.

Darkness obscured the distance, but he knew the drop was at least a dozen feet and there was nothing to break the fall, no piles of hay, no mound of earth.

James knelt and motioned for her to do the same. "You have to make it to the door, Riona," he said, getting to his stomach. "I'll get the horses and meet you there."

When she didn't move, he turned and looked up at her.

"You must promise me," she said, her voice sounding desperate, "if I'm not fast enough, you will jump for safety."

"An easy promise to give," he said, smiling.

Gripping her wrists, he held her as she dangled her legs out the window. He lowered her down as far as he could and only then released her, watching as she fell to the ground. For a horrified instant, he thought she'd been injured, but she scrambled to her feet and raced around to the front of the barn.

James descended the ladder. There was no way to save all the animals, so he made his way to the horses first. Each of them was panicking in its stall, hoofs flailing as they reared and screamed. He managed to grab the reins of his own mount. As one of the double doors opened, he half pulled the horse to the door, surrendering the reins to Riona with a shouted caution before going back for the others.

The second horse had managed to knock some of the boards of his stall loose. James opened the gate and set the animal free, replicating the gesture twice more with the other horses. They shot through the door, escaping to freedom through the choking smoke.

Finally, the horses rescued, he went back for one of the newly born calves just as Riona raced to the other pen. Scooping a sickly lamb into her arms, she made her way back to the door, its mother trailing fretfully behind her.

Everything was oddly muted beneath the fire's growing voice, a low grumbling roar as the inferno consumed everything in its path. If the animals screamed, he could no longer hear; if Riona called to him, the sound was lost.

A movement high above them, a shadow limned by flames, was the only warning they had before a timber fell. The roof beam crashed to the hay-strewn floor with such an impact that the earth vibrated beneath his boots.

He turned, seeing Riona out of the corner of his eye. Lunging for her, he pinned her against the east wall as another part of the roof caved in, falling heavily and blocking the doors.

His eyes were watering so fiercely that he could barely see. His chest felt on fire, each laboring breath more difficult than the last. If they didn't escape soon, they would die here.

The barn was an earthly hell filled with unimaginable heat. The clouds of thick, black smoke were so dense that he could no longer see the doorway. He'd been aboard ship once when a galley fire had spread. The terror of the sailors had been nothing in comparison to what he felt at this moment.

He had no intention of dying, however, or of allowing Riona to perish.

She'd dressed for dinner in a more formal garment than she wore during the day. This gown had an underskirt of quilted fabric. Without explanation, he began to pull on the fabric, cutting it away from her waist with his knife when it refused to rip.

"What are you doing?" she asked, batting his hands away.

"If we're going to survive, we're going to need a way to get through the fire," he shouted.

"My dress?"

He nodded, slicing her underskirt free, leaving her attired in nothing more than her shift and stockings below the waist. After ripping the skirt down the back seam until it was a large semicircle of material, he dipped it into the water trough. When it was soaked, he returned to her side, draping it over her head. Wrapping his arm around her waist, he joined her beneath the dripping cloth. Not an appreciable protection against the fire, but better than nothing.

"Are you ready?" he asked, bending his head so that his lips rested next to her ear. A strange time to feel so exultant. This might well be the last moment of his life.

"I'm ready," she said, her arm reaching around his back.

Together, they raced for the flames.

With God's good grace, they were heading for the back door, but there was no way to tell since the acrid smoke made the disorientation complete. Holding Riona's waist even tighter, James began to pray as they ran. An invocation to God to show pity to those who sailed. The words were wrong, but the sentiment was the same.

Save us.

Suddenly they could breathe again, the smoldering clouds

blown away by a brisk evening breeze. But that same wind fanned the flames atop the barn. The rest of the roof abruptly collapsed, falling within the four walls, immediately killing those animals they hadn't been able to save. Sparks and flames surged skyward like the devil's talons. The west wall abruptly sagged and fell, sending stones tumbling to the ground in a low-throated roar that sounded too much like laughter.

Half naked and trembling, Riona stared wide-eyed at the scene of destruction. "You saved us."

"A narrow escape," he said, turning and looking back at the burning building. "Too narrow."

There was only one way the door could have been locked, and that was deliberately. Only one person wanted him dead: Drummond. They'd both nearly died because of his hatred.

Slowly, he removed the scorched material from his shoulders, did the same for her. Her hair should have been sodden, but the heat had been so intense that both of them were nearly dry.

"You saved my life," she said solemnly, the light from the fire casting an orange glow over her face, rendering her hair red and her eyes dark and mysterious.

"But I probably endangered you in the first place," he told her, wishing that she wouldn't look at him in such a fashion. There was no fear in her gaze, only amazement, and another look that James told himself he didn't see. "An ignoble end to die in a barn. I'd much rather perish aboard ship."

"You've given up the sea."

"That I have," he said, grateful that she was smiling now. But her regard of him hadn't changed. She was still watching him the way Iseabal sometimes studied Alisdair.

Wishes, James. You're only wishing for something that can never happen.

She moved before he could divine her intent. Or perhaps, he told himself later, he knew it well enough but didn't want to halt her. Reaching up with both hands, she pulled his head down and kissed him.

"I owe you a kiss," she said against his lips.

"I thought the debt paid," he said, pulling back and smiling into her face. "But I'm not a fool to question my good fortune."

Hardly a place to lose his senses, scorched, and singed, and smelling of fire. This brief, incandescent second would vanish only too soon. He pulled her closer, and lost himself in a heated, openmouthed, passionate kiss.

Chapter 20

"**A**re you all right?" Susanna asked, rushing up and surveying both of them with concern. She nodded. "And you, James?"

He smiled his response. "But perhaps we should begin to gather up the animals," he said. "And see that the fire is put out."

"Is there any chance of it spreading?" Susanna asked. "The house is far enough away, but what about the other buildings?"

"I doubt it. Most of the structures are far enough away from each other. But there are several precautions we can take to ensure that the fire's contained."

"I would think you'd be more concerned about scandal spreading, Mrs. McKinsey." Mrs. Parker said, her voice escalating in the sudden silence. "After all, it will destroy you as effectively as any fire."

Susanna stared, dismayed, at her daughter and James. It was true that Riona was half-dressed and the kiss they'd shared was not one of friendship.

She was not the only person to have witnessed the kiss, either.

Mrs. Parker stood beside her, dressed in a florid crimson wrapper that trailed on the ground like a queen's robes while Susanna was still attired in her dinner clothes, an apron tied neatly around her waist. Behind her was Maureen, slack jawed and hurriedly dressed, if the askew collar was any indication. Old Ned stood beside them, calmly holding a goat's tether and making no attempt to stay the animal when it looked longingly toward Mrs. Parker's slippers.

Susanna raised an eyebrow at him when the animal moved toward the footwear, then turned her attention back to Riona and James.

"Well? Are you going to allow such behavior? Do something!" Mrs. Parker said.

"What do you suggest I do?"

Riona was looking dazed. She staggered back, blinking, then reached out and grabbed James's arm before evidently realizing that it would be better if there were no contact at all between them. As for James, he simply looked furious.

Frowning, the older woman extended an imperious finger at Riona.

"If you think that I shall allow Captain Hastings to be aligned with such a family, you're mistaken," Mrs. Parker was saying. "One incident might be overlooked, but this behavior is beyond tolerance. Not only is she nearly naked, but she's behaving like a doxy!"

"Perhaps you should return to the house, dear," Susanna said calmly to Riona. "Put some clothes on and we'll talk." She glanced meaningfully at James. "All of us."

"There is no need for that," James said, his voice sounding raspy from the smoke. He turned to Mrs. Parker. "I take full responsibility for what you saw. Riona is blameless in this matter."

"If she were blameless, she would have fought off your advances, sir." Mrs. Parker drew herself up, attempting to frown down her nose at James, but failing miserably since he towered over her.

James looked as if he'd like to say something not entirely pleasant. Quickly, Susanna stepped in front of him, holding up both hands as if to ward off a confrontation.

"Come, Mrs. Parker," she said, leading the woman away. Neither James nor Riona was aiding the situation. She glanced over her shoulder. James was leading Riona away, back to the house. Where she fervently hoped her daughter would dress, and quickly.

"Are you saying, madam," Susanna asked frostily when she and Mrs. Parker were alone, "that you will do everything in your power to dissuade Captain Hastings from aligning himself with our family? I would think on your answer if I were you. I doubt that your reputation will be much enhanced if your part in all of this is learned."

"My reputation?" Mrs. Parker said, pulling herself up. She appeared to Susanna like a banty rooster at that moment, all puffed chest and braggadocio.

"Indeed," Susanna said. "Were you not accompanying Riona on the night she was ruined? Was she not under your tutelage? If the fault for her poor reputation be anyone's, madam, it should be yours. And I will make it known to all and sundry that such is the case. So, before you go bandying your tale about, I would think twice. Otherwise, your own livelihood is bound to suffer. What mother would entrust her daughter to someone with such dubious character?"

"You would not."

"I would. Having been a widow without means, I know only too well how valued a reputation should be."

Mrs. Parker sputtered, but she didn't say a word. Not one word of protest passed her lips, but from the flashing of her eyes, Susanna didn't doubt that she was thinking her to perdition. Everything that she told the woman was true, including her willingness to spread the tale far and wide to even the scales.

"I think perhaps your time at Tyemorn Manor is over," Susanna said. "I will pay you what we agreed to, the remainder of your fee due at Maureen's wedding. On one condition."

"And that is?" Mrs. Parker asked. The words were so brittle that Susanna thought they might break in midair.

"That you give me your promise that not one word of what you've seen at Tyemorn Manor will ever be divulged to another human being."

"You would trust my word?"

"I have it within my power to ruin you. Do you trust me not to use it?"

It was a stalemate, one of equally matched opponents.

"Men are not the only creatures with honor, Mrs. Parker. For all our differences, I think we can agree on that point."

The older woman nodded once to signify her agreement.

"You have my promise," she said a moment later. "And I have yours?"

"You do."

"The inn is no doubt full with visitors for the horse fair," Susanna said as they walked back to the house. "I would not want you on the roads at night. Will you agree to stay until morning?"

"That would be better, I suppose," Mrs. Parker said grudgingly.

"A wise choice," Susanna said.

She saw her guest to her room and then turned and walked to the family quarters, wondering what she might say to her daughter.

Ned's words came back to her. What had she wanted to happen? For James to magically solve her dilemma? In all honesty, yes.

She had hoped that Harold McDougal might give up his suit, but the lure of Riona's fortune was too great. Was there any way out of this conundrum? If there was, she couldn't imagine what it might be.

She knocked on Riona's door, and when her daughter answered, entered.

Riona turned at Susanna's entrance and sighed inwardly. It would do no good to ask for a reprieve. Her mother had a look on her face that brooked no opposition. If she had inherited her stubbornness, it came from the maternal side of the family. She couldn't remember if her father had an obstinate character. All her memories of him were of an easygoing sailor, filled with tales of his travels and gusty laughter. But then, she supposed, he must've been stubborn, to continue following his dream to the detriment of those he loved.

"Would it help if I told you I know what you're about to say?" Riona asked.

"What am I about to say?"

"That my behavior is deplorable, that I have shamed the family, and that I have forgotten I am to be married shortly."

"You have, indeed, saved me a lecture," Susanna responded, smiling.

"Then that is one thing I have done tonight that is to my credit," Riona said softly.

She stood, pushing back the bench in front of her vanity and walking to one of the two windows in the chamber. She pushed aside the curtains and stared out at the view.

"There isn't any hope for it, Riona. Harold McDougal is going to be your husband, and wishes and wants will not change it."

"Do you think I don't know that, Mother?" Riona asked softly. "I have become resigned to it."

"Was the kiss I witnessed a form of your acceptance?"

"I could tell you, Mother, that it was an act of gratitude. After all, James saved my life. Or perhaps I simply forgot myself."

"Is that the truth?"

No, she'd kissed him deliberately and would again, but there were some thoughts that were not meant to be shared.

"Should I be satisfied with your explanation, Riona?"

"You might pretend to be," Riona said, smiling wryly. "Just as I am engaging in pretense about my wedding."

For a long moment, Susanna looked at her. Did her mother see all the reluctance in her mind? She didn't want to try to explain what she felt for James. In the end, it didn't matter. However much she might be fascinated with him, might crave his touch or think forbidden thoughts, he was not for her. Not permanently.

"I have never wanted anything but your happiness, Riona."

"I know that, Mother."

"But I do not see how anyone can conjure up happiness out of this situation. Whatever you do, it can only end in heartache."

If she were a woman given to tears, Riona thought she might cry at this moment. But her tears were better saved for another time.

On the day she married Harold.

"Shall I ask him to leave?"

Whether James was here or gone, the result was the same. She would long for him regardless of where he was.

"No," Riona said. "Nothing will come of this, Mother. I am going to marry Harold. Nothing must disturb Maureen's happiness, after all." There, a little bitterness showing.

"Do you hold your sister responsible?" Susanna asked, frowning.

"No, I don't," she said, her sense of fairness coming to the surface. But it seemed that the past several months had been given up to everyone else's wishes. Mrs. Parker's dictates must always be obeyed, Maureen's happiness must be preserved, even Harold's needs must be considered.

She wanted a few days of hedonism, of sheer enjoyment for the sake of it, with no recriminations. An escape from the reality of her future. A release from being responsible for everyone's happiness.

"No," she repeated. "Do not ask him to leave. My behavior will be above reproach."

How strange to make a promise at the same time she ached to break it.

He was standing in the shadows when Susanna left the room. Moving cautiously so as not to startle her, James came forward.

"The fault is mine," he said.

She turned and looked at him. "Is it?"

"Only mine. Riona is not to blame for what happened."

"Is it honor that makes you say that, James, or guilt?"

"Perhaps a measure of both," he said honestly.

"I know my daughter, James MacRae. No one could have coerced her to such affection. What she did was willingly done."

"I still hold myself responsible."

She regarded him levelly. "This is an untenable situation, James. I am sorry for it. I was wrong to ask you to stay. Forgive me."

"The fault is not yours."

She stared at the far wall and sighed deeply. "At least we've rid ourselves of Mrs. Parker." She studied him once more, smiling this time. "It's already been pointed out to me that I'm lacking wisdom where you're concerned." A surprising comment, but she didn't elaborate.

"I wish Riona had never seen Edinburgh," she said fiercely, and left him, leaving him staring after her.

At first Rory thought he'd died, but the pain was so great that he was certain he hadn't. There was something on his chest, and something else was pressing against his ear and his neck. He brushed at it or tried to. His arm wouldn't work, and a streak of pain traveled from his wrist to his shoulder, answering that question for once and all.

He wouldn't be hurting so badly if he were dead.

He moved his other hand from half beneath him. He was buried alive. A surge of panic made him want to scream, but there was dirt in his mouth. He tried to call out, the sound emerging as a garbled cry. One by one, he picked the bricks off his chest, until he could breathe easier. His arms were next. When he felt upward he finally encountered no obstruction.

It took him nearly an hour, or what he thought was an hour, to emerge from beneath the bricks and crawl a short distance away. He began to shout then, as loud as he was able.

"James!"

He half turned, holding up his hand so that the other men would halt for a moment. The sound of the saws and axes nearly drowned out her voice.

Abigail was running toward him, her skirts held at one side, her hair askew and her cap missing.

"It's Rory!" she shouted. "He's been hurt."

"Where?"

"The barn."

He'd thought Rory was working with one of the teams of men throughout Tyemorn last night. They'd first set up a brigade to extinguish the fire, and then to surround the farm with lookouts. Twice he'd asked about Rory, and twice someone had said that he'd been spotted patrolling one of the pastures.

James should have sought the boy out himself.

He began to run, reaching the site of the burned-out building. He hadn't missed Rory, but he should have. He and the other men had worked through the night, ensuring that the fire was out.

At dawn, he and Ned had set up gangs of men to begin the work necessary to rebuild the structure. The barn was too valuable to do without for more than a few days.

The sagging west wall had collapsed, now nothing more

than a pile of rubble. Rory lay atop it, his young body looking broken and burned. Abigail stood near him, crying softly into the hem of her apron.

James felt a surge of guilt as he knelt at his side. He should have noticed Rory's absence.

Rory turned his head weakly. "Drummond's still out there, sir."

"Did he do this to you?"

Rory nodded. "The lantern exploded. I didn't expect that. Am I burned all over?"

James did a quick appraisal. "One leg, Rory, but it doesn't look that bad."

The young man sighed in relief, looking beyond to where Abigail now stood. "I hurt all over, James." He looked scared and too young. James hastened to reassure him.

"You were buried by the wall," James said, "you're full of bruises. But the bricks probably kept you safe from the rest of the fire."

Susanna moved into James's sight. "We'll take care of him," she said, Riona at her side. Behind her stood Maureen. All three women wore looks of worry overlaid with calm resolve. James realized how much they had come to care for Rory, just as he cared for all of them.

A landlocked home was a strange place for a former cabin boy.

They devised a litter for Rory, carrying him back to the house. Several times during the journey he lost consciousness. Yet every time he opened his eyes, Abigail was at his side, brushing her fingers over his hand.

Without knowing it, the young maid had made a friend. James smiled at her as she hesitated at the door.

"I think he'd like you with him," he said when she

glanced back at him. Abigail nodded and followed the stretcher inside.

"I'll go in search of Drummond, then," he said.

Riona remained between her sister and mother, but the look of concern on her face was reserved for him.

"I'll be careful," he said, in response to her unspoken words.

Ned and a few other men accompanied him on his search for Drummond, a task that James expected to take all day. This time, he vowed to go from door to door in Ayleshire to find the man, if need be. But they discovered him before an hour had passed.

Drummond lay on the path near a copse of trees, not far from where a pack horse stood, its reins tied to a sapling. He was beyond any mortal justice.

James knelt at his side, turning the body over slowly. The dead man's face was long and thin, his ears too large for his head. His mouth hung open, revealing sharpened brown teeth.

"Do you recognize him?" Ned asked.

"Yes," he said finally. "Thomas Drummond." He told Ned the story of the last battle fought between the two clans at Gilmuir. "We turned the prisoners over to the captain of an English merchant ship. He was one of them."

"Reason enough to hate you," Ned said, flinging back the man's leather jerkin. "Pity he didn't care for that cut of his."

A large yellowish stain marred the front of Drummond's shirt, and the stench of a suppurating wound tinged the air.

"A terrible way to die," Ned said. "And a foolish one."

"Hatred killed him as much as his wound," James said. Ned only nodded.

Chapter 21

She dawn breeze fluttered her skirt around Riona's ankles, brushed against her calves as if demanding attention. She wrapped her arms around her waist, tilted her head
up to see the branches of the pine tree towering above her.
The day was perfect, with not a hint of clouds in the sky.

Closing her eyes, she tried to identify each separate scent.
Earth, still damp from the spring rains. Mushrooms, plentiful
now that the ground was wet again. Flowers, the wins and
harebells and heather that marked the season so well.

Life was precious at this moment, special and unique. Especially after they'd nearly been killed in the fire. The calls of
the birds were so much more vocal on this morning, as if they
had something of import to share with one another. Or did
they tally up their numbers to ensure that all of them were
present?

She smiled at her own whimsy, closed her eyes, and

stretched out her arms. In this bright moment she felt a penitent before an all-imposing God, a worshipper at His altar of nature.

Holding her arms out, she began to twirl, a silly movement for a woman of propriety. Her skirts belled up, and she grinned, feeling foolish and too young to be herself. Dizziness prompted her return to decorum, but she was not yet done with dancing.

Here there was no measure to count, no movements to memorize, no constant stream of conversation half understood. No one saw or discussed or judged her as she gripped her skirts with her hands and curtsied to a pine tree.

A most proper companion, Mr. Pine.

Riona grabbed the tip of a low, supple branch, and followed a movement, silent and happy. Not once did Mr. Pine inquire as to how she was enjoying Edinburgh, or if she was discommoded by all the construction in the city. No, the tree was content simply to be itself.

As was she.

She wanted to appreciate each separate moment. To take an hour and savor it. To prize an afternoon or feel joy in a dawn. She experienced every second of her freedom and cherished it, tucking it, used and spent, into a place in her heart.

One day, far into the future, she would pull these hours from her memory and view them again, remembering these days as halcyon and rare, beautiful and splendid.

She attempted to allow nothing into her mind that might tarnish the silver of these days. No thoughts of Harold.

Thoughts of James, however, were harder to expunge.

At times, she'd turn and he would be staring at her, his eyes hooded, as if to hold back any emotion that might have been revealed in them. Occasionally, he'd make a remark and she'd realize it was a goad, a temptation to speech, a comment deliberately made to incite her interest or her answer. But she'd keep silent, concentrating on her plate. Attempting to be decorous. Praying to the dishes.

She turned toward the manor house, wondering what plans he had for today. As she did often, she thought of that moment outside the barn when she'd kissed him. And earlier, when he'd shown her how it was done.

Had he known that she wanted more? Or that her ruin was halted not by temperance or conscience, but by discovery?

She pressed her fingers against her lips. How often in the past year had she attempted to please others by being someone she was not, by holding her own true nature so tightly compressed that not even a shadow of the real Riona was visible? Yet that effort had not proven good enough, had it?

She'd seeped out around the edges, her true nature made visible by comments she couldn't restrain, exuberance she couldn't quite conceal, laughter that sounded too loud, and now wishes that were so far from being proper that they almost shocked her.

Did James know that whenever she was around him she felt more herself than at any time in her life? Or that she was carried away by feelings too strong to be labeled by simple speech?

Even now her cheeks warmed at the memory of those moments in the barn. Turning away, she tried to banish him from her thoughts, but the deed was not so easily accomplished.

Gripping the end of a branch, she pulled it sideways, let it spring back into place with a faint whipping sound. Then, holding it once more, she smiled at herself as she again curtsied to her companion.

Mr. Pine became James MacRae in her mind, and her cheeks warmed even further. When she danced with him, her feet suddenly knew their place, her heart heard the beat of the music clearly and without distortion, and she became witty and charming and urbane.

If she were to engage in foolishness, then she would have all her dreams come true. Not simply a country dance executed in perfect decorum.

She would be beloved and cherished, a woman desired. Her life would be ordained not by rules and regulations, but by the seasons and a celestial clock pushing day into night.

Closing her eyes, she tilted her head back and let the wind kiss her cheeks, pretending that it was James.

James scaled the ladder to the roof of the new barn, intent upon finishing the structure in the next two days. He glanced to his left, then came to a halt, his arms crossed over his chest in a position he often adopted at sea. Those who knew him well said that it was his thinking pose. At the moment he was not conscious of having any thought at all, however, being entranced by the sight of Riona, dancing.

The dawn light captured her hair as it fell from its careful coronet of braids to the middle of her back. With two fingers she held on to the end of a branch, and from time to time addressed it as if it were a partner.

There was something youthful and innocent in her delight. He was content to be an observer for the moment, captivated by the sight of Riona as he knew her to be and not as society and Mrs. Parker would have her appear.

He wanted to seduce her with his mouth, taking his time about it until she directed him with her moans and soft, helpless gasps.

Becoming besotted with a woman soon to marry was foolishness and he'd never been considered lacking in wits.

Turning away, he set about his duties.

"Be careful where you walk," he cautioned Ned as he topped the ladder.

"Do I look the fool, then?" Ned squinted at him. A frown, James thought, or maybe not. With Ned, it was difficult to discern his exact expression through that full beard.

"Are you sure you're up to this?" he asked, glancing at the other man's arm.

"I am," Ned said, his look daring James to argue.

He stifled his smile, and walked to the outermost part of the frame.

The barn was the single most important building at Tyemorn Manor and any number of people could, and had, been recruited to rebuild the structure. Not only were the more valuable animals, such as the horses, sheltered here, but those too young or too old to survive out of doors.

Rolling up the sleeves of his shirt, James knelt and began hammering in the trusses. The framework wasn't much different from that of a ship's hull, only inverted.

There were a great many similarities between his shipboard life and farming, he'd discovered since arriving at Tyemorn Manor. Both occupations required attention to the implements of the trade. Aboard ship, sails had to be mended, decks kept free of salt spray. Here, harnesses had to be repaired, plows sharpened.

A day at sea was regulated by bells; Tyemorn's routine was dictated by the passing of the sun across the sky. The fields must be tended, the animals fed, the cows milked, the slaughtering done. Each day brought its own schedule, as fixed and marked as life aboard ship. But then, life itself was like his grandmother's rosary, each event a tiny gleaming jewel. Spring came and lambs were born. Summer arrived and the crops matured. Autumn brought the harvest, and the winter a dormancy to rest the earth.

Yet there was a curious contrast between the two ways of life. The farms of Tyemorn rewarded hard work with flourishing fields and thriving animals, whereas the sea grudgingly repaid a sailor's efforts by allowing him to survive from voyage to voyage.

He had become, James discovered, a farmer. Yet that was the only revelation he'd made in the past few days. He'd been unable to discover the identity of the thief or even details of the losses themselves.

Susanna, however, seemed to think nothing of his lack of progress. In fact, each time he broached the subject, she waved it away, changing the topic quickly.

"I'm surprised Susanna let you up on the roof. She's so particular about your comfort."

James smiled. He'd heard that tone before.

"She feels the same about you," he said, in an attempt to ease the other man's jealousy. "She's lucky to have you," he added.

He'd studied the ledgers with great care, attempting to discover if the thefts were as a result of simple mathematical errors. Ned's entries had been flawless.

Ned sent him a narrow-eyed look, as if to say that he didn't give a whit what James thought of him. But James had crewed with older sailors before, those who claimed not to want or need praise. A man should know when the job he did was good regardless of his age, so James repeated his statement, adding, "I doubt that Susanna could have settled in here as easily as she has without your help."

"The old barn needed repairing," Ned conceded. "But I never had the time or the manpower. The rain this year only made the damage worse. Not that I'm complaining. A fool would complain about rain. You take what you get and con- sider it a blessing."

"The farmland is rich here."

"Aye, there's more rock than soil away from Ayleshire," Ned agreed. He knelt at James's side, began to hammer. A curious moment of agreement.

"Have you always lived here, Ned?" Today was one of the few times he and the older man shared a conversation that didn't involve the manor or farming.

"Aye," the older man said. "I never went away to war all those many years ago. There were some who call us Ayleshire men traitors because of it, but we didn't side with the prince for all that Scotland seemed to love him. He wa- tered his horse at our well, did you know that?"

"No," James said, sitting back on his heels.

"I guess he thought drinking the waters and making a dis- play of himself would change the villagers' minds. But not one person came to greet him on the day he and his army came here. We all busied ourselves doing what we could to keep our homes and hearth around us. It didn't make it easier that we were right when it all ended."

James nodded, thinking of stories his father had told of the deprivations in Scotland following Culloden.

"Even with help we'll not finish the barn for a good week," Ned said, looking around him.

"A better occupation than looking for a thief who doesn't exist," James said, eyeing the older man.

For nearly two weeks, he'd begun to suspect that there weren't any thefts occurring at Tyemorn Manor. People were too casual about guarding the cattle and sheep. There was no suspicion in their eyes or worried looks. If livestock was missing, he doubted that those who cared for the animals knew it.

Ned didn't even blink an eye. "I told her it wouldn't work."

James straightened. The other man didn't even make an effort to continue the pretense. Nor did it appear, from his wide grin, that he felt any guilt over his part in the ruse.

"If there are no thefts taking place, then what am I doing here?"

"You'll have to ask Susanna that," Ned said.

"Was there ever any missing livestock?"

"To be sure," Ned replied easily. "I sent them to a man on the other side of the village. It cost a pretty penny to keep that creature's lips from flapping."

James couldn't decide exactly what he felt at this particular moment. For some reason, Susanna had decided to lie to him. Yet he couldn't deny that he'd enjoyed the time here. In fact, working at Tyemorn had helped him crystallize his own future.

"Don't tell her that I know just yet," he said.

Ned looked at him.

"If it's an excuse you need for staying, James, there's Rory's healing to do." Ned glanced down at his arm. "And I guess I could use some help."

"Am I that transparent?" James asked, unwillingly amused.

"Let's just say I know what it's like to be bedeviled by a woman," Ned said, looking toward the manor house.

For the moment, however, there was nothing to do but concentrate on the roof.

The summer sun was directly overhead by the time the majority of the roof trusses were finished. The rhythm of hammers and the smell of newly cut wood reminded him of Gilmuir and the new shipyard he'd built there. He might have been with his crew repairing a sail or testing the structural integrity of a mast. From time to time he'd stand and stretch, seeking Riona from his vantage point atop the roof. But she had disappeared, leaving him with a curious feeling of emptiness.

Chapter 22

"Not like that, miss," one of the milkmaids said. "Gently, gently. As if you're combing a baby's curls."

Riona looked down at the scarred iron pot. Her hands were buried to the wrist in gelled milk. Her fingers separated, pulling upward through the curds, cutting the mixture slowly into smaller sections.

"You could do it with a knife, but Tyemorn's cheese is always scored by hand."

Riona nodded, concentrating on her task.

Making cheese was not the easiest task at Tyemorn, but one of the most fascinating. Today she was learning to separate the curds from the whey, one of the first steps in making the hard white cheese commanding such a good price at market. One day's milking resulted in a five-pound wheel, and since so much time was needed to age the finished cheese, a few hours each day was set aside for production.

The building where they worked was at the farthest edge of the outbuildings, well away from any of the animals. A broad oak table in the middle of the room held most of the molds, with a cook fire at one end. The other side of the room was filled with shelves, each one carefully labeled and holding cheese in various stages of ageing.

One of the milkmaids added a small log to the fire below the pot where she was working until the gelled milk began gently to warm. Once the solids had been extracted, they would be pressed into wooden molds and left to age for six months or more. The residue from the pot—what they called day cheese—would be served at breakfast, or sent home with one of the workers. Nothing at Tyemorn Manor ever went to waste.

"Did you ever see such a lad as him?" a milkmaid asked, sighing. The other two girls turned and followed her gaze, each one boldly staring through the open door in turn.

There wasn't any sense in claiming ignorance, Riona thought, glancing toward the barn. There he stood atop the structure, as bold as a mountain, feet apart as if he stood on the deck of his ship. But what fascinated the milkmaids, and disconcerted her, was the fact that James had taken off his coat, waistcoat, and shirt and now stood in the bright afternoon sun bare-chested for all the world to see.

"What is he doing up there?" she asked, the first coherent question that occurred to her.

"Do you care?" one of the young girls asked, smiling. "It's enough to see him there, all tanned and muscled."

In Edinburgh she'd been counseled that a woman never

actually looked directly at a man. One sent a sidelong glance, looked beneath her lashes, or spoke to the floor when addressed. Until this moment, she'd had no idea that women were capable of leering at a man. Riona couldn't decide what unsettled her more, the admiring women and their quasi-lewd comments or the sight of James.

Oh, and what a sight it was. He had done this often, evident from the sun-browned expanse of chest and back. Also obvious was the fact that he had engaged in hard labor before. How else would he have garnered such strong arms, and muscles that rippled across his chest and stomach?

Riona McKinsey, look away. But the sight was almost irresistible.

As she stood watching him, his attention was captured by one of the men on the ground. Or perhaps she moved, or one of the milkmaids beside her giggled too loudly. For whatever reason, he turned his head to see her standing there, mouth agape like a hooked trout.

But he didn't reach to retrieve his shirt. Instead, he placed one hand against his abdomen, the other clenching a mallet.

They exchanged a look, open and aware and filled with more curiosity than any she'd ever shared with a man. How long did she remain staring at him? Long enough to cause comment, evident from the girlish giggles beside her.

Turn away, Riona. A voice so panicked that she couldn't help but heed it. How odd that her conscience should sound so afraid. Face florid, she deliberately turned away from the barn with as much dignity as she'd ever learned from Mrs. Parker.

She concentrated, instead, on her task, dismissing the sight of him from her mind and her memory. A chore made more difficult by the giggling commentary behind her. She knew when James bent down, when he retrieved a board from one of the other workers, when he smiled in their direction. Knew, too, by their longing sighs, when he disappeared from sight.

For a little while, calm reigned in the cheese house. As they grew even more silent, she glanced over her shoulder, pleased that they'd finally gained some sense.

Only to encounter a fully dressed James.

He dwarfed the interior of the building, until all she could see was him.

The worst of his bruises had faded, leaving places slightly yellow in appearance. But from the eternal cooing and lamentations from Polly, Cook, and Abigail, one would have thought him scarred for life.

James handsome or James ugly. Which one was more alluring?

"I've come to take you branch picking. Isn't it a task you need to perform?"

"You remembered."

"I always remember a promise."

"You needn't help," she said. In fact, she'd planned on using a few of the lads from the farm.

"I said I would."

"Can you spare the time from the barn?"

"It cannot be built in a day," he said, smiling.

The milkmaids were looking at her oddly. As if she were a fool to turn down an invitation from James. She would be more foolish to go with him.

"The afternoon is well advanced," he said. "Are you so occupied here that you can't spare an hour or two?"

"We're nearly finished," one of the girls offered. Riona

frowned at her but she was staring at James with that wide-eyed look that most women adopted in his presence. Did he never tire of the adoration?

"It is very nice of you to offer," she said, determined to be polite, "but it's not necessary."

"Have you done the task already?"

Yes. A lie she almost spoke aloud. "No," she said, forcing a smile to her face.

"Then why won't you allow me to help?"

She untied her apron and set it on the table, glanced at one of the milkmaids who came to take her place. Wise or not, she was evidently going to spend some time with James. The saddest part was that she wanted it very much. Reason enough to avoid him, even now.

She nodded, leading the way outside. In the cider shed each of them retrieved one of the tall baskets normally used for harvesting apples.

"How many branches do we need?" he asked, hefting the basket by its leather sling over his shoulder. She did the same, leading the way toward the line of trees in the distance.

"A hundred."

"A hundred?"

"It's not as onerous as it sounds," she said. "Each branch need only be a few inches long. It's the spirit of the tree that's needed, I understand. Not the whole thing."

He only smiled at her explanation.

"Tell me of the last place you visited," she said, bending to pick up a branch. After brushing it clean, she placed it in her basket. James promptly removed it and put it into his. She smiled at his gallantry.

"India. Bombay," he replied. "It's a series of islands that make up a natural harbor."

Picking up another branch, she placed it in his basket.

"It's warm even in winter, but gradually the air gets heavier until June. From then until autumn the rains, or what they call monsoons, arrive."

"Not a place to farm," she said, watching as he snapped a few of the younger branches from some of the older trees.

He shook his head.

"What an odd name, Bombay."

"There are those who say that the name comes from a Hindu goddess, Mumbai Devi. Others who believe it's from the Portuguese, *bom baia* meaning good harbor."

"Which do you think is correct?"

"I tend to think the Portuguese is closer to the truth. The islands were part of Catherine of Braganza's dowry when she married an English king."

"So the English own it now?"

"Specifically, the British East India Company."

"The English are everywhere. Sometimes I think Scotland is more English than England."

He looked surprised.

"Have you not noticed? Mrs. Parker is not the only Englishwoman living in Edinburgh. They're building a city modeled on London, it seems. Our manners are from London, our plays, our balls."

"You would not think that if you'd ever seen Gilmuir," he said. "It's a place as stark and wild as any in Scotland."

"But we cannot all live in places like Gilmuir," she said, picking up another branch from the ground and placing it in the basket. "Some of us must live in towns and villages like Ayleshire. But at least here it seems as if time stands still, defying any changes at all."

"An enchanted village?" he asked, his smile teasing.

"Do you not believe in such things, James? Or witches, fairies, and brownies? As a Scot you should not discount the unexplained."

"You've never seen a more superstitious lot than sailors, Riona. But I don't believe in myth and folklore."

"You mustn't speak in such a way, James, especially not here. Here the spirit of Annie Mull will come and hex you for certain."

"Who is Annie Mull?"

Reaching up, she slid the leather strap from his shoulder, releasing the basket. Propping it against the base of a tree, she added hers to it.

"Come with me, and I'll show you."

"Another Roman wall?"

She shook her head. "A witch's well."

She bent beneath a branch, catching a leaf in her hair. Attempting to brush it free, she only managed to entangle it further.

"Let me," he said.

A tiny twig clung tenaciously to an auburn curl. Gently he extricated it, his fingers tenderly smoothing against her braid until he realized what he was doing.

Her scalp was warm against his palms, her hair seeming to ensnare his fingers. His arms almost surrounded her, creating a hollow for them in the midst of the world. He took one step forward until the tip of his boots met the toe of her shoes.

He glanced down at her. Until he'd seen her in the cheese house he'd had no intention of seeking her out or of spending any time with her. But he'd been transfixed by the sight of her and intrigued by the blush that had suffused her neck and face. She'd not been able to look away from him, and now he felt the same.

Honor had been buried beneath a stronger emotion, one that kept him watching for her, made him lie awake at night thinking of her walk, her smile, her laughter.

Her face was turned up, her gaze silent, and it seemed, in that moment, that the world stilled around them. No doubt in condemnation of his touch. Desire held him rooted to this spot. Riona held him here, captive to a smile and a wish.

She was affianced, and he was transient in her world. Her duty was before her, just as his was, but he couldn't help but wish that each path would change.

"When I marry," she said softly, so very softly that he had to bend his head a little to hear her, "I'll have my hair cut off. It's an incessant nuisance."

"It would be a pity for you to cut your hair," he said.

"It's always in the way."

Her fingers touched his elbows and then trailed down to his wrists. Reaching out, she touched his cuff, her fingers playing on the edge where fabric met skin. Instead of moving away, he simply turned his hand, his finger trailing across the inside of her wrist, his thumb resting on her palm. She looked down at their joined hands, as if engrossed by the sight. But she didn't move away. Nor did he say a word to ease the sudden tension between them.

He could hear her breathe, the sound accentuated in this bower they'd created for themselves. He didn't look up to see if they were visible to any of the workers. At this moment, he didn't care.

"It takes such a very long time to care for," she said.

He'd lost track of their conversation, and it took a second

before he realized she was still talking about her hair. They were so close, he could feel the warmth of her words on his lips. He should be satisfied with that, he told himself, even as he bent closer.

Could he feel her smile?

Her fingers moved from his wrists to rest on the back of his hands.

"I, for one, would hate for you to do such a thing. You have such lovely hair."

"Why does everyone say that? I'm more than my hair."

He smiled at her, forcing himself to pull away. His thoughts were riotous and forbidden, couched as they were in lover's terms. *Yes, you are. You are your thoughts, your actions, and even your smiles. You constantly surprise me, but more than that, you intrigue me. I want to know you, and neither time nor circumstance will allow it.*

"There, you're freed," he said, flinging the twig away and taking the precaution of placing a few feet between them.

She fluffed her skirt and rearranged her jacket. Small, feminine movements that charmed him.

Riona stretched out her hand to him in invitation and temptation. He shouldn't take it, but then he shouldn't have sought her out. Even now, he should claim other tasks to occupy his time.

Instead of being wise, instead of leaving her, instead of offering her a dozen reasons that he should not say, he took her hand.

"Where are we going?"

"To a place of fantasy and wishes," she said.

He was here, he wanted to tell her. Tyemorn Manor was as enchanted a place as he'd ever been.

Chapter 23

❧❧❧

"The Witch's Well is on the other side of the river," she said, leading the way across the footbridge. Once there, they walked to a place at the base of the abbey ruins. Riona enticed him to join her with only a glance over her shoulder. Smiling to himself, he followed her.

In a clearing, marked by a well and a double granite cross, he hesitated. She walked to stand in front of the monument and he joined her, glancing down at the crude inscription carved into. its base.

Here lies Annie Mull, Burned as a witch—1625.

"What did she do to deserve such punishment?" he asked.

"Perhaps she cursed a few people. Or refused to prepare a potion for a lovesick girl."

"Or perhaps she was simply a lone woman without some-one to care for her," he said, turning away. Walking to the edge of the well, James looked down at the bottom of it. He could imagine the myths that grew up around this spot, the whispers about the magic performed here. More than one pretty girl had sipped from its waters, he suspected, and perhaps more than one boy.

"I have seen enough of the world to know that each culture chooses to exclude the unusual or the different. The greatest victims are often those without others to speak for them."

She came and stood beside him, looking down into the well. Gracefully, she sat on the rim, lowering the bucket by its rope.

"Shall we have a drink, James? Gathering Lethson branches is thirsty work."

He bent and lifted the bucket with one hand and placed it beside her on the rim of the well. "A wish, then," he said, holding the dipper for her to drink. "To always having someone to care for us."

Her fingers supported the bowl of the dipper as she drank from it. Then he, too, sipped the cool water. A strange communion, he thought, in a place where magic was supposed to dwell.

"I think the well is older than Annie Mull," Riona said, as if she felt the same odd tension in the air. "The stones look similar to those of the Roman wall."

"What is that place?" he asked, his attention suddenly drawn to the hill above them and the same ruined wall he'd seen upon his arrival at Tyemorn.

"An old abbey," she said, "but the villagers avoid it."

"Yet they seek out a witch's well," he teased.

"Perhaps they are less afraid of witches than of God."

"What about you?" he challenged. "Come explore it with me."

He held out his hand and she took it with ease, smiling up

at him as she stood. A moment later he found an overgrown path winding up to the top of the hill.

Once there, James stood and surveyed the view of the River Wye and beyond to the pastures belonging to Tyemorn Manor. Because of the undulation of the landscape, the manor house was not visible, only a corner of the village and the hills that surrounded the place like the bony elbows of a protective nurse.

For the first time, he could understand what Alisdair had meant when he'd said that Gilmuir had called to him. James had felt ancestral ties to the old castle, but nothing as he did now standing where only one wall remained of what must have been a splendid place.

The spot cried out for structure to be built. Not anything as grand as the fortress of Gilmuir, because there was no further need for defense. But someplace where a man might look out and survey what he owned and be content.

How long had he been thinking of leaving Gilmuir? Perhaps for as long as he'd been there. He needed a place for himself, somewhere to call his alone, where he might be lord. A place where he might find some semblance of peace. Where he might not be regaled constantly with evidence of the deep and abiding love between Alisdair and Iseabal and wonder why it had escaped him.

Here, on this spot almost isolated from the rest of the world, he might find what he sought, especially since there was no view of the manor house.

He turned to watch Riona. Instead of branches, she was gathering wildflowers. Her braid had come loose, and now her hair flew about her shoulders in an almost wicked way. As if she summoned him with a flurry of auburn curls.

In a matter of days she would be gone. Their paths

wouldn't cross unless by accident. Life would be once more as it had been before he'd come to Tyemorn. Seemingly complete yet unbearably dull.

The stones of the abbey wall were blackened either from age or from an ancient fire. Waist-high weeds, waving in the brisk wind, were now the only inhabitants of this place. But there was no sense of sadness, no waste of purpose as he occasionally felt at Gilmuir.

Riona came to stand at his side, her bouquet of flowers too much like that a bride might carry.

"My sister-in-law would study this wall," he said, reaching out to touch the heavily carved lodestone over the one remaining arch. For all its wistful beauty the wall was unsafe. "Iseabal works in stone," he explained, "and has created marvels where before there were only chunks of rock."

"She sounds very talented."

"She is. Her latest work is a bust of my brother. She insists on it being placed in the entranceway of Gilmuir, while Alisdair becomes embarrassed at the thought of his face greeting every visitor."

"I have no abilities to speak of," she said, bending to strip the flower from a sturdy weed. Tall and stocky, the weeds had a beauty of their own, gently swaying in the breeze that swirled around the abbey ruins. "I cannot help but feel lessened by someone else's accomplishment. Is that a foolish way to feel?"

"You shouldn't measure yourself against others."

"No, I shouldn't. But we do, don't we? I always thought I knew my worth. I was reared to believe that as long as I worked hard, that was all that mattered. But now I know it's ability that separates one person from another." She traced a pattern on the stone with one finger. "I haven't Iscabal's gift in carving and I will never be as good a dancer as Maureen. Or even keep a home like my mother."

"Then you will have to find your talent," he said.

She glanced at him, surprised.

"Most people discover their paths in life early. Some must wait until it comes to them."

"What do you think my skill might be? Or should I be brave enough to ask?"

He glanced at her, smiling. "Your way of dealing with people, perhaps. When you smile, others follow suit."

"Really?" she asked, looking pleased at his words.

"You never ask anyone to do something you would not, I've noticed, which makes people want to work beside you. Even Ned does not have that ability to inspire others."

"A trait that I cannot carry to Edinburgh. I wonder what my talent shall be there?"

Instead of answering her, he moved to stand at the point of land, looking down over Ayleshire and Tyemorn Manor.

The doubt she felt made him want to embrace her, reassure her with physical comfort as well as words. The trouble was that he wanted years of her. He wanted her smiles and frowns and observations, humor and complaints, all the untidy parcels of emotion that made life worth living. He wanted to share his secrets and confess his most horrible thoughts, laugh at the unfunny and be ungainly, even rude, with her.

"I want to buy this land," he said abruptly. "I like this place. I feel comfortable here as I never have before."

"Even at sea?"

He shook his head. "I never truly had an affinity for the sea. Not like my brothers. While I believe that anything can be learned, it was difficult to overcome my physical aversion to ocean travel. I'm more like my father in that regard. He would just as soon never put another foot on the deck of a ship."

"You were seasick?" she asked, smiling slightly.

How many confessions would he make to her if given enough time? She might well become the repository of all his secrets.

"Are you such a good sailor, then," he asked wryly, "being a woman of Cormech?"

"I have never been on the ocean," she confessed, placing a blossom on the curving arch of one now empty window. There was a sparseness to this place that oddly suited her, as if, with her auburn hair and gray eyes, she was the most vibrant ornament here.

She turned and looked at him quizzically, and he realized the moments had been spent staring at her.

"I apologize, my mind was wandering," he said, and watched in surprise as color mounted her cheeks.

"I asked if there was another occupation you would prefer?"

"I've discovered that I have an affinity for farming. The land almost reaches out to me, and urges me to plant it."

"I've heard Ned say much the same." She turned, staring out through the empty windows of the abbey wall. "I'll think of you here, then, when I'm in Edinburgh. Building your great house."

"And learning about farming."

"That, too," she said, her smile not matched by the look in her eyes. They seemed too sad. "You'll do well with it, I know. And you'll come to love Ayleshire, I'm sure. From the moment I saw the village, I never wanted to leave it. But I'm glad that I have had this year."

He didn't choose to discuss her wedding, and banished the thought of Harold McDougal from his mind with a surprising alacrity.

A gust of wind blew a few leaves against the abbey wall, capturing their attention. Riona turned her head away, her hands impatiently pushing an errant lock of hair behind her ear.

His fingers replaced hers, his thumb lingering on the curve of her cheek, the shell of her ear.

"Do not be afraid, Riona," he said, feeling her tremble beneath his touch.

"I'm not." Her voice, however, was faint. "I am thinking of decorum and modesty, James, and all those emotions I'm supposed to feel."

He wanted to reassure her that he would do her no harm, but at the moment he wasn't entirely sure that was an honest statement. He felt less protective of her than possessive, wanting to make her his. Once, before she was taken from him.

His honor was in tatters, his will in shreds. He no longer cared.

In his mind, he had sketched out what a perfect woman might say or do, and she had walked into that net of words and thoughts, performing the role with exquisite ease. At any other time such ability would mark her as the one woman in the world he must have. Now, however, all it did was render the moment bittersweet.

He wanted to place his hands against her temples and hold all her thoughts and his at bay. The world would not intrude and there would be only the two of them. Family and friends, soon-to-be husband were all unimportant now.

Nothing was more important than the two of them.

He reached out his hands, pulling her so close that a whisper couldn't come between them. She gasped as he covered her mouth with his. Her hands gripped his shoulders as he swung her around, pressing her gently against the abbey wall.

His mouth was suddenly on her neck, then her temple, burning a trail across her cheek to her lips once more. He murmured something, a word, an oath, an order, she wasn't certain. Her eyes were closed, her head arching back.

She'd thought hunger was reserved for food, thirst for drink. Nothing had prepared her for this. Her hands clenched in his hair, then on his back. Her laces were being unfastened, her bodice loosened, and then his hands, his fingers were on her bare flesh, cupping her breasts.

"Yes, please," she said in a voice barely recognizable as her own. She sighed in surrender, or complicity, as he deepened the kiss.

She had waited for this, wanted it. Dreamed about it.

Her body heated, felt constricted, as if her clothing was an obstruction that must be removed. Her heart felt as if it was in her throat, and her breathing was so fast that she felt almost faint with it.

Her hands joined his in removing her clothing. Her skirt was finally loose, her dress falling to the ground in folds of fabric. She stood before him in her corset, shift, and stockings, wondering at her wantonness. Only for a second, before he smiled and reached for her.

Slowly, she began to unfasten his shirt. His hands covered hers, not to still her actions as much as hasten them.

They shared a look, open and honest. No denial was allowed in these silent moments.

A conquest everywhere he walks. Rory's words.

"You've made one more conquest, James MacRae," she admitted finally, her voice faint.

"If I've made one of you," he said, "then it's only fair. My heart was stolen the first moment you spoke."

He didn't counsel her to prudence, or argue decorum or decency. Instead, he picked her up in his arms, the feeling of being cradled against his naked skin deliciously wicked and decadent.

Had she always been so wanton in spirit? He'd done more than remove her clothes; he'd swept aside any barriers between them. They couldn't be rebuilt with regret.

Love me. Teach me. Touch me. Words she ached to speak. But she was constrained to silence, not by shyness, but by wonder. The moment, sunlit and brilliant, seemed almost perfect.

The only ornament to their trysting place was the abbey wall behind her. The sun was their candle, the ground was her bed, and around them, as if summoning assistance from the wind itself, were the tall swaying grasses shielding them from accidental discovery.

He kissed her again, imbuing their embrace with a sense of wonder. Or perhaps it was simply that nothing at Ayleshire was quite as magical as James, naked and holding her. He placed his thumbs along her jaw, tilting her head at just the right angle to kiss her.

Uncertain yet eager, she flattened her hands against his

chest and felt the muscles dormant there, heard the beating of his heart as it pounded against her palm.

He lowered her so that her feet touched the ground and she stepped forward, until her naked toes touched his. They both lowered their heads, startled at the intimacy of the gesture. Hers whipped up again and she stared at the far grasses, her face warming before she returned to her inspection.

He was so very large.

Curious, she stroked his manhood with one finger, feeling him draw back, then surge forward as if he could not help himself. She measured him, startled to find that his erection was longer than the distance from the tip of her longest finger to the end of her thumb.

She wasn't certain what to do, but some instinct told her that he would gain pleasure from touching her. Reaching out her hands, she gripped his, placing them on her breasts, moving them until her nipples were in the center of each palm. Leaning against him, she kissed him, then entwined her arms around his neck, raising up so that she could deepen the kiss.

James made a sound deep in his throat as his hands dropped to encompass her waist, pulling her closer to him. His legs widened until she was standing between them, his erection, hard, proud, and heated, bumping against her stomach.

She leaned her cheek against his, feeling lost. She wanted to touch him, marvel at the strength of muscles and bones and sinew.

He lowered his head to kiss a breast. His lips encircled a nipple, pulling slightly, exerting a little pressure and then just a bit more. Another lesson, that she wanted the feeling to continue.

She wished her breasts were larger and that she was taller. No, more diminutive. And that her scent was more alluring than barley and summer flowers. Her fingers were callused, and her lips felt almost rough to her own tongue. If he hadn't wound his hand in her hair, she might have draped it in front of her artfully, baring herself to his gaze at the same time she hid her most glaring faults.

Her insecurities both maddened and embarrassed her.

He laid her on the ground, neither of them caring where they were. Neither of them capable of altering the moment or being sensible or prudent.

His hand slid down her body, over her stomach, where his fingers rested for a moment. She buried her face in his neck, wishing that she had more talent and experience.

He touched her then, parting the delicate folds between her thighs. His fingers were tender and gentle, sliding over the dampness. Her mouth opened as she breathed against his throat. Her hands gripped his shoulders, but not to push him away. Rather to hold him close as he softly stroked her, inciting a wondrous feeling.

More, please.

"As much as you want." Until he spoke, she didn't realize she'd said the words aloud.

Her hips arched up, following his hand as he gently caressed her. Her head tossed from side to side and her hands linked behind his head, pulling him down for a kiss.

Hours, moments, years later he slid a finger inside her. She flinched, expecting to feel pain, but experienced only a slight tightening. Curving his finger slightly, he stroked slowly and deliberately against one particular spot as his thumb circled her flesh. The sensation was strange, beginning as a tingle of light, before deepening to become pleasure.

He whispered something, words of instruction, of praise, of inquiry. They were lost beneath the startling feelings he was evoking.

The pleasure was too intense, too much. Too delightful. She felt speared by it. Her vision turned golden and she reached down to hold his hand there. Pure and selfish bliss held her captive as her hips arched and a low, soft moan escaped her lips.

The moment elongated until she couldn't tell how long it lasted. A moment, a year, a lifetime.

She weakly blinked her eyes open as he entered her. Holding her hands, he gazed into her eyes.

"Have I hurt you?"

"No," she said, surprised to find it true. All she felt was fullness. He was too large, or she too small. Neither seemed to fit the other.

"Tell me what you feel," he said, pulling out of her gently, then entering her again a moment later.

Her hands lay against his back. She felt enervated, weakened. Yet the feeling was beginning again. She began to tap her hands against his shoulders in an unconsciously impatient gesture as he moved in and out of her. Patient, yet demanding movements.

"Tell me." He spread his fingers into her hair, pulling her head back gently before kissing her throat.

Her feet brushed up and down on his calves. "I feel too much," she admitted.

"Tell me."

"I want you deeper," she said. "But then to leave me." A contradiction of feelings. As he moved out of her again, she gripped his arms tightly. "And come back quickly."

He entered her again.

"Deeper."

He moved again, a slow, relentless rhythm that had her breath coming sharp in her chest. She'd never felt this way before, as if she were glowing from within like an ember. Her feet felt suddenly warm and tingly, and her hands splayed and lost their ability to grip. Every sensation was focused on where they joined, as if nothing else in the world was more important than this.

Nothing was.

Riona wanted to laugh and weep at the same time. A dozen emotions, a hundred thoughts cascaded through her heart and mind, and yet none of them was coherent.

Only James.

Her mind seemed to expand, even as her body contracted around him. He was hard and huge and invasive, yet at the same time she gloried in his act of possession. She felt herself being stretched even further to accommodate him, but she only pulled him closer, wanting James to experience that same joy she'd felt earlier.

No wonder women were counseled against sin. It blinded her of reason, stripped her of concerns. All she wanted was him.

Gently raking his arms with her nails, she arched her hips, meeting his downward thrusts with a surprising impatience. Again, and her vision darkened. Once more, to his groan. Suddenly, she was there again. Blinded and deafened, inert as the feeling surged through her, then wild as it crested.

Long moments later, he rolled with her, placing her across his chest. She laid her cheek against his skin. Her arms fell, stretched out on either side of them. She was exhausted, beyond tired.

She felt James's kiss to her throat, made an inarticulate

sound to acknowledge the curve of his lips against her skin.

Placing her hand flat against his chest, she felt the rapid beat of his heart. Hers, too, was racing.

Her lips curved beneath his when he kissed her. "What amuses you, Riona?" he asked a moment later.

"I am not amused," she said slowly, her smile not abating. "Merely happy."

"Happy is not a word to be coupled with merely. Joyously, perhaps. Or completely. But never merely."

In a tender benediction of touch, she smoothed her fingertips over his face, touching his cheek, his jaw, his lips. He took her hand, kissing her knuckles before entwining his fingers with hers.

Thank you. A prayer of thanksgiving for the moment, the day, and the man.

James sat up, then stood, granting her an unspoken wish. There he was, crafted of muscle and bone and sinew, naked for her eyes.

His buttocks were perfectly formed, his hips narrow, his thighs strong and fit with muscle. But then he turned to face her in the act of reaching for his clothing, revealing even more wonders.

Her eyes widened as she took in each separate part of his body, one of which was growing.

Riona opened her mouth to speak, but couldn't think of any words to say. What should she do? Apologize for her curiosity? Or her lack of maidenly reserve? Or for being so fascinated that she couldn't look away?

A perfect man, she thought. A creature God might have formed at night, then made the sun for the sole purpose of illuminating His work.

In that instant their gazes locked. She should have been

the first to look away, transfixed by shyness, but she didn't feel as embarrassed as spellbound.

Suddenly, there was a tension in the air, an awareness that was elemental, like the progression of growing things from seed to harvest. Ordained by God and nature, immutable and as fixed as the seasons.

"He shouldn't have you," he said roughly.

"But he does."

He held out his hand to her. "Come with me, instead."

"Where?" she asked, taking his hand and slowly standing.

They stood, brazen and naked and bared for all the world to see. Face to face, with nothing hidden. Not flesh or wishes or wants.

"Anywhere."

The decision was not only hers to make. If it had been, she would never have chosen to marry Harold in the first place.

"I cannot."

He studied her for a few moments, as if to test the resolve of her words. Finally, he turned and began to dress, each garment hiding his body from her gaze.

She couldn't take back her actions. Nor, given the choice, would she. Until the day she died, Riona knew that she would remember this afternoon.

He fastened his shirt with deliberation, as if knowing her sudden reluctance to see him clothed. What would he say to hear her thoughts?

Please, come back and let me reach out and touch you, smooth my hands over your skin to prove that my eyes do not lie.

She'd touched upon magic of her own, she suspected. Something she now knew as truth. His touch brought her delight, but so did the sight of him.

* * *

They returned to the house separately, Riona going first, followed by James. He stood and watched her circle the Witch's Well, wondering why he was not suffused with guilt. All his life he'd been constrained by decency, wrapped in it so tightly that it felt like swaddling. In one afternoon, he'd ignored all the tenets in which he'd believed.

Yet he'd never felt so complete, so whole.

She amused him and delighted him. He'd been disconcerted at her frank inspection of him. She'd not looked away, but studied each portion of his anatomy as if to gauge his height, build, and shape.

An interesting phenomenon, being viewed with such intensity. He'd never before had the experience. Had he proven worthy?

Intimacy had come to them, and it seemed natural and right.

Chapter 24

Edinburgh sat huddled at the bottom of Castle Rock, two miles from the Firth of Forth, on land that looked as if it had been scraped and clawed by some mythological creature. The high, dark buildings gave the city a brooding air, and the narrow streets added to the atmosphere. Edinburgh was, historically, a place of intrigue, where crowns had been bargained or lost, and a country plotted against its neighbor to the south.

The traffic, carriages and pedestrians alike, seemed intent on their destinations, oblivious to the noise and others attempting to make their way through the narrow streets and around the construction.

Strangely enough, James felt unused to the bustle of Edinburgh. Even though he had seen the world and most of its major cities, the peace and tranquility of Ayleshire had affected him more than he thought. Now he heard the carriage wheels on the cobbled streets and they sounded too loud. The cries of the hawkers, the street merchants, the market vendors all seemed equally cacophonous.

It took him some time to find his way to McDougal's lodgings, the address obtained from one of the man's letters to Riona, procured for James by a smiling Abigail. Then on to the gaming hall where McDougal evidently spent a great deal of his time. Money was the universal source of information, and by the time James found the man later that evening, he knew a great deal about Riona's betrothed.

Harold was on the cusp of society, a once respectable young man who had taken to bad habits, and owed some very powerful people. A prosperous marriage was just what he needed to save him.

As the captain of a ship, James had experience in judging men. It wasn't a difficult task to ascertain exactly what type of individual stood before him in one of Edinburgh's more notorious gaming halls.

Harold McDougal did not, evidently, think personal appearance mattered much, else he would have changed his shirt long before now. There were crumbs on his lapel from where he'd eaten, and a yellowish stain on his pocket that James took to be mustard. No doubt he'd considered himself too busy to leave his cards.

His eyes were red rimmed, and a stubble of beard attested to the length of this visit. But what disturbed James the most was the glittery look in the other man's eyes, as if McDougal were reckless and euphoric with it.

Not a man in control of his baser needs. But, then, James wasn't exactly in the position to lecture another.

"Do I have the honor of addressing Harold McDougal?" James asked, forcing himself to be civil.

In truth, he was enraged by the man standing in front of him. He had never before felt such loathing for another human being. He wanted to plant his fist into the other man's considerable nose. Or wipe the smirk from his thin lips. Something atavistic and not entirely civilized made him want to clamp his hands on the back of the man's jacket and send him flying through the doorway.

Yet the man had done nothing to him. His only sin, if one could call it that, was to become engaged to be married to Riona McKinsey.

James decided that it was reason enough for anger.

"You do," the other man replied, surveying him. "You have a message from my intended?"

It hadn't been an easy task getting McDougal away from the card table, but James had done so with the pretense of being a messenger for Riona. Only reluctantly had McDougal left his cards, but he'd taken the precaution of scooping up his winnings and putting them into his pocket before following him.

"Well?" Harold snapped his fingers. "I was on a winning streak, man. Out with it."

"How much do you want to walk away from this marriage?" James asked bluntly.

The other man's eyes narrowed. "Who are you to ask such a question, sir?"

"A friend," he responded tightly. "How much?" Even after buying the abbey land, he'd have enough money left to ransom Riona from a foolish marriage.

"Name your price, and I'll pay it."

"Did Riona send you? You can go back to her and tell her that it's no use. The marriage will still occur."

James named an amount that had the man's eyes widening. "Is that enough? All I ask is that you go to England for a few months, or find another destination equally as distant."

"She's prepared to handle the scandal of being rejected, is she?" McDougal's smile altered in character, turning sly. "If she's that brave, then she ought to pay for it."

"Name your price."

"Tyemorn Manor," Harold said easily. "Promise me that and she's yours."

"I can't do that. But name an amount and I'll pay it."

"Why should I settle for just money? When her mother dies, she and her sister will own a prosperous holding. Who's to know how much more valuable Tyemorn Manor will become in the intervening years? The farm is an investment. In my future."

"Then you refuse?"

"I find the prospect of marrying Riona quite enjoyable. All that money, plus a winsome wife."

"Why would she agree to marry you at all?" James asked, the contempt in his voice audible.

Harold laughed. "She nearly didn't. Stubborn chit. But in the end, she decided that it was best if the world didn't know about her loose behavior." He glanced longingly toward the card game. "As for why, I'm not at all surprised that you don't know. We took great pains to keep it quiet. She's a passionate little number, my Riona. The sooner she's married, the sooner tamed. That's why we're going to be married. To save her reputation."

The man fell like a marble statue.

James rubbed his knuckles, thinking that the other man's jaw was surprisingly hard. Staring down at McDougal, he decided that any pain he felt was worth it.

"She's got herself a protector, then, does she?" Harold

gripped his jaw and winced. "Well, soon enough she'll have herself a husband."

James turned on his heel and left the room before he struck the man again.

"James has gone where?" Riona said, staring at Rory.

"Edinburgh," he repeated, sitting up in his bed. "He came and said goodbye before he left. Didn't he say anything to you?"

She shook her head.

"He said he'd be away for a few days, no longer."

"Why?"

"He didn't tell me that, miss," Rory said, and his tone indicated that she shouldn't have asked, either. "Could you say a word to your mother, miss? She's determined that I'll stay abed, but I truly feel well enough to leave it."

"She's only doing it for your good."

He stared down at his bandaged leg. The yellow salve Susanna had used was seeping through the linen. "I've had worse from the cook's stove aboard ship, miss. Truly."

"Very well," she said, "I'll see what I can do."

She left his room, the chamber that used to belong to Mrs. Parker. It was easier for her mother to tend to Rory if she didn't have to climb so many stairs during the day.

Why was James in Edinburgh? Why hadn't he told her he was going?

She didn't own him. They weren't bound by their illicit act, however much she wished it so.

She had never been wanton, despite her behavior in Edinburgh. But she couldn't say that now. She had been guilty of the most grievous sin, disobeying the teachings of a lifetime.

And she'd do it again.

For the touch of him. For the joy of lying with him.

Now she knew why kisses were forbidden. They opened the door to other more banned acts. Feelings and sensations she had never imagined a few days ago.

Could someone tell? By looking at her, could they discern her wickedness? Or know that she felt different inside?

Riona entered her room, walking to the bureau, tilting the mirror atop it until she could see herself.

She looked different, but would everyone else see the change?

Her hair was tousled as it normally was, the tight coronet having come half undone once again. Her eyes looked wider than they had yesterday and more knowledgeable.

Her gaze traveled from her neck to her chest as she stood at an angle and surveyed herself. Had James thought her shoulders too round or too squared? Her arms too muscled or long? What about her waist? And her breasts? Too large, perhaps? Too small?

Although she'd garnered her share of looks in Inverness and Edinburgh, and had occasionally summoned forth a smile and nod from a male passerby, she wasn't the type of woman who made a man stop and stare wordlessly after her. Or catch his eye as a carriage passed, a slow, dawning smile his delayed reaction.

Suddenly, however, she wanted to be beautiful.

For him. For a man she couldn't have.

A bright, amusing temperament could make a man forget a woman's plain looks. Mrs. Parker's edict.

Even there she had her doubts. She didn't have Iseabal's appreciable talents. Nor did she have as compassionate and gentle a nature as Maureen.

She was curious, had a mind that questioned, and possessed courage to some degree. Her family was important to her, as well as her friends. Other than that? She believed in hope, optimism, and the persistence of possibilities.

Why was she tallying all her assets and liabilities with such vigor? Loving James made her feel vulnerable. Almost weak.

She hugged herself as she walked slowly to the kitchen in search of Susanna. She didn't see the hall she traveled, the staircase she descended, or the various rooms into which she peered. They were nothing but a white backdrop to her thoughts and memories.

How could she feel as if she'd done wrong? Intellectually, perhaps, she agreed that her behavior was foolish. Emotionally, she might even agree. Only because her heart was not hers to give. It was imprisoned in a vow. But how could she regret it physically? How could she possibly want to roll the time back and become, once again, the maiden she'd been?

Yesterday would be her secret for now and forever. James had returned her to the house, parting with a long and tender kiss. She'd stood and watched as he'd rounded the barn, walking his horse back to its stall. What, after all, did a woman say after an afternoon like that?

Love me again.

The words were so easily summoned that she wished James stood before her now so that she might voice them.

He'd touched her and changed her, and as long she lived she would remember that afternoon when they'd been reckless and improvident and unwise. Shortly, she would be a respectable matron of Edinburgh. An honorable woman.

But she didn't want any of these roles. She wanted to love.

After all, no one could chain her heart.

* * *

The journey back from Edinburgh was done in drenching rain. Dark clouds preceded him, while it seemed that lightning was always at his back, sending him away from the city as if it disapproved of his errand.

James peered through the darkness, finally seeing the manor house squatting on the horizon. A few minutes later, he was dismounting in front of the barn and opening one of the doors.

Ned was there, hammer in hand, lips clenched over several nails. As he led his horse inside, the older man removed them, putting the hammer down and moving to close the door in the increasing wind.

"Not a fit night for man or animal, I'm thinking."

"It is not," James said, removing his heavy greatcoat and hanging it on a nail. Rivulets of water dripped from his garments. He didn't think he'd ever been so soaked. Even at sea he'd had a respite from a storm. But he'd been riding for two days straight in bad weather.

He led his horse to his stall, began removing the saddle.

Ned peered over the boards.

"I take it, from your expression, that your errand was pointless?"

He glanced at the older man. "How did you know why I was in Edinburgh?"

"I would do the same if I were you. McDougal refused to relinquish her?"

"He did." James busied himself with rubbing down his horse. They'd taken shelter in an abandoned crofter's hut the night before, but the structure had leaked and was filled with drafts. The warmth of the new barn was welcome.

"What will you do now?"

He was running out of ideas. "At the moment, I don't know."

"There's always elopement."

He eyed Ned with some disfavor. "If she would go, I'd take her from here tomorrow."

Ned nodded. "It would solve the problem." A moment later he spoke again. "Will you be leaving, then?"

"I've no wish to stay and see Riona wed," James admitted.

"But you'll tell the lass before you go? I wouldn't want her to wake one morning and find you gone."

"I'll tell her," James said, not anticipating the meeting. Or the leaving.

Chapter 25

The foot races done, the horse fair finished, the final ceremony of Lethson required the appearance of those from Tyemorn Manor. James watched as the line of villagers formed, thinking that this was not so much a pagan ritual steeped in tradition as a solemn observance.

Most of Ayleshire's inhabitants were lined up behind the parson, who was to walk at the head of the procession. Another example of the present meeting the past. Mr. Dunant's appearance didn't necessarily grant the approval of the church, but his attendance kept Lethson from straying off into pagan paths.

There was a hint of pageantry about the night. Geldings, he'd been told, were the only horses used to pull the peat wagons. They did so slowly, their bridles decorated with flowers. Behind them, young girls walked, crowns of flowers in their hair and ribbons trailing down their backs. Instead of laughter and jocularity, there was a solemnity to this procession.

The villagers' spirit appealed to James. They made no pretense about being who they were, and what was important to them. They believed their home touched with magic, and perhaps it was.

Ayleshire and Gilmuir felt oddly linked. In other places, the English might have made inroads in altering Scottish culture, but in this village tucked among the hills, and at a golden fortress, traditions were valued, honored, and observed.

Placing his hands on Riona's waist, James boosted her up to sit on the saddle of his horse. Her legs draped over one side, her soft yellow gown flowing over the saddle. In her hand she held a nosegay of sorts, woodland ferns that she'd gathered that evening at the edge of the forest.

Fingering the edge of her skirt, he covered Riona's shoe, unconsciously smoothing the fabric over her ankle before realizing what he was doing. He had caught himself in such absent gestures before, as if his body knew he had a right to touch her, stroke a hand over her arm, or brush a wisp of hair from her cheek.

"Why were you in Edinburgh?" she asked, glancing down at him. He turned his head slowly.

He'd returned only the night before, and had been waiting for the question all day. She'd surprised him by waiting until now to ask.

He remained silent for a moment, wondering if he should tell her the reason for his journey.

"I went to see Harold McDougal," he said finally.

"Why?" She looked startled. As well she might be. It had turned out to be a foolish errand.

"To free you from this idiotic marriage."

"I don't know what to say."

"There is nothing to say," he replied stonily. "McDougal refuses to release you."

"I could have told you that had you but asked me. He wants my fortune more than me."

He'd underestimated McDougal's greed, while Riona had evidently never been in doubt of it.

"You look wonderful together," a female voice said. He turned to see Susanna attired in a gown not unlike those of the village girls, with puffed sleeves and a skirt barely coming to her ankles. Around her head was a coronet of daisies.

Without warning, she bent forward to kiss his cheek. Stepping back, she smiled brightly. "It's Lethson, my dear. I have a right to kiss that handsome face."

She tilted her head and narrowed her eyes, looking, he thought, like an inquisitive wren. "Pity that the English took the kilt from us. I'd give a goodly sum to see you attired in one. As your Uncle Fergus was fond of saying, there will come a time when Scotland will once more be into her own. I can only hope that it's in my lifetime."

With a wry grin, James realized that Susanna had been tippling.

"I claim a dance later as well," she said, smiling.

"As do I."

They both turned to see a clean-shaven stranger with graying brown hair standing a few feet away. Something about the eyes hinted at humor. An instant later, recognition came to James, but it took longer for Susanna to realize that it was Old Ned who stood before them.

A man who didn't look nearly as ancient as his appellation.

Her mouth fell open as she continued to stare.

"Well, woman," Ned said impatiently. "Is that a yes or a no?"

She nodded. A moment later she found her voice. "Your beard." She pointed at his face.

"I shave my beard every other year, or did no one tell you?" His smile indicated that he knew quite well that she hadn't known. There was a bit of mischievousness in Ned, James thought, eyeing the couple with interest.

She shook her head.

"I'm a good dancer as well. You'll find that out on your own."

Wordlessly, Susanna nodded again. He extended his good arm to her and she took it, evidently still dazed at his appearance.

The procession began, led by Mr. Dunant and his wife, who tucked her hand into her husband's arm and appeared entirely contented. Together, they began to walk up the path across the hills to the first place the fires would be lit.

The pit at the Roman wall was being set ablaze. The villagers milled around, cheering wildly when the fire was lit. A few moments later, the crowd was on its way, following the path to the Witch's Well where another small blaze was lit. At the abbey ruins, a bonfire was placed at the edge of the abutment overlooking the farms of Tyemorn. The fire illuminated the solitary wall, casting elongated shadows over the arches.   The cheer this time was less effusive than before, no doubt in deference to the once religious nature of the old ruins.

Leaving two lads behind to guard the blaze, they all turned, following the track downward again. Here the villagers separated, their paths clearly delineated with torches as each walked to a separate field.

"Where are they going?"

Riona, silent until now, answered him. "Remember my telling you of the dragons?" He glanced up at her, nodding. "Every man who owns a bit of land is expected to participate in this part of the ceremony. If not, his oats will grow thistles, and weeds will choke his barley."

"Quite a threat."

A smile was her only response.

One by one, young boys separated from the crowds, beginning to beat at the crops.

"What are they doing now?" he asked curiously.

"Daring the dragon to show himself."

"And the torches?" He placed his hand on the saddle, near where she sat. If they had been alone, he would have helped her dismount, taken her into his arms, and kissed her senseless.

"To intimidate the beast, of course," she said, smiling. "Once he sees how bright the blaze is, he runs away, and the crops are safe for another year."

"And who shall I summon to do the beating for me? Am I allowed to select a woman?" he asked.

"I don't think it's ever been done." Her fingers trailed over his cuff. He captured her fingers in his, stood looking at their joined hands. The day had been long, the emotions pummeling him ranging from anger to delight. Now, however, he felt a yearning to be alone with her.

"As our representative," she said, her lips gently curving into a smile, "you can choose anyone you wish."

"Rory then," he said, looking about for the young man. He found him standing near Abigail and her family. The boy's eyes were fixed on the young maid, his feelings only too clear.

"He fancies himself in love, I think," James said, smiling fondly.

"She is a good girl, a good worker, and comes from a fine family," Riona told him.

He signaled to Rory and explained what he needed.

"But only if you feel well enough." Susanna had released him from his bed just a day ago.

"I am. I'm not as fast as I could be, sir, but I can make it around the field."

"I don't even want you running," James said. "Just stand in one place and beat the crops."

Rory grinned. "I can do that well enough."

James led his horse across the footbridge. Those villagers who had already completed running their acreage followed them, as well as those who owned fields to the north of Tyemorn's farms.

Standing at the corner of one of the largest pastures, he reached up, placed his hands on either side of her waist, and slowly helped Riona descend.

"I should learn to ride," she said, her voice sounding oddly breathless. She stood so close to him that her breasts pressed against his shirt. Once again, he wished they were alone, that the celebrations were finished. Or at least that he didn't have a hundred or so witnesses.

"I could teach you." Prudently, he stepped back from her. A diversion was what he needed, and this custom would serve as well as anything else.

"There's not enough time," she said. "I'll be in Edinburgh soon. It won't matter then."

He pushed back her braid from where it had fallen, then watched as she impatiently batted her hair over her shoulder.

Neither of them spoke of Harold, but his name lingered between them as if he stood there.

Nodding to Rory, he took the torch he held aloft. James waited until the boy preceded him, beating at the crops. Slowly, he began to run, increasing his pace as the villagers began to cheer. By the time he had reached the end of one field, James was racing to the sound of their voices. The wind and the sputtering of the torch sounded not unlike a dragon's roar, propelling him backward hundreds of years when this ritual had first been performed.

He felt almost pagan, his blood stirring at the sound of cheers and yells and shouts as Rory beat against the sheaves of barley.

James realized abruptly that he was having fun. His childhood had been filled with laughter and this ceremony seemed to summon memories of similar times when he was filled with merriment and excitement.

Raising his torch still higher, he waved it in an arc above his head as he rounded the final corner, returning to the original starting place.

Riona stood at the front of the crowd, her face wreathed in a smile. Impulsively, he grabbed her hand without slowing his pace. Instead of pulling away or protesting, she grabbed her skirts with her other hand and raced with him.

Chasing dragons.

Chapter 26

"**W**ould Mrs. Parker approve of this celebration?" James asked an hour later. Lanterns were strung on poles around the green, illuminating the dancers. From maid to innkeeper, stable boy to merchant, every inhabitant of Ayleshire seemed to be in the square.

They had danced the first dance and were now resting on the sidelines, watching as the other villagers joined in the gaiety.

"Perhaps not," she admitted. "But she has left Ayleshire, and so we'll have no way of knowing."

"Good riddance."

"She's a very respected member of Edinburgh society," she said in the silence.

"Used to getting her own way," he said dryly.

"She can be rather overpowering," she said, "but I'm sure she means well."

They exchanged a look laced with humor.

"You're more charitable than I," he said. "I am grateful the woman has taken herself off to Edinburgh."

"She doesn't truly mean to be so difficult, I think. She's considered quite proper, although I have never measured up to her standards. Mrs. Parker believes I should be less enthusiastic, I believe she said. And more circumspect." She glanced at him. "Did you know I have the laughter of a braying ass?"

"Mrs. Parker evidently speaks for herself and not for a man. I, for one, like your laugh."

They shared another look. "Thank you," she softly replied. "If you had a marriageable daughter, you would, no doubt, think differently of her."

He raised his eyebrow again. "I cannot think of sending a child of mine off to the care of that woman. It would be like sending a tiny fly off to be boarded with a spider."

"She wasn't all that bad," Riona protested. "I was a very poor student."

"What could she possibly have taught you?"

"How to attract a suitor, for one. How to walk with a gliding gait, how to greet all manner of people. In short, my manners needed to be polished."

"I have no doubt that you would have done equally as well without her tutelage."

"I also learned to dance," she said. "Even though I admit to having no liking for it." Glancing at him, she smiled again. "There, I've told you one of my deepest secrets. I have no grace, Mrs. Parker says."

"The woman is a fool," he said brusquely. "You're a magnificent dancer. You do everything well. Why do you feel the need to defend her when she so obviously disliked you?"

She said nothing for a moment, then finally answered. "Perhaps because I feel sorry for her. I wouldn't like her life at all, spending her time arranging marriages for everyone else while being alone herself. It seems to be an unbearably sad existence."

He didn't say anything, stripped of his irritation toward Mrs. Parker by Riona's artless words.

He pulled her behind a wagon and bent his head and kissed her, giving in to an impulse that had been present all night. Although it was a light, teasing kiss, it hinted at more.

"Besides," she said, her lips curving in a smile when they parted, "you truly cannot blame her. She was only trying to render me more marriageable."

Mrs. Parker hadn't known what to do with her, he suspected. Riona spoke in a voice that sounded like poetry, was forever impatient with her hair. She smiled when there was no reason for it, and her thoughts were years ahead of her speech, leaving him in ignorance and delighted confusion until she shared her musings.

A woman who suited him more than any other.

He raised her hand and kissed her knuckles. There was a scrape on her left thumb. "How did you do this?" he asked.

"Cutting the cake." She stared ruefully at the small wound.

"It looked like a very good cake."

"Luck was on my side. It's the first time I've baked one that didn't fall."

"Perhaps it was because of the midsummer dew," he teased.

"More like it was all the whiskey I used to soak it in as it aged," she said, smiling back at him. "Between it, and the raisins, nuts, and fruits, there wasn't much cake to taste. But what was there seemed to please the elders."

She tilted her head and surveyed him.

"Are you sorry you're not an earl, instead of your brother?"

"Where did that question come from?" he asked, amused.

"Because you look like a prince," she said, her gaze not veering from him.

He smiled at her words. "I wouldn't take the position. I think the only reason that Alisdair agreed to be Earl of Sherbourne was in order to rebuild Gilmuir. The undertaking will cost a fortune."

"Do you think there was once a house on the abbey land? A house as old as Gilmuir with memories of its own, where people laughed and loved?"

"Before the monks arrived and imposed a cloistered silence?"

"For some reason I have difficulty seeing Scottish monks as severe in their religion," she admitted with a smile. "I think they probably wore kilts and sipped whiskey between prayers."

"We Scots do everything to excess. I doubt we were any different in religious devotion. Unfortunately, I can envision more austerity than high spirits."

"Do you think you will be able to expunge their memory, then? Replace it with something happier?"

If he did, another ghost would take their place. A lass with a gray-eyed glance and a teasing smile.

Perhaps it would be better if he left this place entirely, found some other corner of Scotland to call his own. But as Gilmuir called to Alisdair, Ayleshire called to him. Its history was fascinating and its people warm and open and welcoming.

"Perhaps that is the magic of Ayleshire after all," he said.

"That it can grow and transform itself while never losing its past."

"You do the same, James," she said. "Changing from sea captain to builder to landowner."

Her smile was too tempting, almost inviting a kiss. But there were other people around them. He caught sight of Rory and Abigail, each smiling at the other as they danced.

"Will you come with me, to bless my land?" he asked, picking up her hand and bestowing a kiss on it. There, a gesture that he could make in public.

"It would be an improvident act on my part." She allowed her hand to linger in his, her fingers to entwine with his. Neither of them was behaving with strict propriety. He wanted time alone with her.

"Will you come?" he asked again. "Improvident or not?"

She nodded.

They were the loveliest couple, Susanna thought, watching as James kissed Riona's hand. Riona's face was warmed by a blush, and James's bruises had faded completely.

She should have interrupted, perhaps, but she couldn't begrudge her daughter this night. There would be time ahead for her to be as proper as a matron. Perhaps memories of this time would make marriage to Harold palatable.

"You're looking lovely tonight," a voice said. Susanna turned to find herself face-to-face with Ned. His appearance still disturbed her. Who would have thought that beneath that white-bearded exterior lay a handsome man?

Or one who knew her quite so well?

How horrible to recall all those moments when she'd confided in him, told him things she'd never divulged to a soul, only because she thought of him as an uncle.

"Why do you wear that ridiculous beard?" she asked, annoyed. "To make everyone think you're so much older?"

"Everyone in Ayleshire knows my age. It's only those new to the village who make assumptions."

"Then why do they call you Old Ned?" She was unaccountably irritated at the man. Yet, at the same time, she couldn't help but recall those nights when he'd worked on the ledgers in the library and she'd sat on the other side of the room, both of them in perfect accord.

"To separate me from the gardener's boy. Or didn't you know his name was Ned, too?"

His grin was unsettling. She hadn't known, of course, which was why the man was so maddening.

"When did you lose your wife?"

"About the time you lost your husband," he said.

"I wish I'd known you were not as ancient as you appeared."

"Would it have made a difference to the way you treated me?"

She regarded him steadily, but didn't answer him. What would he have said to her confession? She might have flirted more if she'd known he was her age, or taken more care with her appearance?

"Was it a happy marriage, Ned?"

"It was," he answered. "As yours was."

"How very much you know about me," she murmured. "While I need to learn a great deal more about you."

"Shall we begin now?" he asked. "I've got one good arm, and that'll have to do. Will you dance with me?"

He opened up his arms, nodding at the dance floor.

She smiled, placed her hand on his, and accompanied him.

Chapter 27

❧❧❦

Moonlight streamed down on the two of them as they made their way to his land.

Riona sat in front of him, her legs to his left. His arms extended around her, holding the reins in front. Her hand brushed against his, and he turned his palm so that their fingers meshed.

He threw down the torch, and it sputtered, flared, then was extinguished. In the darkness, he slid from the horse, reached up and helped her dismount.

Even in the faint light from the bonfire, he was quite the most beautiful man she had ever seen. Moonlight made him a statue, rendered him a god in shadow.

"Tell me about Harold," he said. "How did you choose him for a husband?"

"What did he tell you?"

"It doesn't matter what he told me," he said. "It's what you have to say that I care about."

She stared it him quizzically, but he turned away, striding toward the bonfire, and dismissing the two boys who still tended it. When he returned, there was enough light to see the fixed expression on his face.

"What did he say to you?" she repeated.

"He said that you were to wed to spare your reputation. Is that true?"

"Is that what you've been thinking? That I've been the wanton with more than just you? You know that's not true, James MacRae." He couldn't be jealous, not James.

"Why would you marry someone like him?"

He took her hand in his and studied it.

Hesitantly at first, and then with greater resolve, she told him the story of that night in Edinburgh. "It was my own foolishness, James. Harold told me that Maureen needed me, and I was silly enough to believe him. I followed him into the garden."

She withdrew her hand.

"Is it that strange that I haven't a care for my reputation with you? I wish some old biddy like Mrs. Parker would declare me ruined, and I would be so happily."

"Is that what happened?"

"Something similar." She decided that it wouldn't be prudent to mention that Harold had been too arduous in his attentions. "Harold pointed out that my reputation would be in ruins if I didn't marry him."

"The man threatened you?" he asked carefully.

"It wasn't for my sake that I cared," she said, "but for Maureen's. Samuel comes from a very strict family, and any hopes of her betrothal would have been ruined if they'd learned of any scandal."

"Yet he's still not offered for her."

"No, but he seems devoted to her."

He caught her hand again, bent to press a kiss on her knuckles.

"If he truly loved Maureen, nothing would stop him. Not family, not reputation. Nothing."

She pulled her hand free and walked a few feet away.

"There is all manner of love, James."

"No, there isn't." He went to her side, and gently turned her until she faced him. "No, there isn't," he repeated. "Love doesn't demand sacrifice, Riona, or that those who feel it give up their family, status, or honor. Love enriches; it doesn't demean."

She smiled. How clear his words; it was a pity people did not always act in such clear-cut ways.

"I can't dictate the actions of others, James. I cannot control what Samuel does or how he behaves. All I know is that my family is depending on me. You should understand. I've heard you speak of your own brothers with fondness. You would do the same."

"Would I?" His smile was crooked. "I think Harold Mc-Dougal should be shot. I should have arranged it when I was in Edinburgh."

"You wouldn't," she said, horrified at his comment.

"No," he said, tipping his head back and staring up at the sky. "No, I wouldn't." But it seemed to her that his voice held a tinge of regret. "But I want to, Riona. Merciful God, I want to."

She didn't want to waste these moments talking about Harold. The fact that James had gone to Edinburgh still surprised her. He'd done that for her.

Instead of saying anything further, she came to him and

placed a hand on his chest. A connection she desperately needed.

Her breasts, pressing against his chest, seemed to know the contour of his muscles. Her body seemed to open and warm, heating as his hips moved against her.

He was going to kiss her and she was going to lose her senses. Just as she thought, her mind went flying to a place of midnight blue. Even the moon seemed too bright behind her eyelids. Then, there was only the taste of his lips and the slow, heated invasion of his tongue.

He ended the kiss, thinking that he'd never been so quickly enchanted as he was when kissing Riona.

He shouldn't have been able to feel her hand through the material of his shirt, vest, and jacket, but he did. He knew the wonder her fingers could perform on his body. He closed his eyes for moments and savored the touch, knowing it would be the last time that she would do so. Or he would let her.

He watched as Riona sat on an overturned pediment, her gown billowing around the stone. Slowly, he leaned over, kissed her lightly once, then again as her smile faded.

There had never been a time when he'd withheld himself from her. From the beginning, he'd spoken his mind and allowed her into previously unguarded places. But on this night, filled with moonlight and shadow, need and impatience, James felt even more vulnerable. As if loving her had made him defenseless.

If she were ill, he would be concerned, and if she were hurt, he'd be angered. Her happiness would enliven him, her humor amuse him. He would never see the world totally through his own eyes again, but also through hers.

Did love open a hole in his soul?

James would never forget the sight of her sitting there in the moonlight, smiling gently at him. He kissed her again and she sighed, opening her mouth to him.

A temptation beyond any that he'd ever been given.

He traced the curve of shoulder to elbow to wrist. How lovely her arms were. How beautiful each separate part of her.

She flattened her hand on his chest, splaying her fingers as if to measure him.

"Be pagan with me, Riona." The words might have been written with his pen, so easily did they come to his mind.

"I am," she said breathlessly. "Haven't I always been?"

Could he bind her to him with passion? Would she stay with him if he ensnared her with desire?

"Close your eyes and tell me what you see," he suddenly said.

"Darkness," she responded, smiling.

He knew that was not quite the truth. People who are quick and intelligent are always thinking, even in the moments before sleep. The mind furnished the eyes with memories or imagination.

He placed his hand over her closed eyelids, feeling the delicate sweep of her lashes against his palm.

"What do you see?"

"Your face," she said after a moment. "I can still see your face."

"Can you? How do I appear to you?"

"You're smiling. Teasing me with kisses."

He pulled her up, began unfastening her laces.

"Now you're undressing me." She opened her eyes. "Is this wise, James?"

"No," he said flatly. "But, then, I've never been wise where you're concerned."

She placed one hand on his chest, the other cupped his jaw. She was alabaster and shadow in the moonlight, her smile enigmatic. Or perhaps only sad.

Closing her eyes again, she continued with their game. "You're very serious now. You have a habit of frowning when you're concentrating. You hold your mouth just so, as if you're not quite certain whether to be irritated, angry, or amused."

His fingers gripped the hem of her gown, pulling it upward. The heels of his hands slid over smooth, sleek thighs to flaring hips, a curving waist, plump breasts, and rounded shoulders. He wanted to know her with such familiarity that he could curve his fingers around a wrist, an ankle, a knee and recognize her from a hundred, a thousand other women.

The gown was finally free from her left arm and he gently extricated her hand, placing a kiss to her fingertips. Then her right hand, where the cut she'd received serving the elders her cake garnered a tender salute.

"Do you know what I see?"

"No."

There had been no fear in her voice earlier, but now there was caution.

"I see a woman graced by moonlight. Whose skin is bathed white and whose auburn hair looks black in the darkness. She has eyes the color of stormy skies and a mouth that dances with words and smiles with amusement but rarely with anger."

"She sounds like a paragon, this woman. A very stiff and proper person."

"Not at all," he corrected, smiling. "On more than one occasion I suspect she would have liked to fly into a temper, stamp her foot, and make a scene, but she didn't. Instead, she simply pointed her chin in the air and stared at me with cloudy eyes."

"I never did."

"Riona," he gently chastised.

"Very well," she said, smiling softly. "Perhaps once or twice."

"This woman has a will of iron, did I tell you that?"

She shook her head from side to side.

"And a very strong character," he added, placing a gentle kiss upon her bared shoulder. "One that I admire."

"Do you?"

"Oh yes," he answered. "She has a kind heart, I've noticed. She treats each person the same and never seems to favor one above the other.

"She might have known what it was like to have been poor at one time in her life, and consequently realized that character has nothing to do with wealth.

"Perhaps," he said, "in addition to her heart, she has a facile mind. One that questions more than it accepts."

"She sounds like a difficult woman."

"Not difficult, but beautiful."

She said nothing in return for that compliment. He smiled at this sign of her reticence. He'd not often caught Riona without a word to say.

"She has lovely features and a lush figure."

"Do you think so?" she asked faintly, as if she weren't standing before him naked but for moonlight. "I was told that a gentleman never comments upon a woman's form."

"Perhaps gentlemen do not," he said, delighted with her. "But this man will."

He bent, placing a kiss to her temple. His fingers trailed a pattern around her ear, wondering why he had never noticed that such a useful organ might also be a pretty one.

"Tell me what you hear," he whispered.

A Highland summer pressed against them, the night heavy with the heat of the day. Somewhere, a bird called to its mate in a low and forlorn summons. The wind, once mischievous and playful, had matured. Now gusts echoed through the arches of the lone abbey wall, stirring the tall grasses with invisible fingers. Above them, a full moon was suddenly trapped in a filmy gauze of clouds.

He'd never known a night as enchanted.

"I can't hear anything."

"Then listen." A moment later he spoke again. "What do you hear?"

"The villagers are singing," she said, smiling.

He lowered his head, kissed her lightly in reward.

Her smile broadened as if she had reasoned out his game.

"I hear the last of the bonfire. The wood is nearly gone, but it still makes a sputtering sound."

Another kiss.

"The waterfall," she said, amazed. "I can hear the falls from here."

He reached down and began to unwind the plait of her hair. Only when her braids were loosened, and her hair tumbling over her shoulders, did he speak again.

"I visited the falls the other day," he said. "A place to reflect. I know now why it's your favorite place at Tyemorn."

"Did you hear the voice of God?" she asked softly.

He shook his head. "If He spoke, I wasn't listening. But are you? What else do you hear?"

She tilted her head, a smile curving her lips. "Your breathing. I can hear you breathe." She placed her hand flat on his chest. "You sound as if you've been running, James."

He smiled.

The silence between them was complete, not awkward as much as aware.

He bent and lowered his head, kissing her between her breasts. His thumbs gently pressed against each impudent nipple, his mouth against her warm skin. She seemed to taste of the night itself, of fertile fields and hedges, flowers blooming in secret places.

"You are so beautiful," he murmured, his command of the language departing him. In its place was a cavernous space filled with longing. How did he convey that to her? How did he tell her how much this moment meant to him? How much she meant to him?

She was a goddess of the moon, a silvery-blue washed creature that he had conjured up from imagination, lust, and desperate desire.

"You are so beautiful," he repeated, impatient with himself. The words were not the ones he'd wished to use. They were lacking, falling short of all he felt. But nothing rushed in to take their place, and in the end, he lost the ability to speak at all.

He wanted her breath against his lips and his name in her mouth.

As she stood there, chin tilted up at him, James realized that she was the essence of all that he wanted in a woman. Not because of her beauty or even because she was articulate, witty, and intelligent.

All his life he'd been surrounded by love, from his parents and his brothers. He'd explored the world, becoming used to those patches of solitary time, yet never becoming accustomed to solitude. Something had been missing from his life, and until now he hadn't known what it was.

A peace that he knew only she could give, answers to his curiosity, an end to the loneliness he'd felt during the past years.

This was the woman his spirit craved, who lived in his mind when she was apart from him. Who expanded his heart when she joined him. This was the woman who completed him in ways that he had never imagined. But then, he had never thought himself lacking.

He stroked one finger across a gently curving breast to a nipple. She closed her eyes slowly, then opened them again when he feared she would hide her reaction from him. Where once her gray eyes had been stormy, in the moonlight they were deeply mysterious and enchanting.

Bending his head, he took a nipple into his mouth, then breathed upon it, giving her the sensation of both chill and warmth. She shivered beneath his ministrations, encouraging him to continue.

He touched her breasts, and they puckered and tightened as if accustomed to the sensation he offered. He placed a kiss on her stomach and the muscles there fluttered, as if anticipating more to come.

Slowly, he lowered her to the ground, not far from where they'd lain before.

His fingers seemed to know her, retaining memory in their callused tips of intimate touches. The underside of her breasts, the front of her ankle, the arch of her foot, the back of her neck. Soft, swollen folds that ached when he kissed her and throbbed now at the silken stroke of one delicate finger.

His kisses were candies dropped upon her tongue, one by one. She grew to anticipate their delight and then simply became part of them, her breath and body growing heated.

How many hours did he touch her? How many enchanting minutes did he spend tasting her skin and brushing his warm lips across her breasts? How many times did he kiss her? Too many to count and not enough.

He moved over her, all warmth and strength. Gently, he widened her thighs.

"Are you very experienced, James?"

He drew back and framed her face with his hands as he stared at her wordlessly. Finally, he spoke. "Why would you ask that, Riona? Why now?"

She closed her eyes against his gentle inspection.

"I wish I knew more," she said, opening her eyes. "I wish I could please you."

He looked at her quizzically as if he heard more than the words she spoke, discerned the near desperate love she felt for him.

"I don't want you to be anything more than who you are, Riona," he said tenderly. "Just to be you. That is pleasure enough."

He entered her then and she was overpowered by the sensation. Wordlessly, he slid from her, then returned, the slow undulation of her hips beginning as if by magic or sorcery.

Her hands were on his shoulders, her fingers curving to grip him with her nails. Her lips were clamped over a soft moan, but when he kissed her, she heatedly returned it. The feeling grew within her until it was more powerful than reason or reputation, graying her vision and flooding her body with light. A siren's call to bliss that she couldn't help but obey.

Hours, or minutes, later, they dressed again, neither speaking amid the tasks of tucking, lacing, braiding. Yet the mood between them had changed subtly. Neither joyful nor condemnatory, rather it had become solemn, as if the darkness around them had colored their thoughts.

But Riona didn't speak and neither did James, for which she was profoundly grateful. What could she have said to him?

Stay with me and be my lover. This shall be our trysting place. Ours alone.

Not a role a man like James would accept. Not a road she should travel.

"It's late," she finally said.

He nodded, agreeing wordlessly.

He retrieved his horse, and they descended the path to the Witch's Well and beyond, to Tyemorn Manor.

"We never blessed your land."

"Yes, we did," he said, and they exchanged a look. She was the first to glance away.

The rest of the journey was made in silence, both of them walking with his horse trailing behind. From time to time their hands would brush, and cling, then part. Once, he pushed a tendril of hair back from her face and she brushed at his jacket sleeve to remove a blade of grass.

Back at the house she waited until he'd removed the saddle from his horse and settled it for the night before walking in companionable silence to the rear of the house.

They entered by the kitchen door to find that Abigail and Polly had returned before them. Both women were still dressed in their finery, and each of them was staring down into a deep bowl of wine where two blocks of charred wood rested.

"I didn't think you would believe in that custom, Polly," Riona teased. "I thought you said that it would take a rare man to coax you into matrimony again."

"It would at that," Polly agreed, retrieving her block from the wine and placing it on a stack of old toweling to drain. "But I see no reason not to be prepared just in case it happens."

At James's look, Riona explained. "The wood comes from one of the bonfires," she said.

"In the morning," Polly added, "we'll break the wood open and the color inside will be the shade of our true love's hair."

Abigail fished out her block and stood staring at it, smiling.

"Would you like to try, Riona?"

She shook her head. What was the use? The shade of her true love's hair would be black, his eyes would be blue, and he would be the most handsome man she'd ever seen.

But he wouldn't be the man she'd marry.

Chapter 28

"You look so beautiful, Riona," Maureen said, an expression of awe on her face.

"Indeed she does, my dearest," Susanna replied from a similar seated position. "When you wed, Maureen, we shall have a dress as lovely made for you."

Two seamstresses knelt on the floor, waiting for instructions. It was the final fitting of the dress and it fit perfectly, even if the dressmaker frowned and ordered everyone about with an insistence reminiscent of Mrs. Parker. Riona fingered the pale blue garment at the throat. The high neck of the gown felt as if it were choking her.

"Please do not move, Miss McKinsey," the seamstress said. "If you do, we shall just have to take longer at this task."

Obediently, Riona dropped her hands to her sides, staring through the parlor window. Beyond was the expanse of lawn and the path leading to the village. Still farther was the road that led to Edinburgh. Or Inverness. South to England, north to Gilmuir. She was not, however, inclined to flee. Only in her imagination could she give rein to such wicked thoughts of stepping down from the small pedestal, grabbing her skirts in her fists, and racing from the room. Any destination as long as she was no longer here, poked and prodded and pushed into the role of an Edinburgh wife.

No more waking at dawn. No more standing on the hill and watching as the sun crept shyly over the horizon. No more greeting the day with excitement and enthusiasm and a huge swelling feeling of anticipation.

Her life had come full circle, and once more she would be a city woman, expected to be but one of a thousand proper wives. Expected to dance and to hold polite conversation while hiding her boredom. Perhaps she would entertain on a modest scale, although she would be more comfortable birthing a calf than acting as hostess.

If she were wise, she'd consider marriage to Harold an adventure, something akin to piracy. She was as little suited for that profession as she was for being a wife.

Would he waste her money? She might well find herself back here in time, dependent on her mother's charity to survive. If that were the case, she would convince Harold to become a farmer and instruct him as she had another man.

No. She would not think of James, and certainly would not voluntarily recall those moments of lessons given in such amusement. The first time he'd milked a cow, or helped in the weeding. In fact, it would be better if she did not remember him at all, pretending that memories of him did not cling to every separate room or spot at Tyemorn.

Recollections of Lethson night stood out. Images of James, limned by moonlight, flashed into her mind. Her fingers curved as if to touch a shoulder, smooth down a thigh, hold his erection cradled in her hand.

Her mother stood, addressing the seamstress with a question.

"Whatever are you thinking, Riona?" Maureen asked her.

Riona blinked at her sister.

"You have the most unholy look of glee on your face."

Riona motioned to Maureen, who leaned forward.

"Did you ever wonder what Captain Hastings looks like without his clothes?" she whispered.

Her sister blinked slowly, her expression changing to incredulity. "Is that what you were thinking?"

She nodded. "Do you never think of it?"

Maureen stared down at her interlocked fingers. "I like the feel of Samuel's arm beneath his sleeve," Maureen confessed.

Riona eyed her sister with impatience. That wasn't exactly what she meant.

"Are you wondering about Harold?"

For a horrified moment, Riona tried to envision Harold without his clothing, but the image would not come to her. Yet it was all too easy to recall James. Perhaps Mrs. Parker was correct after all and she was hopelessly wanton.

Maureen was looking at her strangely, and Riona hurried to reassure her. "I'm going to be a bride," she said. "Of course I would think such things."

Her sister looked doubtful, but she was silenced now that the seamstress was returning to her side.

Riona was made to lift her arms, round her shoulders, all to allow the seamstress to inspect her creation. The boredom of the fitting was momentary and barely noticeable, however, in the wake of her thoughts.

Pity was an emotion to be spent on those more unfortunate than she. The lame war veteran, the mother who cradles a dying child, a young boy with the pox. A hundred examples of worthwhile candidates, two in her own family. Her mother, for example, losing the husband she dearly loved and being told the story of his loss at sea nearly a year after it happened. Or Polly with her daughter, lost to her since she'd emigrated.

She wasn't an object of pity, for all that her future wasn't what she wished.

Suddenly, she heard James's footsteps in the hall. Why didn't the other women in the room seem to note his approach? Riona froze, waiting, her breath trapped in her chest as he entered the room.

Even plainly attired as he was during the day, in his dark breeches and white shirt, he had an almost commanding appearance. Yet there was more to him than his attractiveness, more than simple physical beauty. He was a man to come to in need or lack. A leader, someone to inspire confidence and hope. Old Ned and the other men of Tyemorn had nothing but praise for him.

He had suggested that the irrigation channels be cut deeper, and the main sluice emerging from the River Wye dug at a different angle. The upper pasture had been left as grazing land for the cattle, and sheep moved to a different location. He and Ned had met with the other villagers, and they'd agreed to plant oats in twice as many fields next year. For a man who had known little of farming before coming to Tyemorn, he'd learned much.

Was it being a ship's captain that gave him such an aura of power? Or was it the man himself, beneath all his roles?

"Forgive me," he said, bowing and taking a step out of the room.

"Not at all," Susanna said, standing. She went to the doorway and, taking his hand between both of hers, drew him back into the room. "Will Riona not be the loveliest bride?" The question gave him permission to turn his attention to her.

Look away, she told him silently as he regarded her. *Look away and I will pretend not to see you, either. So that the thought of you is not placed on the inside of my eyelids and in my heart as I take my vows.*

He held his thoughts inside most times, making her wonder at them. Some were transparent and could be divined by the curve of his lips. Some were deeper still, as if his studied expression was deliberate in order to hide his opinions.

She could not fault him for his silence, because she felt the same caution with her speech. With James, words could not be taken back. A casual rejoinder could not be erased with a smile. She could not easily tease him as Maureen did. Each sentence seemed important, each separate voiced thought mattered.

A look stretched between them, and she wondered if all other voices faded away for him as they did for her. She no longer heard her mother's voluble chatter or the seamstress's disapproval or Maureen's comments. She heard nothing, and in that strange and silent tunnel that stretched between them she spoke, finally, of what was in her heart.

Forgive me.

Forgive me for being foolish before I met you. Forgive me for being rash before you came into my life. Forgive me, if you will, for seeing the hurt on my sister's face and wishing her happiness more than my own. If I had known that you were to come, I would have been more cautious. But what is done is done.

But words didn't flow between them, only a silence that grew larger and larger as neither spoke.

Abruptly, he was turning on his heel with military precision, gone from the room without a word to anyone.

Pressing her hand against her waist, Riona forced herself to breathe.

Susanna gazed after him before turning and glancing at Riona.

"Are you finished?" she asked the seamstress with uncharacteristic abruptness. When the other woman nodded, she waved her hand in the air in an almost rude gesture of dismissal.

They began to remove her dress, Riona actively helping them. More than once she looked in the direction of the doorway. Once attired in her simple day dress, she hurriedly left the room. A moment later the seamstress and her helpers departed Tyemorn Manor.

Susanna moved to pick up Riona's wedding dress, smoothing her hand over the pale blue silk. She frowned at the mess the seamstress and her helpers had made.

"Harold McDougal is a grasping lout, and if your sister had no funds at all, he would be looking for another plump pigeon," she said angrily.

Maureen looked a little surprised at her vehemence.

"She can't marry Harold. You saw that yourself, Maureen."

"But she's betrothed to him."

Susanna nodded. "Then I suggest we both start praying for a miracle."

Chapter 29

R iona had escaped to the village church. In a matter of days, her wedding would be held here.

"Dear St. Margaret," Riona began softly, well aware that she was committing a sin in beseeching a saint here in this lovely, shadowed church where people did not believe in such things. The altar, dappled by the muted colors from the stained-glass window, had been transformed to a communion table. If there had once been statues in this place, they'd long been discarded, leaving an empty, cavernous space for only God to fill.

Riona wondered how many other women before her had considered St. Margaret a patron of sorts. The woman who had found refuge in Scotland a thousand years earlier had been welcomed by the man who would become her husband. A match made due to power? Or the heart?

Clasping her hands in front of her, she bowed her head.

Dear St. Margaret, she began again, this time silently. *I need some intercession, please. God has not seen fit to answer my prayers, and a word from you would not be amiss, I think. I have made mistakes in my life, not all of which I have confessed, but you and I know that God sees all. So I cannot claim purity in all my deeds and thoughts. In fact, I have sinned, and enjoyed it.*

No answer was forthcoming. St. Margaret did not whisper to her, but thunder rumbled overhead, as if the approaching storm was the voice of a stern and admonishing deity. She had a sudden sinking feeling that perhaps God was displeased that she'd gone to St. Margaret instead of directly to Him.

Please, take the vision of James from me, so that I might not remember him. I want not to recall the day we loved, or his smile, or any of his kisses. Or think of all those times we've met and talked. Or if he must remain in my heart, God, then let me see him as only a friend, a dear and valuable and cherished acquaintance. Do not let me wonder what my life might have been under different circumstances.

Something was wrong with her chest because it felt so tight that she could barely breathe. There must be something in the air, some dust or pollen from the flowering plants. That was the only reason her eyes felt gritty and near to tears.

She opened her eyes, her gaze fixed on the stone floor, pocked in spots and worn smooth in others by generations of worshippers. Had any of them prayed as selfishly as she?

Leaning forward, she lowered her forehead to rest against the backs of her hands. For a long time she simply sat there, waiting for the peace of the sanctuary to heal her. But peace couldn't enter where tumult lived, words she'd once heard the pastor speak. Then how did she quiet her mind? Become resigned to the future?

She hoped James would be leaving soon. She didn't want him there for her wedding. The sharing of vows was a sacred thing. She could not stand before the communion table and say the words binding her to Harold when he was in the room.

Do I wish this man for my husband? No. Do I want to bind my life to his? No. Will I promise to be a good wife? Yes, but only reluctantly. She would not lie to God.

Agreeing to marry Harold had been a necessity, but not a disaster, all the same. Granted, if he'd not threatened ruin she would never have considered his suit, but there wasn't anyone else she'd wanted to have as husband among all the men she'd met. No one to tempt her humor or her curiosity. No one to impress her with his judgment, fairness, and strength.

She'd found him too late.

Riona heard a sound, an intrusion in this world of silence, and sat up straight. Glancing behind her, she saw James. Did God have a sense of humor that He would send her the very person she did not wish to see?

"I didn't mean to disturb your prayers."

Riona stood, arranging her skirts. At least she hadn't given in to tears. There would be no sign of weeping to explain away. "Did you follow me here?"

"Yes." Was she to receive no more an explanation than that? A moment later, he spoke again. "You left the house very quickly. I was concerned." There, too much of an explanation. He shouldn't be so kind.

If he had flaws, let her see them now. Let him be parsimonious to a fault, or uncaring for the poor, or cruel or hateful. Let him be arrogant and vain. Or let him be more like Harold.

She glanced at him, wondering if he knew what she felt.

But the expression on his face was guarded. Perhaps she should ask him how he masked his emotions so well, and do as he did.

"Sometimes I think I know why mankind creates churches. So that God can come and rest here. He can blow His breath and give life to this place, yet never needs to prove anything."

He smiled, an almost encouraging expression. Two small words were all she needed to speak, and he would accede to her demands. *Please leave.* But she didn't say them.

"Do you think God gets tired of the endless prayers He must hear?"

"I doubt He has the impatience of mortals," James said with a smile. "He is, after all, omnipotent."

"When I was a little girl, I believed that God only gave you a few prayers at birth. As if He said, Here, I bequeath you twenty prayers, Riona. If you waste those there are no more. Feel free to keep saying them, for devotion is a wondrous thing, but do not expect them to be answered."

"What if you were a greedy child? How unfortunate if you'd expended all your prayers in your youth and have nothing left."

She considered his remark. "Perhaps, in that case, a person could be the recipient of another's prayers. A mother's prayer that you are happy, for example. Perhaps you're even the answer to a prayer. A woman might pray for an end to loneliness, and a man without any prayers left finds himself happily married."

"Perhaps I have none left, according to your premise. I've prayed my way through enough typhoons and gales."

She smoothed her hand against the wooden pew, finding the wood warm to her touch. "But they must have been granted, James, else you would not be standing here." How adept she was becoming at hiding her emotions. A few moments earlier, she'd wanted to weep. Now she was discussing religion.

His smile grew broader. "You make God sound finite and prayers no more than wishes."

"Do we not use them as such?"

"Your pastor would not approve of your thoughts," he said.

She nodded. Not many people would. "The kirk holds that you must accept all that you are told without questioning the why of it."

"Perhaps they believe that freedom of thought is a dangerous thing."

"Sometimes that's the only freedom we have," she said, thinking of the choices she had in life. To marry. Or remain a burden to her mother.

"I once found it easy to be free," he said, surprising her with that declaration. Perhaps it was the church itself, a structure dedicated to worship and contemplation, that encouraged such candor. "You must be part of society in order to live by its rules. As the captain of a ship, I was free to choose no one's company but my own and my crew."

"Yet now you're no longer a ship's captain," she reminded him.

"Instead of the sea surrounding me, I'll have fields."

"Will you be as free, however?"

"A man's freedom is in his heart, Riona," he said softly.

A moment passed, silent and serene, marred only by the furious beat of her heart.

"You looked very beautiful in your wedding dress," he said unexpectedly.

A comment that had the power to halt her breath.

"Thank you." She stiffened her shoulders and pasted a smile on her face.

"Don't marry him."

She looked up, startled at his words. His expression had altered. Gone was the surface affability. His eyes hadn't left her, and now they seemed particularly intense. His mouth, that beautiful full mouth that doled out mind-numbing kisses, was thinned. His face was still, his features immobile. As if he had simply become frozen.

"You can't marry him. You're mine."

He took a few steps toward her, bending his head to speak against her temple. If someone had seen them, James would have been viewed as solicitous. Two worshippers, one standing, one seated in a pew beside the aisle.

But his words were wicked, salacious. "I know how you feel when I enter you, all hot and wet and welcoming. I know how your breasts feel against my palms. Each night I relive how you shuddered against me in your release. How can you think of giving yourself to anyone else?"

"James . . ." Dear God, she couldn't breathe.

"Come with me, Riona. Live with me on the abbey land. I'll build our home, and we'll be impervious to scandal or whispers. Let the biddies say what they will. We simply won't care."

"I can't." She lowered her head, closed her eyes. "Please do not ask it of me."

Nothing had changed. Nothing but her love for him.

"Do not marry him, Riona. Don't turn your back on happiness. Do not turn your back on me."

She stood, slapped both hands against his chest, and

shoved with all her might. He barely budged. "You don't understand," she said, her voice thick with tears. "It isn't just me. It's not just my happiness. It never has been."

Her voice seemed to carry, echo strangely across the church as if she'd shouted the words. A repudiation, but not because of honor or decency but rather due to guilt.

How could she deny Maureen the happiness she deserved by taking her own? Her sister had done nothing, was innocent in all this.

"I can't," she softly repeated. Her heart was breaking, and still he regarded her with those beautiful blue eyes.

"I'm leaving, then," he said. "Do not expect me to stay and see you wed. I've no stomach for it."

"When?" Wasn't it odd that she could still speak? Her heart had stopped as well as her breath, but her body didn't seem to know. How strange to feel so distant from herself.

"Today," he said. The word was too vague. She wanted to know in hours and minutes.

"You've bought the abbey land," she countered.

"I need to return to Gilmuir to tell Alisdair of my decision."

"But then you'll be coming back."

"Not until you're in Edinburgh."

"I'll think of you here," she said. Mild words that didn't begin to hint at what she truly felt. She would do more than think of him. He would forever be in her heart and in her mind.

Even now she ached, as if her body suffered for his absence, preparing for the long months and years to come.

"We haven't been the wisest people, have we, James?"

He didn't answer. His face was suddenly a mask; no

emotion shone in his eyes. He held himself so stiffly that she felt as if he'd disappeared and left only an effigy of himself behind.

"Would you change it?" he asked. "If you could go back and change my coming here, would you?"

"No," she said honestly and perhaps unwisely. The word thawed him. He smiled softly, charmingly, devastatingly. "I will always cherish the memory of these days. As long as I live, they will always be with me. Even if I were given a chance to remove them from my mind, I never could, James."

He turned on his heel and left her.

She watched him until he walked through the door of the sanctuary. Only then did she allow her tears to fall.

Chapter 30

In the library, James packed up his quills and ink, wrote a short note to Ned about ideas he'd had for the north pasture. Leaving Tyemorn Manor was more complicated than arriving here. There were details to oversee and things to be finished.

James looked out through the library window.

From there the view of Tyemorn was spectacular, bathed as it was with the golden light of a setting sun. Below him the northern pastures, green and yellow squares of land, lay like nature's quilt. A few birds flew overhead to give life to the panorama, or else it might have been a painting entitled *An Idyllic Day at Tyemorn Manor.*

The place had a sense of peace about it that James wished he could replicate in his mind. Sometimes, in the morning, he would saddle his horse and ride over the farms. More than once, he'd followed the trail back up to the abbey ruins and dismounted, surveying everything before him with a pride of ownership. Before coming to Ayleshire, he'd never understood what rooted a man to one place. Here he had knelt on the ground and buried his hands in the earth, helped to find a lost lamb, and cut trees in the forest. The bruises and cuts on his flesh were marks of what this land had done to him. Yet the growing crops were evidence of his influence on the land.

A life sailing the oceans left a man with weathered skin and watchful eyes. But as soon as a ship passed, the waves obliterated all trace of its passage, the sea unknowing and uncaring that men had once sailed there.

Susanna opened the door, peering inside with a smile. "Am I interrupting?"

"Only my dour thoughts," he answered honestly.

She slanted a look at him as she entered. "About what, exactly?"

"The thefts, for one. We both know the workers of Tyemorn Manor are honest and diligent."

Her cheeks appeared a little pink, but other than that Susanna didn't look the least bit chagrined. He smiled at the innocence of her expression, and she smiled back in perfect accord.

"So you discovered my little ruse," she said. She studied the floorboards intensely before looking back at him, as if gathering her courage. "But surely you don't regret your visit?"

He shook his head.

"Riona says you've bought the abbey ruins."

"Yes, and the pastures to the south of you."

She looked stunned, as if she'd no idea of his wealth. The trade he'd engaged in had profited both him and his crew. For years, he'd invested his earnings, and with few needs his fortune had grown.

"The time here has shown me that I have an affinity for the land, Susanna," he said in the silence. "I am looking forward to owning my own property."

She hesitated, and he wondered what else Riona had told her. A moment later that question was answered.

"You're leaving us, then, James?"

He nodded.

"So you'll come back and look down upon us from your fine place on the hill."

"Not for a few years," he said. "It will take that long to build my home there." He smiled, confiding in her a thought he'd had often in the past few days. "We've remained away from Scotland for thirty years, but now the MacRaes are doing their best to build it up again."

"When you return to Ayleshire, I hope you will do me the honor of staying here as my guest until your own home is finished."

"It would be better, Susanna," he said soberly, "if I made other arrangements."

He wouldn't be gone long from Ayleshire, but when he returned, Riona would be married and in Edinburgh. Memories of her, however, would remain with him. Everywhere he'd look, she would be there, as if she were a hundred women, all shadow and wraith, marking each place at Tyemorn and Ayleshire. He'd see her on the village road, smiling beneath an oak, straddling a furrow and laughing at something a companion had said. There again, tilting her head in an inquisitive look and offering advice on the line of the barn wall, or at night, when he could only see the outline of her form.

He was not a man given to yearning, and it made him impatient to feel this way. His forefathers had been reivers and plunderers and had taken pride in their thievery, seen as just and proper in a wilder and less civilized Scotland.

What would Riona say if he threw her over his saddle and raced with her across the fields and through the glens to a place where the mountains grew higher and starker? There would be no propriety in the place they'd live, no rules to break, only freedom.

He and Susanna shared a look, and he wondered if she suspected his thoughts.

"The only person who ever uses that desk is Ned," she said finally, "and he constantly grumbles the entire time he works on the ledgers."

"He's a fine steward for you, Susanna," he said, compelled to defend the older man.

"I know that well enough," she said. "He is a good man, and I have a great deal of admiration for all that he accomplishes. However, he manages to make himself rather bothersome with his attitude. We engage in a game of pull and tug, James. I fuss at him, and he ignores me. Together we will see each other through well enough. We are both as stubborn as donkeys."

"Fergus never mentioned that particular character trait of yours," he said, amused.

"Perhaps Fergus didn't know," she said surprisingly. "For the longest time, I believed that perseverance was not a feminine trait. I now believe otherwise."

"I have met few females without it," he replied.

She said nothing, only placed both her hands on the arms of the chair, surveying him with an intense and almost regal look. "I will be very sorry to see you go. You have been a great help to me. I shall communicate as much to Fergus."

"It isn't necessary," he said kindly. "Anything I did was done because I wished to do it, not because I felt obligated to do so."

"I know that, which makes it doubly difficult to see you leave."

"I appreciate your hospitality," he said, looking around the library. "And the use of this room in addition to every one of your generosities."

She surveyed the chamber, her gaze returning to rest on him. "Few people ever come in here. Riona told me once that she wanted to read all the volumes, but it's Maureen who has more time for reading."

He'd often seen her in the garden or in the parlor with a book. She did not, evidently, choose to occupy herself as Riona did. Susanna's wealth made her indolence possible. Or perhaps, he amended silently, it was not so much indolence as it was aptitude. He couldn't envision Maureen directing the flow of water in the sluice, or hopping from row to row over the seedlings.

"As for myself," Susanna was saying now, "I find the place almost sad," she said, surveying the bookcases lining the walls. "Sometimes I feel as if all the previous owners of the manor congregate here at night to marvel at the changes of the present day." She glanced at him again. "Perhaps they don't entirely approve of me, a seaman's widow made rich by one of their own."

"They would if they knew you," he said, surprised at her whimsy. In a lot of ways, Riona was very much like her. A core of sentimentality overlaid by a surface of practicality.

"Did you know that this place was originally built by a war hero?"

"Is he the one who had the tower erected?"

"The better to be on guard for his enemies? Perhaps he was, I don't know." Standing, she smiled at him once again. "Perhaps I, too, should have a goal of reading all these books. I have not had the time before, but once my girls are married off I shall have plenty of opportunity."

He stood also, coming around the desk. She surprised him by embracing him in a quick hug. "I do so wish you'd stay with us, James," she said, a further surprise. "Are you so impatient to be about your own life?"

He only smiled, unable to tell her that he couldn't stay and watch Riona wed another man.

Susanna nodded and went to the door, turning as she grabbed the latch. "I bless the day Fergus sent you to us. I hope you know that. You will always be a friend." She hesitated, glanced at her hand, then back at him.

"I feel the same, Susanna."

He sat again at her departure, staring out at the view again, trying to envision what his life would be like after Riona's marriage. Tyemorn Manor wouldn't be the same without her. Even Ayleshire would be stripped of some of its charm.

He picked up the account ledger where it rested in the center of the desk, next to his journal. Opening the aged leather binder at random, he studied the figures. A sum for etched goblets purchased in Inverness, another amount paid to the tanners for a hide dyed to match an old chair. Still another, larger expenditure for the annual clothing allowance for those employed at Tyemorn Manor. The estate was prosperous, Susanna was wealthy, and her daughters quite obviously heiresses.

Closing the ledger, he picked up his journal. Whereas another man might have chosen spirits, words were his form of escape. Between the leather covers of his journal he could express his thoughts as he could to no one else.

Perhaps it would be wiser not to write in it; the revelations might prove to be too difficult to read in the future. He might happen upon an entry that chronicled all his emotions and wonder at the man he'd been. Once, his journal had been used to impart those memories of places he had once seen and might never visit again. Lately, however, the passages had been a recitation of his regrets and a word painting of a woman he could never have.

He opened the journal at random, and read what he'd written earlier.

I cannot live comfortably with thoughts of what might have been. Mine is not the nature simply to accept. Even now I chafe at a future given to me by circumstance and not one of my own making.

There are times when I seek her out during the day, simply to see her and refresh my eyes with the sight of her. She will be smiling, and my own heart feels enlivened. On some occasions, I have seen her with a book, her hands curled protectively over the covers, the pages parted for her eyes. I am tempted to go to her in order to discuss the book's contents or her thoughts on it. But wisdom tells me to limit the hours I spend with her.

I find myself increasingly envious of Alisdair and his Iseabal. Now I am doubly grateful about my decision not to live at Gilmuir, knowing what I will forever miss. How do I live with this hollowness, as if I were missing a limb, like Fergus?

I shall build a house with her in mind. Direct the planting of an herb garden that she might have enjoyed. In the middle of it, at its most fragrant point, I shall install a bench where she might have sat in the sunny light of a bright spring day. My chamber will be large, with a broad fireplace in ebony marble.

He slammed the book shut. He was damned if he was going to allow her to marry Harold McDougal. Even if he had to make Maureen miserable in the process. A not entirely honorable thought, but his honor had been in tatters ever since meeting Riona.

Kiss her. Kiss her again and again. Until the night obliterated the sun and once again morning came. Kiss her until Harold went away along with any man who might look at her with favor. Kiss her until he shocked them all and scandalized the proper world. To hell with their rules and regulations. To damnation with their dictates and their mores.

He wanted her, more than anything in his life. She was his future and his past, and quite possibly his present. Give him a woman who changed her life out of loyalty, one who walked the fields as though she ruled the earth itself, and whose thoughts wandered along paths that fascinated him. Give him Riona and he was supremely happy.

Yet in a matter of days she would walk away from him. She would say the simple words that obligated her to another human being and become, for Harold McDougal's lifetime, his wife and helpmate.

He wondered if Fergus knew what a great and ironic gesture he had performed in sending him to this place.

In that instant, James knew what he had to do.

Reaching the new barn, he sent one of the stable boys after

Rory, waiting with barely leashed impatience until he arrived.

"Do you feel like traveling?"

"We're leaving for Gilmuir, then?" Rory asked, disappointment coloring his voice.

James wished his own courtship was as uncomplicated as his cabin boy's. "No," he said. "For Inverness."

"Inverness?" Rory asked, his crestfallen look changing to one of confusion.

It seemed to James, as he readied his mount, that he'd traveled throughout Scotland for one woman. Edinburgh and now Inverness. What was one more destination when his happiness was at stake?

"Are you certain you're feeling well enough?" he asked when he saw Rory limping toward the door.

Rory smiled, reassuring him. "I'll go and pack our things."

James nodded. If their errand proved successful, they'd be traveling all night. If not, he'd stay in Inverness, do those errands for Iseabal and Alisdair, and return to Gilmuir.

"Why are we going, then?" Rory asked, turning at the door.

James glanced over his shoulder at him. "We're going to kick some sense into an Englishman."

Chapter 31

Inverness, located on the shores of the Moray Firth, sat at the head of the Great Glen, and the mouth of the River Ness. The most populated town in the Highlands, Inverness had a long history, beginning with its origins as a Pictish capital in the sixth century.

The rounded Ben Wyvis in the distance commanded an impressive view of the countryside. But the challenging cliffs of Glen Affric warned the traveler not to think himself too comfortable. This was, after all, the Highlands of Scotland.

The remains of a castle, blown up by the Jacobites to prevent it from falling into the hands of the English, sat above the peaceful River Ness. The town proper was surrounded by mansions and fine houses, close enough to the city so that entertainments might be enjoyed, but far enough away that the noise and bustle wouldn't intrude on the pastoral beauty of their parklands and waterfalls.

James and Rory passed the clock tower, the remains of a large citadel built by Oliver Cromwell a hundred-plus years ago. At another time, James would have pointed out other sights to Rory, but he was in the mood for a confrontation, not conversation.

He asked the way of a shopkeeper and was directed to the barracks of the Fencible Regiment. There he dismounted, glancing at Rory as he did so. The young man wore a decided look of reluctance to enter an English encampment.

"You can stay here if you wish," he said.

Rory looked relieved. "I'd prefer it, sir, if you don't mind. I can't help but remember all those times that Alisdair and I challenged an English ship."

He should urge Rory to tell him about some of his shipboard adventures with his brother, James decided. He nodded, stifling his smile, and went inside.

Captain Hastings would be summoned, he was told by a young subaltern who looked younger than Rory. In the intervening moments, James strode up and down the corridor, thinking that one English fortress was not unlike another. They had a tendency to build similar structures in every outpost from India to the colonies. Such devotion to pattern was not necessarily a bad thing, but it revealed an underlying inability to accept change. No doubt why the English were now experiencing such difficulty with the American rebels.

A quarter of an hour later, he heard footsteps echoing on the cobbled floor. A tall blond man emerged from the shadows, attired in a bloodred uniform. Another irony of his life, that his happiness relied upon an Englishman.

"I am Samuel Hastings," the man said, halting in front of James. "You were asking for me?"

After he introduced himself, James extended his hand.

The other man took it in a warm and solid grip that reassured him somewhat.

"I understand that you know Maureen McKinsey," he said.

Samuel nodded. "I do. Is Maureen well?"

"Very well when I left her yesterday."

Another good sign that the man cared enough to ask about her. But James was done with tact. He was running out of time.

"Do you love the girl?"

Hastings didn't answer. Instead, he drew himself up, frowning at James.

"Is that any of your concern?"

"Or is your family more important than she is?"

Hastings's expression was becoming decidedly frosty.

"I think you'd better state your business with me, sir," he said in a formal, clipped tone.

So James did, in words that even an Englishman could understand.

Nothing could be worse, Susanna McKinsey thought. Everything that could possibly go wrong had done so.

Polly was ill with a cold; Cook had come down with some kind of fever. The wine she'd ordered had finally arrived, but half the bottles were vinegar. The ham she was planning on serving for the wedding supper had gone bad, and the chickens were refusing to lay any eggs.

Even Ned was being taciturn, more than usual. He had barely said five words to her since dancing with her on Lethson night. She had not been able to stop thinking about him, a bit of foolishness on her part. But she sincerely hoped that he kept his beard trimmed. As if she would ever be able to forget that youthful face.

It was enough to give her hives.

But the greatest disaster was the fact that it looked as if there was nothing to preclude Riona's marriage to the insufferable young man who sat in front of her in the parlor, drinking her whiskey appreciatively. He acted as though the bond of kinship had already been formed, and he was entitled to anything she owned.

There was no dust to be seen, and everything was arranged perfectly, as if Abigail had just finished cleaning the room. But she scanned the room just in case, taking in each detail. Better to concentrate on her housekeeping than her annoyance.

She couldn't fault Harold's appearance; he was very well dressed today without a speck of dirt about his person. He'd politely presented himself to her in an agreeable manner.

Pity that she'd disliked him from the moment they'd met.

"Another glass?" she asked, hiding her irritation behind a hostesslike smile.

"Thank you, no," he said. "But I would like to see Riona. I've not seen her for weeks, it seems."

Since Polly was feeling poorly, and Abigail was busy with the wedding supper preparations, she excused herself and went in search of Riona herself.

She found her daughter in her room, staring listlessly in the mirror.

Riona turned at her entrance. "I am practicing smiles," she said. "Which do you think looks more genuine?" She demonstrated a selection, and despite her resolve, tears came to Susanna's eyes.

Sorrow, however, would not make the situation better.

"Harold is asking for you," she said.

"Oh, has he arrived?"

"A few minutes ago. He is an impatient bridegroom, Riona."

"I would rather not see him until tomorrow," Riona said.

"You should at least greet him."

"Why?" Riona said. "I may practice smiles, Mother, but I refuse to pretend this marriage is my choice. I will see him tomorrow, isn't that soon enough?"

She had no words for Riona, no wisdom that would make the situation any better than it was. She knew quite well how her daughter felt about James, and experienced a pinch of guilt every time she thought of it. She had interfered, and look what had happened. Her daughter was miserable, and James was gone.

The only person in this entire situation who was happy was Harold McDougal.

She closed the door silently, thinking that her own marriage had been one of such joy that she could not imagine entering into a union with anyone she did not love. What a pity her daughter had to learn that lesson.

In the end, Riona went to dinner only because she decided it wasn't fair to inflict Harold on her mother and Maureen.

She sat opposite him, thinking that if the situation had been different, she would not have been displeased with her choice of bridegroom. He was of average height, and had a pleasant smile. His features were proportional and made for a pleasing countenance. He neither laughed too loudly nor was officious in his manner.

But he reminded her of the rind of a cheese that had gone bad. Outwardly, there was no sign of rot.

She couldn't forget that he had threatened her into marriage. But by his manner, one would think that theirs was a love match.

She watched him from beneath her lashes, uncaring if she made any further conversation. Let Maureen and her mother be polite to him. She had years in which to be so.

How was she supposed to let him touch her? Their wedding night would be a revelation to him, but she had no regrets. If she could not be married to the man of her dreams, at least she'd loved him.

"Ayleshire is a lovely little village," he said. "I have few duties in the country, and I find that I miss it from time to time."

"Perhaps you and Riona can be counted upon to visit us often," Susanna said, smiling pleasantly.

If they did, Riona thought, she would see the abbey ruins on the hill and know herself almost home. Perhaps she could even visit there, to witness the building of James's house. She might even see him, only a glimpse to last for the long months in Edinburgh.

"I doubt that will be possible," Harold said. "Business will keep me in Edinburgh, and Riona should not journey anywhere unaccompanied."

She exchanged a glance with her mother and then looked away. Now she was to be a prisoner, subject to her husband's whims.

Yet if James had made that remark, she would only have smiled fondly at him and thought him concerned for her well-being.

"Will your family be attending the wedding?" Maureen asked.

"Alas, they will not," Harold said. "My three sisters do not like to stray from our ancestral home, and Peter has business that keeps him occupied in the city."

"You have just the one brother?" Susanna asked.

"Just the one. But you will never lack for company, dear Riona," he said, glancing at her. "Not with all those sisters of mine."

Maureen looked at her and smiled.

A common joke between them. Riona would be happier with a field of flowers or a pasture filled with cattle than she would a group of women.

Perhaps if she spoke to him, and told him exactly what kind of wife she would be, he would finally relent. Give up this thought of marriage between them and seek another heiress, one with whom he might be more compatible.

The endless dinner finally done, they adjourned to the parlor. After a few moments of desultory conversation, Riona abruptly stood.

She glanced at her mother and Maureen. "If I may but have a few moments alone with Harold," she said.

Her mother nodded, standing and gesturing to Maureen. The double doors closed, leaving the two of them in silence but for the sputtering of the candles.

Harold remained seated on one of the sofas, looking at her complacently.

"I cannot be the kind of wife you wish," she said, the words spilling from her lips. "I cannot be acquiescent all the time, any more than I can be sweet and demure. I have more faults than attributes."

"I am sure we will do well together, regardless of your flaws, Riona."

"Will my money make everything acceptable, Harold?" she asked him impatiently. "I have no great talents. And although I like my needlework from time to time, I do not excel at it. I laugh at silly things and I become angry at the oddest circumstances. Groups of giggling females give me a headache, Harold, and I would rather be alone than irritated by my companions."

"I have felt the same when surrounded by my siblings," he said. "There, you see, a bond of commonality already." He stood and advanced on her.

She remained where she was, hands clasped together. At his approach, she clamped her lips together and regarded him stonily.

"Nothing you say or do will end this marriage, Riona. It didn't work when you sent that man to Edinburgh to beat me up, and it won't work now. If we do not suit, then I doubt it will matter to any significant degree. Regardless, we will be married tomorrow."

"What did you say?" She frowned at him, intent upon only a few words. "What man?"

His lips twisted in a grimace. "James MacRae. You deny you sent him to pummel me?"

"Did he?" The most outrageous amusement was stealing through her. A bit of the story James had neglected to mention.

Harold didn't answer her. Instead, he left the room, leaving her alone.

A noise at the window startled her. Sitting up, Maureen gripped the sheet and pulled it to her chin, staring at the shadow that suddenly appeared behind the filmy curtain. For a moment, she wanted to hide beneath the covers, feeling as she had as a child afraid of storms and the dark.

"Maureen?" A whisper. "Maureen?" Louder this time. She knew that voice.

Silently, she slipped from the bed, taking the candlestick with her. Standing at the side of the window, she peeked around the curtains.

"Samuel?"

Raising the window, she knelt, propping her elbows on the sill.

"What are you doing?"

"Obeying an order," he said brightly. "I'm coming to claim you."

"You are?"

"It has been pointed out to me that I've been lax as a suitor, my dear Maureen. Will you come away with me, and marry me in Gretna?"

"Tonight, Samuel?" she asked, wondering if she were dreaming.

"This very night."

"It sounds a bit impetuous, don't you think?"

"Or passionate," he said softly, smiling at her in a way that made her think of kissing him. "Will you?" He held out his hand. Without thought, she placed hers in his.

She began to smile, a feeling like lightness expanding from deep inside until even her toes tingled. "Yes," she said, pushing open the window. "Of course I will, Samuel."

Then she drew back. "Give me a moment to change."

After closing the curtains on a smile, Maureen turned and stared at her wardrobe. What should she wear?

There had been times, in the past, when she'd envied Riona. She seemed so much more alive. Riona had adventures. Even her marriage was done in high drama, with James leaving without a word. Not, however, after tonight.

She'd never thought that she would be eloping with Samuel, or that he would be so daring as to propose such a thing. A wild and wicked thing to do, and on the eve of Riona's wedding. But how could she refuse?

The clothes flew on as she laced herself and rolled up her stockings. Finally, she bent down to see herself in the mirror. A more thorough appraisal could be done if she took the time to light a candle, but she didn't want to waste the moments. She ran a brush over her hair, tucked it into a bun, and pressed her bonnet down over her head.

She was going to be married!

Pushing open the window, she escaped her room, feeling like a princess in a fairy tale off to meet a prince. Or better than that, Maureen thought, a giggle escaping her. She and Samuel were behaving like reivers of old.

He helped her from the window, embracing her before her feet touched the ground.

"This is so unlike you, Samuel," she said softly.

"Do you regret not having a wedding in the church, my love?"

"Not at all," she said softly, placing her palm on his cheek. "I am enchanted by your daring."

He led her to his horse, and helped her mount, and it was only then that she saw the other figure.

James stood in the shadow of the moonlight holding the reins of his mount. Behind him was Rory.

She understood in that instant, tears coming to her eyes. She raised her hand and he responded in kind, bidding them farewell. Samuel mounted and then they were off, following the road to Gretna Green like a highwayman and his bride.

Chapter 32

A wedding was a somber occasion, but nature had decided to gift the day with beauty. The afternoon sky
was a brilliant blue, the hills surrounding Ayleshire were an
emerald green. From the nearby trees came the sounds of
birds, blithely unaware that people congregated in the village
church to celebrate the union of one of their own to a stranger
from Edinburgh.

The day was marred by her mood, of course, one so dour
that Riona remained silent rather than betray her state of near
tears. Susanna had seemed the same, but Riona wasn't sure,
since her mother wouldn't meet her eyes as she bustled
around, attending to last-minute details.

She was dressed and ready, waiting only for her hat, a tiny
scrap of lace and flowers. A silly thing, almost frivolous, and
since she was not in the mood for frivolity, Riona decided
that she wouldn't wear it. Tossing it to the chair on the other

side of the room, she turned and surveyed herself in the mirror.

Her eyes looked bruised, the dark circles attesting to a night filled with troubled dreams. Her face was pale, her lips almost bloodless. Hardly the picture of an ecstatic bride.

Her hair was almost beyond hope. Abigail had used the curling tongs on it that morning, and the resultant frizz was a disaster. She could tuck it up into a bun and lace flowers through it. Or braid it into a coronet with a few ferns. Or she could leave it as it was and simply not care. She opted for the last course.

For the first time since he'd left, she was grateful for James's absence. She wouldn't be able to do her duty today if he'd been sitting in the congregation. How could she pass him on her way to the communion table?

Too much temptation, to give up James MacRae.

He shouldn't have you.

You make prayers sound like wishes. His words on that day in the church. How long ago it seemed. And how wrong he was. Not wishes, but desires, deeply felt. Needs, perhaps, but nothing as simple or easy as a wish.

Dear God, how could she go through with this?

If Ayleshire were truly the magical place the villagers thought it to be, she could take herself away merely by a thought. Or by clicking her fingers together, she could change this afternoon. But she did not believe in magic, however much she wanted it to be true now.

It wasn't that she wanted to become someone else. She simply wanted Harold to disappear.

Solemnity and laughter, joy and heartache, all emotions she'd felt around James. She closed her eyes to savor it all for just one more moment before she pushed his memory resolutely from her. How could she perform this duty with his smile dancing in her vision, or the recollection of his blue eyes boring into her mind?

How can you think of giving yourself to anyone else?

Oh, but she couldn't. Tonight, when Harold came to her, she would close her eyes tightly and think of something else. The roof of the chicken coop that needed repair, the new dating system for the cheese, the irrigation channels James had suggested be dug.

No, not James.

Then she would think of needlepoint stitches, the pattern she'd envisioned in her mind, the lovely embroidery on Maureen's nightgowns, the blue the exact color of James's . . .

Not James.

The scenery? The thick forests that reminded her of the time they gathered branches? Or a verdant glen that recalled that afternoon of abandon? Even the ocean could bring him to mind, sea captain that he was.

Nothing she could envision would be free of him.

Retribution issued by a celestial hand. *Sin, Riona, and you'll be reminded of it a hundred times, a thousand times over.*

She pressed her hand on her abdomen. Was there another reminder waiting even now? A child, with brilliant blue eyes and an engaging grin?

"Where is Maureen?" Susanna asked crossly, as she entered the room. A frown wrinkled her brow. "Where is your sister? She's not in her room and no one has seen her."

Riona shook her head. "I don't know. I haven't seen her since dinner last night."

Susanna looked around, then flew to the side of the room where Riona's hat lay.

"I've decided not to wear it," Riona said.

Susanna held it in her hands, looking first at Riona and then at the scrap of material, lace, and feathers. Sighing deeply, she placed the hat back on the chair.

The only time today, Riona thought, that she would get her way.

"Harold is waiting."

Riona nodded, squaring her shoulders. Together they would walk to the church, followed by the people of Tye-morn Manor. A ceremony to be duplicated by Maureen when the time came.

She was enveloped in a hug, and Susanna held on when Riona would have withdrawn.

"Be happy, my dearest. There are ways."

"Yes," she said. An agreement issued for the sake of politeness.

Susanna handed her a nosegay of flowers from her garden. She thanked her and left the room, her mother following.

Entering the parlor a few minutes later, she turned to Harold, presenting herself with a small curtsy.

"You look beautiful," he said, standing. "The loveliest bride I've ever seen."

For a moment, she could almost believe him sincere. But how like him not to realize that her coloring was too pale and her hands trembled. Or maybe he didn't care. She would have told him that nerves kept her stomach lurching, and that she felt decidedly ill, but all she did was force a smile to her face and thank him in a wooden voice.

She was strangling the flowers. The stems were damp, crushed by her fingers.

"Are you ready?"

She nodded, resigned to her fate. Together they left the house.

The procession was delayed while another search was made for Maureen.

"I cannot believe your sister would do something so inconsiderate," Susanna said, when she couldn't be found. "What with everything else happening today."

"Maybe she left for the church early," Riona volunteered. "Or she's gone to pick some mint for my stomach. She knew I was ill last night." There were a dozen or so reasons why she couldn't be found.

"You're right, of course," Susanna said. "She'll just have to catch up with us."

They walked silently, forming a procession. Behind them were Susanna and Ned. Polly was still ill, but in attendance, but poor Abigail had been left behind to finish the wedding supper since Cook's fever had not abated. But following them were the men and women who worked at Tyemorn Manor.

The kirk was crowded, the happy faces of the villagers beaming back at her as she and Harold entered. Slowly, they made their way to the communion table as those from Tyemorn Manor found their places among the congregation.

The afternoon sunlight filtered through the stained-glass windows, bathing the front of the church in soft hues of red, blue, and green. The windows were from another time, when the church had first been constructed and the service was more ornate. Popish, she'd heard it called.

This ceremony would be plain and unadorned. A simple declaration from them both and blessed by the church.

Mr. Dunant smiled in approval as they took their places before him.

Her dress was strangling her. Nor could she breathe. It wasn't the constriction of her laces as much as a growing feeling of utter horror.

What was she doing?

Sometimes, as a girl, she'd dreamed of her wedding. Her imagination had furnished the day with sunshine, singing birds, smiles and laughter. Although her childish visions had a shadowy figure as the groom, she knew only too well that this bridegroom was not the man he should have been.

She couldn't marry him. She glanced at Harold, feeling as if she were waking from a nightmare. Except, of course, that this was real.

If James had never come into her life, she would have accepted this marriage. Not with good grace, true, but she wouldn't have felt the sense of despair she was experiencing now. But he had come into her life, and despite the fact that he had left Tyemorn Manor, he was still here. Simply because he would always be in her heart.

Once she'd loved like that, how could she forget it? How could she ignore it? How could she trade that for Harold McDougal?

She looked wildly around for Maureen. She needed to talk to her sister, explain why this marriage couldn't continue. Surely James was correct. If Samuel really loved Maureen, wouldn't he want her? Scandal wouldn't matter.

It hadn't mattered to James.

Live with me on the abbey land. I'll build our home and we'll be impervious to scandal or whispers. Let the biddies say what they will. We simply won't care.

She couldn't do this. She couldn't marry Harold.

A few weeks ago, the idea had been repugnant but necessary. Now it seemed even more loathsome and not quite as important.

She turned and looked at Harold, staring at him full face in front of the congregation.

Frankly, she no longer cared that he'd once threatened her with scandal. Or still posed a danger. She would no doubt horrify her mother and the rest of the congregation by doing what her heart decreed. But she no longer cared about that, either.

All that mattered was that she loved James. As soon as she could, she was going to travel to Gilmuir, to beg him to forgive her.

But first, she had to stop this marriage.

"Do you love anyone in your life, Harold?" she asked him. He turned and looked at her, surprised.

"Are we at that again, Riona? I had thought we'd settled that."

"I don't care what you feel for me, Harold," she said shaking her head. "But tell me this, is there anyone else in your life whom you love? Truly, completely, absolutely? Someone who makes your heart beat faster just by being in the same room? Someone who makes you smile? Someone who makes you daydream?"

He impatiently turned back to Mr. Dunant, nodding for the ceremony to begin.

She held up her hand, and the minister stopped in midword, frowning.

"I do," she said, hearing the words echo through the church. "I love him beyond any measure." Beyond sin or society's dictates. Eons past propriety or even reason.

She scanned the congregation once again. Her mother sat there, and beside her, Ned. But of Maureen, there was no sign.

"I cannot do this, Harold," she said, feeling an absurd desire to laugh. She compromised by smiling. "I can't marry you."

"Have you forgotten our arrangement, Riona?" His eyes narrowed as he whispered the words to her.

"No," she said, sending a silent apology to her absent sister. "I haven't forgotten. But it doesn't matter. You can say what you will to whomever you will, whenever you will."

"Then you leave me no choice." He was threatening her, and yet she still felt almost buoyant with relief.

"I doubt anyone will care what you have to say, McDougal," a voice boomed out.

Riona turned and looked up at the choir gallery, empty save for one figure. James stood there, attired in his captain's finery. A commanding presence, one who now had the attention of every pair of eyes in the church.

Riona's smile widened.

He turned and disappeared from sight, and she heard his boots on the steps. A moment later he appeared at the end of the aisle. The members of the congregation turned and looked at him, then at her.

She left Harold's side, dropping her bouquet on the floor.

"Tell the story far and wide," James said, his voice booming throughout the church. "Maureen and Captain Hastings were wed this morning at Gretna Green."

Slowly, Riona walked down the aisle toward him, ignoring Harold and the minister, and the avid eyes of those who watched. She noticed only one person. James.

"You didn't leave me after all," she said, reaching him.

"How could I?"

She stretched out her hands, but instead of taking them, he placed his hands on her waist. "Will you be my bride, Riona McKinsey?" he said, loud enough so that anyone in the church could hear him.

"Oh yes, James," she said.

He startled her by picking her up and holding her above him while he turned in a slow circle. She braced her hands on his shoulders, thinking that now was a strange time to begin to weep. But perhaps tears came with joy as well as grief.

"You once asked what were my weaknesses," he said. "I've only one. You."

She began to smile through her tears, startled by his words and his wild and reckless mood. She'd never seen him this way, with his smile flashing bright and a lock of hair falling over his brow.

"And you're my temptation," she said, bending her head, still smiling even as he kissed her.

Chapter 33

~~~⌒◯◯⌒~~~

Susanna decided that it would be more proper to move from the church, to hold the wedding in the parlor at Tyemorn Manor, which meant, of course, that few people would witness the nuptials. But since she and James had given the village of Ayleshire enough to talk about for months, the private ceremony was more to Riona's liking.

Harold was sent on his way, which was just as well, since it looked as if James would cheerfully pummel him again. The moment the carriage left, a pony cart arrived, bearing the minister and Mrs. Dunant.

"I cannot believe that you don't have to marry that odious man," Susanna said, smoothing the folds of Riona's dress. The second time she'd done so today. "I am so very pleased."

"Why didn't you tell me?" she asked. "I thought you approved of Harold."

Her mother looked disconcerted. "How could you think that?"

"Because you urged me to marry him, that's why," Riona said in disbelief.

"That was before James arrived."

She raised her eyebrows at that. But her mother didn't add to the comment.

"Just think, both my girls married on the same day." Susanna looked inordinately pleased with herself.

James had answered all her questions. "Captain Hastings assures me that he'll bring Maureen back for a visit before they settle permanently in Inverness. At the moment, they're staying with his parents."

Susanna's look changed to concern and he reassured her. "I believe that Mrs. Parker's worries on that score were greatly exaggerated. According to Hastings, his parents have no objection to the match."

"Or to the wedding? A most romantic thing for him to do," Susanna said, smiling at him.

"Yes." But that's all he would say.

A spot had been cleared before the fireplace, and the large family Bible placed on the table. Behind it stood the parson, Mr. Dunant, and his wife. Her gaze was pleasant yet curious while the pastor, evidently irritated about the change of venue, glared at everyone in the room. In punishment, perhaps, for moving the wedding from the church, he'd retreated into an uncharacteristic sermon about sin and its consequences. Mrs. Dunant merely patted him on the arm from time to time, and he'd finally ceased.

Her mother and Ned stood behind them, with Polly, Abigail, Rory, and Cook behind them.

But it was James who was the focus of her attention, tall and overpoweringly male.

Riona recited her vows in a voice that held laughter in it, unable to hide her joy. James's voice sounded firm and sure. She slanted a glance at him as he stood there, unable to believe, even at that moment, that he was to be her husband.

When the ceremony was over, he looked down at her, his impossibly blue eyes twinkling. "Are you up to a journey?" he asked.

"Now?"

"Now," he said.

Of course she was. Anywhere he wished to go.

"Where are we going?"

"Gilmuir."

A wedding trip to a castle. What could be more enchanted?

Less than an hour later she found herself in their coach, her bags packed, and James beside her.

"We'll stay in Inverness tonight," he said, after they'd waved goodbye to her family. "At an inn I know."

They reached the city after night had fallen, the journey surprisingly swift. But it might have been because she was with James. They'd sat together facing the horses, his arm around her. She couldn't keep from patting him from time to time, or stroking her gloved hand across his sleeve, small touches that reassured her he was really there.

"How did you arrange their elopement?" she asked, under no illusions that Captain Hastings had devised the plan on his own. It was the perfect solution to their problems, and yet it had taken James to ensure that it happened.

"I merely told the good captain that the woman I love was determined to sacrifice herself for him. He agreed with me that such an event could not be allowed to happen. Even an Englishman has a sense of honor, Riona."

She smiled at him, shaking her head.

"A very dramatic way of proposing, James."

"I was in the mood for a bit of claiming, Riona," he said with a grin. "Call it public passion, if you will. We do fine in private, but I think the world needs to know how I feel about you."

That declaration earned him a kiss.

The innkeeper's wife and the tavern maid were as goggle-eyed as the women of her household around James. Riona didn't bother frowning at them, knowing, from prior experience, that nothing she could do would have any effect.

They were led to a chamber that startled her with its appointments. The third-floor room boasted a dressing table, a wardrobe, and a large fabric-draped screen in the corner. The fireplace, with its chiseled white stone mantel, dominated one wall. But it was the bed that commanded the room. Four tall, carved mahogany posts stretched upward to the ceiling, left undraped by curtains so that the ornate carving was revealed.

James closed the door behind them, placing her valise near the vanity and putting his own bag next to it.

"I can arrange a bath if you'd like," he offered.

"Perhaps later." She opened her bag, removing her nightgown and her brush from the top.

He stood at the edge of the screen erected in the corner. "This inn boasts a clever tub."

She walked to where he stood and peered around the screen. There, a tall armoire with a rounded top rested on a marble pedestal. James went to open it, but instead of it being a place to hold clothes, the unit tilted down until it rested on the floor, becoming a bath.

"How marvelous," she said, raising and lowering it herself. "But how did you know? Have you stayed here before?"

He nodded.

She pushed back the tendrils of hair from her face as she sat at the dressing table. Staring at herself in the mirror, she saw his reflection behind her. He was so large and the room, although commodious, was not built to house a MacRae.

He was smiling at her in perfect accord. As if he understood every thought she had, including a feeling of shyness she'd never before felt around him.

She stood and moved to him, beginning to smile as she neared him. "The innkeeper called me your wife."

"That he did," he said easily, reaching for her. She went into his embrace easily. "Riona MacRae."

"It has a nice sound," she admitted. "Will we be happy, do you think? Or will we argue and disagree from time to time?"

His smile grew in scope. "We are neither of us saints, dear wife. If you thought yourself married to one, I must change your mind. Quickly."

"Oh, but you could be an angel," she said, teasing him. "An angel with black hair and heavenly blue eyes. At least the barmaid thought so. And the innkeeper's wife."

"And I never saw the one of them," he said, smiling. "How foolish you women are, to judge a man by his appearance."

"And you men do not?" She frowned at him. "We are constrained to our corsets because of men's idea of beauty. We must purse our lips just so and never seem to notice that our bodice barely covers our breasts. A woman's hair must be long, however unruly it becomes. No, it is the men who judge a woman upon her appearance. Either that, or her fortune."

His smile faded. "Like Harold?"

"Exactly like Harold."

He released her, stepping back and surveying her. "While I care little for your fortune. Thus I must have judged you solely on your character and your charm."

"Did you?" She felt her cheeks warm at his words.

"I was entranced by your mind first, I recall. When we walked in the darkness together."

"A forbidden thing to do."

"Then I'm grateful for your wanton streak."

"I would be happier if you were not so handsome," she told him, a confession from the depths of her heart. "It is easier, I think, to love a homely man than an impossibly beautiful one. A wife should not have to worry about women stumbling over themselves in an effort to see you."

"They do not," he said, his face deepening in color.

The sight of his discomfort made them equals in this moment of revelation.

"Oh, but they do," she said, smiling.

"Would you prefer that I had a scar and a limp?" he asked.

"Yes." Her answer disconcerted him, she could tell. "Or if you had some flaws. Any that might be apparent."

He shook his head, his smile back in place. "Perhaps I can arrange a duel with Alisdair after we return to Gilmuir. Or fall down the stairs to the shipyard," he added wryly.

"I don't want you hurt," she was quick to say.

"Then perhaps I can inquire if there are any faux scars for sale, like beauty patches."

"Or you could scowl more," she suggested. "Look fiercer than you do. Or blacken one of your teeth."

He laughed, the sound echoing through the room. "I think you exaggerate, but my esteem has grown by it. Thank you."

She busied herself with unbraiding her plait, wishing for the thousandth time that she wasn't cursed with such unmanageable hair. A few gold pins dropped to the ground, and both she and James bent to pick them up.

"I hate my hair," she said when they stood. The frizzed ends flared around her head. "Nothing else represents my life so much as my hair. Its length is measured by propriety, and it doesn't matter how unruly it is, I must fashion it as society decrees."

He smiled. "I am partial to it, myself."

"Are you?" She sighed. "But I truly hate it."

"Then cut it," he said.

She glanced at him, the thought skittering to a halt within her. "Cut it?"

"Yes," he said folding his arms and looking down at her. "Didn't you say that when you married you would?"

"I was jesting. Or it was only a wish."

"Why should it only be a wish?"

"Because it isn't done, for one thing," she said.

"You're sounding too much like Mrs. Parker."

She looked up at him wide-eyed. "Truly? That is an incentive, if nothing else."

Reaching out, he gathered the ends of her hair in his hand. "If this is, as you say, representative of any constraints, then change it. Your life has changed, perhaps your hair should reflect it."

"I couldn't," she said, but she turned and went to the dressing table. Sitting on the bench, she stared at herself again. "I truly couldn't."

"Shall I do it for you?"

She glanced up at him, amazed that he should offer. "Would you?"

"If you wish."

She had never considered that she might rid herself of her

burdensome hair, but now the temptation seemed almost too wonderful to resist.

Grabbing a handful of hair, Riona stared at the riot of auburn curls that were forever frizzed. Thick and unruly, it marked her days with its care. An hour was spent combing it in the morning and another hour was wasted brushing and braiding it at night. What would it be like to be freed from such a chore?

"Yes," Riona said quickly, before she could change her mind. "I will do it. Cut my hair, James."

He came to stand behind her, and all she could see of him in the mirror was the lower half of his body.

His hands reached out to rest on her shoulders, pulling her back until her shoulders rested against his legs. His fingers thrust into her hair, dislodging the rest of her carefully placed pins without thought to their cost or to the effort of finding them later. But she didn't open her mouth, didn't speak the words that might have cautioned him.

Bending, he withdrew his dirk. The fingers of one hand trailed in her hair, lifting up the tresses. The silver knife glinted in the other hand, promising death to the mess of her hair. With a stroke, her appearance would be changed.

He hesitated just a moment, but Riona took a deep breath and spoke, "Go ahead," she said in a surprisingly steady voice.

"Are you certain, Riona?"

"Yes." She stared at her image in the mirror. The woman there looked resolute.

As one lock was severed she took a deep breath. Then another tress was cut, curling around his hand. He extended his fist toward her, and Riona covered his hand with both of hers, feeling the warmth of her hair between them.

"It's not too late," he cautioned.

Cutting her hair was a symbol of her new status, her freedom from a society restrictive toward unmarried women.

"People will think I've had a fever," she said. "I'll tell them it's a recurring one."

One by one the locks were snipped, falling to the floor as she watched. His hands were warm and large, the actions of his knife relentless as her hair was cut to just below her shoulders. The weight on her neck eased as he continued.

Once he stopped, he placed his hand against her forehead gently, pressed her head back so that she looked up at him. They shared a surprisingly somber upside-down look. How strange that he should be so formidable in his silence.

Now she glanced at the floor, stunned to realize how much hair lay there. The vision in the mirror had altered to become someone else. Someone she had only dreamed about in her wildest and most wicked fantasies.

Her hair fluttered around her shoulders, curling at the ends. Her lips were tempting. Her eyes were wide, holding secrets in their depths.

The knife clattered on top of the dressing table as James reached out with both hands to spear through her hair, bringing her head back once more to rest against him.

"Is this enough, Riona?" he asked in a hoarse voice unlike him.

"Yes," she said, threading her fingers through her hair. Tiny hairs clung to her bodice, and she flicked them away. Standing, she turned and faced him, only to encounter his look.

His face was almost severe as he studied her. Self-consciously, she raised her hand, pulling at the ends of her hair.

"Don't you like it?"

"It suits you."

She brushed away the loose hairs at her neck and cheeks.

"Let me," he said, removing her hand to retrieve a hair clinging tenaciously to her nose. That done, his fingers dusted like feathers across her cheeks and brow, down her neck. He blew gently against her collarbone, causing her to shiver.

His palms smoothed over her shoulders, down her back.

They were man and wife, yet at this exact moment, what was between them didn't feel blessed as much as simply exciting.

Her breaths alternated with her heartbeat, both at a rapid rate. Cogent thought had flown from her mind at his appearance, and the only thing remaining was a need that recalled the pleasure of the moments they'd shared together.

"You are so beautiful," he said.

There was no sorcery at the Witch's Well, or in the Lethson ceremonies. There was magic, however, in his voice.

Stretching out his hand, he touched her shoulder, leaving a warm path to her elbow. She shivered, and he smiled.

"Are you cold?"

She shook her head, thinking that he knew as well as she that it wasn't a chill that caused her response.

He opened his coat, pulled her close. Riona linked her fingers at the back of his neck, staring up at him.

Slowly, in the silence, he bent his head and kissed her.

Her hands framed his face as she deepened the kiss. She could see starlight and blackness behind her eyelids, felt the surge of excitement being near him always caused in her. Reaching down, she moved his hands from her waist to press against her breasts.

Suddenly, he broke off the kiss and stood with his chest heaving, his chin resting against her temple.

She leaned against his chest, nodding. Her hands gripped his upper arms as she pushed herself away.

But she didn't want to be cautious or prudent or even wise at this moment. She only wanted to feel.

Something wanton and wild and not altogether understandable made her want to remove her clothing in front of him and stand, one hand on hip, to let him look his fill.

There, Mrs. Parker, that is true wantonness.

Rory stood in front of the mirror in the room he and James had shared, slicking down his hair with some water from the ewer. He had on a new white shirt that James had given him. He hadn't been able to afford new trousers and a coat, and didn't feel that he should be asking for an advance on his wages, but the old ones were presentable.

On his shirt he'd pinned a MacRae clan badge, an emblem he prized above all others. Through it, he'd threaded a piece of moss, another symbol of the MacRaes.

He was feeling quite well, Rory decided. The journey to and from Inverness hadn't worsened the state of his leg. In fact, it didn't sting as much as before. Although it would always be scarred, it wouldn't show below his trousers. His hand was a different matter. He'd lost the use of two fingers. But, he reasoned, he might have done the same damage in a carpentry accident. At least he still had them. It wasn't as if they had been sheared off with a sharp saw.

That was the bad. As far as the good, he had quite a future ahead of him, working with James MacRae to build his new great house. He would be occupied for years in good honest labor. If one of the buildings he constructed happened to be his own cozy home, then perhaps he should be doing some thinking about who should occupy it besides him. Even a snug little place could get lonely in the winter months.

Abigail had danced with him at Lethson, and she'd giggled, too. She'd even introduced her parents to him, and a brother and sister. A good start, he thought.

He smiled at himself in the mirror, the expression fading the longer he stared. Perhaps she would be offended if he addressed his comments to her.

This business of courting was a terrible thing, filled with all sorts of rules and regulations. Would she think him old enough? If not, he'd be willing to wait a year or so. After all, one didn't find a girl like Abigail in every corner of Scotland.

Giving himself one last look, Rory smiled again, threw his shoulders back, and strode across the room. He opened the door and closed it with firmness, walked downstairs with resolve in his very footsteps. He sat at one of the tables waiting for Abigail to be finished with her duties.

A few minutes later, she came bustling into the kitchen, a tray in hand. She stopped at the doorway and stared at him. As if, he thought, irritated, she'd never seen him presentable before.

He stood and bowed slightly to her.

"Abigail," he said.

She, in her frilly little cap and apron, performed a small curtsy.

"Rory."

"Are you planning any entertainment this evening?" he asked, wishing that his throat felt less tight and that his heart wasn't beating quite so fast. It made his words sound breathless, as if he'd run down the stairs.

"No, I'm not," she said.

"Are you seeing anyone else, Abigail?" he asked, wondering if it was permissible to ask such a question.

She shook her head, still looking bemused. "I'm not, Rory."

"Would you like to walk out with me from time to time, then?"

"I would," she said, finally beginning to smile. "It seems a lovely evening tonight."

He grinned back at her, thinking the world a wondrous place.

He offered her his arm, and they left the room, their destination uncertain. All each of them truly cared about was that they were together.

Susanna held her shawl tightly around her shoulders and slipped from the kitchen door. What she was about to do would, no doubt, horrify Polly, and most definitely shock Abigail. Cook, she suspected, would understand.

Why, then, was she doing something so wicked? Because it had been fifteen years since a man had touched her with desire in his eyes. Because tonight she wanted to forget she was a mother, a matron, an heiress. All she wanted to be was a woman.

Her feet flew over the ground, the dew seeping through her slippers. At his door she hesitated. Before reason could surface, before she could think further about the consequences of her actions, Susanna raised her fist and pounded on the door. Not a ladylike gesture as much as a demanding one.

Ned opened the door.

For a moment he said nothing, simply stood there in his shirt and trousers, his eyes narrowed. "You've come."

"You knew I would."

He smiled. "I hoped." He held the door open, and she entered his cottage, the first time she'd done so. The space was tidy and surprisingly comfortable. In front of a fireplace rested two chairs, and behind them a small table bearing a vase of Tyemorn's roses. A doorway led to another chamber, filled with a bed on which lay a multicolored quilt.

"I've no daughters at home to worry about," she said.

"So you've a yen to be a little irresponsible."

"Is that what I'm being?"

"A little bit wicked, I'm thinking," he said, grinning at her. It seemed to Susanna that his smile had a little bit of wickedness about it as well.

"Should I leave?"

She clutched the shawl more tightly, glanced up at him, and smiled. How many months had they worked closely together? How many times had she met with him and never noticed the intelligence in his brown eyes, or the humor resting there? His face without the beard was strangely unlined, and his smile was as youthful as she felt at this moment.

"Only if you wish it," he said, the wicked man, as if knowing how desperately she wanted to stay.

She glanced at his arm. "Are you feeling up to visitors?"

"I've powers you'll never know, lass," he said, grinning at her.

"Then I'll stay," she said.

"Then come in, my dear Susanna," he said.

Slowly, without taking her eyes from his, she pushed the door closed.

Riona's skin felt too warm and tight as she sat, smoothing her stockings from ankle to thigh. Was he going to stand there and watch her? Evidently so, since James made no movement toward the door. Instead, his gaze was fixed on her movements. She removed each garter before slipping off her stockings.

Her stays were next, and then her shift.

He startled her by kissing the nape of her neck as she bent her head to undo the bow at her neck. When she turned to face him, he stepped back, wearing a rueful smile.

"Love me, James. Please."

"No." He reached out and pulled her to him. "Never ask. You never need to ask."

She rose up on her knees, entwined her arms around him. "Can I encourage?" she asked, smiling. "Spur you on, perhaps?" She nipped at his earlobe with a teasing bite.

With one swift movement, he tossed her onto her back and loomed over her. "No need."

She'd never thought that lovemaking might be fun, or that she might be naked and laughing in James's arms. But as he rolled with her until she was atop him, both of them were smiling.

Dear heavens, how she loved him. Was there anything as wonderful as the sight of James smiling? Or laughing with his deep, melodious voice?

As she watched him, her amusement leached away, leaving only a warm wonder. How precious this moment, and how fortunate she was. His arms were around her as she lay on his chest. "A gigantic rock, that's what you are. A warm rock. You're hard all over."

She realized, suddenly, that other parts of his body were quite solid as well.

Raising up on her knees once again, she surveyed him.

"A stallion?" he asked, teasing her. The words she'd ut-

tered on their first meeting came back to her as she smiled at
him.

Their couplings had been done in bright sunlight or in
moonlight, but never in the soft glow of flickering candles.

His chest was broad, tapering down to a narrow waist and
hips. His thighs and calves were well muscled, leaving no
doubt as to his fitness. His erection was as solid as a pillar.

She held him lightly between both hands, marveling at the
size of him. Slowly, her fingers encompassed him. So large
and so beautiful.

His indrawn breath indicated that he liked her touch. Glancing at him below her lids, she smiled inwardly, feeling a surge
of pure feminine power. He sat up, his hands braced behind
him, his glance on her face and not on what she was doing.

Her hands were suddenly talented, smoothing around the
curves of his body, flattening against a flank, his muscular
chest. Her palms ached to press against his skin, learn him in
some ancient and almost mystical way.

Her fingers closed more fully over him as she stroked
down the length of him. Again. And again. From base to tip,
circling the breadth of him in a relentless and enticing touch.

"Are you milking me, Riona?" he asked incredulously.

"Oh yes," she said, breathing the words through her delight. "Does it hurt?"

His bark of laughter was unexpected. "Do I look as if it
hurts?"

Each movement of her fingers had made him hotter and
harder in her hands. "No," she agreed, shaking her head
slowly.

She hadn't noticed before that James's body was so hard.
The expanse of his arms, the length of his thighs, even his
buttocks as she cupped them, were tight and taut, and su-

perbly masculine. He was beautifully made, an elemental and perfect creature.

She hadn't realized that she had the power to alter his breath, make his heart beat faster with a simple touch. Nor had she ever considered that this joining, this coupling, might be so filled with thoughts and feelings that had nothing to do with love or even passion.

A feeling of possession stole over her, startling her in its fierceness. He was hers, just as she had given her life over to him. Their fates and futures were inexorably intertwined. Whatever happened to him would happen to her. Never again would she feel that sense of loneliness, strange and unsettling as it had been, especially in the midst of a loving family and friends.

How utterly powerful she felt at this moment, as if she'd been given a secret strength.

Suddenly, James toppled her, forcing her onto her back in a movement she hadn't anticipated. Pinning her wrists to the bed with his hands, he lowered himself over her.

"I want to be inside you," he said, his words as potent as the look in his eyes.

But instead, he stood, his erection so magnificent that she couldn't help but reach out and touch it, pull it down from his belly where the tip rested.

"Soon," he said, stepping cautiously away from her. "First, let me indulge in a fantasy only hours old." He held out his hand in invitation.

She rose from the bed, taking his hand and following him to the bench before the dressing table.

Sitting down, he moved his legs apart, guiding her to stand between them. "Put your hands on my shoulders." Wordlessly, she did so as he placed his hands behind her legs, raising her until she sat on each of his thighs. She was exposed and open, facing him. In front of her was the dressing table and above it the mirror. All she could see of herself was her hands and knees. But his muscled back and buttocks were readily visible as well as the powerful arms supporting her.

Suddenly, he was slipping inside her, her body heated and ready for him. Her hands clenched on his shoulders and her eyes half closed in pleasure. A moan escaped her as he separated his legs farther. Bracing his hands behind him, he moved, thrusting himself deeper.

Glancing at herself in the mirror, she was shocked at the face of the woman she saw. Abandoned, flushed, with her hair cut short and her fingers clenching James's shoulders, she seemed a stranger. A moment, an instant, a second later and all thought vanished as he continued to move, leading her into a labyrinth of delight. There was nothing more than her and him; everything else fading into nothingness.

She kissed him, held his head still so that she could deepen the kiss, her tongue exploring his mouth. Her hands speared through his hair, nails sliding along his scalp, fingers linking at the back of his head. His hands moved to explore her as he mouthed her breasts. He surged within her, hungry for her capitulation, demanding her surrender.

What choice did she have? The feeling was in her, part of her, submerging her beneath a powerful wave of sensation. A single spear of bliss so powerful that she felt faint with it.

Long moments later, she felt him carry her to the bed. She turned toward him, content when he curved an arm around her.

Epilogue

James toyed with a tendril of Riona's hair. Curling around his hand, it seemed to welcome his touch, summoning a stroke of his finger. Soft, almost like silk.

The day was fully advanced, but Riona slept deeply, only occasionally moving. Even the movement of the coach as it traveled over ruts in the road didn't disturb her. They'd remained in Inverness for a day or two, in order for him to complete those errands entrusted to him by Iseabal and Alisdair. The nights, however, had been reserved just for them.

She'd not slept much the night before.

Smiling, he traced the edge of her bottom lip with the tip of his finger, thinking that kissing her awake was a temptation.

Bending his head, he breathed softly against her lips, smiling again when she moved her head restlessly. One hand brushed at her cheek, and he kissed the spot she'd rubbed.

"Riona." A gentle whisper that had no effect on her.

Finally, he kissed her, laying his lips gently on hers. Another kiss to incite her to wakefulness. Then another.

She made a sound deep in her throat, her arms stretching out to wind around his neck.

"We're almost there," he said gently. "At Gilmuir."

She woke gradually, rubbing her eyes and yawning. "We're here?" she said sleepily, peering beyond him. "It's very large. You never told me it was quite so big."

He bent and kissed her on the cheek as she looked at Gilmuir. "It's a castle," he teased. "What else would a castle look like?"

"Less imposing," she said, evidently awed by the sight of the MacRae ancestral fortress. "What are those wooden structures?"

"Scaffolding. Gilmuir's being rebuilt from the ground up. The walls are almost finished, but the masons are adding the finishing touches. The interior will take much longer, however."

"Why were you at Tyemorn, James?" she asked suddenly.

"I was wondering when you would ask," he said, smiling.

"Surely you'll tell me now?"

"Your mother's idea, I'm afraid. I was to investigate a series of thefts."

"Thefts?" she asked, frowning.

His smile deepened at her look. "Supposedly, some of the livestock were missing."

"We've never had any missing livestock at Tyemorn." She began to yawn, then quickly held her hand over her mouth.

"Yes, I know."

Pulling back, she gave him an arch glance, one filled with humor. "You had only to ask me and I would have told you."

"But then there would have been no reason for me to remain."

"True," she said, and gave him a kiss.

He glanced at Gilmuir, smiling faintly. "I've only been gone a few weeks and already I feel like a stranger."

"That's because you have your own home," she said, placing her hand on his arm. He immediately covered it with his hand, looked down at their linked fingers.

"Yes, I do. And my own place in the world."

"Somewhere safe where gales don't threaten and shipwrecks never happen."

"And where there's a lass with short hair who waits near an abbey wall for me." He reached up and fingered the ends of her hair resting on her shoulders.

Another kiss and then they sat close together, watching as they neared Gilmuir.

"You'll have to tell them about Rory."

"They'll miss him, but I need him too much." Even now, his former cabin boy was beginning to mark out the foundation of their new house. A home that needed a name. Before she'd fallen asleep, he and Riona had toyed with ideas, but nothing had seemed right.

A moment later, she spoke again.

"Do you think they'll be surprised that you've married?"

"Dumbstruck," he said, beginning to smile again. "All the MacRaes will be. I'm known to be a solitary sort."

She eyed him suspiciously. "I doubt all the women of Gilmuir feel that way. I am certain there will be a great many tears shed at the news."

He laughed at her look. Didn't she realize she was a beautiful woman? He'd felt his own share of jealousy.

He glanced out the window, narrowing his eyes. The loch

he viewed was long and narrow, deeply blue and topped with white frothy waves.

"I think you'll have a chance to meet more than Alisdair and Iseabal," he said, turning to her.

She looked where he pointed. There, on the horizon, were two ships in full sail, heavy bellied like the ocean-going vessels she'd seen often in Cormech.

"My brothers," he announced, his grin widening as he stared.

"Gilmuir and all the MacRaes." She sounded bemused.

"You're one of us, my love. You're a MacRae now."

"I am, aren't I?" A moment later she spoke again. "Dachaigh," she said, the word just now popping into her mind.

At his look, she smiled. "That's what we should name the house we build. It's a perfect choice."

"Dachaigh," he repeated.

"Home," she said simply, smiling as he pulled her closer.

Author's Note

The village of Ayleshire is actually a compilation of three Scottish villages, all of which have their unique characteristics. In one small hamlet stands a Celtic cross. At its base is an inscription listing the name and date of the woman who was burned as a witch on that spot. As with Annie Mull, the actual tale remains a mystery.

Lethson is a word I unabashedly created, from several Gaelic words meaning half year. The actual ceremony of Lethson, or Midsummer Night, or St. John's Eve, was taken from similar observances in the northern part of Scotland where Viking influences were the strongest.

During the American Revolution, the English were very concerned about the French invasion of Scotland. Therefore, several Fencible Regiments were called up, their sole duty to patrol the Scottish coastline. After the end of the war, they were disbanded.